SILICON HEARTS

Robin Miyashita & R. K. Moravec

Five are in.
One will stay.

SILIC♥N

A Novel

HEARTS

HYPERION
AVENUE

LOS ANGELES   NEW YORK

First Hardcover Edition, August 2023
First Paperback Edition, August 2023
10 9 8 7 6 5 4 3 2 1
FAC-004510-23167
Printed in the United States of America

This book is set in Hoefler Text, Lust, Chalet Comprine.
Designed by Amy C. King

Library of Congress Control Number: 2023931121
ISBN 978-1-368-08113-9
ISBN 978-1-368-08116-0

Reinforced binding
www.HyperionAvenueBooks.com

SUSTAINABLE FORESTRY INITIATIVE

Certified Sourcing

www.forests.org
SFI-01681

Logo Applies to Text Stock only

To the brave ones who believe in an optimistic future and those who have the conviction to build it. Succeed or fail, you make the world a better place.

Chapter 1

"AH! NO, NO, NO, NO!" Cam screeched, leaping across her cramped room to catch the wall shelf as one side sagged and collapsed. A partially disassembled power supply slid off and hit the floor with a metallic crash.

"Cam, honey, are you all right?" Rosa Diaz's muffled voice filtered through the front door of the apartment. A frantic jangle of keys and a clatter of footsteps preceded Rosa's head popping through a crack in the door. The room had been small to begin with. Under Cam's electronics-hoarding regime, the space had only gotten more cramped. Rows of mismatched shelves, stacks of empty computer cases, and boxes full of components labeled "salvage?" occupied the vast majority of available floor space. Posters of fan art for various TV shows, a framed magazine cover of brilliant engineer Lee Baker standing in a holographic sphere of streaming binary, and a permanently unmade bed helped complete the look. Cam met her mother's eyes with a look of mingled dismay and relief as she struggled under the weight of the wall shelf that was desperately overburdened with various tech jetsam.

Cam tried to project cheer, but her voice had an edge of desperation. "Hey, Mom, how was class? There's carne guisada in the pot. Don't worry, I've got this." A plastic bin slid off the shelf and various-sized screws exploded everywhere.

As Rosa hopscotched over tools, parts, and clothes strewn on the floor, Cam experienced a flutter of anxiety. With each step, Rosa came perilously close to crushing some piece of equipment or other that Cam had acquired at great personal cost. System on a chip microcomputer? Only $25 after using the coupon code Cam had acquired via trawling discount forums. Capacitance touch screen? Just $6, salvaged from a car's used backup camera display she had found for sale online. Digital oscilloscope? A huge investment at $135 and her absolute pride and joy. It was acquired by haggling with the seller and, eventually, explaining to him how to solve a thorny cross-talk problem with a circuit he was constructing. A pile of breadboards? Cheap, but Cam had constructed test circuits on several of them over endless long nights in the preparation process for her application to the Beekor Accelerator Program, and she would not appreciate seeing them smashed.

To Cam's great relief, Rosa successfully navigated the cluttered floor to grab the other end of the shelf. Cam started unloading the shelf and placing boxes and loose gear on the scant remaining inches of bare floor space.

"Cam, mi amor, you know these walls are made of sawdust. I told you not to put anything too heavy on these shelves."

"I know, I know," Cam said, setting down the final item before assisting her mother in lifting the shelf off the wall to lean against the window. "It's just that they're sending out the acceptance letters today. And I could either keep refreshing my phone or I could put some more work into building my new prototype. Then I got so in the zone I didn't realize what I was doing until the shelf was already collapsing."

Cam flopped back down at her desk. She looked like a near-identical copy of her mother, aged down to her early twenties. They both had wavy dark hair, round cheeks, and pointed chins. But Cam traded Rosa's wispy brows and warm skin for thick straight eyebrows and a smattering of freckles. And while Rosa's brown eyes crinkled with laugh lines, Cam's eyes burned with a bright zeal. That passion was on full display as Cam eyed her act of creation in progress with a mixture of pride and worry.

The surface of Cam's desk looked like the eye of organized calm in the maelstrom that was her room. There, the guts of a disassembled phone lay butterflied out, components and pieces arranged meticulously.

"I thought you already finished this weeks ago as part of the submission process," Rosa said, peering at the mechanical carcass.

"Yeah, but that was only the first prototype. I was able to nab a few parts I had been missing from the last flea market. Can you believe someone was throwing away an old phone with a perfectly good projector lens assembly?" Cam laughed at the folly.

"So, how's it coming along?" Rosa asked. Cam recognized her mother's often-used "supportive but totally clueless about what her daughter was talking about" expression, going all the way back to that time as a kid that she had been absolutely certain she could upgrade Rosa's e-bike to recharge the battery better while going downhill. Cam had eventually gotten it to work, but looking back, the most impressive thing was Rosa's patience with the whole endeavor, which had left her without a functioning bike for the better part of three months.

Cam perked up. "Great! I only need—" She was cut off by the screeching sound of the 9:23 p.m. train passing by her window. "Twenty minutes," Cam mouthed. Her mom gave her a big thumbs-up and left, passing the foldout couch that served as Rosa's bed to the corner of the one-bedroom apartment that acted as a kitchen to eat her belated dinner.

The sound of the train faded into the distance, leaving behind a ponderous silence. Cam flipped open the beat-up old laptop on the corner of her desk, squinted at the schematic on-screen, and gently slid aside a pile of colorful plastic bits, striated and rough from the cheap 3D printer, to clear some elbow room to work.

She compared the last join she had soldered to her schematic. "Hmm." She broke out a strip of solder wick and pressed it against the silver clump of hardened solder with the iron. The board hissed and crackled as the solder soaked back into the wick, clearing away the erroneous connection so she could resume assembling. Bit by bit, the contraption on her desk went from a flayed and pinned insect back to a recognizable piece of consumer hardware. With patience and expert precision, she converted the chaotic piles of plastic and metal bits scattered across her desk into a complicated assembly that both attached to and emerged from the phone. Exactly as she had envisioned in her schematics, screws slid into shafts, plastic shapes interlocked, hinges attached, and ribbon cables connected.

Finally, triumphantly, Cam held her handiwork aloft and laughed like a comic-book villain. It looked as if her phone, a standard, featureless rectangle of glass and metal, had been half-eaten by a spider made out of 3D-printer plastic. The coarse, ribbed plastic hinged open on the top and bottom of the phone's surface. Held within the grasp of those hinged spider's legs was a tiny projector assembly with a wide ribbon cable running into it from a slot Cam had rough-carved into the chassis of the phone itself. She sat up straight and stretched her aching back as she examined her creation from all angles. It certainly wouldn't win any awards for compactness or elegance, but it was beautiful. It was hers.

Long accustomed to her daughter's signature laugh of victory, Rosa peeked her head back in her daughter's room holding a bowl of the carne guisada that Cam had prepped for the two of them while Rosa was busy at her night classes all the way across town at Greenview Community College. "How's it looking?" she asked between bites.

"Let's see," Cam replied expectantly.

Carefully, she reached for the power button and pressed.

A strange noise burst out of the phone's speaker, and the back of the phone sparked and flashed. "Shit," she exclaimed as she hastily cracked the case open again and disconnected the battery. Taking a second look at the battery, swollen nearly to bursting, Cam let out a disgusted groan and threw it into an overflowing box labeled "waste." She crawled under her desk and began riffling through a mesh bin full of batteries. She managed to find two of roughly the right dimensions and brought them back to the top of her desk. A quick voltage test revealed one of the batteries was dead, landing it unceremoniously into the waste bin. The last one appeared fine. At least Cam hoped it was fine. Second- or thirdhand batteries had a habit of bursting into flames, as the scorch marks on her desk could attest.

As her mom watched, she reattached the battery and pressed the power button. The screen's backlight came on as expected; no bizarre noises were forthcoming. Suddenly, a boot-up graphic appeared. Instead of merely being visible on-screen, the three-dimensional icon made of light hovered several centimeters above the phone. The stylized silver "S" of the phone manufacturer's logo, converted to a hologram, floated in the air and spun in place. Cam's holographic adapter worked. She leapt to her feet cheering, sending a heap of salvaged computer parts crashing down. Cam's mother looked shocked for a moment, then began clapping happily alongside her daughter.

"Introducing Specio!" Cam flourished her hands like a used-car salesman. "This piece of hardware can make any cheap old phone display holograms just like one of those expensive Beekor holophones. Now you too can join the future!"

"You decided to call it Specio? Like a little speck?" Rosa asked, puzzled.

Cam made a face. "No. 'Specio,' as in 'to spectate or view,' *in Latin!*" Completely undeterred by her mother's question, she pushed on. "We'd have to work three more jobs to save up for the latest generation of Beekor phone. Or . . . we could just use Specio!" Cam laughed maniacally again.

Cam slid a finger across the exposed segment of screen that wasn't occupied by the plastic bits that comprised Specio's hardware and launched a custom app she had programmed. "And this," she said as the app launched, "is an app that allows the phone to access the Beekor network, join holographic video calls, get mail—" Cam was cut off by a sudden loud chime. Her app had launched, and she already had a pending notification.

There was a piece of mail there, waiting for her.

With trembling fingers, Cam poked the space above her phone where the notification prompt appeared. At her hand gesture, the notification unfolded like an old envelope, wax seal and all. A tinny fanfare sound played, and virtual confetti burst into the air. The words "You are accepted!" appeared in large font.

Her body began vibrating uncontrollably with excitement as she frantically scrolled the text. In smaller font, it continued.

Dear Camila Diaz,

Congratulations!

I am pleased to inform you that Beekor is proud to accept you into this year's Beekor Accelerator Program.

Admission to the Beekor Accelerator Program is highly selective, with over 227,000 applicants from across the globe competing for only five openings. This year's candidates were our most remarkable yet, and the decision-making process was not easy, and still you impressed us with your project submission. We are excited about your potential for success and look forward to what you can create with Beekor's extensive support, details to be discussed after your acceptance, as a member of this year's batch of pages.

Attached you will find details for travel, accommodation, and orientation. We cannot wait to see what profound things you create to build an exciting tomorrow, and we at Beekor are honored to help you bring your ideas to life.

With best wishes and congratulations, we look forward to seeing you on campus soon.

Cam was stunned silent. Outside, the rail crossing bells chimed.

Her mother swept her up into a forceful hug, and they bounced in place together. Through a blur of tears, Cam took in her cluttered room over her mother's shoulder and all the by-products of the hard months of struggle she had been through. The hours of scavenging, the sleepless nights of building, the long and painful submission process, the exhaustive interviews. Suddenly, her space seemed like it could barely contain her. This town, where nobody understood the things that excited her or where she was going, had grown too small to contain her and her gigantic ambitions. She was going to Beekor.

Chapter 2

"I AM GOING TO MISS you so much." Cam's mom went in for yet another bone-crushing hug, which Cam returned with enthusiasm.

"Excuse me, ma'am? This is a drop-off zone only. You need to move your . . . car." The harried traffic agent interrupted their farewell and eyed their rust-flaked vehicle dubiously. The departure area of the airport was five lanes deep of honking cars, rattling luggage, dashing passengers, and hastily shouted goodbyes through open windows.

"Oh, sorry! Sorry! I'll go!" Rosa sprang apart from Cam. "Do you have everything? Your jacket? Your ID?" she asked her daughter anxiously.

"I think so? I'm pretty sure— Wait, where's my wallet?" Cam began frantically patting her oversized green plaid thrift-store jacket with her right hand, then riffling through the outer pockets of her patched-together army-surplus duffel bag. Panic was about to truly set in as she reached to open her cracked and duct-taped suitcase, when her mom cleared her throat.

"In your hand, honey." Her mom pointed to Cam's left hand, which clutched her wallet.

"Oh, right, thanks. Okay, yes, I have everything." Cam straightened and pushed the flyaways that had escaped her frayed ponytail back out of her face.

"Ma'am, I'm really going to need you to move." The traffic agent circled back to them.

"All right, I have to go now. I don't want to get a ticket on Rudy's car," Cam's mom said as she pulled Cam in for one final, tight hug.

"I love you so much, tell Rudy thanks again for letting you borrow his car, tell him I'll fix his radio when I get back, I'll call you when I get there, I miss you already, I love you, I love you, I love you, okay, bye!" Cam leapt away, grabbed the handle of her giant brick of a rolling suitcase, and dashed toward the entrance doors, ready to begin her new life.

"I love you so much! You're going to do great!" her mom shouted after her with tears in her eyes.

Cam half spun to wave and nearly tripped over a Beekor auto-suitcase. Over $750 new, Cam's appraising eye couldn't help but append. It was decked out with an incredibly powerful custom ASIC optimized to run machine learning tasks, for a discerning set of scavenging hands. The suitcase beeped a warning, and its owner turned to glare. "Watch where you're going!" snarled the man, straightening his blue pin-striped suit with a brisk fury. He brusquely strode away, and the autonomous suitcase followed behind. It trilled huffily.

"Sorry!" Cam yelped at the man's back. She turned to wave to her mother one final time, who looked chagrined on her daughter's behalf, then Cam wrestled her baggage inside, once again embarking on her new life.

Inside the enormous departure hall, Cam quickly found her airline and the long line of passengers waiting to check in. She pulled out her phone and examined the ticket Beekor had provided for her. She eyed the dense line of harried-looking economy-class passengers snaking back on itself. Two children simultaneously erupted into screams. Cam triple-checked her ticket, and tentatively, almost embarrassedly, stepped into the welcoming, empty business-class queue and right up to the desk. Pleasant music played.

"Hello," greeted the apple-cheeked attendant in a disturbingly chipper tone. "Can I have your name and destination?"

"Um," Cam stammered, "Camila Diaz, San Francisco?"

"Excellent, Ms. Diaz. Put the bags you'd like to check right here, and please show me your ID when you're ready," the attendant said with a smile, never breaking eye contact as she clacked away on her keyboard.

With a vague anxiety that she might be demoted back to economy at any moment, Cam quietly complied and was handed a thick ticket in exchange for her suitcase. Her disintegrating black square on wheels, which contained all her belongings, was placed on a conveyor belt next to the slick white designer auto-suitcase she had collided with earlier. The auto-suitcase beeped once, smugly. Meanwhile, she was ushered through a private first-class security screening and personally escorted to her gate with a wish she have a pleasant flight.

The whole process was over quickly, and Cam was surprised to find herself standing in front of her gate three hours early. To bleed off some of her anxious energy, she decided to distract herself with some work. Cam found an outlet on the floor near the gate entrance and pulled her creaking laptop, frayed attachments, and cobbled-together phone out of her duffel bag. She assembled them into a scattered array before her. If she had some time to kill, she might as well get a few more lines of code into her prototype.

The current problem she was trying to solve was image file opening. Her jerry-rigged tech sort of worked, and it was definitely very affordable to fabricate, but it was full of bugs, hiccups, and gaps in what features it could support. Like now, when all the images attached to her acceptance letter from Beekor weren't opening properly. Probably because it was being sent from the latest Beekor tech. The text of the acceptance letter was fine, but the attached images of herself and all her fellow pages were opening up blurry and unidentifiable. If one squinted, it was possible to intuit that the other four people in her cohort had two eyes and a mouth, each. But even that was guesswork. She opened up the software and began tinkering with the code.

With her highly personalized coding tools open, the airport around Cam disappeared as she sank into intense focus. Complex problems gave way to clear, logical frameworks of her own devising. She realized there was a boundary case that had been neglected in the code she had just been about to write, stepped back, and attacked from another angle that would handle it elegantly. She smiled smugly to herself. From her vantage point within a deep flow state, Cam's code was a vast, conceptual edifice that she was conjuring bit by bit, laboring to bring each piece into greater alignment and clarity. Every improvement brought her work satisfyingly closer to her perfect vision. This was the exact sort of endlessly rewarding work that Cam loved to disappear into over the long nights.

"Superfluous."

Cam's head snapped up. She had been so deep in the zone that she hadn't even noticed the tall, young woman leaning over Cam's shoulder, viewing her code. She appeared to be about Cam's own age and looked chic in an off-white mock-neck cashmere sweater tucked into crisp tan slacks, and stylishly sensible flats

"Superfluous," the woman said again. She pointed at a line of code on the screen.

Cam looked back over her code and realized the woman was right. Cam had been repeatedly initializing a file handler, causing it to reset while it was already in the process of loading media. "Huh," Cam replied, nonplussed. "You're actually right." Cam quickly punched in the fix and triggered recompilation. Her computer set to work preparing a fresh build and pushing it to her phone.

Cam tamped down her surprise, and the subtle note of irritation that naturally came to her voice. "Thanks for that." Cam turned to face the woman, who had straightened up, and said shyly, "I'm not used to even having anyone around that can understand what I'm doing, let alone point out a problem in my code."

"Made the same mistake before," the woman said matter-of-factly. "Sofia Ly. You're Camila Diaz."

"Oh, uh, yes, I am. I'm Cam," Cam stammered, bewildered.

Sofia nodded again with satisfaction and tapped the frames of her glasses. "AR facial recognition plus identification." Cam peered closely at Sofia's eyewear. There was flickering light from a minuscule projector in the frames, displaying a tiny image of her face along with what looked like a news article on one of the lenses. "It's my application project for the Beekor Accelerator."

Cam's phone pinged as the new build was installed and loaded, and suddenly she was able to view a freshly legible holo of five young faces above the words "Incoming Pages" in all their high-resolution glory. "Yes!"

One face belonged to Cam herself. Same self-cut brown hair and freckles. Another face had straight dark hair, pulled back in a tight ponytail, and the same meticulously shaped eyebrows over an intense stare as the real Sofia, who looked down at her. The holo definitely didn't capture her towering height, though. Standing over Cam, Sofia projected a stiletto sharpness.

Cam pushed her laptop aside and leapt up to shake Sofia's hand. "Wow! It's really great to meet another page."

"Agreed." Sofia took the proffered hand and gave it a firm shake. "What are you working on?" She gestured back down at Cam's array.

"This is my Beekor project." Cam puffed herself out in pride. "It's an adapter that you can slap on a non-Beekor phone or an older Beekor model in order to display holographic content. And this"—Cam gestured at the code on her screen—"is my software that makes it all possible."

"I saw you open the acceptance letter with holographic content support." Sofia looked thoughtful. Cam could see the gears turning in Sofia's head; then, suddenly, her eyebrows raised. "But that implies ... Impressive," Sofia said. Even though the change in her expression was minute, it seemed to speak volumes.

Cam beamed with restored pride. "That's right. I reverse-engineered Beekor protocols."

"This is for flight 993 to San Francisco International Airport. We will begin boarding business class at this time," the loudspeaker intruded.

Cam started and threw all her electronics back in her duffel bag in a frenzy, causing other belongings to pop out. As Cam dealt with her chaos, Sofia blithely bent down to pick up Cam's ticket.

"Seatmates," said Sofia, comparing the seat number on her own ticket.

"Really? That's great!" Cam gave up stuffing the bag and finally resorted to sitting on it to get it to zip closed. She got up, swung the massive bulk onto her shoulder, stumbled a few steps from the momentum, and gratefully took her ticket back from Sofia. Together they proceeded to the gate, Cam resembling a scuttling hermit crab; Sofia, a delicate crane pulling a single small white bag behind her. They made their way down the runway and onto the airplane.

As they reached their large reclining pod seats, Cam attempted to puzzle out how to actually get into the seat. She tried in vain to recall which voice command opened the tank cockpit in *Battlequeens: Apocalypse*. Cam watched Sofia stow her tiny bag neatly under the seat and tap a button to close a shutter over it and expose the seat cushion. Cam tried to play it cool and mimic the motion, but her massive bag didn't fit beneath the seat without significant stuffing, and the shutter emitted a mechanical whine of protest as it struggled to close over the bag. She heard a soft crunch and prayed it wasn't anything important.

"So," started Cam as she flopped into her seat and pointed at Sofia's glasses. "Can you tell me about your project?"

"I have moderate facial-recognition difficulties. As a child, my classmates just assumed I was just very rude. So, I made these"—Sofia tapped her frames—"to connect to this." She lifted her phone, the latest Beekor model, sleek, shiny, and made out of some exotic purple metal. "The camera in the glasses scans faces and runs them against my contact list, then against my calendar, social media, and email to present me with the name and context of each individual." She smiled slightly. "Now I am only rude when I intend to be."

Cam's eyes grew wide. "Incredible! Can I see?"

Sofia nodded and took off the black frames to hand them to Cam, who examined the tiny camera hidden in a false screw design over the right eye, and the microscopic projector in the right temple.

"Default Beekor smart glasses. Code is my own," Sofia stated. Cam held the glasses aloft. They were, indeed, the latest Beekor smart glasses, unmodified. She had only ever seen them on websites or reviewed on tech streamers' channels, never actually touched a pair. They were sleek, beautiful, and hideously expensive. At least $2,600 new. For the cheapest model. These were not the cheapest model. "Try them," Sofia encouraged.

Cam gingerly put the glasses on her face as Sofia swiped through an app on her phone. Suddenly, Cam saw her own face in a pop-up window with her name below it, projected onto the right lens of the glasses. Beneath her name was a sequence of tiny bullet points, notes that listed that she was a Beekor page and that Sofia had met her today at the airport.

"Amazing!" Cam turned to look at Sofia. As she observed her travel companion, the glasses identified Sofia's face and rendered a loading bar beneath her as it began fetching her info. Finally, it resolved with a subtle beep and presented a pop-up projection with her face and name. Sofia Ly, and another set of tiny bullet-point notes.

Cam read aloud. "'Flawless genius. Talented engineer. Favorite movie: *Dance Nights 2* . . .'?"

"Thank you for the compliments. And yes, the sequel is far superior," Sofia responded without hesitation or embarrassment. She pulled the glasses off Cam and placed them back onto her own face.

"Hello, can I get either of you something complimentary to drink before we take off?" Cam looked up to see a flight attendant softly smiling at them.

"Champagne, please," Sofia replied, and looked at Cam.

"Oh, uh." Cam had never had complimentary alcohol, let alone champagne. She had no idea what the options were. In a panic, she just said, "Uh, two, please. Thank you!" The attendant nodded and came back shortly with two fluted glasses on a metal tray. A tray? On a plane?

Both girls took their drinks, and Sofia lightly clinked Cam's glass (actual glass!) with hers. "Cheers to pages."

"To pages!" Cam sipped tentatively. It fizzed and bubbled in her mouth, tart, sweet, and stronger than she anticipated. Cam started to think she might actually like champagne.

"Would you like to see the code for my glasses app?" Sofia offered, placing her barely sipped glass down on the table-like area between them and pulling her razor-thin laptop out from her bag.

Cam took a bigger gulp of her complimentary champagne and responded enthusiastically, "Yes, please! I'd love that!" And the two delved deep into discussion about programs and algorithms and preferred languages to code in. Cam was so engrossed she didn't even notice them taking off, or the last vestiges of her familiar home disappearing in the window.

—

"How about this one?" Cam gestured at yet another Beekar.

Sofia merely looked at her, and Cam sighed, resigned to letting the fifth perfectly good car pass them.

They were standing on the curb of the arrival area of San Francisco International Airport. They had already grabbed their bags—Cam's hulking behemoth and Sofia's neat white roller, which interlocked and matched the smaller one she had brought on board—and were currently watching a fleet of cars swoop in to take people away. Some of the cars picked up what looked like family members, but just as many cars were of the autonomous variety from four or five competing self-driving taxi companies, as well as a rare few that were privately owned. Beekor had its own fleet of self-driving cars, Beekars, ranging from small commuter cars to minivans for families.

Sofia had let about a dozen of these cars get claimed by people behind them, merely saying "Inadequate" over each one.

Cam was about to give up and grab a car regardless of what her picky companion wanted, when Sofia pointed triumphantly at a slick white whale of a Beekar pulling up to the curb two cars down. She walked over to the car with such confidence and poise, three pale men in jeans and hoodies that had pounced on the same vehicle backed off. One even apologized to her. Sofia ignored them as she opened the gull-wing door and stepped in with her suitcase. Taken by surprise by the sudden action, Cam scrambled after her and barely hauled her bags into the car before the door shut behind her. Inside, there were two cushioned seats that looked closer to couches facing each other, side tables with storage underneath for their suitcases, large windows with curtains pulled open, and what appeared to be faux hardwood floors with a neat rug in the center. Was she supposed to take her shoes off inside the car? Toward the front, behind one of the couches, was an array of sensors and readouts along with a steering wheel that could be taken over by a human driver in an emergency. Cam could not even begin to calculate what a ride in one of these would cost normally. Sofia was already pulling up the QR code they had received in the orientation email and putting it on the scanner on her armrest. Cam noted that she kept her shoes on.

"Hello, Sofia, your destination is . . . Beekor Offices Omni Building. Your travel time is . . . twenty-seven . . . minutes. Please buckle your seat belt and enjoy the ride. Thank you for choosing Beekor," the car chirped at them.

"Conference car model, best seats," said Sofia. She pulled out two complimentary bottles of iced tea from the mini fridge hidden beneath her seat and handed one to Cam, who promptly dropped her bags in a heap in favor of the beverage.

"I've never been in an autonomous car before—well, I've used the semi-auto public buses around town—but not a private car." Cam buckled into her seat as the car pulled into traffic and sped away.

"Watch." Sofia, who sat into the seat opposing Cam, picked up her phone and tapped a few times before appearing to swipe a window from her phone onto the big window of the car, which promptly turned into a screen, causing all the other windows to dim and become opaque, rendering the outside world barely visible.

"*Dance Nights 2?*" Cam read the title on the screen aloud.

"Watch," Sofia repeated, and the movie began to play with surround sound.

Twenty-six minutes and forty-eight seconds later, Cam and Sofia's vehicle pulled up to the Omni building, right near one of the entrances to the Beekor campus.

"Don Julio can't keep running a double life as a veterinarian and the leader of a gang of exotic male dancers—the rival break-dancing gang is too good!" Cam leapt out of the car, absolutely energized.

"Wait until his mother dances," Sofia replied, stepping smoothly out and pulling her suitcase along with her. "I must handle a small visa issue. I'll see you at orientation shortly." And with that, Sofia waved and walked off across the campus with determination.

"Oh, uh, see you soon!" replied a dazed Cam. Then the sudden realization of where she was kicked in. She had been so enthralled with Sofia's movie, she had forgotten to be nervous, but now it was hitting her all at once. She had finally arrived at the headquarters of Beekor, the most powerful tech company in the world, the beating heart of the holographic computing revolution. She took a long look around her. The Beekar had deposited her in the exact location from which any number of magazine photos, article headers, and MiTube campus-walkthrough videos had been shot, which Cam had pored over through the years. Finally standing there in person, she experienced a momentary, intense déjà vu. Although the smell of the much-vaunted "meticulously cultivated scent landscape" was somewhat less impressive than some of the vlogs had made it out to be. . . .

The Beekor campus was a manicured landscape made of imported old trees, trimmed hedged pathways, and a profusion of flowers rolled between pristine buildings made of brushed steel, white-painted walls, and expansive windows. People circulated through the idyllic open space in singles or groups, on foot or by electric scooter, quickly or lazily taking a nap on the grass. There was also a metal sculpture that Cam thought looked like dancing noodles.

Cam got some puzzled looks as she held up her heavily modded phone, 3D-printed parts and all, and consulted the campus map Beekor had sent her. With finger gestures in the air, she rotated and zoomed until she was able to align the buildings in the hologram to what she was looking at and could zero in on where she was supposed to go. It looked like she was headed to a crushed juice box of a building.

Cam navigated the relentlessly pleasant campus. She passed Beekor employees milling about who were mostly well dressed, if a bit uniformly. Cam observed no small number of button-down shirts of a tastefully restrained pattern or trendy, ostensibly charitable internet shoe brands. However, there was an undercurrent of the extremely poorly dressed. A separate group of the old T-shirted, the besweatpanted, and the unkempt. Both subcultures filtered in and among each other and seemed on cordial terms.

She arrived at the hulking auditorium and encountered a sign on the ground: "New Page Orientation." The path terminated in a secured entry point with a bored-looking man in a blue uniform and cap sitting guard. He browsed his phone listlessly beside the security gate. Cam squeezed her bag strap tightly and walked up. She eventually managed to wrest his attention from a woodworking live stream with a tentative wave.

"Badge?" he asked.

"Oh, sorry, I'm part of the Beekor Accelerator Program," Cam said, by way of explanation. She tried to exude confidence and friendliness but had the sinking suspicion she resembled a stray dog, bedraggled and unwelcome. She tried to covertly straighten her jacket.

"Congratulations," he declared with minimal cheer. "In that case, you should have a temporary badge attached to your mail. Just activate that and I'll ping you." He held up a handheld near-field receiver device expectantly.

"Uh . . ." Cam began, and held up her phone. She swiped to the end of the acceptance letter and found some bizarre data that didn't work with her homemade device. Apparently, the image fix hadn't helped with whatever this was. The guard grimaced and attempted to ping her phone with his scanner. It made an unhappy noise and pinged red.

"I don't think it will actually—" She was cut off by the scanner pinging again as the guard attempted a different angle. It still pinged red. "Look, this isn't going to work." It pinged red a third time. "Is there somebody that you can talk to that will let you know they're expecting me?" She could feel herself on the edge of embarrassed panic.

"I'm sorry, I can't just let people wander into restricted areas," the guard began, not seeming sorry at all.

"Hey, maybe I can help?" A tall young man, impeccably dressed in a tailored gray suit with a white tee and holding a compostable coffee cup, strode up beside Cam. He smiled down at her with palpable confidence and incandescent charm. Cam heard herself involuntarily gasp. From his meticulous high fade with short, thick twists down to his crisp white trainers, with just a peek of fuchsia for his socks, he looked like he stepped out of a catalog for young businessmen. Cam became suddenly and intensely aware of how sweaty and disheveled she probably looked after all the travel. Her posture canting sharply at an angle under a straining duffel bag that was customized with patches of pentagrams, cartoon dinosaurs, and several breeds of pocket monster. All this while hauling a crumbling suitcase the size of a freight train.

The man held up his own gleaming Beekor badge for the guard, who pinged it dutifully. The security gate slid open. He didn't enter.

"Look, I can verify that she's one of the new pages." The man held up his phone and tabbed to a news article about the latest cohort of Beekor pages. He swiped about until he came to a picture of Cam. Despite having been taken with an old webcam and compressed a minimum of seventeen separate times, the picture was still recognizably her. "You see? Camila Diaz. No harm letting her in." The guard's resistance wavered under the young man's self-assuredness and affability. "Besides, if she causes any trouble, I'll take responsibility." He winked.

The guard's resistance crumbled. "Go on ahead," he said, defeated.

The man in the suit turned back to Cam and smiled. "All right, follow close so you can pass through with me before it closes." As he strode through at a measured pace, Cam stuck close enough to feel the heat from his body. From behind, it was abundantly clear to Cam that he did not skip leg day. Or ass day.

On the other side of the gate, he turned and grabbed her duffel from her with his free hand. "Here, let me take that." He lifted the heavy bag with easy grace, and Cam felt her spine straighten gratefully.

"Thanks for helping me out!" she burst out. "Are you running the orientation?" She wondered how he had known about her, and if she'd be seeing more of him while she was here.

He laughed, caught off guard, and a dimple appeared in his right cheek. "No, I'm one of the pages. I'm Marcus."

Chapter 3

MORE THAN A LITTLE MORTIFIED, Cam clutched her suitcase tightly and silently followed Marcus. They passed through a lobby full of large paintings that looked like bathroom-stall graffiti to a bank of elevators and up to a floor that appeared to be made entirely of novelty decorated meeting rooms. The furniture in the rooms seemed to vary wildly. As Cam passed down the hallway, she peered past the glass walls to rooms that looked like forests with toadstool chairs, a coral reef with jellyfish lights, and a cornfield with UFO-shaped screens.

"It's better in Wei-Yu," stated Marcus.

"What?" asked Cam, distracted by a room that was made to look like a destroyed city. The conference table was a concrete slab balanced on a mangled car. Were these fully custom pieces? Her internal price appraisal system shorted out.

"The coffee. It's better in the Wei-Yu Building. It's why I was outside to buzz you in; I just came from there. At Beekor, each building has a different brand of coffee and different food hall options. It's supposed to encourage movement between divisions and a free exchange of ideas," Marcus recited, as if he were giving a book report.

"Uh," Cam responded eloquently.

"But it really just means the whole campus is taking long coffee breaks waiting in line at one shop." Marcus looked over his shoulder and shot her a wry smile, like they were in on something together.

Cam's heart skipped a beat with that little smirk. It was the right level of irreverent and playful to make her blood hum with delight. It was the same taunting grin her ex-boyfriend had used to lure her into the woods with him for a hookup. But where Nick's cheeky ways had always induced a giddy little thrill, Marcus's look had her whole body tingling down to her very toes. Suddenly, she wanted to do anything to see his dimple again. "Maybe they should put the coffee on a train so it serves the whole campus," Cam began.

Marcus responded practically, "It would always be stuck at one stop."

"Right," said Cam, "which is why it would never stop." Marcus turned fully toward her and eyed her evenly. Cam felt her breath catch having his full attention focused on her. She became all too aware of her limbs, which felt heavy and uncoordinated. She worried she was being too weird, too other, too awkward next to his immaculate perfection. But with the memory of his devious grin, she stepped tentatively forward into the conversation. "It'll be going at a good clip, so people will have to run to catch up. And if you manage to get on, you can ride it to a new building or back to yours."

Marcus's dark eyes lit up, clearly delighted at Cam's frivolous banter, and she internally breathed a sigh of relief. "How would you disembark?" The corner of his mouth quirked up.

"Jell-O, lining the tracks. You just roll off onto it," Cam said easily.

"What flavors?" Marcus egged her on.

"Anything but cherry."

"Agreed. And I think we should add trampolines along the tracks to provide an easy boarding process. Help you jump over the Jell-O," Marcus said.

"Yes! You'll run after the train, jump on the trampoline, and launch into an open door."

"No, windows only."

"And the reward better be the best coffee you've ever had in your life." Cam laughed.

"Here, try some. I got a latte." Marcus offered Cam his coffee cup.

"Oh, uh, thanks!" Cam took the cup, suddenly flustered and shy again. She took a tiny sip, almost unable to taste the drink as Marcus watched her to gauge her reaction. "Oh wow," she said, surprised. "This *is* pretty good." She wasn't even lying. She handed the cup back to him.

"Is it trampoline good?" Marcus teased.

"I don't know. I actually haven't tried a lot of coffee." She usually spent her stimulant budget on twelve-hour energy shots ($25 each) that she rationed out in quarter-bottle increments.

"We should fix that. Have to know what you're willing to defy death for." Marcus flashed her a full-blown smile. And there it was, dimple on the right. "Here we are." He opened a door and ushered her through.

Under the megawatt glare of Marcus's smile, Cam couldn't even attempt to puzzle out whether she had just been asked out on a date—or if she would even entertain the thought. She stood awkwardly in the doorway, struggling to take in her surroundings.

The large room contained structures around the perimeter that looked like they belonged in a playground. Only, it was a playground entirely in white and shades of gray, sized to fit adults. There were swings, a teeter-totter, a jungle gym, rocking horses, and a roundabout. The pièce de résistance was a slide that started somewhere upstairs and terminated in a ball pit filled with white and gray balls. In the middle of the room, there were several tables that resembled large white picnic tables. Three of the tables were occupied by small groups of people.

A hush came over the room as every occupant simultaneously turned to look at Cam and Marcus. Everybody was ridiculously good-looking, and

Cam couldn't help but imagine each and every one of them judging her and finding her wanting. She was reminded forcibly of the time in the third grade when she had to tell her teacher, in front of the whole class, that her mother couldn't pay the fees for the class field trip to the zoo. She felt her classmates' pitying stares as she went to bed that night, and many nights after. She tucked her hair anxiously behind her ear.

"Excellent. You must be Camila Diaz. I'm Jessica." A high-efficiency functionary slid into Cam's field of view and neatly interjected herself into the silence. "I'm a senior PR manager and also the primary coordinator for the Accelerator Program. Marcus, thank you so much for taking the time to guide Camila here. Camila, you can put your bags in this corner here. We just have some paperwork for you to go over while we wait for our last page." Jessica delivered her speech in one seamless, hyperefficient pass, shaking Cam's hand, gesturing her toward a table, and dismissing her all in one go.

Cam woodenly followed orders, rolling her suitcase next to where Marcus leaned her duffel bag and making her way to the indicated table, where several other efficient-looking functionaries with white-and-blue Beekor badges awaited. Marcus thanked Jessica with a smile. Cam noticed there was no dimple.

Once at her assigned table, a young woman with blown-out bouncing hair leaned across to Cam and slid her a stapled stack of paper and a specialized green Beekor badge with that same cheap webcam photo on it. "Hello Camila, I'm Jennifer, and I'll be your daily coordinator! I'll be handling your event schedule, and I'm also the one you should reach out to if you have any questions or concerns. Here's my contact information, here's your initial itinerary, which is subject to change, please note you'll have your first one-on-one with Wyatt tomorrow morning—so exciting, he normally doesn't see the pages until they're here at least a week—here's the address of your residence, who you can call if you have any issues with the location—I don't think you will, it's absolutely gorgeous, I'm so jealous of all of you—this is the security desk, which will answer twenty-four/seven. Here's a list of all the places to eat on campus—I circled my favorites; they are free for all Beekor employees and guests, so just scan your badge. Here are some of my favorite places to eat in the city, but please ask me for any more recommendations, that's what I'm here for." Cam swore Jennifer didn't take a breath through the entire monologue as she flipped through and pointed to each page with an increasingly upbeat attitude. "I also emailed all of this to you!"

Cam leapt at the conversational opening. "Um, actually I had a hard time opening some of the previous files you sent me. Could you possibly make sure it's all backward-compatible?"

Jennifer blinked at the unexpected deviation from her script. "Oh? Which generation do you have?"

"Well . . ." Cam pulled out her non-Beekor phone, covered in grafted-on 3D-printed parts and exposed ribbon cables. "It's . . . intergenerational?"

Jennifer visibly recoiled. "Oh, no, no, that won't do. Beekor canNOT have you running around with that." She began furiously typing on her phone. "You'll have a new one before you leave this room. What's your favorite color?"

"Ah, I like . . . green? I think? But really, it's not necessary—"

"I have to make a few calls. Jerry, can you please take over?" Jennifer tore out of the room like a comet.

The slightly portly man in a suit seated to her right, who had been silent up until now, opened up his suitcase and pulled out a thick blue folder that put Jennifer's stack of papers to shame.

"Hello, Camila. I'm Jerry, and I'm from the HR department. I've got a few simple documents for you to sign so that we can get you started. It's all fairly boilerplate. Please sign here, here, fill out this form with your address and social security number, initial here, here, here, and here. Then sign here, here, initial here, sign here, and your address along with your signature one more time." Jerry flipped through each of the pages, pointing to what Cam needed to fill out before handing her a pen. "Let me know if you have any questions," he finished, in a tone that seemed to expect no questions.

Cam looked around the room. She was able to discern her fellow pages by process of elimination. They were all in their early twenties and at least a decade younger than anyone else in the room. Marcus was chatting quietly with the two employees at his table, pen resting on a stack of already-signed documents. Sofia was still absent, presumably dealing with visa issues. The other two pages couldn't have been more different from each other.

One had neat blond hair with a pair of black earbuds poking out and was dressed simply but comfortably in a worn gray sweater from a developers conference that had happened a decade prior. He seemed to be making determined progress on his paperwork while avoiding much interaction or eye contact with the Beekor employees assigned to him. The toe of his sneakered foot tapped away rhythmically

The other page was strikingly dressed in a teal leopard-print zoot suit with gold accents, a button-down shirt with bright fuchsia flowers, and flaming-red hair slicked back to the nape of the neck. This page was exchanging quips with their Beekor employees while signing papers they didn't even bother looking at. Seeming to sense Cam's gaze, the page suddenly looked up, made direct eye contact, smiled sparklingly, and waved. Their purple eyeliner was in the shape of lightning bolts. Cam waved back and set to work on her legal documents.

One was an NDA, which basically said she couldn't disclose the proprietary information she was inevitably going to see while walking around the campus to anyone else, especially competition. Easy, signed. The next asked about her tax information. Easy, signed. After that the documentation got confusing with a lot of legal jargon. She felt out of her depth as she asked question after question. It felt like all the attention in the room was on her.

"What's this part here, about entering into a contract relationship with . . . Grow Unlimited?" Cam asked. "I thought the program was run by Beekor."

"Ah, don't worry about that. The program is run by a separate 501(c) (3) charitable organization called Grow Unlimited, for tax purposes. It in no way affects your experience; it's only for internal accounting, and staff on loan from Beekor comprise the entire org," Jerry responded with the same subtly fraying patience with which he had answered every question.

"All right," said Cam, wilting under yet another of Jerry's laconic responses, and signed the final page. She leaned back, mentally exhausted. Jerry shook her hand and thanked her as he assembled the paperwork and got up to deliver it wherever it was intended, before, Cam presumed, setting himself down in a docking station to recharge for the rest of the day.

"Done signing your firstborn away to Beekor?" came a playful voice from a table away.

The page in teal grinned and waved Cam over as they took a seat across from the blond page. Both appeared to have completed their paperwork, successfully dispelling their respective handlers.

"Avery. They/them/emperor," the page declaimed with a dramatic gesture of one kaleidoscopically attired arm. Cam walked over.

"Hi, uh, good to meet you. I'm Cam. She/her." Cam tried not to squirm too much under the other page's intense scrutiny. "Can I sit here?" Cam asked the blond page, looking away from Avery's thousand-watt gaze and gesturing to the bench to the right of the page.

He didn't look up from his hands, which were folding some paper, but he nodded curtly. "I'm James. Nice to meet you both."

"Is that a grand piano?" Marcus asked, sliding next to Avery and hip-checking them good naturedly farther down the bench. Cam followed Marcus's pointed finger. James had been slowly turning Jennifer's pages of phone numbers and recommendations into a set of intricate, tiny origami musical instruments.

"Wow! That's fantastic!" Avery made to grab what looked like a finger-length paper saxophone before Marcus lightly smacked their hand.

"You have to ask. You're not five anymore," Marcus chastised.

"Oh my god, you're never going to let that go, are you?" Avery pouted as they withdrew their hand. "It was literally over fifteen years ago."

"And you literally ate my birthday cake before the party even started," Marcus replied in what was obviously a thoroughly worn argument, with more gentle ribbing than resentment. "Hey, I'm Marcus. Can I pick this up?" This last was directed at James, who paused in his folding to glance briefly at Marcus before giving a small nod.

Marcus gingerly picked up what indeed looked like a miniature piano. "You're really good," he said, delicately spinning the piece to admire the precise craftsmanship.

Cam heard the soft click of the door opening and looked up to see Sofia swanning gracefully in with her interlocking suitcases. She handed off her own stack of signed papers to a functionary.

"Sofia!" Cam called to her, relieved to see a familiar face. She waved for the tall young woman to sit next to her.

Avery leapt up and halted Sofia with one outstretched palm. With a flourish, they bowed. "I wasn't aware that angels were accepted to the Accelerator Program," Avery flirted shamelessly. They insistently claimed Sofia's luggage and deposited it precisely at the table, then returned to her side.

"Apparently peacocks too," Sofia responded dryly, as she allowed herself to be escorted to the table with the rest of the pages.

Marcus started coughing in a way that sounded suspiciously like a laugh. Avery's eyes gleamed with a mischievous light.

Before they could say anything, Wyatt Ecker strode briskly into the room. *The* Wyatt Ecker. Beekor CEO. Industry titan. *Time's* Person of the Year (and not the year when everybody got it). Cam's breath caught. He appeared as if he had stepped straight off of a magazine cover. Wyatt's accomplishments stacked up and itemized themselves in Cam's brain, all the way down to that satisfying *click*. In person, the man projected an almost-palpable glow of power and fame, as if he were in his own personal spotlight. Cam's hands shook. "All right, everybody, take a seat. Let's get started, shall we?"

Chapter 4

WYATT STRODE PURPOSEFULLY TO THE front of the room. Assistants, people with cameras, employees with tablets full of notes, and caterers carrying bar height white mini tables for people to cluster around streamed in behind him to take places around the space. As people shuffled in, Wyatt looked up pensively and pursed his lips. Ruggedly handsome in his early fifties, Wyatt's long salt-and-pepper hair was swept back in waves from his deep widow's peak. His outfit, despite appearing to be a casual black sweater and slacks, projected an air of high quality and cost. As everybody quieted expectantly and the shuffling ceased, Wyatt turned to face the pages. He smiled warmly and began. "Hello and welcome. I'm Wyatt Ecker, the CEO of Beekor Industries. It's my honor and privilege to induct a new cohort of pages into the Beekor Accelerator Program!"

Somebody yelped a cheer, eliciting a grin from Wyatt. He began to walk slowly around the cleared space as he spoke. "When Lee Baker and I founded Beekor, we envisioned a company that would act as an inspiration and a haven for those with the will to think unconventional thoughts and try unconventional things." Wyatt punctuated his points with hand gestures, as if he were attempting to seize those new ideas and drag them into existence. "We planned to create a space where new ideas could flourish and under-represented talent could shine." Wyatt paused dramatically. "You pages are the distilled-down essence of that vision." He turned toward them, and his gaze swept past each of them. "You're young and ambitious, from a broad range of backgrounds, and just at the start of your careers. Fresh ideas and different perspectives like yours are exactly what an established company like Beekor needs." He began to pace again. "And in return, we will empower you to build! We will set you on the best possible career trajectory.

"As pages, you will have unfettered access to our innovation lab and our design teams, including tools, technologies, and processes that are not yet available to the public. Do you want avionics-grade 3D printers? Help yourself." James adjusted his glasses, and the overhead light flashed off his lenses. "Need a meeting with the elusive artist Banksy?" Wyatt winked at Avery. "Sure, we can get you an invite to his birthday party. In addition, you will have access to our team of advisers, which includes some of the best minds in business." Wyatt grinned. "And by that I mean myself." Everyone chuckled. "And some of our other executives.

"We will run regular office hours to discuss the progress of your projects. Over the next six months, we hope to hone your instincts, develop your ideas, and build new products, tools, and businesses together." He made brief eye contact with Cam. She felt as if he had perceived her down to her very core. "Midway through the program, Beekor will host its annual conference, The Beekor International Developer Conference." He raised his eyebrows. "No doubt, you're all familiar with it, and you'll all have invites to attend, take part, and meet industry greats from around the world! That's just one of the many perks you'll get access to throughout the program." He laughed. "Impress us, and there's a lot more where that came from."

He continued. "At the conclusion of the program, we'll host a public commencement event, where some of you will get to share your projects with the world. At the end of your term, all of you will have a place here at Beekor as a member of one of our existing teams, but for the most successful of you—the page who has demonstrated the most ingenuity and capability—we will be provide a three-million-dollar budget with which to build a brand-new team all your own here at Beekor, with full access to all our resources for hiring, marketing, and distribution, so we can continue to execute on your project, together." Cam gasped. That's what she wanted more than anything. Being able to lead a team at Beekor, working on her dream project, bringing Specio to the masses. "This early in your careers, the Accelerator Program is an unparalleled opportunity." Wyatt spoke with energy and gestured expansively. "Which is only fitting for unparalleled talents!"

He took on a reflective tone. "First and foremost, however, we expect you to be independent thinkers. We are not looking to produce cookie-cutter clones of our current staff. So shine on, you crazy diamonds." He grinned self-effacingly. Sofia quietly snickered.

Earnestly, he finished, "I look forward to working closely with you to build a better world."

The assembled staff around the pages broke into applause. Cam joined them. Exhilarated, she felt like she had found herself at the center of the universe. A tap on her shoulder brought her out of her reverie. She looked up to see Jennifer smiling and a little out of breath.

"Sorry that took so long—here's your new phone!" She handed Cam a slender box. Cam's eyes widened as she realized that this was not only the latest model, but it was also a proprietary one with maxed-out stats. It was one of the limited-edition models, individually numbered, with only five thousand total issued worldwide. And it was indeed green. $6,300. More than she had made at her old part-time job in six months at the computer shop back home. Cam held the box gingerly and looked up at Jennifer, dumbfounded.

"I can't possibly—" Cam began, pushing the phone back toward Jennifer.

"We want to make sure you have the tools you need to succeed!" Jennifer beamed, cutting Cam off and putting her hands behind her back. "Welcome to Beekor!"

Cam suddenly felt the seed of something big and beautiful taking root. Her heart felt full of promise as she began to glimpse the bright future that lay ahead of her here at Beekor.

"All right, let's gather for the group photo now!" Jennifer called out in good cheer. Instantly, a photographer and two assistants with light boxes and reflectors leapt to the forefront. Cam and the rest of the pages were ushered forward to surround Wyatt, Jennifer, and several people that radiated some power or other. The photographer immediately began to take pictures and bark orders, and the session was in full swing before Cam had time to realize that *she* was about to be in the same exact cohort group picture she had studied in tech journals every six months. The assistants dove in between the group, adjusting lights, directing angles, changing people's positions, all to frame Wyatt. Without even realizing what had happened, Cam found herself in the back, partially hidden behind Sofia's statuesque figure, to which the camera seemed to naturally gravitate, as the group photo period wound down.

"Cameo shots," ordered the photographer, and Cam was unceremoniously thrust out of the limelight. She found herself at the edge, blinking in confusion, as Wyatt leaned in to speak cordially with Marcus and Avery. Avery laughed photogenically. The photographer continued to circle them taking pictures.

"Your first photo shoot," stated a deep baritone voice. Cam looked up, and up, and up, to a tall, broad man who looked like he had more muscles than his blue-gray suit could handle. She thought he looked vaguely familiar.

"Yeah, actually. That obvious?" Cam laughed.

"You don't know your angles." A woman with tight box braids and a light pink suit who also seemed familiar smirked. "You'll need to figure those out before the next publicity shoot. But"—her gaze swept up and down Cam's appearance—"you probably won't have to do that many."

Cam felt her face heat with a wave of self-consciousness. She compared her frayed clothing and crudely chopped hair to this flawlessly crisp woman as a caterer bearing a tray of pink drinks decorated with tiny sprigs of lavender in cut glasses interjected his tray into the group.

"Lovely." Avery descended from nowhere and grabbed a drink for themselves before thrusting one at Cam. They downed their drink like it was a shot, put the empty back on the tray, and grabbed a fresh one.

The woman took a glass for herself, and the man gestured at the caterer without looking at him. "Whiskey, rocks."

Cam went to thank the caterer, but he had already left.

"Amari, you bitch, good to see you," Avery playfully greeted the woman next to Cam. "I didn't know you'd be here."

"Well, you know, they like to prop us past successes up in front of the new crew. Give you a goal to aspire to and all that." Amari grinned wryly, flashing bright white teeth framed by dark red lipstick.

Her face suddenly clicked for Cam. "You're Amari Davis. You were part of the Beekor Accelerator Program a few years ago." Cam looked to the man next to her, "And you're Keloa Ogawa. You were in the program a few years before that."

Keola winced. "I was only the year before. I'm not that old."

As Amari laughed with relish at Keloa's discomfort, Cam took a swig of her drink and almost choked. From the way Avery had slung back their drink, Cam had assumed it was lemonade. It was not. Cam was used to 40s and plastic-jug vodka mixed with off-brand sodas. Her experience sneaking out to drink with friends after high school in the ponderous hulk of a rusted-out Cadillac had not prepared her for the delicate but deceptively strong cocktail of sweet flavors. And she hadn't drunk much at all in the past couple of years. She had been too busy juggling community college classes, transitioning to full-time work at her cousin's computer shop, and building her own prototype for more than the occasional bonfire in the woods.

Avery laughed and patted her back. "Take it easy. St-Germain can sneak up on you if you're not used to it."

"I've never tried that before," Cam admitted, taking a smaller sip this time. It was delicious, whatever it was.

"Aww, a bumpkin," Amari cooed at Cam, and Cam felt herself stiffen. "That explains your . . . sense of fashion." She favored Cam with that calculating, sweeping look again. "You're this year's PR opportunity."

"I'm sure all of this is very new and exciting for you," Keloa said to Cam.

Cam hesitated as the air went out of her. "I mean, yes?" she eventually replied. She was at a loss for how to respond. She could practically feel him placing his hands on his knees to lean down to address her like she was a small child. Cam felt herself looking down at her feet, at her ragged sneakers, next to their glossy leather loafers, patent black heels, and boots laden with shiny buckles.

"So, did you know you'll be joining my team?" Amari turned to address Avery, apparently having dismissed Cam.

"You're part of Outreach now?" Avery asked. "I thought I would be with Bailey."

"They got sniped by TrySpace, so I moved over."

"Really?" Avery scoffed. "That company is still running?"

Amari shrugged. "You know how it goes—they'll probably be hired back to Beekor next year with a raise. But in the meantime, it freed up space for me. You play these next six months right, Avery, and you'll have my spot when I get promoted."

"Not if I don't leapfrog you and get that promotion first." Avery grinned ferally.

Amari's eyes glinted like a shark that tasted blood in the water.

"Don't mind them—they've been like this since we were children," Keloa sighed exasperatedly to Cam.

Cam was trying to figure out a response when she felt a tap on her shoulder. It was one of the photographer's assistants. "Can you please move aside so we can get a picture of this group?" she asked, gesturing at Avery, Amari, and Keloa.

"Oh, sure." Cam tried to slip unobtrusively away.

Before she could get too far, Avery grabbed her sleeve and gave her a look that read as charitable, generous, and pitying all at once. "Hey, don't worry. I'll help you get up to speed, okay? It'll be our side project." They winked and released her before she could decide how she felt about that prospect.

Set adrift, Cam saw the meet and greet had shifted in general tenor to unstructured conversations. The executives and VIPs had filtered throughout the room and were chatting loudly. Their looks ranged from business drag, suit and tie, to informal but professional button-downs. Two of them were barefoot. Platters of drinks and hors d'oeuvres circled the room, carried by catering staff in iconic black-and-white suits.

With everyone's attention finally off of her, Cam realized she was absolutely ravenous. She practically pounced on the first tray she saw.

"Bacon-wrapped peach with goat cheese?" the caterer asked, offering the tray to Cam.

"How many can I take?" she asked, practically salivating.

The caterer laughed. "As many as you want. It means I can go back out faster."

Well, when they put it like that, she was only being helpful, taking two. She was also helpful to the tray of small bags of deep-fried zucchini strips, to the scallops with a strawberry salsa, extra helpful to the cashew chicken lettuce wraps (a tray so good she decided to circle back and help it twice), to the fluffy pastry filled with mushrooms, and to a cup made of fried wonton filled with a creamy soup.

Her nerves, which had started to fray in the airport and only continued to frazzle with each completely new experience, finally began to settle. Cam let her guard down and began to enjoy herself. Which was when, leisurely reaching for what appeared to be a miniature hamburger, she collided mid-grab with somebody else's hand.

"Sorry!" She looked up and experienced a full-body shock as she made eye contact with Lee Baker, cofounder of Beekor and her personal hero. Wyatt may have been the face of Beekor, but the brains were all Lee. Cam had heard that she was on some sort of long-term sabbatical, although she hadn't said much to the press. Lee was in her midforties. She wasn't particularly tall or beautiful, but her green hair, shaved on the sides, her absolute confidence, and her legendary reputation as one of the most technically capable humans to have ever walked the planet contributed to a palpable solar flare of intimidation.

"You gotta give it to him, that asshole never skimps on the spread." Lee Baker plopped the tiny burger in her mouth as the server moved on. Even the way she chewed and enjoyed her burger was imbued with a sort of wry humor.

Cam tried to think of anything to say, but in the presence of her idol, her brain was completely short-circuiting. She gave up and opted to laugh nervously instead. All Cam could think about was the poster of Lee on her wall, with the quote "The future is decided by optimists!"

"Can't fault him for his taste, at least," Lee continued, then stared daggers across the room at Wyatt. She sighed and glanced at Cam with a sip of her beer. "So, what got you here?" She gestured at Cam's bulging pocket, where some of the wires from her phone poked out.

With a mixture of pride and trepidation, Cam slowly pulled out her baby, her Frankensteined phone with all its attached parts. Lee Baker looked at the heap of parts, nonplussed. Her eyes roved the haphazard assemblage critically, until she spotted the type of phone that it was, intuited the utility of the parts, and understanding dawned. Her eyes went wide, and her mouth formed an O shape.

"What did you say your name was?" Lee queried, her eyes seeming to focus on Cam for the first time.

"Camila Diaz. Cam," she stammered.

"Turn it on. Let me see it," Lee commanded excitedly.

Cam tried to still her shaking hands as she put her drink down and booted the phone up. "There are still a lot of bugs in messaging and media playback interop. Figuring out the way the Beekor protocol sends and receives some types of content has been hard."

Lee waved her concerns away and took a sip of beer. Finally, the phone booted successfully and the off-brand phone manufacturer logo began hovering and spinning in space above the phone. Lee laughed aloud and clapped Cam on the shoulder. "It looks like a chastity cage and a Transformer fucked, but I'm impressed!"

Lee looked up and stared intently across the room. Cam glanced over Lee's hand and saw Wyatt staring right back at Lee. His characteristic thousand-watt smile was absent from his face.

Lee squeezed Cam's shoulder and said, almost offhandedly, "You and I will be meeting every two weeks on Wednesdays. It'll be our secret." Lee began to hold up her Beekor phone to exchange contact info via near-field communication, realized it wasn't going to work, and scrounged in her pockets to retrieve an old-fashioned business card instead.

Cam dropped her phone back into her pocket and took the card with both hands. As she gazed at it, Lee practically jumped a server, swept their whole tray of tiny lobster quiches onto a plate, and turned to leave. "Text me your info. I gotta get out of here. Great to meet you, Cam!" she called over her shoulder as she walked determinedly out.

"Great to meet you," Cam called back even though Lee was already long gone. She clutched the card to her chest and stared flabbergasted at the place the industry legend had vacated.

"Lovestruck?" Sofia wandered to Cam's side at the table. James followed, meticulously arranging snacks by color on his plate.

"I can't tell if I'm drunk from this incredible cocktail or if I'm hallucinating, but I'm pretty sure I just embarrassed myself in front of my personal hero.

Anyway, look! Lee Baker just gave me her business card!" Cam flourished the card with manic disbelief.

Sofia smiled. "I'm envious but happy for you." Sofia held up her glass. "Cheers!" And Cam could tell that Sofia was genuine in her celebration.

Cam grabbed her drink, clinked glasses with Sofia, pocketed Lee's card, finished her cocktail, then snagged another off a passing tray. "Don't worry, now that me and Lee Baker are besties, you'll be first on my list for the slumber party invites," she teased.

"I never understood how people are meant to party while sleeping, but I hope you all enjoy your bed together." James made brief eye contact, then looked away. He began eating his hors d'oeuvres in the order he had arranged as the corner of his mouth folded up into the tiniest smirk.

Cam hesitated, then burst out laughing. "So it looks like we were all chosen for our sense of humor." She took a joyful bite from a tiny toast with chicken salad and let out an audible moan. It wasn't chicken, it was crab, and it was one of the best things she had ever eaten in her life.

"With sounds like that, exactly what is happening over here?" Avery grinned a Cheshire Cat smile as they sidled up to the three of them from one side. Amari and Keloa, thankfully, were nowhere in sight.

"And can I join?" Marcus asked as he approached them from the other side.

"We were just working out how we're going to be running this company within two months," Cam preened.

Avery arched an eyebrow. "That long? What say we set our sights a little bit higher?" They held up their glass. "To world domination!"

"To world domination," the other pages all cheered back. James took a measured sip, Cam and Marcus took a gulp, but both Sofia and Avery tossed the remains of their drinks back in one go. A fire lit in Avery's eyes, and they looked appraisingly up at the six inches Sofia had on them.

"Shall we get another?" Avery quirked a brow up at the tall young woman. Sofia tilted her head, assessing Avery. Cam had a delightful moment to see

.the bombastic page squirm uncomfortably under Sofia's scrutiny. Sofia finally nodded once with a smile. The two walked off in search of a drinks tray while James moved on after a passing server pursuing savory bites. Suddenly, it was just Cam and Marcus.

"So, about that coffee invite . . ." Cam began, tucking her hair nervously behind her ear.

"Yes, let's set up a time after you've become accustomed to your team."

Cam recoiled in hurt at his polite, formal smile, dimple nowhere in sight. His eyes slid to something over her shoulder.

Wyatt intruded from behind her and took Marcus by the arm. "Marcus, I was looking for you!" He addressed Marcus as if they were already well acquainted. Cam spun in surprise. "We need to get you in front of Pascal. He's going to be heading up a new business unit of ours, and I think you should get some exposure to him and the team." Marcus let himself get pulled away without a backward glance, leaving Cam confused, in a state of emotional whiplash, and alone.

Chapter 5

"AND THIS IS WHERE YOU'LL be staying!" Jennifer chirruped as the self-driving SUV pulled up to a beautiful restored Victorian home on the edge of the Beekor campus. Jennifer had fairly bludgeoned the pages with a continuous upbeat patter the entire time they were in her presence, from when she gathered Sofia and Avery away from the bar, unstuck Cam from the table where the tiny toasts with crab lived, fished James out of the ball pit, *and* delivered them all to what would be their accommodations for the duration of the program. Cam was exhausted just listening to her. Marcus had been asked to remain behind in the meeting rooms with Wyatt and some of the other VIPs.

The house was three stories tall with a garage below, but not very wide. The building had a round tower in the corner that extended all the way to the top and was perforated with enormous bay windows. Elaborate wooden patterns ran around the trim, windows, and beneath the roof overhang. It looked beautiful and old and wildly out of place on the futuristic campus of sleek steel and glass. "Lee Baker grew up in this house!"

They all exited the vehicle and grabbed their bags. Jennifer led them to a wrought-iron gate between tall hedges that enclosed the house and a front yard. "Lee had the house brought here on a giant truck bed and had plumbing and electricity run out to the place after Beekor first broke a billion dollars in market cap."

"Vanity?" Sofia whispered to Cam as Cam tried to figure out what that would even begin to cost.

Jennifer overheard and delivered a strained laugh, and for the first time, her animated voice flattened a little. "It wasn't that she wanted to move her home just for the sake of it. Several elderly neighbors successfully lobbied the city of San Francisco to declare the house a historic landmark, and the only way Lee could build a larger building with space for multiple families on the lot was to also promise to preserve the home in its current form."

"She wasn't allowed to build more housing unless she could afford to move and preserve the old building?" Cam was overwhelmed by the convoluted implications. "How is that sustainable? Aren't there tons of people trying to move to the city all the time because of the job opportunities out here?"

Jennifer nodded and made a sour face. "One battle at a time." The well-oiled gate opened without a squeak as she walked through it and led them to the front lawn. "The house was painted in these shades of pink and purple just last year," she trilled with an expansive gesture, her pep returning.

Avery slid in between Cam and Sofia to jerk their chin cheekily at a small memorial stone set in the grass to the side. "They say that's the exact spot where Lee Baker envisioned the lensing system that would enable Beekor holographic technology, during a particularly productive mushroom trip." Sofia took out her phone and snapped a picture.

If Jennifer overheard this bit of gossip, she chose to ignore it, instead ushering the group through the front door.

The interior of the house was beautiful. The floors were all hardwood, finished to a high gloss. Molding decorated every trim, and tasteful wallpaper hearkened to the Victorian house traditions while still looking modern. "This is the living room." Jennifer gestured to a space off the right of the entryway as she and the pages all took off their shoes to enter the house. The entertainment system was terrifyingly modern, with full support for large scale in-air projection ($3,500), massive fully custom speakers ($???), and a laser disc player (cheap, but really cool to see one of these still floating around). The couch was gigantic and just old enough to be comfortable without looking worn. The ergonomic Swedish conversation chairs looked less comfortable but more suave (definitely unreasonably expensive).

Avery dropped onto the couch. "This is my stop."

"We haven't gotten to the bedrooms yet. They are an absolute delight!" promised Jennifer.

Avery waved Jennifer off. "I'll just take whatever bedroom is left unclaimed. I'm figuring out which party I'm going to tonight. You want in?" This last was directed at the three pages.

James shook his head no. Cam, beginning to feel the exhaustion of the day settle into her bones, also shook her head. She just wanted to take a shower and fall asleep.

Sofia, however, nodded. "Let me change first."

Avery's eyes lit up. "Wear something to dance in."

Jennifer proceeded with the remaining pages. "This is the kitchen, fully restored a couple years ago." The kitchen gleamed with marble surfaces and stainless steel. The stove had five burners and an enormous brass hood. Cam rummaged around in awe. There was even a warming rack set into the kitchen island, disguised to look like the same wood paneling as the rest of the drawers. One wall was made of floor-to-ceiling sliding glass doors, indicating they could be opened to merge the kitchen seamlessly with the large deck and grill outside. It was, by a fair margin, the most incredible kitchen Cam had ever seen in person.

"Down these stairs is the garage. We keep tools, 3D-printers, the CNC machine, all that stuff in there."

James stopped tapping his foot and looked down the hall. "What about metal printing? Smelting furnace? Vapor deposition fabrication chamber with vacuum bell?" Cam thought these were all really good questions. She was practically salivating.

Jennifer beamed, by all appearances ecstatic about any chance to answer questions about Beekor. "Anything that isn't here can be found at the main workshop on campus, to which you all have access. I'll take you there tomorrow!"

Jennifer started up the stairwell. "Bring your bags! Up here we've got four bedrooms, two full baths, and the game room." Jennifer opened a door onto a richly decorated space with dark wooden panels, heavy carpets, a massive pool table, and a fully stocked bar in the corner. Cam didn't know much about liquor, but the way Sofia eyed the bottles appreciatively, she assumed that they were top shelf.

"The bar is yours to enjoy as well. Email me if you need a restock." Jennifer led them back out of the game room. "Lastly, there is a room up these stairs in the attic. It has a sloped ceiling, which makes it a little tight, but your reward is a completely private full bathroom. It is, in my opinion, the cutest room in the house!" Jennifer clapped her hands in her enthusiasm. "This is where I head back. Please make yourselves comfortable and consult your packets if you are looking for somewhere to eat or visit during your time off."

As Jennifer descended the stairs back to the first floor, the remaining three explored the bedrooms. At least, Cam and Sofia did.

"I want this one," James said decisively, walking into the first room on the right after a brief examination. Cam caught a fleeting glance at a dark room with metal accents and a chandelier that looked like an Alexander Calder kinetic sculpture, before James waved the other two an abrupt good night and closed the door behind him. Cam peeked into a room farther down the hallway. It was wallpapered in a dark green floral pattern, held a large four-poster bed, a wooden rolltop desk and a matching wardrobe. It was also already occupied. Looking at the blazers hanging up neatly in the open wardrobe, Cam assumed Marcus had been here and fully unpacked. How much earlier had he arrived, anyway?

The third room had a mural of a giant bird-of-paradise on one wall. Cam met Sofia there, and they both looked at each other and simply said, "Avery."

The fourth room was painted in a tasteful light blue with ornate white trim everywhere. Sofia looked around with pleasure and put her bags down. "Wedgwood aesthetic." She sounded utterly charmed. Cam didn't know what that was, but she knew that meant the attic was for her.

She turned and hauled her stuff up a precariously narrow flight of stairs to a landing with a single door. Opening it was like stepping into a grown-up version of a childhood fantasy of living in a tree fort. Wallpapered in soft green, there was a cozy bay window with cushions in front of it, a large platform bed, a built-in closet, a small bathroom with a smaller shower, and even a private patio with just enough space for a love seat.

"This is going to be the best time of my life," said Cam. Though if it was a realization or declaration, she didn't know.

Chapter 6

CAM SPRANG AWAKE WITH A start, hyperalert. She looked around her room pensively. Early sun poured through her new, enormous bay window, lighting the room with a brilliant glow. Though Jennifer had called it tight, the room was still bigger than the entire apartment Cam had shared with her mother. Its size, and the hushed silence of the surrounding campus, had actually made it hard for her to fall asleep. And the lack of train noises had left her feeling oddly jumpy all night. Or maybe it was just her nervousness about meeting Wyatt one-on-one.

When Jennifer had mentioned the meeting yesterday, Cam hadn't been able to process it under the barrage of other information she had been inundated with. But last night, she had finally gotten the chance to go over Jennifer's extensive packet and had found that she was indeed scheduled to meet with the cofounder of Beekor in the morning. In fact, he was going to personally walk her to her new work space. It was a level of direct interaction that Cam hadn't anticipated. The prospect of being so close to one of the most powerful people on the planet was terrifying. Cam had spent half the night ruminating on ways to show off Specio. A demonstration of some kind?

Cam threw off the covers and walked to the closet that was filled with the contents of her suitcase she had unpacked in her insomnia the night before. Dismayed, she realized she just didn't own anything that seemed up to the occasion. She finally pulled out a dressier-feeling pair of jeans, a black shirt with only a tiny logo for the puppy-playdate place she worked at one summer in the corner, and pulled a very slightly rumpled plaid button-down on over top. A pair of worn but clean sneakers completed the look. Cam looked at herself in the mirror as she brushed her hair. Workable.

Grabbing her creaking laptop and stuffing it into her patchworked backpack, Cam headed downstairs. Laughter filtered up both flights of stairs from the kitchen, where Cam found Sofia and Avery seated at the counter, chatting.

"Morning," Cam called, surprised to see the two up already. She had actually been awake when the pair had come back last night, and it had been late.

"Help yourself to some coffee." Avery gestured with their cup to a half-full pot in the coffee machine on the counter before turning back to Sofia. They wiped tears of laughter from their eyes. "But seriously, when you called that guy an overplayed Greek tragedy, I nearly lost it!"

"Better than you throwing your drink on the art," Sofia deadpanned to Avery while giving Cam a nod of acknowledgment.

Avery barked a laugh. "Debatable. Still, the DJ was good. Here, take another one. You look hungry." Avery snapped another banana off the bunch Cam had tentatively plucked at and handed it to her. "Jennifer said they restock weekly, so eat as much as you want."

Cam gratefully took the fruit and used it as her cue to riffle through the overflowing pantry, finally settling on granola, yogurt, juice, coffee, a cheese Danish, and the ripest strawberries she had ever seen.

Cam sat down at the counter next to the other pages and was content to listen to them. Their conversation about what sounded like a roller coaster of a night helped to distract her from her anxiety over the upcoming meeting. And also made her feel a twinge of jealousy. Dancing on a boat sounded a lot better than rearranging her minuscule wardrobe repeatedly.

"You'll come out with us tonight, yeah?" Avery asked Cam as she cleaned her dishes.

"Oh, tonight?" Cam was surprised Avery was planning on going out again.

"Yes, James too." Sofia added with authority as James himself came down the stairs wearing another hoodie with a pair of large black-and-gray headphones draped around his neck. He paused and looked a little bit like a deer caught in the headlights.

"Marcus?" Cam wondered aloud in a way she hoped sounded casual.

Avery scoffed. "Don't think so. He's probably booked out for the next month."

"Um, yeah, okay, that sounds great." Cam didn't know if she was relieved or disappointed by this information, but she did know she was warmed by the invite.

"James what?" he asked at the threshold of the kitchen. Cam waved farewell to them all and stepped out of the page house with a little more pep in her step, leaving them to apprise James of what he had been committed to.

While she stood outside the house attempting to boot her homemade holographic phone and bring up the Beekor map, she became dimly, then all at once, very aware of what sounded like a chorus of cybernetic angels singing a descending note, like the final trumpet call winding down the last age of humanity. She stepped back just in time as the black autonomous vehicle slid to a smooth stop in front of her. The angel chorus engine noise ceased. The door automatically opened, and one angel said, "Camila Diaz. Meeting with Wyatt Ecker." Startled at the unexpected ride but deciding not to question it, she hopped in and slammed the door.

As the Beekar took her smoothly across campus, Cam reviewed yet again what she planned to say to Wyatt. Cutting through her intense nerves was a vein of pure, unmitigated excitement at the opportunity to go over Specio and figure out what she could build with serious resources at her command. Lost deep in thought about 3D printers and technical possibilities, she almost didn't notice when the car came to a stop in front of a gigantic metal-and-glass building that looked like it should house interdimensional portal research. She stepped out, and the Beekar closed its own door and drove off, futuristic angel choir harmony fading into the distance.

With her jerry-rigged holographic phone, Cam reconsulted the map. It looked like she was at the correct place to meet Wyatt, in front of a statue of what looked like a pile of square concrete tubes titled *Loathsome Monstrosity*. The feeling of excitement and a bit of nerves still fluttered in her stomach, and she felt a sudden, intense need to pee. Thankfully, she was on time. She waited one minute. Then another minute elapsed. At around the five-minute mark, she began to truly panic and believe she was somehow in the wrong place. She busied herself by imagining the ways she could ruin this. Frustrated, she checked her phone again and muttered, "Keep it together, Cam!"

"Camila!" Wyatt cried jovially as he appeared in front of her, hand extended. Cam jumped in surprise. Wyatt. *The* Wyatt Ecker was looking at her. Making eye contact with her. Speaking to her.

She started to ask to be called Cam rather than Camila, but the request died on her lips. She felt too self-conscious to contradict him. She shook his hand and frantically hoped hers wasn't too sweaty. A note-taking functionary at his shoulder wrote something down.

"Let's walk, Camila." He spun and began taking long strides across the campus. Cam gripped the straps of her backpack and rushed to catch up. "Welcome to Beekor. We are so incredibly jazzed to see what you can do. How are you settling in?" Wyatt looked her in the eyes, artfully tousled salt-and-pepper hair swept back, suit immaculate.

"A-all right," Cam stuttered. "Thank you, Mr. Ecker!"

"No need for formalities, please. Call me Wyatt." He smiled indulgently and with a honed polish.

As they walked, he gestured at a batch of blob-shaped bench tables where a collection of Beekor employees were drinking coffee and discussing some work esoterica. "Look at this. This is humanity flourishing. You know, I've read up on you. We truly relish the opportunity to give people from all sorts of backgrounds new opportunities. And I'm sure this feels *very* different for you, right?"

"Uh." Why did everyone keep saying that? It was technically true, but Cam didn't feel so great about hearing it said like that.

They came to a stop. "Look over here—this is where you're going to be working, Camila." He had a hand on her shoulder and pointed at the front door of yet another steel-and-glass building. This one looked like an egg hatching to reveal another, smaller egg emerging from it. Cam took the building in. Excitement thrilled through her. This was it, she was here, and she was going to build a whole new generation of accessible holographic technology with the help of some of the world's smartest and most knowledgeable people.

"Come inside!" His assistant leapt ahead to hold the door open. Wyatt strode through, and Cam made to follow. The assistant released the door and spun to take his position at Wyatt's shoulder again. Cam awkwardly caught the door before it could close.

Inside, the vast lobby space was host to a three-story, floating holographic projection of abstract waves of water flowing through invisible vessels. Cam looked on in awe as purple waves crashed against the walls of an invisible cube, before squirting into an invisible tube that deposited the now-fuchsia water into an invisible teapot shape. They came to a separate layer of building security gates that blocked access to the office spaces. All lights turned green and the gates instantly opened as Wyatt approached. Cam scurried through behind him.

Wyatt led Cam through a vast, open area full of desks, interspersed with micro kitchens stocked full of snacks, drinks, and high-end espresso machines, as well as towering bits of abstract architecture. It resembled an enormous indoor city. Cam looked around, trying to take everything in while also keeping up with Wyatt. This was going to be the place she changed the world from. The two different types of employees that Cam had noticed on first arriving at the Beekor campus were on full display. The well-dressed types had minimalist desks, gestured in front of whiteboards, and, in one case, had a surfboard mounted on a wall. The ill-dressed types scowled at dark code terminals, had to move their anime figures aside to use their mouse, and looked, generally, as if they would do anything to not have people interrupt their train of thought for the six-hundredth time that day. Group conformity was by no means universal. There was plenty of crossover between the two groups, but some trends were discernible. Everyone, regardless of affiliation, looked up as Wyatt came through. Cam watched as a wave of terror and awe preceded Wyatt through the building. She understood exactly how they felt. Wyatt seemed not to notice.

Wyatt came to a stop at a well-lit corner made of four desks, three of which were occupied, in a circle shape with a half wall surrounding them. The three employees in the area sat up straight, rapidly minimized any non-work windows on their monitors, and momentarily froze. As Wyatt walked past them to the full-length glass window and looked out at the campus, the three of them spun to face Cam, one with a welcoming smile on his face, one appearing pleasantly neutral, and one looking slightly irritated at the interruption in her day. Wyatt spoke without looking at any of them. "You'll be sitting here, Camila." He turned. "Travis here helps to liaise with the hardware and software engineering teams."

Travis, the smiling one with tousled dark hair and a trimmed beard, got up and greeted Cam with a warm handshake. "Good to meet you!"

Wyatt continued. "Terry works with our official comms teams as well as graphic designers and artists who help to put together outreach packets." Terry, the polite-looking one of the trio, had strawberry blond hair in a ponytail, and freckles. They tilted their head empathetically and gave Cam a welcoming wave.

"Outreach . . . ?" Cam began.

Wyatt bulldozed through. "Theresa builds the funnel. Theresa, we're gonna want your help hooking some real whales that Camila can work with!" He laughed.

Theresa looked even more irritated. She fiddled impatiently with her bright lavender hijab. She had thick, dark eyebrows and wore a long, flowy cardigan over a shirt and slacks. "We're so glad to have you on the team," she said, sounding only slightly glad, at best. "There's a massive backlog that I can't wait to get you tackling!" That sounded a lot more sincere.

Wyatt spun to leave. "It's great to have you working with us, Camila. I've got another meeting to get to, but I'll see you at our next sync-up."

"Uh, Wyatt?" Cam ventured. She was utterly confused by what she was doing in this office, with these people, but she rallied. She was sure she could handle whatever Wyatt was throwing at her. She continued more steadily. "What do you mean by 'whales'?"

Wyatt stopped and grinned at Cam. "Influencers, the rich big spenders, of course! We want your hardware in the most watched hands. We want to drive envy." He clenched a fist in the air to emphasize the last word.

Cam tilted her head and brandished her phone. "This hardware?"

Wyatt looked briefly pained by the crude assembly. "No, Camila! You're joining our influencer customization program. You're going to be finding and working with the wealthy, influencers, and celebrities to get personalized, limited-edition Beekor devices in their hands and on their social feeds. We're talking a whole tier above what's available at retail. Solid palladium devices. IMAX-level projection strength, an operating system that they accidentally fall in love with!" He laughed at his own joke.

Cam was shocked. "But . . . I thought I was working on Specio, building hardware to make more phones compatible with holographic content?" She gestured at her phone. A piece fell off.

Wyatt blinked. Then he walked into a small, two-person conference room and beckoned for Cam to follow. Theresa promptly turned back to work, Terry met her gaze, and Travis shrugged. Bewildered, Cam entered the room with Wyatt and closed the door behind her.

Wyatt crossed his arms. "Look, Camila, here at Beekor, we care about user experience above all else. That means minimalist design. Easy and intuitive to use and, above all else, gratifying." He gestured forcefully. "Every object that comes out of Beekor should be aesthetically pleasing, both to interact with and to look at."

Cam just looked confused. Sure, her device didn't look pretty, but it worked. Kind of. Sort of. She looked at it again, then back at Wyatt.

Wyatt sighed and appeared vaguely frustrated. "We all loved your little submission." Cam felt the wind go out of her. "You can really feel the passion you have for everything you do. And that's energy we desperately need here." He put his hand on her shoulder, "But if I'm going to level with you, you don't have anything approaching the experience needed to operate a team working on a project with as many moving parts as that." Wyatt laughed, but he also smiled warmly to soften the blow. "Not even close. Even compared to the other pages, you're really behind."

Was that true? Cam calculated in her head. Sure, she got the impression that the others were more than self-taught. And her job at the computer shop owned by her cousin in the strip mall near her home didn't exactly give her a lot of corporate knowledge. But what had the others accomplished? So what if Sofia didn't seem fazed by anything, if Avery had an international background, if Marcus appeared to have been born here, and if James looked like half the staff walking around the campus. So what? Her natural confidence warred with her wilting dismay.

"But listen, when I saw what you're doing, even in the circumstances you're coming from, I knew I had to take a chance on you." Cam began to protest, but Wyatt rushed in to cut her off. "You have *real* potential. And when you've worked with as many people as I have, you'll know how rare that is." Wyatt squeezed Cam's shoulder lightly and looked into her eyes with disarming earnestness. Cam attempted to tamp down her rage. He was the CEO of one of the largest tech companies on the planet, she reasoned. He built Beekor from the ground up. Maybe she should at least listen to his insight on this. She gripped the straps of her backpack painfully tight.

"That's why I'm giving you the influencer project. It's a great match with your unique skill set. You've been at home building customized hardware with a unique software stack? The influencer project is exactly that, but supercharged! I think with just a little more experience under your belt, you could really go places."

This wasn't what she had anticipated, but maybe Wyatt had a better understanding of how her capabilities could be developed. Cam felt herself nodding woodenly.

Wyatt sighed. "How about this: Take on the influencer project I'm giving you and prove to me that you have what it takes to deliver real products to real customers, and then we can talk again about you building your own product, all right?" He gave her a tiny, hopeful smile with open, beseeching eyes.

Cam thought about it. It did seem like a fair deal. She would work on Wyatt's project, learn what she needed, and would be ready to lead her own project in no time. She nodded a little less stiffly. "So just learn some things and then I can get back to working on Specio?"

Wyatt looked exasperated again. "You're calling it Specio? Camila, we have a team responsible for product names and overall style guides. There's no chance in hell anything that looks like that"—he gestured at Specio—"and with a name like Specio would go out under the Beekor name."

Cam recoiled and looked at her phone with wounded pride. Rather than attempt to soften the blow, Wyatt looked at Cam evenly. "I respect your abilities, and that's why I'm not sugar coating my feedback. You can do *so* much"—he imbued it with enthusiasm—"but you're going to have to learn to accept harsh truths and learn from them. And to accept your own limitations." Cam took a deep breath and tried to quell the hurt and fury welling up. With significant effort, she attempted to reassert to herself that Wyatt, a genius in the field, was only telling her things she needed to hear because he respected her. Eventually, she met Wyatt's eyes again and nodded.

Wyatt paused a beat, then more quietly said, "I noticed you spending some time with Lee Baker at the party." Suddenly on far less shaky ground, Cam opened her mouth to enthuse about her meeting with Lee, but Wyatt, pivoting once again, rode over her, back in his energetic sales-pitch mode. "The influencer program will be the place for you! There will be plenty of *good* network opportunities there! You're going to be rubbing shoulders with the greats!" Was Wyatt implying Lee wasn't a good connection? The cofounder of Beekor? Wyatt patted her back once and straightened up, abruptly an intimidating tech giant again. He held a hand up, palm outward, before Cam's eyes, as if he were revealing a brilliant landscape to her. "You'll be in contact with powerful people across all levels of society." Quietly, again, "I can't stress how advantageous those sorts of connections are. Stick to them." Cam nodded slowly. "Your crossover talents for hardware and software will get an incredible workout as you manage cocreation of limited-edition devices for our most affluent customers," he spoke excitedly.

He was right; she would get *tons* of chances to design and build things too.

"Not to mention the opportunity to learn how to handle business development, outreach, communications, and project management with a team of Beekor professionals." Wyatt punctuated the last point by punching his fist into his open palm. "Do you see how exciting this is, Camila?"

After all the bruising revelations, Cam felt relieved as she began to be borne along by Wyatt's enthusiasm. She didn't know what business development or project management were, but she knew she could learn fast. She couldn't wait to get started and prove herself. "All right, I'm ready for this! Thanks, Mr.—uh, Wyatt."

He smiled warmly at her. "No problem, Camila. When you've been in this business as long as I have, it's a true pleasure to meet young, new faces with a fire for the work." Wyatt exited the small conference room. "Please reach out to me if you've got any other questions," he said as he strode away. "I can't wait to hear your insights!" His assistant scurried after.

Cam made her way tentatively back to the circle of desks and looked at the unoccupied one. *Her* desk. There was a brand-new set of Beekor displays on it, both flat panel and holographic. Travis, Terry, and Theresa all stood around her with looks of varying excitement and warmth. Cam felt beat after the emotional whiplash of her talk with Wyatt. Perhaps noticing the look on Cam's face, Travis sidled up to comfort her.

"Hey, so Wyatt is known to be a bit . . . harsh from time to time."

Theresa made a pained gesture. "Ruthless, painstaking control down to the finest detail of user experience is what got Beekor where it is."

"But is it normal that I'm scared that he actually knows my name?" Travis shivered visibly.

"Right?!" Theresa gestured forcefully. "There are over fifty thousand employees! How does he do that?"

Terry looked pensive.

Travis went on. "I think it's some kind of CEO superpower. Or something he practiced after reading a self-help book. *How to Gain Trust and Manipulate People.*"

Cam laughed. "Maybe he got ocular implants and has an earpiece so he's constantly being fed insider info?"

Nobody else laughed. Travis just tilted his head thoughtfully. Theresa actually nodded once.

Terry broke the moment. "Hey, look, just so you know? This project has been struggling a bit." Terry sounded embarrassed.

"Yeah, it turns out customers often don't know what they want until they actually get it," Travis continued. "And the hardware and software teams are *hella* busy. We need black magic to get them to prioritize anything. But hey, that's why we get paid the big bucks, right?"

Cam smiled proudly. "The weekly stipend is more than I've ever gotten paid at my old job at the computer shop!" They looked at each other blankly.

"Oh, honey," Terry began.

"Free meals too! And I get a place to live...." Cam petered off, somewhat confused at their sympathetic expressions.

Travis's face looked pinched. "That's no small thing in SF, at least."

"How about we let you settle in?" Terry asked. "I can help you get up and running on our project so you can become familiar with the task board and Theresa can start giving you leads."

"Uh, yeah. Leads . . ."

Terry explained, "Those are the people that you're hoping to sell to. We have a list compiled. Theresa will help you choose those people and set you up to work with them. And I"—Terry gave a small, empathetic smile—"will always be here to talk about things if you're struggling."

"All right." Cam felt herself returning to solid ground. She was going to be the best employee there ever was. With a renewed lightness, she pulled out her laptop and placed it on her desk, eager to get started.

Her new coworkers looked on in mute horror at Cam's massive, battered laptop as she sought a cable to connect it to the monitors on her desk. As she was about to crawl under the table in her search, Terry took pity and pulled out the cable from a slot in the table designed for just that use and handed it to Cam.

"Seriously, just *ask* us for help," Terry said as Cam took the cable gratefully. "We're coworkers now. We support each other."

As Cam's laptop opened up with an audible creak, Theresa turned to her computer and began aggressively clicking and typing. "I'm supporting you right now by getting you a laptop that was built more recently than the Pyramids of Giza," she said with fervor, and continued filling out a form.

Cam connected the screens to her laptop using the cable she'd gotten. "I think my old laptop should be just fine. I have everything set up how I like it. . . ." The laptop connected to one of the two screens briefly. A browser window full of embarrassing search results for body-hair removal was plastered on-screen. Then the laptop lost the monitor connection. All at once the laptop's main screen also turned off. It beeped plaintively. Theresa made prolonged eye contact with Cam. Cam quietly nodded her assent.

"Hey, how about we all head to lunch early?" Travis asked the group. "There's a Michelin-star chef in the Tyrell food hall today, and we'll need to get there quick to beat the crowds. We can deal with your laptop and onboarding afterward. C'mon, Camila."

Cam gave up on setup for the moment and left with her new coworkers. "It's Cam."

Terry nodded, then asked offhandedly, "By the way, have you met that page, Marcus, yet?"

"My God. *I* want to meet him," Theresa lamented. They all laughed while Cam just wondered how they all seemed to know who Marcus was already.

Chapter 7

CAM STRUGGLED TO FINISH YET another piece of ibérico ham on her plate. Travis, Theresa, and Terry, whom Cam had taken to calling the Three Ts in her head, had brought her to one of the many campus food halls, where she had had easily the most incredible free lunch in her life. She couldn't even pronounce half the food options available.

Theresa rose with mild impatience. "All right, Cam. It's time to get you acquainted with what we do here. Travis is going to take you to meet the engineers first. Meet back at our space after." Cam gave the gnocchi with mascarpone cream on her tray one last mournful look as Theresa took the initiative of depositing it on the conveyor belt with the other dirty dishes.

Theresa and Terry headed back to their building, while Travis and Cam proceeded to where the hardware team worked. The enormous work floor of the hardware space instantly felt like a paradise to Cam. It was a vast, high-ceilinged garage with polished concrete floors where the hardware team assembled and tested devices. There were electric outlets and mounting equipment hanging from the ceiling, and rails with sliding gantries to mount new camera assemblies on for focus calibration testing. Shelves against the walls had thousands of different components for use in different devices, such as phones or tablets. Cam's eyes widened, and she instantly ran over to see what they had available. There were little 2D cameras ($5 each but you could only purchase them in lots of five thousand or more), structured light-depth sensors ($8 each, batches of 2,000), laser microphones ($750), inertial measurement units ($3 each, minimum 10,000), and holographic projector arrays of all types, from consumer grade all the way up to hardened, military-grade components. Everything was brand-new too—none of the batteries had that explodey look!

"Cam, this is David."

Cam became dimly aware that Travis had been talking and that she had been laughing with mad glee. She reluctantly dragged herself away from all the equipment she had dreamed about for so many years and spun to introduce herself to David. David looked dour, almost sad. His hairline had badly receded, and he wore a somewhat ill-fitted button-down shirt. He looked a bit put-upon, as if Travis had interrupted him in the middle of his workflow for something that wasn't that important.

"Hi, David, good to meet you!" David accepted her handshake somewhat lethargically. Cam could feel herself talking a bit too fast and loud, but she couldn't get over her excitement. "I can't believe what I'm seeing here! Is this actually a bin of *neutrino detectors*?!"

David's eyes brightened, as if he was seeing Cam for the first time. "Yes . . . Are you interested in exotic physics?"

"Not exactly . . . But I read an incredible breakdown of the Beekor partnership with NASA," Cam enthused. "When you guys built that hardened sensor package to take onto the space station—"

David cut her off excitedly. "Oh, you mean the interview with . . . this guy?" David pointed over to a workbench where a man with a beard like a wizard and ancient, ratty T-shirt advertising drinks at a space bar was seated.

Cam's eyes somehow went even wider, and she inhaled sharply. "Lewis Travers?!" The bearded man met Cam's gaze and smiled warmly. "The guy that remote-piloted a drone to fix the solar arrays on the space station and saved those astronauts?!" Lewis Travers stood up, took a bow, and basked in Cam's adulation.

A long conversation about various legendary hardware-engineering achievements and several introductions later, Travis had to forcibly pull Cam away to go meet the software team. As Travis led her across the campus, Cam realized suddenly that she had never met a group of people that shared the same excitement and zeal for building hardware and software in person before. It was a warm feeling, a feeling of actually belonging. She also finally understood the division of people on the Beekor campus—the well-dressed types versus the people in old T-shirts who mostly just wanted to be left alone: the engineers. Cam was proud that she was one of them.

After a similar set of excited introductions and exchanges of stories with the software team and their lead, Kevin, a portly man with glasses and jet-black hair that stood up in clumps, Travis finally led a terminally enthusiastic Cam back to their building and into a conference room a floor above their own desks. It had four gray office chairs, a small table with a tray of multicolored sticky notes, a wood wall with fake moss spelling out "Beekor," and a large digital whiteboard. Terry and Travis flanked the whiteboard and began writing vocab on it with a stylus. As they finished writing, Terry's swooping letters and Travis's jagged scrawl resolved into a tidy uniform Times New Roman font.

"All right, so let's try to keep this as simple as possible. Tech Company Project Management 101 time! Do you know what a KPI is?"

Cam just blinked in response.

The barrage of new info came in hot and heavy. Travis kept taking them on tangents in an effort to make the lesson light and fun, while Theresa cracked the whip and snapped at them to get them to refocus. Terry regularly checked in with Cam to see how she was taking it all in. For her part,

Cam desperately tried to keep track of all the new terminology. She took cramped notes on a pad she had found in the room as the Three Ts walked her through the structure of how a project worked. Ultimately, it boiled down to a couple simple ideas that were then warped utterly beyond all recognition by the unique needs of every single team. Task management software allowed them to create tickets that would track what was being done, by whom, and when. It was like a big to-do list that other people could assign to you. Except that it also had estimated completion times. And the items in the to-do list could link to other tickets that needed to be done first in order to move forward (a "blocker," Cam wrote down). Plus, the whole thing in its entirety could be used to compile a vast chart showing the progress of all the parts of the project, which parts had dependencies, and how that all combined to comprise a schedule. The rate at which tasks were closed against that schedule often figured into metrics of team progress toward a specific goal, or "KPI" (key performance indicator, Cam learned).

Cam had only ever worked on projects by herself. In those cases, she always knew exactly what needed doing, so it was easy to keep in her head. "What's the point of all this?" She tried not to sound too know-it-all-y. "Can't we just remember what we're working on and tell that to higher-ups?"

Theresa stopped cold and looked Cam in the eye. "Just keep it in your head?" She began quietly. "Keep an active list in your head of all the UI team's conflicting priorities for tasks given to them for six separate projects across the entire company, in order to track when they might be ready to hand off work to the software team so that we can fairly estimate an overall time frame in order to set up sequencing with marketing?" Cam shrank in her chair. "Keep a complete checklist of all changes in your head so you can just . . . regurgitate it all to QA so they can figure out exactly where to target testing in the run-up to launch?"

"Well, I guess write *some* of it down," Cam squeaked out.

"Do you have a clue how many moving parts there are when you build *anything* at a big company?" Theresa asked forcefully. Cam slowly shook her head. Over the next ten minutes, in brutal detail, Theresa worked to impress on Cam just how complex it was to plan and execute highly involved tasks that required many people across different teams at a gigantic company to work together. Cam had the sudden, unexpected sense that maybe there were one or two things about building technology that she didn't understand. The feeling of being out of her depth, in what she had considered her absolute wheelhouse, rattled her.

Theresa continued acerbically, explaining the difficulty and importance of also figuring out ways to measure how well things were going, in order to continually update timelines, spot weaknesses or obstacles in the process, and refine the strategy. To illustrate, Travis had pulled up a dashboard showing the overall progress of the influencer customization program. "This is what a higher-up can glance at to see how well we're doing," he said.

Every single KPI goal showed red or "at risk." Travis winced, and Theresa just pursed her lips angrily. "Things haven't gone so hot since we lost our team lead, Terrance, two months back," said Terry.

"God rest his soul." Travis held a hand to his heart and looked solemn.

Wildly off-balance, and uncertain how to respond, Cam said quietly, "I'm so sorry for your loss."

Theresa shook her head and looked sour. "He's fine. He works at OccuTask now. He just got fired for scheduling a tequila tasting and a blood drive for the same day."

"An honest mistake," said Travis.

"That's good." Cam sighed in relief. Then scrambled to recover. "I mean, it still really sucks that the world was deprived of a fourth T—" Cam stopped herself short and laughed nervously. The Three Ts looked at each other.

Travis smiled and shrugged. "No worries. Everybody calls us the Four Ts."

"Alas, now Three," mourned Terry. The Three Ts sighed in unison.

Terry quickly swiped on the whiteboard to switch back to the vocab they had been writing down. "At any rate, returning to the user acquisition funnel—"

A knock on the glass interrupted the lesson. "Paperweight delivery!" A woman with straight dark hair leaned in. She had on black eyeliner, a spiked collar, a band T-shirt, shorts over ripped tights, and her sneakers had grinning ghost faces drawn on the toes in Wite-Out. Cam had never seen anyone who was a stronger embodiment of "cool." In one hand, she held up a shiny, new Beekor laptop. In the other, she held an earbud from which Cam could hear tinny but nonetheless intimidating death metal blaring.

"Oh, thank God," Cam gasped, thankful for a reprieve. She went to take the laptop but started when she realized it was a fully loaded platinum model that cost more than every car her family had ever owned. "How much . . . ?" she began.

The woman from IT snickered. "It's billed to your Beekor Accelerator Program. So, it's yours, gratis."

"Drinks this weekend, Daphne?" Terry asked.

"Ask me on Thursday," Daphne called as she walked off. "Later, nerds." She gave them the finger.

"Well, looks like I'm gonna have to go set up all the software I need on my laptop. So we'll have to continue this lesson another time . . ." Cam began, absolutely flabbergasted at the pile of gold in her hands and also beginning to feel her brain turning to mush from all the new jargon.

"You wish." Theresa grinned evilly. "We didn't even scratch the surface about how we gather information on *what* to make for the customer," Terry explained. "We run regular research sessions with users. I'll get you a user interview sheet so you can see what sorts of questions we ask."

Cam nodded defeatedly.

Chapter 8

LIVING IN THE BEAUTIFUL ATTIC studio might actually be a double-edged sword, thought Cam, as she dragged her exhausted body up the final steps. Marcus, Avery, and Sofia appeared to be out. James's bedroom door was cracked open and his satchel was on the big, square, modern-looking desk with underlighting, but he himself was nowhere to be found. Her head was hurting all over. She felt as if she had been drinking from the fire hose all day, trying to come to terms with everything about how a big company worked. She was starting to realize what Wyatt meant when he said she was drastically inexperienced. All the terminology was new to her. All the tools were new to her. Even her phone was new to her. She had started the setup process three separate times throughout the day but had gotten distracted with other things.

Utterly wrung out, Cam stripped out of her clothes and stepped into comfortable pajamas. She pulled a Tupperware full of extra food she had grabbed at the lunch line out of her bag and took it out onto her little patio. She munched on Michelin-star pasta leftovers and watched the sun slowly set on the hill. It was studded with thousands of house lights. A vast antenna Jennifer had called Sutro Tower, with three prongs pointed up to the heavens, stood at the peak. A massive wall of purple-lit fog rolled up the back side of the hill and back down toward her, obscuring first the base of the antenna, then the little houses, and then the entirety of Sutro Tower up to its top, until Cam could just barely make out the hazy glow of the red lights at its tips from within the fog. The sky exploded into a profusion of purples and oranges.

She took out her trusty old phone, removed all the extra bits of hardware, and rang her mother for a plain-old call.

"Cammy! Mi amor, how are you? Have you made friends? Are you eating enough? I miss you so much." Rosa Diaz's voice came through warm and nourishing, like hot soup on a cold day, or a heavy, warm blanket you were tucked into while it rained outside.

Cam felt herself relaxing. "Mom, I've only been gone for two days."

"That long?" Cam laughed. "But seriously, little lamb, tell me about Beekor. How was your day?"

Cam hesitated. She wasn't sure how to feel about the day. All the new things she learned were exciting and exhausting, and she was sure Wyatt was right. Getting to work with a team on hardware and software, all while learning how to do business development and marketing, was *seriously* exciting. There was no way she would've ever learned any of this back at home. But at the same time, it didn't look like she would be working on Specio anytime soon. Even though she had thought that was the reason she had come to Beekor in the first place.

In the end, she was too disheartened to admit it. "Well . . . everyone here is really nice," Cam decided to go the safer route. "And I'm staying in a huge house. I'll have to show you the kitchen! I'm thinking of making breakfast for my housemates one day."

Rosa's voice perked up. "Housemates?"

"Yes," Cam said. "The other pages."

"Are any of them boys?" Rosa questioned.

"Uh . . ." Cam knew where her mother was going with this, and she didn't like it.

"Are they cute?" Instantly, Marcus's dimpled face flashed in Cam's mind, and she blushed. Then she remembered his strange coldness. This was no longer the safe topic she had hoped it would be.

Rosa picked up on her silence. "So, there *are!*" She laughed.

"I've got homework." Cam practically threw the conversational gambit into the ring, desperate to distract her mother. "I'm supposed to be doing user research, and I got a list of questions that I'm supposed to ask customers. Can I practice on you? It would really help me out with my new coworkers."

"Cammy, you know I'll do anything to help you. Yes, yes, ask away!" Rosa replied, sounding enthusiastic to assist her daughter, and Cam silently sighed with relief.

"Hold on." Cam dashed back inside, pulled out her new laptop, and flopped onto her bed. She pulled out the user research questionnaire and opened a note-taking app before putting her mother on speaker. "Okay, let's see, first question, what current Beekor products do you own?"

"Cam, you know we don't have any. They're too expensive," Rosa chided.

"Right, sorry, um . . ." Cam skimmed through the questionnaire. The next few questions were all Beekor specific. Like how many years the user had been with Beekor, their first Beekor item, if they owned any of the limited-edition Beekor drops, and what Beekor products they planned to purchase in the future. Finally, Cam got to a question that was a little more open-ended. "Can you tell me a friction* you have in your daily life?"

"A 'friction'?" Rosa sounded confused.

Cam looked at the asterisk next to the word "friction" and found a note below. "'Something that causes difficulty or requires multiple work-arounds to complete,'" Cam recited.

"Well, I need a Beekor phone," Rosa admitted with a sigh.

Cam's heart squeezed as she thought about the expensive phone that had been handed to her so casually and now sat in her bag waiting to be set up. Then she looked at the questionnaire and noticed the italics below the question she had just asked. *Don't allow the users to answer with a solution. Instead make sure you learn about the root of the problem.* Cam thought about that.

"Mom, can you tell me why you need a Beekor phone?"

"Well," Rosa started, "I guess I really need holographic capabilities." She went on to describe the nursing courses that she had been taking at night, the latest of which had her and her classmates examining virtual patients. "Honestly, it's amazing to be able to zoom in and see all the internal organs just by gesturing with your hands. It makes understanding some of the underlying pathologies so much simpler. The problem is that the school only has two shared Beekor phones available for students to use. And they are always occupied." Rosa sounded exhausted and frustrated.

Cam began taking notes as her mother spoke. This was exactly what she had been thinking about. Holographic technology was incredibly powerful, with unexplored possibilities to help people, but it was too prohibitively expensive for some of the people who needed it the most to use it. It was unexpected but not surprising to learn that her mother had been using holographic technology for classes.

"'Can you tell me some of the work-arounds you're currently doing to alleviate the problem?'" Cam asked, reading the next question on her sheet.

"Right now, I have a study group. We all go in together early on Saturdays and wait for one of the machines to open up, and then we take turns and compare notes."

"I thought you said you were doing a baked-food swap!" Cam exclaimed, thinking about all the delicious foods her mother wouldn't let her touch on Friday night and the equally delicious meals that came home with her mother every Saturday afternoon.

"We do both," Rosa admitted with a laugh.

Suddenly, Cam's brain was whirling. A plan began to form in her mind. What if she kept Specio going, to provide something for her mom's study group? What if during the day she went to work and learned everything she could? Became the most badass product manager/technical specialist/project manager/marketer Beekor had ever seen. Then at night, she would take all her learnings and keep working on Specio. She could use the machine shop in the garage downstairs to make prototypes she could send to her mom, which would help her mom study and give Cam an opportunity to collect user feedback, all at the same time. Subsequently she would have so much more to present to Wyatt the next time she saw him. He would be so impressed by all her work on the side, he would be begging to give her a team. It certainly helped that the thought of working on Specio, something that was fully hers, and that she understood completely, felt almost like a refuge after all the uncertainty and new concepts she was struggling with.

"Mom, if I send you a couple of my latest Specio prototypes, can you and your study group use them and help tell me what I need to improve?"

"Will this help you with your job?"

Cam wavered. Technically it was eventually going to be her job. "Yes, it would be a big help."

"Then yes! I know we'd all be so happy to help," Rosa effused.

"Awesome! All right, I have a few more questions for you, and then I want to talk to a few of the others in your study group to learn about their experiences too."

—

Cam was suddenly jolted out of the last of her note-taking from the call with her mom by Sofia's knock on the doorframe. She stood statuesque in the open doorway, looking expectant.

"Ready to go?" she asked with a raised eyebrow, and Cam remembered Avery's invite from this morning. She was drained from the day, but the prospect of a night out in this new city sounded exciting. And, if she was being honest, she was driven by more than a little FOMO.

Sofia and Cam walked downstairs and joined a jovial Avery, who appeared to have cornered a reluctant-looking James. Marcus was, as Avery had predicted, nowhere in sight.

"Thank you all for gathering, my friends! It has come to my attention that all of you are unfamiliar with the delights of this city. But you need not worry; I have decided to take you all under my wing." They struck a grandiose pose. "Prepare yourselves for a night of debauchery!"

"This sounds like a lot of trouble," muttered James, fidgeting with some knobs on the headphones slung around his neck. Cam had never seen headphones like them before. Up close, she realized what she had taken for stylistic decorations were actually cleverly hidden controls for functions she couldn't comprehend. She had no idea what they would cost.

"No, it sounds like an adventure." Avery gleefully rubbed their hands together which made James, if anything, more uncomfortable.

Just as James looked ready to make a dash back to his room, Sofia spoke up. "If this is unenjoyable, I will leave."

Avery gasped theatrically. "Me? Show you a bad time? Never. But if I somehow fail to entertain you, I will immediately assist in a strategic retreat. Merely say the word." The interaction was purely between Sofia and Avery, but out of the corner of her eye, Cam saw James relax a smidgeon.

"Where are we going?" Cam tentatively asked.

"We're going to get thoroughly, apocalyptically shredded at the bar my friend has rented for the evening over in the Mission," Avery purred. "It's his birthday and he's got more money than God. We're the guests of honor, and it's an open bar. All you can drink?! Challenge accepted. We will drink all, my friends. We. Will. Drink. ALL.

"And our carriage awaits!" Avery revealed a holographic map from the Beekor phone in the palm of their hand. It showed a vehicle on a rideshare app, waiting just outside their front gate. Avery laughed madly and spun, pulling on a long orange sleeveless coat with a pattern of tiny tigers that billowed like a cape behind them. They strode out the front door as if it were a runway and they were the whole show. They didn't bother looking back to confirm the others followed.

Sofia serenely glided out in Avery's wake. James gave one final forlorn look at the stairs that lead to his room before slouching after. Cam hiked her backpack higher on her shoulders, mentally preparing herself for anything, and skipped outside.

The carriage turned out to be a large black SUV. Cam, Sofia, and James slid into the back while Avery got into the front, where the driver turned to face them. "Avery! How goes?!"

"Incredibly, Rob. It goes incredibly." Avery turned to Rob. "How's the app progressing?"

The three pages in the back exchanged surprised looks that Avery seemed to know this man. Rob, for his part, needed no more prompting and launched into a long spiel about his idea for a food-delivery app for pet tarantulas as he drove them to their destination.

"There can't be that many pet spiders," Sofia muttered, appearing horrified as they were inundated with tarantula facts. Cam had to stifle a laugh, and James cracked a small smile.

Chapter 9

THE BAR WAS SEEDY IN an extremely horny but comfortable way. Inside, vintage pornography magazines covered every inch of the walls except for those spaces occupied by tablet screens. On the screens, randomized compilations of old commercials and snippets of more porn played. All the seating areas resembled classic make-out spots, like a movie theater, the back of a car, a hot tub, or a couch.

Cam was temporarily separated from the rest of the group when she stopped to gape in amazement over the corner set up with a live sloth dangling from a faux tree. The sloth waved two long claws at her.

"Hey, aren't you one of the Beekor pages?" Cam spun and saw a tall, skinny man with a Mohawk and pure black rings tattooed on his forearm.

"Um, yeah." Uncertain what to do with the attention, Cam just anxiously gripped the straps of her backpack. "How'd you know?"

In answer, he pulled out his phone and showed Cam the front page of TechMudder, prominently featuring the group shot from the meeting with

Wyatt, as well as a deep dive on each of the pages, hers featuring that same low-res headshot image she had been using for years, blown up far beyond reasonable scale for the number of pixels it contained. Excitement warred with embarrassment in her mind. She could already see this entire article, framed, on the living room wall over her mom's couch.

"Congrats," he said, pocketing his phone and walking away. "Tell Avery that Ian said hi, and thanks for helping me get my Winnebago dating service launched!"

Walking farther in, Cam soon found Sofia on top of a massive waterbed set into a large wooden frame in the corner of the main floor of the bar and joined her on it. James stood beside the bed nursing a soft drink and looking stiffly uncomfortable with his headphones over his ears, his fingers tapping on his thigh erratically. Avery was on their way back with a round of drinks for the group, when they were waylaid by a statuesque figure in heels and a black sequin dress. "Avery! What are you doing?"

Avery spun but did not spill a single drop of the three drinks they held. "Georges!" They pronounced it with a flawless French accent, or so Cam assumed. The two of them air-kissed. "I'm currently on a mission, but we will have to talk later. I have somebody that requires your services!" Avery gestured with their head toward the three other pages. Georges nodded and patted Avery's shoulder, then headed to the bar.

"That dress is Georges's design. He's an absolute virtuoso!" Avery exclaimed, delivering the drinks to Cam and Sofia's waterbed redoubt. Cam attempted to stabilize herself on the bed in order to receive the drink, instantly lost balance, and spilled on the mattress. Sofia gracefully grabbed a napkin from a side table and mopped it up. Avery held up their glass to initiate a cheer, when suddenly an extremely handsome blond man poked his head into their little space and grinned broadly.

"Oleg!" Avery cried. "Happy birthday! We are availing ourselves of your generosity at present. Thank you!" Oleg leaned his upper body in, and Avery hugged him warmly.

"Anything for you, Avery. I owe you big-time!" Somebody began shouting "Happy birthday," and everyone in the bar was handed a shot of tequila. Cam felt obliged to accept the shot pressed into her hand and tossed it back with the rest. She soothed her burning throat with the other free cocktail. The entire bar broke into raucous cheers and began to sing in an off-kilter way. Cam had never before been to a bar or a party like this, but buoyed with alcohol, she soon became infected by the revelry and began to sing along. Oleg waggled his eyebrows at the four pages and turned away to dutifully receive his serenading.

Sofia looked at Avery and quirked one perfectly manicured eyebrow.

"Oh, it's nothing. I introduced him to some friends." Avery explained that their friend Oleg was a founder who had recently secured a gigantic funding round to build a company around an extremely promising cell rejuvenation therapy that could potentially result in people being healthy, strong, and disease-free for decades longer. Cam and Sofia were impressed. Even James looked surprised.

Avery raised a glass. "To eternal life!"

The four of them cheered and another round of shots was distributed. If this was just a glimpse of Cam's future, she wasn't sure if her, or her liver, would survive. But she downed the shot with a wide grin on her face.

—

Eventually, the bar owner turned the revelers out for the night. A lot of the party left with the birthday boy to continue the celebration at his Russian Hill apartment. "Rent-controlled since 2006," he boasted.

Cam was completely drunk and extremely hungry at that point. Just outside the bar, the most heavenly smell on earth wafted into Cam's nostrils. She began salivating. Not half a block away, the sidewalk was occupied by a hastily erected hut with functioning grill, table full of condiments, and two abuelas preparing bacon-wrapped hot dogs for a crowd of laughing, excited partiers. Cam took off running, and Avery and Sofia trailed her, laughing.

James made his way more doggedly behind them, with a look of slightly alarmed chagrin, his headphones back around his neck.

Nobody in the food line protested as Cam cut them and slapped a five-dollar bill on the table, too drunk to calculate her bank account, for a hot dog heaped with every conceivable topping. She took one juicy bite, sautéed onions, mayonnaise, and hot sauce running down her chin, and experienced an intense wave of full-body satisfaction. Sofia snatched the dog away to steal a bite.

Avery didn't bother using their hands; they simply finished the entire hot dog in one enormous bite, right from out of Sofia's fingers. "C'mon," they called as they started down the street with purpose, coat swishing behind them with the flair of royalty. "There's more!"

As Avery led the three of them several blocks to a—they swore—legendary burrito spot, the three of them encountered no fewer than five separate people that Avery appeared to know intimately. On that short walk down Mission Street, Avery hugged a crew of three twenty-somethings in tech worker drag, a man in an extremely worn suit, protesting with a densely annotated sign declaring the collusion of multiple government figures with alien cabals from several other galaxies, and a woman walking four dogs, each groomed to resemble a different geometric shape.

Cam found herself trailing behind Avery and Sofia, who laughed and engaged in repartee with a man that had twisted his hair into antennae. She cast a bloodshot eye at James, who momentarily met her gaze and looked away again. "Hey," Cam began, trying to keep the drunkenness out of her voice. She was not succeeding.

"Yes?" James replied, and took an awkward sip on the soft drink he had managed to retain from the bar.

"Hey," she continued, more confidently. "I saw you ogling the CNC machine." Cam waggled her eyebrows in what she assumed was a gesture of subtle impertinence. She looked exactly like the woozy face emoji.

James laughed tentatively. "Yeah, I do hardware."

"Are we talking 3D-printing? Or circuit board design? Or mechanical stuff?" Up ahead, Sofia laughed at something Avery said.

"Yes." James nodded his head and took another sip.

"So, like, mechanical stuff?" Cam tried to walk in a straight line but kept veering to the side.

"All of it," James said. "I particularly like designing speakers and headphones."

"So wait"—Cam attempted to focus her brain more firmly—"did you make those?" She pointed at James's giant black-and-gray headphones.

"Yeah, I did," James confirmed, touching them affectionately. "I finished painting them right before I left home."

Cam was impressed and envious of his skill. His headphones looked nothing like her own projects, which resembled scrap heaps. Highly functional, but scrap heaps, nonetheless. His looked sleek, high-tech, functional, and just plain cool.

"So why'd you come to Beekor? They don't have a big headphone department. How did you get here?" She leaned in close. "With me!" she practically shouted.

James winced but softened it with a smile. "I'm an industrial designer. I like making lots of different objects work for lots of people. My headphones, for example. I couldn't find a pair that had all the sound-dampening and music-enhancing qualities I wanted. Or ones I could adjust to fit me comfortably. So I made these for myself, but I want to make this kind of customization available to a lot more people.

"Beekor is the best in the world when it comes to industrial design," James continued. "There is no better place on the planet for making things that are both beautiful and functional, and reach so many people." James sounded passionate. "For my Beekor project, I made an adjustable hardware chassis that can fit multiple grip types. Large and small hands of course, but also single hand, missing digits, feet, and ways to attach it to mobility devices."

He looked pensive before saying, "I haven't always been so good with people, but when someone holds something I've made and it fits them . . ." With seeming effort, he met Cam's eyes. "It's a great feeling," he said with relish.

Cam nodded with drunken earnestness.

"Plus"—James's gaze fell away again—"I like working with machines, they make sense. And I like when everything I've made just clicks together perfectly the way I designed it. Beekor is the best place for that, it has all of the most top-notch equipment."

Cam was too drunk to experience embarrassment about gaping at James. His project sounded amazing; she desperately wanted to try it out. She sensed a kindred spirit in someone who wanted to make something that lots of people would use. And she understood exactly what he meant about the simple joy of losing yourself in the act of creation. When you built something, the rules were clear—you got back exactly what you put in. The driver software you coded didn't suddenly realize it had stopped loving the network interface years ago, and that it had been living a lie and needed to get a divorce, leaving you and the network interface to make your own way.

"What about you? Why are you at Beekor?" James asked.

Cam stopped for a moment, subtly swaying as she looked around at the street full of drunk partiers. She took in the buildings and lights around them, the activity. "Where I come from, nobody knows what industrial design even is." She laughed. "It gets tiring being the 'smart one.' I can only fix so many computers." She stuck out her tongue. "Small place, small dreams." She clenched a fist. "Not me, though. I came to Beekor because I'm going to do something big!" She shouted the last, and several bystanders flowing around the two of them on the sidewalk cheered her on. Cam put her hands on her hips and laughed maniacally. "I'm never going back!" The bystanders cheered more effusively for her.

"Fuck that place!" somebody yelled along with her.

Avery took that opportunity to intrude on the two of them. "This is where you went! C'mon, we're almost there!" Cam laughed imperiously and resisted Avery's attempts to pull her away. Sofia arched one eyebrow at James, who shrugged and followed her tall form through the crowd of people, which effortlessly parted as she moved through them.

The burrito spot in question had a lighthouse logo and a line out the front to the end of the block. Sofia and Cam balked, but Avery cautioned patience. "Believe me." The four of them joined up at the back of the line.

"So how does everybody know you?" Cam asked Avery.

Avery took a moment before answering. "There's nothing in the world more important than your relationships." They had a keen and calculating gleam in their eye.

Sofia nodded her assent. Cam just looked confused at this seeming segue.

"Silicon Valley in particular is a world built on relationships," Avery continued as they moved with the line. "It's a place where jobs constantly change and there's no better asset in a job interview than having worked with somebody before who liked working with you. Investors and founders swap places so often, neither tries to alienate the other no matter the business proposal." Cam was surprised. She had always assumed one group came from wealthy families and one had no money at all.

"The vast majority of investors are not professionals; they just do angel investing on the side." At Cam's confused look, Avery clarified. "That means mostly writing small checks for founders and companies they really believe in. Investors frequently start companies of their own, and founders angel-invest on the side all the time."

In the meantime, the group had slowly shuffled into the restaurant. Loud drunken laughter, hissing griddles, and vaporized fat filled the air. James looked strained in the tight space, fidgeting furiously. Cam and Sofia held one hand each on either side of a greasy, laminated menu before Avery seized the menu and threw it aside. To the person behind the counter they said, "Four California burritos, please." The four of them squeezed into a tiny nook of available space to wait for their order.

"Look," Avery continued from where they left off, "if you want a big slice of pie, you can always try to take an unfairly big slice right now and piss everybody off and get booted from the game. But out here, we learned that you can all flourish and eventually get as much pie as you want if you all work together to continually grow the pie over time. So, we all pay it back, forward, and sideways to keep each other building and prospering. Keep the pie growing.

"We're all engaged in a game of iterated prisoner's dilemma. We'll be playing with each other again at the next turn, so learning to cooperate, or at least not to backstab each other *too* egregiously, is the greatest skill." There was so much more to this world than just designing hardware or coding. Cam was really starting to think Wyatt might've been right about her inexperience. Not that she would ever admit that out loud.

The call finally came. "Avery!" The four of them grabbed their burritos, each roughly the size of an aluminum-foil-swaddled child, and made their way back out into the cool night air. Cam opened a hole in the top of her burrito right there and tasted her first bite. Growing up in a Mexican family, Cam was no stranger to burritos, or even Mission-style burritos, which had become the norm across the country. But California style, with guacamole, sour cream, and french fries on the inside, was a whole different ball game. Cam felt herself tearing up. It was like touching the face of God. Her stomach lining silently thanked her.

"You are good at the game," Sofia said to Avery contemplatively as she delicately chewed her burrito.

"Well, I try." Avery looked away with uncharacteristic bashfulness.

"You must be the BEST," Cam slurred. "I'm pretty sure we just passed a street named after you. Number one prisoner!"

Avery barked a laugh and led them to a minuscule playground. While sitting and eating on the swings, they had front-row seats to a Big Wheel race taking place across the street between a woman dressed as the Statue of Liberty and a mustachioed plumber in overalls.

"So then, how do you know Marcus?" Cam asked. She mentally kicked herself. Where had that question come from? Too much tequila meant her brain was chasing behind her mouth.

"Asking after our golden boy again?" Avery teased playfully.

Cam felt herself going red. "I just— I mean, you're the only two that seem to know each other from before this, and I was curious." The sliver of her brain that was still sober observed her floundering and begged her to stop. Cam took a giant bite of her burrito and almost choked.

James looked concerned, but Sofia calmly reached over and patted Cam through her coughing fit while Avery laughed.

"It's all right, kitten; I get it. Marcus is cute if you're into that classic Adonis look, cheekbones and all," Avery consoled Cam.

Sofia cocked her eyebrow at Avery, and suddenly Avery was on the defensive.

"I have eyes! I know what he looks like. But he's also like a brother to me," Avery rushed out, not looking in Sofia's direction. "Our parents have known each other since their college days. We've never gone to school together—my parents moved me around too much for that—but we've spent holidays in resorts together frequently enough to be utterly uninterested in each other."

"So where have you lived?" Cam wheezed, eyes still watering from the bean currently stuck in her esophagus.

Avery started to list off places on their fingers: "San Francisco, New York, Rio de Janeiro, LA, London, Munich, Seoul, Johannesburg, and Mumbai."

Cam gaped. "How old are you even? That's too many places!"

Avery laughed, "I only listed the places I lived for at least six months. Anything less and you can't possibly get the vibe of the place. One year I changed schools four times!"

"Hong Kong ever?" Sofia asked, tilting her head.

"Only visited; would love to live there for a bit. That's where you're from, right?" Avery asked. Sofia nodded, and the two of them launched into an exchange of places they had been and people they knew. Cam was content to be soothed by their voices. She ate her delicious burrito as they swapped stories, and James fiddled with his foil-wrapped feast, attempting to ascertain some way to eat it with a minimum of spillage or mess. Looking up at the stars, Cam thought about how small her world had been back home and how much it had grown in only the short time she had been at Beekor. She couldn't wait to see all the new universes that were waiting to be unlocked.

But first she had to finish her burrito.

Chapter 10

IT HAD BEEN SURPRISINGLY EASY for Cam to tell Travis, Terry, and Theresa the next day that she was spending the afternoon with a mentor, though she didn't specify who she was going to meet. She didn't want to say it aloud, afraid that it would somehow jinx her unbelievable good fortune. She kept rereading their text exchange, expecting it to have all been a fever dream. If she was also still confused about the strange way Wyatt had brought Lee up in their meeting, she opted to put it out of her mind for the moment.

The Three Ts, for their part, had simply waved her off and continued clacking away at their respective keyboards. "IT still needs to get you access to a couple other pieces of software for you to really get to work, but that should be done by tomorrow morning," Travis reassured her. It felt weird to just up and leave in the middle of a workday.

Cam headed out and hailed one of the autonomous Beekars that circulated among the campus like cells in a bloodstream. A small, sleek, three-wheeled car came to a smooth stop in front of her, and she hopped in. The door closed behind her, enclosing her in a warm, utterly silent, plush interior.

Aloud Cam recited, "Meeting, Lee Baker, Chinatown gate." Something on the dash at the front seat flashed green, and the car departed. "Yes!" It appeared she even had free rides across the entire city if she wanted.

She closed her eyes and took deep, even breaths. Time to get her head in the game, she thought. She ran through several mantras. She recited some aspirations. She tried to recall the litany against fear. She was about to spend real quality time with Lee Baker, and she had no clue what to expect, but she wanted—no, *needed*—to make a fantastic impression. She idly fantasized about actually working with the living legend, maybe appearing on a magazine cover alongside her. And perhaps Lee could assist with getting Specio prioritized again, since Wyatt had seemed disinterested. She decided the best way to get on Lee's good side was effusive compliments. Everyone loved compliments. Wyatt seemed to thrive off them. She struggled to push down her nerves. She didn't think there was anything else she could do to prepare at this point. She had even reviewed Lee Baker's career achievements the night before, just to ensure she had things to talk about.

Cam marveled at how incomprehensible her life had already become. Free transport across a new city. Incredible free food. The campus also had a free barbershop, laundry service, and multiple gyms. To top it off, nobody tracked her time or gave her trouble if she got up from work to avail herself of any of these services. She took out the Beekor phone that she had received and admired it. Cam realized that at Beekor she had access to basically anything she needed to live or work. Back home, she had scrabbled and scrounged for tools and parts. Cam and her mother clipped coupons to afford food. They borrowed neighbors' cars. Then she had gotten into this giant company and suddenly had all those problems completely solved for her.

Outside the car window, Cam ascended a vast hilly area full of mansions. At the peak of one particularly steep hill, she was able to see the entire city arrayed before her. A carpet of low-density housing, many single-family

Victorians, like Lee Baker's former abode, covered the landscape and unfurled down the hill, until it gave way to increasingly dense and tall buildings downtown. The Transamerica building, a tall, thin acute isosceles triangle, thrust up to the sky. There was also another one that Cam thought looked suspiciously phallic, with some sort of animated sequence playing on the tip.

The car tipped over the hill and headed downtown. As Cam got closer to her destination, her nerves returned. What if she made a fool of herself and ruined everything? What if Lee regretted agreeing to meet her? What if Lee hated her so much, she personally kicked Cam out of the program and made sure she never worked in tech again? The fluttering in her stomach reached a crescendo as the car pulled up to its stop. She got out by a wide red-painted gate with tiered pagoda roofs that spanned the road into Chinatown proper. At either side of the gate sat an enormous stone guardian dog, defending the entry. An endless procession of tourists took photos of the dogs, the gate, each other, and each other with the gate and the dogs.

The city all around her looked like modern Western architecture. Upscale airy retail spaces, expensive-looking restaurants, and broad streets. But passing through the gate revealed a whole different world. Chinatown was a maze of narrow alleys, drastic inclines, dense clusters of pedestrians, and small shops bursting at the seams with tourist merchandise like massive bronze turtle sculptures and throwing stars.

Cam felt a hand on her shoulder and spun. Lee Baker had walked up beside her in sunglasses, a patterned button-down T-shirt, slim-fit gray jeans, and loafers. She looked casual, approachable, and not at all like someone whose net worth was probably nine figures. "Cam!" she called. "Coffee?"

She strode across the street to a coffee shop, and Cam scrambled after, clutching her backpack. "Thank you so, so much," Cam effused. "I am *so* appreciative of this opportunity." Lee held the door open for her, and Cam went through. "I've been such a huge fan of your work for so, so long."

Lee put a hand on her head and looked chagrined. Cam worried she was screwing up everything. She resolved to gush even harder. "I mean, that thing you did with the first tablets where you made the entire case into a single massive heat sink to get low-cost passive cooling to offset the overclocked CPUs . . . Genius!"

"Uh, sure," Lee said. She looked at Cam expectantly. Cam looked back. Lee pointed at the counter, where a barista waited patiently.

"Oh, oh! Sorry!" Cam selected a coffee and size at random.

Out in front of the shop, Cam had begun her effusive praise yet again, but Lee silenced her by pushing the coffee cup into her hands. Cam sipped her coffee and waited at the corner for the crosswalk light to turn with Lee. A homeless man began to sing in a rich tenor. Lee had a wistful look on her face.

"Wyatt and I had our first office right out here," she said, gesturing vaguely at an office window overlooking the street. "The rent was free. Some friend of his." She made a small, private smile. "We used to joke about how the tops of our heads are in thousands of tourist photos." Lee and Cam walked through the gate and started up the hill.

Cam decided to try a different approach. "I'm really grateful to have been chosen for the Beekor Accelerator Program." They pushed up the hill, frequently getting separated and coming back together as they navigated through walls of people filtering through in both directions. "I've never actually worked at a real company before," she continued when she had reached Lee's side again.

"A bit busier than usual," Lee mused.

Cam infused her voice with the utmost of grateful cheer. "It all feels like I got invited to some kind of secret world. I can't thank you and Wyatt—"

Lee cut Cam off by grabbing her shoulder and pointing to a more secluded alley. "Let's cut through here. Get out of the crowd."

Lee led Cam determinedly deeper into a series of increasingly tight alleys. Cam had to pay attention to avoid tripping on the uneven brick roads. Finally, they came to an alley with a line leading all the way out and around the corner. The line terminated at a shop that smelled incredible.

Lee made a little frown as she took in the length of the line. "Hmm, shit. I should've expected this," Lee said. "Wait here a sec."

Cam watched in confusion as Lee found a tourist right near the entrance and handed her some cash, then gestured at something in the dark store interior. The tourist looked hesitantly down at the money pressed into her hand, back up at Lee, then nodded. Lee smiled winningly.

Cam gave the appearance of waiting dutifully, while silently racking her brain for some way to turn this all around. She hadn't gotten to talk about any of her work, and she felt like she was *seriously* failing to impress Lee. She considered her holographic upgrade prototype in her bag. Cam steeled herself to make a last-ditch effort.

The tourist came back out and handed Lee two large discs. Lee thanked her warmly, before coming back to Cam and handing her one. "Try this out," she said gleefully as she pressed one of the brown discs into Cam's hand. Then she bit into her own. "It's a fortune cookie! Before they fold it!" She spat crumbs everywhere.

Cam took a bite of hers. It was quite good—still warm, but crunchy and just the right degree of sweetness. "Wait, so do we not get a fortune if we eat it like this?"

"No clue!" Lee exclaimed. "Maybe it's a 'no fate but what we make' kinda thing? Let's find a place to sit."

Lee led Cam out of the alley, around a corner, and to a park where groups of elderly Chinese men and women were playing mah-jongg, practicing tai chi, or otherwise sitting around and laughing. Lee watched the benches like a hawk and instantly descended on one as its occupant made to stand up. She patted the seat beside her, and Cam joined.

Lee reclined and looked peacefully about them. Cam reached into her bag to pull out the prototype at the same time Lee reached into hers to pull out a vape pen. Lee took a puff, then exhaled a broad plume of something that definitely wasn't tobacco. She smiled and looked over at Cam. "Just like old times." She patted Cam's hand. "Eat your cookie," she admonished.

Then she offered the vape pen to Cam. Cam shook her head.

Defeated, Cam put her prototype back in her bag. She mournfully chewed as she felt her hopes of impressing Lee Baker collapsing around her. She sank into a solemn certainty that she had just failed utterly.

After a few moments of silence, punctuated by Lee toking up a few more times, Lee excitedly asked, "So, what did you think?" A group of elderly men hunched over a mah-jongg game erupted into laughter and cries.

"I— What?" Cam stuttered.

"Thanks for giving me the chance to just hang out a bit!" Lee chattered. "It's great to see the city again through new eyes! Don't forget to enjoy it while you're here, you know? It's not all just work."

Cam gave a small, stiff nod. She had no idea what Lee was talking about.

"Why so glum?" Lee asked.

Cam sighed. Trying to flatter Lee had gotten her nowhere, and she was frankly emotionally exhausted from the past couple of days. She felt a dam break inside her, and a burst of hot feelings came rushing out. "Honestly," Cam admitted, "I thought I was joining the Accelerator to work on my holographic adapter, Specio."

"And?" Lee inquired, lazily watching a group of older women in the corner slowly flow from one athletic pose to another.

"Wyatt put me on this influencer-customization-program thing. I'm just kind of confused."

Lee looked over with unexpected sharpness, all her attention on Cam. "He tasked you directly?"

Cam nodded, pinned under Lee's laser focus. Suddenly, Cam saw her, Lee Baker, the genius who had built Beekor from nothing: a titan and a force to be reckoned with.

"Son of a bitch," she muttered, gazing grimly into the middle distance. Acidly, she continued. "Wyatt is used to treating the entire company like his own little kingdom nowadays. Even more so for the Accelerator, I'm sure."

Cam was confused. "So, where do you fit into his kingdom?"

Lee snorted. "Haven't you heard? I'm on fucking 'sabbatical.'" A familiar feeling began to creep over Cam. She was no stranger to being caught between divorcing parents. Less angrily, Lee continued. "Wyatt can appear amicable enough, and his instincts are absolutely second to none. And that bastard can certainly make you rich, but you need to keep this in mind: He'll always do what benefits him and his own bottom line."

Lee looked up and gave Cam a calculated look, then seemed to shrug to herself. She relaxed her posture, folding back in, until she was once again just a regular person, not the engineer who had led the righteous coup to liberate the FreeCam software project from sexist leadership. Cam had some of the articles taped on her wall in her home. "You need to make sure to protect yourself when it comes to working with Wyatt."

Feeling as if she had tattled on somebody, Cam attempted to walk things back. "Look, I'm an adult; I know how to deal with people. And Wyatt has already given me great advice, a chance to learn, all these opportunities...."

"And a bunch of perks, like a nice house and free toys," Lee commented wryly with a relaxed puff.

"I'm really thankful for all of that," Cam said, partially to herself.

"That's fair." Lee nodded, spinning her vape in her hand distractedly. "But you should keep one thing in mind. People in Wyatt's orbit profit, but only as long as they reflect well on him. He will never champion you to grow on your own, or to exceed him." Lee took another massive toke from her vape pen. "He'll pursue his own vision without tolerance for deviation. From anybody. And what he sees is usually right." She blew out a giant cloud. "*Usually*. But you're correct; you're an adult. It's up to you to figure out how to deal with that rat fuck." She proceeded to blow rings. "What about your invention?"

An old man laughed gleefully as he slapped down a mah-jongg tile. The people around him groaned. Cam watched thoughtfully.

"I'm still working on it on the side," she said in a distracted tone. "My mom and her study group could really use it."

Lee clapped Cam hard on the back like a jolly, overenthusiastic uncle. "Holy shit, you've got customers?!"

Staggering under the blow, Cam realized hadn't thought of it like that. "I guess I do, don't I?" She sat up a little straighter. She had a product.

Lee smiled. "Don't give up on it, all right?"

Cam nodded, resolved.

Lee stowed her vape pen, stood, and straightened her clothes. "I've gotta get outta here, but I'm giving you an assignment. Do some fun shit before our next meeting. I want you to tell me all about it when I see you in two weeks!" She waved, spun, and walked jauntily off through the park square, leaving Cam to process.

Chapter 11

"YOU ARE JUST *SO* GREAT to chat with!" Karrygold's animated golden bear head reconfigured into an exaggerated anime wink, three-fingered paw in a peace sign by her chin. A big pink heart erupted from her head and floated leisurely up, rotating back and forth like a balloon, and out of the field of the holographic display.

"Thanks, you too!" As far as Cam could tell, things were going swimmingly. She sat in a tiny conference room that mimicked an old-timey red phone booth but with soundproofing and a cozy desk. She leaned personally over her new laptop to speak with Karrygold. Karrygold was a gamer who live streamed entirely as a virtual character, or a VTuber. She appeared as an animated golden bear while playing popular video games. She was also a wildly successful influencer, having over 2.8 million subscribers on MiTube and 4.5 million followers on TicTak. Cam had had no clue what to expect going in, but the VTuber had appeared for the holochat in character as her animated golden bear avatar and was so incredibly personable that the entire conversation had been a delight from the start.

"Anyway," Cam said, consulting her list of questions, "going back to some of your future plans and where Beekor might fit into them, what's something you think we could help with right away?"

Karrygold's golden bear avatar face pinched in dramatic, cartoony thought and made a thinking noise, then gasped. "Well, I was just thinking how I would love to branch out into IRL streams." She spoke in a mournful rasp; then her voice pitched wildly back up. "How *cool* would it be to stream a cooking show with my avatar applied in real time?!" Her avatar took on a theatrical thoughtful pose. "Not that I'm particularly koala-fied, but you get the idea."

Cam began to walk through how she would solve the problem in her head. She could see exactly how she would go about building a feature to allow a real person to map their expressions and motions onto a virtual avatar from within a live camera feed on a phone as it moved around, as opposed to the stationary position Karrygold had to stay in and the powerful computer she used to run her current live streams. She did some mental math, then decided what the hell. If Cam could picture just how to build it, it would probably be no snap for the Beekor software team. "You know what, we can *definitely* get you that. I'll get the engineering team working on it."

"Woooow!" The bear avatar's eyes became dinner-plate-sized circles, and both pupils disappeared. "You and Theresa are really polar opposites! In all my conversations with Theresa, she usually just made that sour face and said, 'I'll check in with our execution teams and get back to you with feasibility info.'" Karrygold took on a huffy, humorless tone, capturing Theresa's brusque voice flawlessly.

Cam laughed.

"And is it pawsible to get more battery life?"

"We'll see." Cam smiled, feeling like an indulgent parent.

The golden bear avatar screamed joyously, then fell over as if dead. A small golden bear ghost erupted from the avatar's cartoony corpse. Then the ghost also died. Karrygold recovered instantly and began to thank Cam profusely.

Cam exited the meeting with the sense that this whole gig was going to be pretty easy. Her very first influencer interview, and it had been a complete success. She did some research about the way that virtual avatar streaming worked, compiled a couple links for specs that broke down the file formats and protocol info, and wrote up a task for the software team. "Enable on-device avatar streaming." She attached her links.

While she was at it, in a spirit of good cheer, she also wrote up a ticket for the hardware team. She could totally see a way to downgrade the camera and replace it with some more battery. Boom, battery life: granted, she thought. She wrote up the ticket and assigned it to the hardware team. Then she got up to go to lunch. At this rate, she really would be on her own project in just a week.

The conversations with the hardware and software team leads that followed were not pleasant. Cam found herself having to sit down and explain what the goals of the new features were, who they were for, and what sort of time frame she expected them on. The software team lead, Kevin, had all but screamed at her. His black hair had the patchy look of someone who frequently pulled out chunks in frustration. There were multiple silent periods in the conversation where she was pretty sure Kevin had muted the call and hidden his video feed in order to curse Cam's name. David from the hardware team, on the other hand, resembled a basset hound. Cheeks practically melting off his face as his eyes looked sadder and redder. He spent the entire call mournfully requesting more information, sighing, and then defeatedly agreeing to commit himself and his team to the new work.

Cam finished the calls feeling guilty for turning up the charm to get her way, but she figured, this must be the hard part of the job. Honestly, she had expected more capability from one of the best funded and most talented engineering teams in the entire world. She couldn't imagine why they were complaining about building something she could have done with a hundredth of their resources. Maybe they hadn't been pushed to innovate recently, she reasoned. Or maybe she was just that good.

Cam went back and forth with Karrygold and the engineering teams once more that week, tacking on yet another set of new features. To herself, she began to wonder when things might get difficult.

Cam spent a relaxing weekend unpacking and moving more fully into her gorgeous attic room. She made herslef at home in the game room at the page house with Sofia and Avery, who seemed to be enjoying working on their facial identification software and user acquisition, respectively. When Cam asked for clarification on exactly what Avery meant by "user acquisition," they had simply laughed and said a wall of tech and finance jargon that sounded intimidatingly complex. Although Cam had a funny suspicion that it might have been a politic way of saying "nothing." James made a few brief appearances, coming out of the garage to grab snacks and hastily return to his weekend tinkering. Marcus was nowhere in sight. Cam also spent some time cheerfully printing and assembling a new Specio prototype for her mother.

Next Wednesday, Cam met with Karrygold again. One more hardware ticket with a new feature request later, Cam suddenly found herself embroiled in a crisis. David had initiated an immediate holochat with Cam upon ticket assignment. Cam accepted it, but what she saw in her holographic display was not David. It was the view from inside the hardware building. Whoever was holding the device, David she presumed, was bringing it around the space to show Cam what was going on. The space looked to be in complete disarray.

As the camera explored the space, it revealed new, disorganized heaps of various tiny microphones and cameras. The miniature OEM components that might eventually be slotted into a Beekor phone were scattered across many tables and spilled onto the floor. A collapsing pile of test-pattern sheets leaned against a broken rail-mounted frame in one corner of the space. Fast-food wrappers were strewn everywhere. Lewis and the others working the floor looked like zombies. They all had dark circles under their eyes and greasy hair. David took extra pains to bring the camera around to the cots and sleeping bags employees had assembled on the concrete and under desks over the course of the weekend. Several of them were currently occupied.

David finally appeared in view of the camera, his normally dour, hangdog expression transformed to a look of incandescent rage. Rather than speak, all he did was emit one loud, long scream. Cam jumped. The Three Ts all looked up to see what was happening. She brought her laptop to a conference room.

"Haven't you ever heard of scope creep?" David bellowed, his eyes were bloodshot, and he had what appeared to be a forty-eight o'clock shadow's worth of stubble.

Cam looked on, horrified. Had she been the cause of this? "But I thought all the changes were easy! I know exactly how to build them!" she attempted to explain.

"You know how to build them?" David began menacingly. "You know how to select and test a range of components for quality, compatibility, and supplier availability? You know how to create a calibration test bed to ensure all new devices that use the new camera come off of assembly functioning as expected? You know how to retool an assembly line to prepare to work with the new hardware? You know how to do that over and over again every three days, forcing us to throw away our work each time and start over, all while trying to hit an arbitrary deadline you put in place so we could help a cartoon bear fail at making omelets?!" By the end of it, David's voice had transitioned to an enraged bellow.

"Oh my God," Cam began, mortified. Suddenly, she realized that what she had assumed was just an ice cube was actually the tip of an iceberg, and she had steered the ship right into it. "I had no clue!"

"I *know* you had no clue." David's rage petered out, and he just sounded sad again. His face lost its rictus grimace and melted back into its customary hangdog expression, but somehow even more tired than ever before. "How about we start over? We'll stop all work on this project. I'll leave it up to you to figure your way out of this mess."

"Yes, please, everybody should stop! Everyone should head home and ... maybe take the rest of the week off?" Cam said the last hopefully, unsure if she even had the jurisdiction to do such a thing and braced herself.

David just nodded frigidly. Then he hung up.

Cam returned to her desk feeling absolutely awful. She had barely set her laptop back down when another holochat came in. This time it was Kevin from the software team. Cam took the precaution of rushing back to the conference room before accepting the call.

"So. When were you going to tell me?" Kevin asked angrily. He was missing fresh patches of hair.

"Tell you what?" Cam asked.

"Tell me that we've been building your feature—consumer-grade face tracking and avatar remapping, which, by the way, relies on detailed and precise camera calibration—for the *incorrect* camera."

"Oh fuck."

"Oh fuck is *correct*, Cam." Kevin sounded pissed. "You know what wasn't correct? Asking us to build a feature that relies on very specific interactions with the camera while also changing the camera, and then neglecting to tell us!"

Cam felt worse than ever. The tasks she thought she had been effortlessly juggling came crashing down around her. "Oh, I'm so sorry."

"Sure, you are." Kevin sounded unconvinced.

"Look, I'm going to sort this out. Please, take the rest of the week off!" Cam said frantically and in full-blown damage control.

"Done," Kevin snapped and cut the call.

Chapter 12

CAM FELT TERRIBLE. THE GUILT over what she had inflicted on the hardware and software teams kept washing over her in waves, like a tide pushing a rotting whale corpse onto the beach. She was the rotting whale corpse, and her chosen beach was the living room couch in the page house. She didn't have the will to try to climb up the stairs to her room. Maybe she could just stay on the couch forever and be absorbed into the cushions to become stuffing for the next person to sit on. She would be of more use as stuffing than as a person.

Deep in her self-pity spiral, Cam didn't notice Sofia come in and look at her contemplatively. She only became aware of the other girl's presence when the sounds of *Dance Nights 2* began playing on the TV. Sofia scrubbed it right to where they had stopped watching in the car ride from the airport and sat down next to Cam with a bowl of popcorn. The two watched through the rest of the movie not saying a word, just the quiet sounds of munching as they both consumed the salty treat. Without comment, Sofia tapped her phone and started streaming the film *Dance Battle Island 3* to the TV. It was only partway through "Take My Hand 2Nite" that Cam finally broke the silence.

"I really messed up." She felt her throat tighten on the words.

Sofia lowered the volume on the movie, but let it keep playing and turned to look at Cam expectantly. Cam, for her part, continued to lie on the couch and watch the movie.

"So many people are so mad at me now, and it's all my fault, and I don't know how to fix it." Cam felt frustrated tears start to prick at the corners of her eyes. She had been so recklessly confident that she knew everything. That she knew better than anyone else. That cockiness had made two whole teams miserable and resulted in promises to Karrygold that she couldn't possibly keep. Wyatt was right: She was way out of her depth. She was going to get kicked out of the program for sure.

"Make a list," Sofia said.

"What?" Cam looked up at Sofia.

"When I need to figure out something, I make a list of what I *do* know. Then I can see the gaps I need to fill," Sofia said succinctly.

Cam thought for a moment. Then she sat upright, got her laptop from her bag, and opened up a blank notepad.

Sofia returned her attention to the movie as Cam typed away, deleted, thought, and typed again.

In the end, Cam's list looked like this:

- *Assumed the time it takes to build a consumer product is the same as a prototype I would make to test something out for myself*
  - *Did not consult with engineering before committing to work, assuming I knew exactly what it entailed*
  - *ASK ENGINEERING HOW HARD THINGS ARE BEFORE COMMITTING*
- *Kept agreeing to new work, forcing engineering to start over or change direction*

- *SCOPE CREEP*
- *Did not foster communication between hardware and software, despite dependencies between their work, resulting in wasted effort*

She looked up at Sofia. "I need to apologize."

Sofia looked over her shoulder and read her notes before nodding. "And?"

"And," Cam said, "I need to make sure it doesn't happen again."

Sofia nodded again.

Cam pushed her laptop aside and gave Sofia a powerful hug. Sofia was initially stiff with shock but quickly warmed and returned the gesture.

"Thank you so much, Sofia. I really appreciate it." Cam pulled away. "I'm going to make this right." She bounced up and headed toward the kitchen before hesitating and turning back. Cam realized that Avery was right; Cam could only do so much on her own. "Actually, do you think you could help me? I'd love the company, and we can watch more movies? It's totally okay if you don't want to; you're probably busy. You've done so much already, and—" Cam cut off at Sofia's waving gesture.

"Yes." Sofia got up to join Cam in the kitchen.

Chapter 13

CAM WOKE UP TO THE sounds of a drumroll being pounded on her door and a person that could only be Avery singing at the top of their lungs. Through a groggy haze of sleep, Cam threw on some pajama bottoms under her oversized sleeping shirt and opened the door, interrupting Avery's percussion recital. Undeterred, Avery finished their routine on the wall, belting out a final "Tacky Tourist Tiiiiiiimmmme!!"

Cam stared at them. "Avery, it's ten in the morning on a Saturday. What are you doing?"

Avery posed, looking positively chipper in a calf-length pleated black leather kilt, large zebra-patterned blazer, peacock-feather-patterned button-down, and knee-high, shiny gold boots. "We're going on an adventure. I know you haven't left your hometown that much, so I'm making it my responsibility to show you the big city. Remember?"

"I actually did go to Chinatown already," Cam said a little defensively. And yeah, her hometown was small, but it wasn't a backwater or anything.

"Oh, I'm impressed!" Avery did look mildly taken aback. "Already did some exploring, and here I thought you hadn't left the Beekor campus at all."

"Well," Cam relented, "I went to meet someone there. I haven't actually gone anywhere else. But I'd like to."

"Great!" Avery's buoyant good cheer returned. "Get dressed. I'll gather the rest." With that, they bounded down the stairs three at a time. Cam had no idea how they managed it in those shoes.

Back in her room, Cam got ready. As she washed her face and caught a glimpse of herself in the mirror, she contemplated the shadows under her eyes. She had spent the last few days and nights stressing over Kevin and David and her general bungling of the entire Karrygold situation, reworking her list of mistakes over and over. But eventually, she realized she had worried over that bone enough. The past was the past, and she just had to move forward. And that particular hurdle of an apology would have to wait until Monday. In the meantime, she should enjoy her time in the city with the other pages, just in case she got kicked out of the Accelerator Program on Monday for screwing everything up. No, she berated herself, she wasn't going to think like that, not today.

Cam finally got down to the first floor dressed in patched jeans, a navy sweater with the name of a high school she had never gone to stamped on it, and sneakers that had once been red but were now a dusty-brown color. She dropped her backpack by the couch and turned to see Sofia pouring herself coffee in the kitchen in a sleek knee-length knit beige cardigan and flats, while Avery attempted to cajole James into joining them on their day trip.

"I was planning on working downstairs today," James protested as he pushed around the remainder of his breakfast on his plate.

"Come on, James, you've been holed up in the basement this whole time. Come out with us—you'll have fun," Avery promised.

"I am going to have fun. Downstairs. Building a new piece," James muttered, fiddling with the sleek white pair of headphones with gray ear foam around his neck. He had also made those, Cam suspected. She abruptly realized the garage must be where he had been all those nights she had seen his empty room. He hadn't been there the one time she went to print a few Specio prototypes for her mother, but that wasn't surprising considering how fast the 3D printers were.

Just then, the front door opened and Marcus walked in. Cam hadn't been within six feet of him since the first night, and she realized she had forgotten how attractive he was. It wasn't her fault, though; he seemed to wake up early and constantly be out late. She would occasionally spot him across the campus from her, walking with Wyatt, but if it hadn't been for the appearance and disappearance of his shoes by the front door, Cam would have thought he didn't live in the house at all.

This particular morning, he was in fine form. Looking as though he had just been out for a run, sporting a light sheen of sweat, with a loose-fitting tracksuit open over an extremely tight shirt. His pecs looked like they were straining to escape, and Cam restrained the urge to leap over there and help set them free.

"Good, there you are." Avery waved at Marcus, who popped one earbud out of his ear. Sounds by Charlene, $500 for a pair. "We're going to explore the city—want to come?"

"You're leading?" Marcus jerked his chin at Avery, who nodded. He appeared to think for a moment as he glanced around the room. His eyes finally landed on Cam, who had started to prepare a bowl of cereal in an effort to distract herself from staring at Marcus's hips, where his long-fingered hands rested lightly. Cam tried to pour the Frosted Flakes as loudly as possible. "Yeah, okay. Let me take a quick shower."

Avery crowed, "We achieved the impossible. The elusive Marcus is coming with us. James, that means you have no choice; you're joining." James looked defeated as Marcus climbed the stairs to his room.

Cam pulled out the list of ideas Jennifer had given the pages on the first day. "So, where do you want to go? I was looking over Jennifer's suggestions, and I—" Avery snatched the paper out of her hands and ripped it into pieces before throwing it all with a flourish in the compost.

"We are not doing that basic bullshit. I'm in charge."

Cam looked a little despondently at the compost. She thought a few of those things had sounded fun. She felt a hand on her shoulder and looked up at Sofia, who smiled down at her.

"You can have my copy," Sofia said quietly. To Avery she asked, "Where are we going?"

"Everywhere of course! This is Tacky Tourist Time. We will be tourists, ergo, we needs must be tacky. Here—" They reached into a large gold snakeskin bag that had been resting on the counter and pulled out five sets of gigantic sunglasses in gaudy colors that absolutely fulfilled the requirement of being tacky. "GlaucoDyne was handing out this company swag at a concert last week."

A brief exchange of glasses and a quick breakfast for Cam later, and Marcus was walking down the stairs again looking fresh in slacks—light beige with navy pin-striped—white shirt, white high-tops, and blue-gray heather thigh-length coat.

"These are yours." Avery tossed the last pair of glasses, square flattops in a shade of neon purple, at Marcus and shouted, "Let's roll out! I've got a car outside."

Outside, they were confronted by Avery's vehicle. "I got it for free for agreeing to join a trial for some service or other. I dunno, they said I was 'good signal.'" Avery waved them in.

It looked like no car Cam had ever seen. It looked like the type of car Soviet Bloc nations imagined Americans might drive in the future. It had six doors, three rows of seats, and fabric curtains. Sofia inspected the vehicle from several angles, a look of oblique horror on her face.

James simply opened the door and claimed one of the back seats. He began applying sunscreen. Cam, used to cars that didn't look like they had any right to move, got in. Avery was their usual cheery self as they took the driver's seat. Marcus slipped into the passenger seat with the long-suffering look of someone used to Avery's ways. Sofia, with the air of a princess sleeping on a pea, got in as well.

The inside of the car was more bizarre. There was an enormous tablet screen mounted on the dash, but it didn't work. There were actual loose wires hanging out of various panels throughout the interior. In the front passenger seat, Marcus opened the glove box. Loose fuses fell out.

"Don't touch those," Avery said. Then they sparked two wires together, and the sunroof slid mechanically open. Avery jumped. "Cool!" Various other fumblings eventually resulted in the engine starting.

Cam relaxed back and looked out the window at the changing landscape. In between views of corner groceries, busy restaurant parklets, and buildings Avery called beaux arts architecture, Cam spotted glimpses of streets swooping down hills into the waters of the bay. It was, Cam realized, an absolutely beautiful day.

"So, where are you taking me this time?" Marcus asked Avery as he put the sunglasses on. Cam could only see his profile as she sat in the seat behind Avery, but she was disturbed at how good the glasses looked on him. "This better not be like the time you took me to that underground run-with-the-bulls club in Dubai."

"Come on, they weren't actual bulls. And we had a great time getting that whole group of crown princes to gamble on a game of musical chairs," Avery cajoled.

"*You* had a great time. I had to explain to my parents why I was missing half my clothes and a three-thousand-dollar watch." Marcus grimaced, to which Avery only cackled.

Before Cam could ask what exactly had happened to Marcus's clothes, Avery was parking the car and kicking them all out. In short order, they stood before the enormous crab sign of Fisherman's Wharf, which Cam recognized from movies and advertisements for the city. It was a maze of wooden buildings built on an enormous pier out over the water. Signage for restaurants, shops, galleries, museums, tours, and an aquarium stuck out at colorful angles, and Cam could hear the sounds of a carousel drifting from somewhere farther down.

"This place is probably on Jennifer's list," commented Sofia dryly, to no one in particular.

"Look, the classics are classics for a reason. Now let's see the wax statues," Avery said breezily.

The four pages followed Avery into a museum of uncanny-valley look-alikes of famous celebrities. The pages fell into a stupor, wandering about and vaguely appreciating all the dead-eyed figures. Cam leapt as a loud, tuneless crooning erupted.

"It's been a hard day's night, and I've been jerking . . . off a fro-og!" Avery was using their phone to project a hologram of their face over John Lennon's, belting for all they were worth. The rest of the pages shrieked with laughter. Soon they all joined in and ran around projecting their faces onto statues and telling jokes, loudly making up ludicrous backstories for characters, and generally being a menace to any poor tourist caught in the same room as their antics. Even James got in a few punchy one-liners.

Cam was in tears by the time they were in the third room, and Sofia grabbed Avery's phone to sing the bawdiest song Cam had ever heard with the voice of a siren and the serene expression of an angel. Avery looked at her, wide-eyed. For once, they seemed at a loss for words.

"That's both beautiful and almost certainly a war crime," said James. "But you're projecting your face over Bruce Lee, not David Bowie."

Sofia turned to look at the wax statue. "I knew that." Cam's head hurt and her abs ached from laughing.

With the tenor for the day set, the gang stumbled back outside to explore the rest of the wharf.

Avery showed Cam a place serving crepes rolled like a cone and stuffed with red bean mochi ice cream, and chocolate sauce. The $12 price tag pained her, but she reasoned she did have a sizable paycheck now and this was a special occasion. It ended up being unlike anything she had eaten before. It was unbelievably good. James had what looked like an ordinary cup of noodles, but it had been bolstered with a fried egg, sauteed veggies, seasoned bacon, and other garnishes Cam couldn't identify. Avery held what could be loosely described as an ice-cream sandwich that had gone through a unicorn factory. Sofia delicately sipped at a monstrosity of an iced coffee that appeared to change colors as she consumed it. And Marcus ate crab cakes coated in breadcrumbs and stuffed with shallots, parsley, lemon zest, and topped with an avocado mayonnaise.

The group began to meander around, checking out the various stores.

Cam found Sofia in the corner of a tiny store that sold doe-eyed statues of children. She was contemplating a miniature statue of a samba dancer.

"For my desk," Sofia explained to Cam. "I'm lonely; I could use the company."

Cam was surprised. "Aren't you seated with teammates?" She thought of her own seating arrangement in the tight pod of desks. She was practically in Theresa's lap half the time.

"The mentor I was assigned explained that I would be contributing to the Beekor Glasses in a different way, working on support tools for content creators," Sofia began. "But the entire team is based in Eastern Europe, and my mentor has also been difficult to get ahold of on a regular basis." Sofia sounded peeved.

James walked in partway through Sofia's explanation. "I don't have an assigned desk," he said. "They move me depending on the project. They put me in machine shops across the campus. It's been very instructive to see how different teams, on different projects, do things."

"You don't have an assigned project?" Cam was astonished. "But what about your multi-grip chassis?"

"I'm helping with different design components of multiple products now," James said. More tentatively, he continued. "The tasks do appear to be rather menial. I can't deny that I'm learning, though."

"Why don't we get you a figurine?" suggested Sofia serenely. "Something small you can take with you when you move desks."

James looked around him, seemingly noticing the angelic figures for the first time. His face melted into a look of revulsion. "No, thank you." Cam, and only Cam, laughed.

After Sofia paid for her dancer, the three wandered to a museum/arcade/shop much more to James's taste. The display out front was a complex mechanical figure, animating and waving, beckoning the pages inside. Avery found them out front, and they went in together.

It was a visual hodgepodge of a place. Mechanical knickknacks and toys, old pinball machines and singing animatronic displays from family pizza restaurants long past were juxtaposed against modern dance games, light-gun games, and holographic games for groups of players. By one wall, Cam saw a bizarre mechanical vignette from some old war, featuring little soldier puppets that, at the drop of a penny, would wobble forward and perish one by one on a tin re-creation of a European countryside. Right beside it, she saw a boxing game that used lidar to track user body motion, enabling players to box with holograms of historic greats. Cam found herself lingering farther and farther behind the main group as she looked at all the various contraptions both mundane and mysterious.

"Hey, Cam, over here." Cam turned and saw Marcus standing on a platform beneath a large dome. She glanced around and realized the rest of the pages were nowhere in sight. She felt a small thrill of nerves and joined him as Marcus explained, "It's a two player co-op game."

"What are we supposed to do?" Cam asked as he tapped a card to the screen in front of them and quickly ran through the selections.

"Keep the spaceship from crashing." Suddenly, holographic projections of fake space equipment appeared before them and cartoonish alarms flared.

The next several minutes were spent in frantic action, too chaotic to think, as one catastrophe after another befell their illusionary spacecraft. Everything from asteroid bombardment to deadly plants growing from the vents. Cam and Marcus were forced to dodge back and forth, playing action-based mini games to resolve the various issues, nearly colliding with each other on numerous occasions. The game finally ended when Marcus failed to repair the engines in time to keep them from falling into a star.

They were both panting and laughing when Cam asked, "Again?"

"Yes!" Marcus's eyes shone with a childish delight, his dimple on full display.

Cam's breath caught on his smile before she laughed, a little embarrassed at herself.

They played again, somehow managing to score worse than the first time, with Marcus failing to deal with the alien infestation in the dormitories. The third time, Marcus began to sabotage Cam while she tried to reaffix the oxygen tanks.

"I thought you said this was co-op!" Cam half yelled, half laughed as they died.

Marcus shrugged with a rueful smile. "I was tired of being the reason we lost. How were you so good at putting out the fires? You got all of them."

"Lots of practice. A bunch of us used to blow stuff up in the field behind my school. I got really good at using the fire extinguisher." Cam pointed an imaginary extinguisher and blew on the nozzle like it was a smoking gun.

Marcus looked stunned, then tilted back his head and issued a full-throated laugh.

Cam found herself admiring the curve of his neck, his deep laugh vibrating her body. Mentally, she took hold of herself and shook violently. *Focus!* When she had broken it off with her ex Nick during the Beekor Accelerator application process, she had told herself no boys, they were only distractions. No matter how cute.

But Marcus isn't a boy . . . he's a man, a contemplative voice said in the back of her head. Cam quietly strangled that voice.

"Come on, let's try something else," Marcus beckoned with a grin. Cam felt compelled to follow.

They wandered through more of the space. The two of them passed several fortune-telling puppets in glass cases, an ancient mechanical game that tasked players with destroying submarines, and a mechanical bull that Marcus eyed with apprehension. What had actually happened in Dubai? Cam wondered.

A freestanding machine from the 2000s caught Cam's eye, and she squeaked, "Oh look! It's one of those old photo machines!" She dashed over with Marcus following closely behind.

"What is it?" he asked, looking at the big box with a room cordoned off by plastic curtains.

"We had one of these in our pizza place, but it stopped working when I was a kid and no one ever bothered to fix it. These were popular before everyone had phones with good cameras," Cam explained. "You stand in this little room with the green screen and take pictures, then you go to this booth on the side to edit them." She gestured to the box.

Marcus nodded. "Let's do it," he said, corralling Cam in.

She put up a show of resistance but then shrugged and gave in. Inside the photography area of the booth was a green screen and a small set of monkey bars. Cam laughed, and when the photo countdown began, she surprised Marcus by climbing up it and hanging upside from her knees. Laughing, Marcus joined her for the next photo. Cam found herself leaning into Marcus to fit in the photo frame. He smelled like amber and cinnamon. For the next few photos, they tried to top each other with increasingly ridiculous poses around the small space. They were falling over each other laughing by the time they got to the photo editing phase.

The editing area consisted of two screens side by side with stylus attached and stools bolted to the floor. Cam grabbed a stylus and began adding stickers of panda bears and funny hats to their photos. After a while, she realized that Marcus was working intently on his screen. She looked over and saw he had opened up a separate screen she hadn't known existed with various brushes and a fully customizable color palette. He had chosen a photo of them fake screaming in the foreground and was proceeding to draw a faithful re-creation of the spaceship holo game they had been playing earlier, complete with space flames and fire extinguisher.

"Whoa! You're really good," Cam marveled, looking over his shoulder.

Marcus startled. "Oh, uh, thanks. Drawing is a hobby of mine," he explained, a little bashfully.

It was the first time Cam had seen Marcus portray anything other than perfect confidence. "Wow, if I was that good as a hobby, my mom would have had me paint murals on the walls of our apartment."

Marcus replied shortly, "Yup, just a hobby." He looked over at her screen. "What have you got?"

Seeing his blatant attempt to change the subject for what it was, Cam decided to let it slide and showed him.

"Why did you give me a monocle and a cigar?" Marcus inquired.

"Because you're too rich to spend time in the house with the rest of us rabble," Cam joked. But as soon as the words left her mouth, she regretted them. She tried to backpedal. "Oh, not to imply that you're snobby or any-thing—" Somehow she was making it worse! She had seen the stickers and thought they were funny—a light dig at Marcus after they had had a good time in the arcade. In her head, it had sounded like gentle ribbing. But now, saying it out loud, she felt like it was a mean accusation after an enjoyable time where he hadn't been snobby in the slightest. "Never mind. I'll erase it. I saw a blobfish hat I'll use instead."

She went to change it, but Marcus put his hand over hers, stopping her stylus.

He appeared to struggle with words before finally haltingly saying, "You're right—I can be a bit of a snob." He looked away from her and took his hand away to rub the back of his neck. Cam's hand continued to tingle where he had touched her.

"Look"—he turned back to her—"I've wanted to apologize to you for giving you the cold shoulder at the meet and greet that first night. There are a lot of expectations on me right now from a lot of people, and I was pretty stressed. But that's no reason to take it out on you. I think you're awesome, and I'd like to get to know you more if I haven't completely blown my chances."

Cam was surprised. This was the most sincere apology she had ever gotten from a boy before. Man. Definitely a man. She considered a moment before giving him a light smile. "I'll forgive you if you take me to some trampoline-worthy coffee."

Marcus grinned back with his whole dimple.

Before he could reply, the plastic curtain was ripped away. Avery stood there with Sofia and James looking over their shoulders.

"You guys are doing purikura without me? These Japanese photo booths are my favorite. Come on—print yours out and let's do a group photo!" Avery demanded.

Marcus and Cam complied, and soon the five pages were in the green-screen room posing with their tacky sunglasses. Cam donned her pink cat-eye sunglasses, Avery an octagonal set in tiger stripes, Marcus his purple square tops, and Sofia removed her Beekor lenses in favor of an oversized tortoiseshell pair. James didn't take off his own glasses, but he did place the round lavender lenses on his head as a grudging compromise.

If the process of taking the picture with the five of them crammed into the small room had been riotous, the entire group compacted into the tiny editing area was pure chaos. Sofia took charge of one of the screens and indulgently acquiesced to Avery's demand for a mullet on their photo. Cam took charge of the other screen, and Marcus asked for the sticker of a pudding with a face. James got into the spirit and requested insistently to have a robot body sticker in one of the photos. He also did an extremely precise job manning the scissors when it came time to cut out the photo stickers from the sheets the kiosk printed.

After a little more exploring around the pier and some quality time with the famous sea lions, the gang finally decided to head home. They all traipsed back to the car with bags of knickknacks, food, or candy as was their want. The ride home was quick and enjoyable, as Avery pressed Sofia about the exact lyrics of the song she had sung earlier.

Later that night, as Cam lay relaxing in her window seat in her room thinking about the day, Avery came in and handed Cam her share of the photos from the photo booth machine.

"Here, these are the ones of all of us," Avery said, handing a pile of colorfully silly photos to Cam. "And these are the ones of you and Marcus." They winked at her. "I've already given him his half of the pics."

Cam felt herself redden a little and grinned back at Avery. As Avery turned to leave, Cam called out after them, "Hey, Avery?"

The other page turned back to look at her questioningly.

"Thanks for today. For taking me off campus. I had a lot of fun," Cam said sincerely.

"Yeah, I did too." Avery actually looked a little surprised before giving a toothy grin. "We'll do Tacky Tourist Time again!" They waved jauntily and left.

Cam looked down at the photo of her and Marcus hanging upside down, laughing. It had been a really good day.

Chapter 14

CAM SPENT SUNDAY RUNNING AROUND shopping, doing errands, and coordinating with Sofia for her return to the Beekor engineering teams on Monday, before finally collapsing on her bed for a relaxing call with her mother.

Cam pulled out her old phone, which looked even more sad and beat-up than ever before next to the slick limited-edition Beekor phone she had been using. But there was something comforting in using the familiar old brick to talk to her mother. She took the Specio adapter off and gave her mom a call. The phone rang and rang. Eventually, she got Rosa's voicemail. Cam called again, to the same result. Cam was puzzled and beginning to feel concerned. But then her mom called her.

"Cammy!" Her mom sounded breathless but cheerful.

"Is everything all right, Mom?" Cam asked.

Rosa hesitated before replying. "Oh, fine. I was just trying to take your plastic spider off of my phone again."

Damn, Cam thought. She hadn't figured on how annoying that might get. She cast a wary eye on her own hastily disassembled phone.

"About that," Cam began, "how are you liking it?" She was practically bouncing in her seat with all the energy of a child on Christmas morning.

"Oh, it's great!" Rosa said. "I think I really started to figure it out! I'm learning so much!"

"Figure out what?" Cam asked curiously, getting ready to take notes.

"Well, I had to take the phone apart three times to reconnect that one piece." Her mom sounded distracted. Cam could hear the sound of chopping vegetables in the background. "When it came to the software part, I had a lot of trouble understanding the instructions, but I did the things with the terminal the way you said." Cam heard vegetables being dropped into a pot.

"I think I mistyped the commands a couple times, but it eventually worked. I got it to show the 3D spinny thing in the air, and I was so excited! Now I know how my little Cammy feels!" Rosa sounded incredibly pleased with herself.

Cam, on the other hand, was becoming increasingly distressed. "So, uh. Did you get to try out any of your coursework with it yet?" Cam prompted.

"Not yet, mi amor. I had to stop after the spinny part. I think I can get your list done in a couple more days!"

Cam scrubbed at her face with her hand. In her mind, she went over the fifty-one-step installation instructions and realized that Rosa hadn't even made it past step eighteen yet.

"What about your study group?" Cam began hopefully. "How are they liking it?"

Rosa was quiet.

"Oh."

"I'm sure they'll get around to trying it, Cammy! You did a great job!" Rosa effused. "But all those steps you wrote down so nicely are a little daunting." Rosa's attempt to be comforting did not succeed. Cam was struck with the dawning realization that her list of installation steps was something that Cam, a highly technical person, could understand, but must have been so much nonsense to a regular person. In many ways, she was thinking of herself and ignoring her mother, the actual customer, as she was building.

Both her day job and her side project were conspiring to make it distressingly clear just how much harder it was to deliver an actual product that regular people could use than it was to just get something working on her own. After her massive failure at work, some time out with the other pages had done a lot to help her regain her equilibrium, but facing another setback, this time in her personal project, the one in which she took refuge, took the wind right back out of her sails.

She began to do the internal calculations for all the hardware changes and software changes it would take to convert her batch of rough ideas and test components into something that a regular person could just plug in, install an app, and use. As she thought through it all, she realized the amount of work ahead of her was staggering. She thought she had done the hard part, but getting things to work in a limited fashion on her own device was just the beginning.

Cam considered the Beekor user experience, and just how easy and smooth it was to use all their hardware. She was starting to gain a true appreciation for Wyatt's genius. It wasn't just Lee Baker's smarts, but also Wyatt's consumer insights that made the company the giant that it was.

No, she had to stop focusing on the amount of work for now. Her new muscles for damage control and fixing things kicked in. She took a deep breath and directed herself to write a list, like she and Sofia had done together. Cam gritted her teeth and began itemizing the key gaps in her work. She opened her laptop and began furiously typing.

- *Failed to understand customer*
  - *Did not take into account actual level of customer technical capability*

- *Thought I could just present a questionnaire, then drop products and they would be useful*
- *Can't even learn what's good/bad about the product if the customer never gets through the install process*
- *WORK DIRECTLY WITH MOM/STUDY GROUP TO FIGURE OUT PAIN POINTS IN INSTALLATION PROCESS*
- *Lack the expertise to create a smooth/easy install user experience*
    - *Seriously, this is not my wheelhouse. I type green text into black windows all day.*
    - *START STUDYING . . . OR FIND SOMEBODY TO HELP?*
- *My vision of Specio may be specific to me, and it may not be what the customer actually wants*
    - *Maybe not everybody is just like Cam*
    - *RUN SESSIONS ACTUALLY USING SPECIO TOGETHER WITH CUSTOMERS TO FIGURE OUT HOW THEY WANT TO USE IT AND WHERE IT FAILS THEM*

She would convert the Specio prototype into a simple kit that anybody could use. She vowed then and there to build something that could help not just people like her mom and her study group take advantage of the opportunities of holographic technology, but to also bring it to a level of polish and user experience that even the completely technologically illiterate could install and use it.

"Uh, Cam?"

Cam realized she had been quiet for far too long. She took a breath and addressed her mother like a client. "Mom, I'm sorry for not actually taking your needs into account with what I built. It hadn't occurred to me just how complicated that install list was. If you're still open to working on this with me, I'd really like to improve the install process and go over it with you directly in order to figure out how to make Specio better for you."

Rosa sounded concerned. "Don't beat yourself up." After a pause, she laughed. "That was really, really hard, yeah." More warmly, she continued. "Of course I'll help you. It helps me with my classes too!"

Cam had expected that, but she momentarily felt thankful for just how continually supportive her mother was. She dropped the formality entirely and asked casually, "How are things going back there?"

Rosa needed no more prompting and launched into a long update of the whole neighborhood, who was working where, whose child passed their math test, the outrageous deals she had gotten at the supermarket, and on and on. For the first time since she arrived, Cam experienced just a twinge of homesickness.

Chapter 15

CAM KICKED OFF HER APOLOGY tour in grand fashion on Monday morning. Both the hardware and software teams were coming back that day from the time off they'd taken after she'd run them ragged. Cam set up a meeting for both teams as well as the Three Ts on the hardware floor for 11:00 a.m. Sofia had agreed to be her assistant and helped her carry an enormous pot from home to the hardware building work floor. Together, the two had scrounged a burner to put the pot on to heat it back up. Sofia set to retrieving dishes and serving implements from the cafeteria while Cam got to work tidying the space.

Some engineers from the team showed up partway through and offered half-hearted assistance. Together, they collected all the various little test cameras and microphones and organized them into the correct bins. Cam rolled up several of the impromptu cots, collected discarded food wrappers, and pushed workbenches back into ninety-degree angles. Under Cam's ministrations, the space became significantly neater than the last time she had seen it, via David's distressed holochat inspection.

By 11:00, all the rest of the engineers began slowly filing in.

David and Kevin showed up last. Cam made sure to get the heat going, checked the contents of the pot, gave it a stir, then turned around to address the assembled team.

"Hi, everybody. As you are all no doubt aware, I basically made your lives a living hell for the last two weeks, and for that I am sincerely sorry." Cam's voice quavered. One of the engineers coughed. "David and team especially, I owe an extra apology," she began. "I had no clue just how much prep work, testing, and calibrations were necessary for any new hardware changes, and there is no excuse for that ignorance."

David cleared his throat. He had returned to the generally somber aspect Cam was familiar with. He was also freshly shaved. "I take responsibility for that too. I should have said no on behalf of my team, and I should have more directly expressed our workload and boundaries."

There was a muttering rumble from the seated teams that sounded distinctly antagonistic. Someone stage-whispered, "They both suck."

Cam nearly wilted under the onslaught. She took a deep breath, put a hand on her head, and forced herself to make eye contact with the assembled teams. "I deserve that," she said. "But I never suck the same way twice!" Somebody snickered. "To ensure this doesn't happen again, I'm doing a couple things. First off, I'm going back to the client and drastically revising expectations." Someone from the hardware team started to say something, but Cam quickly rushed to get out, "This time around, I'll check in with you guys *before* actually committing to anything. Engineering will be firmly in the loop." They nodded, satisfied. Cam continued. "We're also going back to the client with a firm commit to *one* set of features. No more continual, evolving feature updates. No more scope creep."

The room was quiet. Somebody clapped sarcastically. Cam grinned self-consciously.

"We'll also set up a brief, daily morning meeting with the team leads and myself so we can stay in consistent communication. These stand-ups will make sure we let each other know about problems before they result in lost work or wasted time."

Lewis, the wizardly, bearded engineer in only the most ancient of shirts, raised a hand. Cam pointed at him. "What's in the pot?"

Cam looked chagrined. "Well, back home, I always expressed my caring through cooking. So, in light of the difficulties I put you all through, I wanted to do something to let you all know that you're appreciated. So I made a beef stew called carne guisada. It's no Michelin-star quail-egg soufflé, but it's a comfort food specialty in my family and I really hope you all enjoy it. Please, line up and grab some!"

The tension in the room broke as people rose and started chattering. As employees got in line for food, Cam pulled on an apron and grabbed a serving ladle to dole out stew to everybody. Sofia set out bowls of seasoned rice, sour cream, and some avocado, and uncovered a heap of tortillas that Cam had warmed that morning and placed in an insulated pizza-delivery bag.

Cam served the employees one by one, doing her best to project cheer as she explained how to eat it—alone or with rice and tortilla. The ugly atmosphere slowly dissipated as the engineers seemed increasingly mollified, especially those coming in for seconds. All of a sudden, there was even scattered laughter around the room. There was nothing some effort in the kitchen couldn't solve, Cam thought. When Kevin and David finally came up in line, they both got their bowls, then shuffled awkwardly in front of the table. Cam tried to give them an opening.

"Hey, look, I know the last couple weeks have gone badly, but I'm trying to learn, and I'd really love it if you guys felt empowered to give me feedback and share information."

Kevin kicked at nothing. "I gotta apologize too." David nodded along with him. "I was out of line with the way I responded to you. Also . . . I took a look at what we had done, and I think a lot of the work could still be salvaged if we switch cameras. We'd just need to do a lot of additional testing."

Cam nodded. "I'll go back to Karrygold and figure out what features are high priorities versus what's just a nice-to-have. We might be able to cut a lot."

David jumped in. "I respect the way you've taken responsibility." He looked abashed. "I get that you're new. We can help save you from yourself." Kevin nodded.

Cam laughed, eyes stinging. "Please stop me before I destroy your lives again." She took off her apron and came around the table, and they exchanged a group hug.

After the meeting, which had started with the air of a funeral but had ended in a state of moderate cheer, Cam was emotionally exhausted. She went back to her desk and flopped into her chair to take a moment to recharge. She still had to set up a new meeting with Karrygold.

"Good job," said Sofia with a satisfied nod. She and the Three Ts had also come back to their pod of desks.

"I couldn't have done this without you. Thank you, seriously," Cam said to Sofia. To the Three Ts, she said, "I'm sorry again for getting everybody into this mess."

Terry came to hover over Cam. "Making mistakes is normal. Owning them is a sign of a good leader."

"I'm basically George Washington, if that's the case," Travis declared.

Theresa jumped in. "It doesn't count if you don't actually try to learn from your mistakes."

They laughed, and Cam breathed a silent sigh of relief.

Chapter 16

"IT LOOKS LIKE A TORNADO hit this place," Avery said over the top of the dividing wall that separated Cam's division from the rest of the open-floor-plan office space. They weren't wrong. It had been a couple of weeks since her failures and eventual success with Karrygold, and Cam had started in immediately on new influencer partnerships. She wanted to prove to everyone that she could do better and was eager to implement her new project-management protocols. Avery had come upon Cam in the process of juggling customizations for two influencers while interviewing a third. Piles of sample hardware lay scattered across her deck. Two pushcarts with overflowing drawers of color-coded papers were wedged in on either side of her chair. A whiteboard with "KPI" written on it with animating blood pouring down leaned against the half wall next to a corkboard full of notes about users and Venn diagrams of overlapping desires. And every last inch of available space was layered in sticky notes, some places three or four deep.

"I know exactly where everything is," Cam replied with the perfect confidence of a teenager who was absolutely not going to clean their room.

"Sure you do, love." Avery grinned. Today, they were wearing a long red duster with a half cape and more buckles than a Japanese video game character, snake-print faux-leather pants, and shiny red platform loafers with tiny silver spikes. "Come!" They beckoned with a flourish of their hand. "I'm taking you to meet someone."

Cam checked the time on her phone. It was four p.m., which was a little earlier than she would usually leave, but it was Friday, meaning the office-wide happy hour was about to begin. Nothing ever got done except by the most determined of workaholics during that time, as the office grew more raucous with each new beer and wine poured.

"Okay." By now Cam realized it was just easier to agree with whatever Avery suggested. She got up and waved to the Three Ts before stuffing her laptop into her tattered backpack and following Avery.

"Where are we going?" Cam asked as she and Avery got into the back seat of a Beekar.

Avery tapped the QR code on their phone to the scanner on the armrest between them, and they whizzed off into the city. "We'll be there soon," Avery responded airily. "But tell me, how's work?"

Cam was honestly a little surprised by such mundane small talk from Avery. "Good," Cam replied.

Avery looked at her evenly, clearly wanting more information.

"Well," Cam started. "It's not what I expected. If I'm telling the truth, interviewing uber-rich socialites is something I never saw myself doing. No offense," she added.

Avery grinned a little wryly. "None taken. I know what I am. Go on."

"But I am learning a lot. I just hope I can use these networking skills to do something a little more meaningful."

"The only meaningful thing *is* people," Avery replied. And then, "We're here."

The two of them stepped out onto a narrow cobblestone street and stood before a brick building with a single unmarked metal door. Avery went up and pressed the doorbell. The electric buzz of the door unlocking sounded.

Inside was a bright and airy space two stories tall with light filtering through windows on the second floor and diffused skylights in the ceiling. Several comfy-looking white chaise lounges ringed a slightly raised platform with a white curtain. Racks of clothing lined the walls.

"Avery, you are finally here," trilled a deep masculine voice with a thick French accent from the balcony above them.

"Georges." Avery ran up the steps to greet their friend and air-kiss. "Always good to see you." Avery spun to gesture to Cam. "Georges, this is Cam, the friend I was telling you about. Cam, this is Georges. He is a fashion designer with an impeccable eye for individuality and character. He understands apparel like no other, and I trust him with my very life."

Georges laughed as they both began to descend the stairs, "I love you too, Avery." He wore a balloon-sleeve blouse with a Peter Pan collar; a long, pleated black skirt; and glittery gold heels. He leaned down from his considerable height to air-kiss Cam's cheeks, a gesture she stumbled to mimic. "Cam, it is good to meet another friend of Avery's. They tell me you are in need of some fashion direction?"

Cam's face heated. As she beheld her own dirty sneakers, free volunteer T-shirt from a fundraising event in her neighborhood, and jeans that had lived five lifetimes before she got them at Goodwill, she began to squirm uncomfortably. She squeezed the straps of her backpack tightly. "Well, we hadn't really talked about it." Cam glared daggers at Avery.

Avery smiled back with a maddening, indulgent beneficence. "You can thank me later," they said. "Besides, we're having a page-mentor dinner tonight and Amari and Keloa are going to be there. You'll want some armor."

Cam blanched thinking about being stuck at a dinner with those two's subtle jibes all night.

"Do not worry." Georges led Cam to the platform in the middle of the room and pulled back the curtains to reveal a set of full-length mirrors. "We are all always becoming, evolving. As the bird grows, she must molt. Now tell me, where do you get most of your clothing?"

Georges had such a soothing, nonjudgmental aura, Cam began to feel a little less embarrassed. "Well," she admitted, "mostly thrift stores." She looked at the racks of clothing and felt positive that a single shirt cost at least eight times what she had spent on her entire wardrobe.

"Ah, vintage, I love it. It is more sustainable, and you can get some truly unique looks. I am a fan of upcycling myself. The trick, though, is pairing the pieces sensibly." He turned and pulled a few things off the racks before hanging them up beside Cam. "Keep your shirt and try the rest of this on." Cam looked at the pieces as Georges closed the curtain behind her.

A short time later, Cam pulled the curtain open and showed her new look to a reclining Avery, who whistled appreciatively, and an expectant Georges, who practically cooed.

She was wearing her same volunteer shirt but now paired with jeans that fit her well, cute white booties, and a purse that looked like a pear. The shirt somehow looked elevated and intentional. Cam had to admit, she looked really cute.

She looked longingly at the pear purse. There was no way she could afford this outfit; she would search for similar items next time she went to a thrift store, but maybe she could spring for the purse. She had just received her first stipend payment, and it was more money than her account had ever held at one time before. "How much is the pear?"

Georges waved her off. "This whole session is on the house. You can take everything you want today. Avery has already been doing so much work to promote my boutique. I'm currently in the process of training three new designers." He looked at her with a twinkle in his eye. "I also know that you'll be attending many events. If anyone asks, tell them you're my client. Now put on the pants you arrived in and let's try something else."

The next hour flew by as Cam tried on outfit after outfit and Georges gave her some quick tips and guidelines to consider next time she shopped. It turned out over half the clothes Georges handed her were actually originally thrifted and just altered or repaired.

"We should look more into fixing what we have than always chasing what is new and shiny," Georges said sagely as Cam marveled at a denim jacket that was made out of a patchwork of old jeans.

Cam could have stayed for even longer talking to Georges, but Avery had already turned to leave. "Sorry, Georges," they called over their shoulder. "But we have another appointment to keep. Exchange numbers, Cam, and get in the car."

"It was a true pleasure meeting you, Cam. I will send the rest of what we picked out to your address." A Beekar pulled up, and Georges and Cam exchanged waves as she was hustled into it by a polite but firm Avery.

Cam sat in silence for a moment absorbing everything that had happened. In her mind, frustration at being treated like Avery's doll and commanded about warred with legitimate gratitude for the incredible wardrobe revamp Avery had arranged for her. In the end, gratitude won, and Cam smoothed her face.

"Avery, what are you doing at Beekor?"

Avery grinned their mischievous grin. "What do you mean?"

"You know everyone, you have tons of contacts, you understand this industry intimately—why are you here? What do you possibly have to gain from all this?"

Avery looked at Cam appraisingly, seeming to measure her up before coming to a decision.

"Do you remember how I said connections were important?" Avery queried, uncharacteristically stoic.

Cam cocked her head sideways, unsure where this was going.

"Well, I meant it," Avery pressed. "Talent, skill, work ethic, those are all important. But they mean nothing if you don't have connections to people who can give you resources. Resources like money, customers, opportunities, whatever. You can be the world's biggest genius, but if you don't have connections, you're just wasting away in your basement.

"So," they said in a more chipper tone, "where is the best place to make connections?"

"Beekor?" Cam guessed.

"Well, not Beekor precisely. But Beekor is a fantastic place because it's a hub. Not only does Beekor employ incredible people, but it also works with tons of incredible people from lots of different industries. It's a magnet for people with potential." At this, Avery looked at Cam pointedly.

"You mean the pages," Cam said, understanding Avery's meaning.

Avery nodded. "Not every connection is viable today, some take years to bear fruit. But it's important to plant the seeds today." They tapped Cam's nose playfully.

Cam suddenly realized that Avery was referring to that first drunken conversation over burritos when the pages had just met one another at the start of the program. Avery had been deadly serious about cultivating a network from the very start. And they were methodical about how they went about it.

Cam rubbed at her nose and asked, "Where did you learn about all this anyway?" She herself had never considered the importance of networking. But, she thought, that was probably because she already knew almost everyone in her small community.

"I had to. When you move as much as I have, you discover the fastest way to get situated in a new place is to make connections and to use the ones you already have. And the second best way"—at this Avery gestured at their own attire—"is to get some good armor."

Cam eyed Avery's highly impractical red duster dubiously.

Avery laughed at Cam's look. "My whole life I've always stuck out, wherever I went," they said by way of explanation. "So I figured, if I'm never going to fit the mold, I might as well embrace being as loud as possible.

This is me. I want to be seen. And it has the added benefit of more people seeking me out. Because you can't possibly miss me.

"That's what clothes are," Avery went on, "a way to project your personal energy outwards."

Cam began to see today's outing in a new light. These clothes were Avery building a link between the two of them in the form of a favor that Cam would try to repay in the future. But more than that, Avery was investing in Cam. They were giving Cam the weaponry to succeed and be able to form successful connections of her own.

"Thank you for all of this." Cam waved to her new outfit: dark cutoff jeans, a gray jersey blazer, high-tops, and a bag shaped like a pizza box that had been just big enough to fit her laptop—Georges and Avery had refused to let her leave with her ratty backpack. "You didn't have to help me out, and I appreciate it. Seriously. Let me know if you ever need anything from me," Cam said.

"I know you're good for it. I don't know what exactly you're doing in the office each day, but you look as if you've been run ragged. Anyone who is working this hard at a tech job with this many relaxing perks is going places."

It's probably because she was basically working two jobs, Cam mused to herself, thinking about the latest iteration of Specio she was working on at night.

"Here we are." Avery hopped out of the car before it had fully stopped.

Cam looked out the car window and saw a brightly lit salon with red barber chairs before Avery opened her door for her and gestured magnanimously.

"Let's get you a haircut." They grinned. "I just adore makeovers."

Chapter 17

BACK IN THE PAGE HOUSE, Cam looked herself over in the tall mirror on the inside of her bedroom door. The broad strokes of her appearance and personal style hadn't changed significantly, but the sum of the minor adjustments somehow made a big difference. Her hair was no longer a shaggy, shoulder-length cut, but an effortless-looking nape bob that framed her face and made her eyes look brighter. Her clothes were no longer a mismatched hodgepodge of worn-down items, but a curated thesis of patina fashion. The subtle tweaks did a lot to allow her to feel like her old self while also somehow elevating her. She felt like a whole new being.

Cam smiled, and a sophisticated young woman smiled out of the mirror back at her. Despite feeling like a charity case, she had to hand it to Avery and Georges—they knew their stuff.

Someone knocked on her bedroom door. Cam opened it to reveal Sofia, looking chic in houndstooth slacks, a cropped knit sweater, and a long ocher cardigan coupled with pearl earrings and her customary sleek ponytail. Sofia blinked at Cam. Then she leaned back and adjusted her glasses while taking in Cam's full appearance. Sofia made a little twirl motion with her finger, and Cam dutifully spun in place.

Sofia straightened up, satisfied. "Magnificent."

Cam's cheeks warmed with pleasure. "It's all thanks to Avery," she said, attempting to deflect the compliment.

"Good raw material," Sofia responded, undeterred by Cam's modesty. "Ready?"

Cam took a steadying breath and nodded. Tonight was the first of the mentor dinners Beekor had arranged. Jennifer had sent a bubbly group email to the pages informing them of the dinner location and the time. There was also a note at the bottom in a much crisper tone that the dinners were mandatory. Cam had a suspicion that the last bit might have been directed at James. . . . It had the feel of the final word in a long argument.

Sofia, Cam, Avery, and a reluctant James took a car from the house to the restaurant. Once there, they were ushered by a host in a suit past a dining area full of eating patrons, through the chaos of the kitchen, and onto a private patio nestled in a small, secluded garden of pink roses. The long wood dining table was already mostly filled. Wyatt sat at the head drinking a glass of red wine. Marcus was seated just to Wyatt's left in a dusty-evergreen-colored suit that seemed to make his warm skin glow. It was the first time Cam had seen him since the pier. He had once again disappeared into a schedule that seemed to completely disconnect him from the rest of the pages. He was conversing pleasantly with a sleepy-eyed man with wavy golden hair who sat to Wyatt's right. The next two seats were occupied by two loud, jovial men in business suits who looked like they had already been drinking for hours. Beside them were Amari and Keloa, looking sharp in a rose-colored and pin-striped gray suit respectively. Avery instantly sat down next to Amari, and Sofia sat next to Avery. James quickly grabbed the chair across from Sofia at the end of the table, which left Cam with the remaining seat next to Keloa. Sitting down among all this opulence, Cam was suddenly more grateful than ever for Avery's makeover and Georges's professional styling. She didn't feel like she fit in exactly, but in her jersey blazer, she wasn't hyperaware of her appearance, either. She felt her shoulders relaxing ever so slightly.

In fact, if anyone stuck out, it was Avery. They were still in their outfit from earlier, which looked like it had been ripped right out of a visual kei band's closet. But they seemed utterly unfazed by how loud their clothes were. If anything, they seemed to revel in it. Cam thought back to their earlier conversation, and seeing Avery in action, she had to agree—there was a certain power in being the boldest in the room.

"This is surprising. The little PR project cleans up nice," Amari said, eyeing Cam up and down.

"My name is Cam," she said steadily, looking Amari dead in the eye. In the month since Cam had last seen Amari, her ego had been shredded more deeply than anything this beautiful woman could manage. But she had also persevered, grown, and flourished with hard-won experience. And surprisingly enough, these clothes did make her feel more assured. It was still her, but polished. She would not let this woman walk all over her again.

Amari looked vaguely surprised, as if at a frog that had suddenly tried to bite her.

"Oh, little PR project has got a backbone. All right, *Cam*"—Amari smiled like she was indulging a child—"who was responsible for your makeover? I know you didn't put this together yourself."

Dinner hadn't even started, and Cam was already fed up with Amari's antics. But, she also reasoned, she had promised to be good press for Georges. He had, after all, comped her one entire wardrobe.

"Avery introduced me to Georges Dubois," Cam admitted.

Now Amari really did look surprised, and even Keloa turned in his seat to look at Cam.

Amari recovered quickly and turned to Avery. "Avery, you snake, why didn't you introduce me?"

Avery just smirked. Cam secretly hoped that if Amari did ever meet the fashion designer, Georges would kick her to the curb.

As Amari bickered with Avery, two members of the waitstaff came out from the kitchen bearing a whole roasted boar and placed it in the center of the table. Cam watched as side dishes of roasted beets with goat cheese, miniature baked potatoes with mint, and macaroni and cheese with truffles were brought out to encircle the roast, in the manner of a royal feast.

The sommelier came out and poured Wyatt a small sample of a red wine from a bottle. He swirled the glass pensively before giving the liquid a small sip. He thought for a moment, then beamed magnanimously, and the sommelier poured him a full serving. Wyatt waited until everyone had a glass of wine, then got up and addressed the table like he was a king and they were his subjects.

"Everyone, I want to thank you for coming to this gathering. As you know, the Beekor Accelerator Program represents our future! It represents our continued commitment to independent thinking. There has never been a better home for innovators than Beekor, and of that, you are all exemplars." Wyatt made sustained eye contact with each of them in turn as he spoke. Cam had the bizarre feeling that Wyatt knew her down to her soul. "Let it never be said that Beekor, institutionally, is content to rest and rely on prior successes. Thanks to all you pages and former pages for allowing Beekor to supply the resources, *the fuel*, to propel you into the firmament, and, in turn, to hitch a ride on your respective stars.

"Finally, I want to thank Birmingham for this exquisite boar." Wyatt looked to the sleepy-eyed man to his right. "Really magnificent shot, old sport."

Birmingham nodded passively. "They can get out of hand on the family estate."

Wyatt laughed, like he too understood perfectly what it was like to have an estate in Northern California that would get overrun with wild boar frequently enough to necessitate that he and his rich friends go hunt them and then bring them to restaurants to be roasted. Cam stared at the boar.

"Cheers!" Wyatt lifted his glass, and the rest of the table followed suit. Cam took a hearty swig. The waitstaff then returned and pulled the roast pig off the table and to a sideboard where a chef began carving out delicate cuts of tender meat and placing them on serving plates that were then brought back to the table. In the meantime, even more platters of stuffed quail, deviled duck eggs, some kind of baked squash, and other dishes the likes of which Cam had never seen were laid in the recently vacated space. Apparently, the boar had only been there for the toast.

The two suited men in the middle of the table, who had been quiet during Wyatt's speech, reignited their loud conversation with each other and the other three at the head of the table. They created a blaring wall of sound that effectively cut the lower half of the table into their own conversational group.

Amari shrugged in a way that seemed to indicate she had fully expected this and didn't even attempt to engage in conversation with the man next to her. Instead, she turned to Avery.

"So have you given any thought to The_FlamingTomato's party?" she asked, scooping some couscous onto her plate.

"Ugh, please, no work discussions outside of office hours," Avery groaned, taking three slices of steaming roast boar.

"Work?" Cam questioned, and looked at all the plates before her, completely at a loss as to where she should start.

Avery sighed. "Yeah, Amari is my supervisor. Here, try the bacon-wrapped figs." They handed Cam a plate, and she took it, mouth watering.

"Amari and I have been working at Beekor since our respective Accelerator Program stints ended," Keloa explained as he took a bacon-wrapped fig for himself. "So we're sort of poster children for life after. We get brought in to these dinners to encourage you to join the team."

"Or the cult," Amari quipped, and took a big bite of her food. "You know," she said, looking at Avery, then at the head of the table, where Marcus sat, and back to Avery, "I was sure you were going to be the star pupil of this year's group. Did your parents piss someone off?"

Avery waved Amari away. "You know I don't want the responsibility. I just want the parties. Besides, I hardly look the part."

"Well, you never know. After all, Wyatt worked with Lee," Amari said with a shrug.

Cam hadn't really been able to keep up with the exchange between the two, but at the mention of Lee Baker, she recognized a topic she was comfortable with. She jumped into the conversation like it was a game of double Dutch. "Lee is amazing. I've been learning so much about her history. Can you believe she actually got holographic video calls up and running in a single day?"

"Yeah, she was really something in her heyday. But she burned out, like most stoners," Amari said flippantly to Cam, and turned back to Avery.

Cam felt herself trip on the conversational jump rope and fall flat. *Was* Lee burned out? It was true Lee was supposedly on sabbatical. And she hadn't been exactly keen to talk about tech when Cam had seen her.

While Cam worried about Lee, the conversation moved on to the other former Accelerator Program pages who were now full-time employees at Beekor. It sounded like all of them stayed at Beekor, save for the odd exception. "Tamira got snatched up by OneTap at commencement. At *commencement*. Right under Wyatt's nose, they offered her a CTO position, and she took it on the spot," Amari whispered scandalously. "You can ask Andrew about it; he was part of her year. You'll probably meet him at one of these mentor dinners. He's usually in the rotation."

The rest of the evening was filled with gossip from Amari and the occasional explanation from Keloa. Avery seemed to be used to this and encouraged Amari as necessary. Cam tried to participate a few more times, but each of her attempts were soundly rebuffed. Sofia listened intently but stayed silent for the most part. James spent the entire evening with his eyes glued to his plate, fidgeting with a pair of black wraparound earbuds shaped like stars.

A couple times, Cam looked down the few feet of the table to Marcus. She thought she felt his gaze on her a few times, but whenever she turned to him, he was deep in conversation. He seemed as if he was on an entirely different planet, circling the star that was Wyatt Ecker. Cam saw him smile, but she never saw his dimple.

Chapter 18

THE NEXT AFTERNOON, CAM, THE Three Ts, David and Kevin from hardware and software, and the rest of the engineering teams gathered together atop a tower overlooking the campus. The vast observation deck, despite being several stories up, was fully landscaped with hills, trees, and a gigantic wooden lawn chair that at least six people could sit in, side by side. When Terry had told Cam they would have a space to host the launch party for the Karrygold limited-edition custom phones, she had no clue that they had meant this. And there were caterers! The Three Ts let Cam know that the higher-ups had allocated some budget to reward the teams for a successful release. That looked like a whole team of caterers, circulating with drinks and food, staff lighting up and manning the Ferris wheel for people to ride, and an enormous holographic projector.

At first, Cam had been absolutely agog. She had arrived at the roof and just stared, slack-jawed, at the garden space, gazebos and garden trellises done up with lights, food stations, and drinks prepped and ready.

"Perks of success," Travis had said with relish, striding out as if this wasn't abnormal in any way. Theresa had followed.

Terry had hung back next to Cam and said, "Welcome to big-tech-company life. They really do reward victory."

Cam grew increasingly used to the opulence as she explored the space, got a drink—a highly custom, elevated margarita with top-shelf tequila and a flower floating in it—and mingled with the assembled team members. As the drinks flowed, people were in good spirits. Eventually, people began to assemble near the projector for the big moment.

Getting the Karrygold limited-edition Beekor phone live had not been without some further mishaps, but everything had gotten far easier to navigate once Cam had reoriented everybody toward continual communication and effectively managed the way she worked with Karrygold.

In the conversion from a fully overhauled phone to just the custom live-avatar software and a slightly modified shell with Karrygold engraving, Cam had been subjected to a flood of bear tears and the words "bear-trayal" and "un-bear-able." But after much groveling and open admission of mistakes on Cam's part, as well as an impassioned breakdown for how she was going to prevent these problems from ever happening in the future while still promising to deliver on some of what Karrygold really wanted, the streamer relented. By their last meeting, Karrygold had even seemed happy!

Most important of all, Cam had successfully built and shipped her first product as a member of a big company! It felt like a huge milestone. "To shipping!" Cam called out. The gathered teams on the lawn erupted in cheers, and people threw back their drinks. Cam couldn't wait to start applying all her new learnings to her work turning Specio into an easy-to-use upgrade kit at home.

Cam joined the loose cluster of Travis, Theresa, and Kevin, who were exchanging anecdotes about prior catastrophic failures they had experienced. Kevin seemed buzzed and was speaking effusively. "Back when I was a quality-assurance test engineer at a game company, we had a new game coming out and were instructed by the higher-ups to do a company-wide test. We're talking ten thousand employees. I thought I was being clever, so I made my name a line of text that included some SQL code in it as an injection exploit and submitted it." Kevin looked pensive. "We all launched the game, and it seemed to work fine. Everybody was playfully trash-talking. Then I sent a message in chat." Kevin started snorting with barely restrained laughter.

"And?" Theresa asked, clearly not understanding what he was talking about. Meanwhile, Cam and Travis were choking on laughter.

"And the next thing I knew, all the trash talking and jokes died down. The whole building became quiet. Then, one after another, people all over the room around me started complaining that nothing was working. I tried to cover my head and hide. The whole damn game dropped." Kevin started cracking up. "All because I put in a messed-up name!"

Theresa started laughing uproariously. "Oof," Travis said.

"So let me get this straight," Cam began. "They weren't properly sanitizing their inputs in their code, so somebody with nothing but a weirdly formatted name could bring the whole game down?" Travis nodded. "And you spotted it in a company playtest, effectively allowing them to catch that catastrophic bug and fix it before the game went live for real users, saving them from having it happen at a larger scale, with actual paying customers." Kevin nodded more profusely. "Sounds like you were doing your job—testing!" Cam said.

Kevin nodded most profusely. "That's what I said! But the team couldn't fix it. The database was just totally nuked. I started packing my desk up immediately."

After the laughter died down, Travis said into the quiet, "I think I got you beat."

"Oh?" Kevin asked.

"I once tripped over a wire that caused an entire social network to go down for six hours."

"What did you do?!" Cam asked, horrified on his behalf.

"I plugged it back in and ran away!" The group became hysterical. "Somebody fixed it eventually."

The laughter died down, and Cam asked, "What happened after that?"

"Well," Travis began, "we lost nearly five percent of our users in a single day. The manager of the infrastructure team was fired for allowing critical pieces of our tech stack to be so vulnerable." Travis looked thoughtful. "Honestly, I don't think it was anyone's fault. We were growing so fast and had so little bandwidth to focus on anything but meeting new feature needs to support the influx of users." He brightened. "On the plus side, we immediately began the process of upgrading and securing any of our legacy systems that still had a single point of failure, so that forced us to mature as an engineering organization and a company. We also began to put into place systems and protocols to manage outages quickly and effectively."

Cam couldn't believe the scale of screwups that pretty much everybody had been party to at some point or another. It was actually really comforting to know she wasn't alone, and that she had responded, if anything, with more integrity than most.

Terry got a ping on their phone. They called out to the gathered crowd, "Quiet, everyone! It's starting."

The space took on an expectant hush. Terry fiddled with some controls and then, finally, got a holographic video stream displaying on the giant projector in the center of the lawn. Karrygold was live!

Karrygold's golden bear avatar appeared in the middle of a real kitchen, wearing a custom apron and a chef's hat. "Hey, Honeys, welcome to my very fur-st cooking stream!" Karrygold panned the camera around so the audience could take in her entire bear body for the very first time, from multiple angles. The bear's face contorted into an extreme cartoon version of a handsome smirk. "You're probably noticing that I'm not just playing a video game, but I'm actually streaming myself in the real world, *live*"—she raised an arm in the air and virtual fireworks erupted into the air in her kitchen—"for the fur-st time anybody, on the face of the planet, has ever done, *ever*." The bear threw up a bizarre three-fingered-paw version of devil horns, and a guitar sting played. Karrygold's chat was going wild. They'd never seen a virtual avatar appear in a real-world stream like this before.

"And it's all thanks to the team at Beekor, who set me up with this *insane* custom phone that lets me go live as my beautiful bear self. When. Ever. I. Want." The bear did an arm swipe motion, and a graphic showing the Karrygold limited-edition phone slid on-screen. It was shiny, like all Beekor phones, but it had the Karrygold bear avatar etched into the metal. Karrygold swiped again and dismissed the phone image. "This ain't something you could buy at the *maul*." Karrygold winked. "Thanks, Cam!"

All the employees in the garden erupted into cheers. "Thanks, Cam," they called back as one, and the drinks flowed.

The party grew increasingly raucous as the team reveled in the product they shipped. They laughed and joined in with the stream chat as Karrygold did, in fact, attempt to make an omelet and fail.

Chapter 19

AS THE WEEKS PASSED, CAM slowly began to get into the rhythm of the influencer team, communicating with other groups throughout the company, working with influencers, and managing the complex moving parts involved in building and releasing products. One day, unexpectedly, while helping the Three Ts solve a supply chain mix-up, she realized that they had come to depend and rely on her. It dawned on her then that she was, in fact, quite good at her job. The feeling was like a warm light in her gut. And it came with increasingly extravagant perks, from the company card to the "business development" events (renting out arcades to throw parties with streamers).

But it won her no progress at the intrigue heavy mentor dinners with Wyatt. Cam found herself stuck on the wrong end of the table, an impossible, exorbitantly expensive squid-ink-gnocchi-banquet's distance from Wyatt's light, in which Marcus routinely bathed. In contrast, meetings with Lee Baker persisted in defying Cam's expectations. Lee still dropped nuggets of wisdom during trips to castles, redwood forests, and cult buildings with running creeks inside, usually while high. Maybe Amari was right that Lee was burned out, Cam thought. But she was sharp as ever when Cam posed technical problems. And crass as ever when Wyatt came up.

At least Cam's mom had finally succeeded in installing her Specio prototype, though. Long nights simplifying and improving it finally paid off. Rosa happily reported how often the rest of her study group borrowed her phone to look at engines or circulatory systems. Buoyed by finally having a real customer using something she'd dragged into existence from scratch, Cam set her ambitions on a KPI of her own—seven users for Specio. The rest of her mom's study group.

Cam's relationship with the other pages deepened. Cam, Sofia, and Avery were inseparable, but even James joined them with increasing regularity. They spent plenty of weekends joining Avery at parties in bars, penthouses, and even a Napa wine tour once. There seemed to be no limit to Avery's connections. When Cam asked if Beekor was sending them to some of these parties, Avery had seemed affronted. "You think a bunch of suits would send us here?!" They gestured at the drag king lip-synching battle their friend was hosting while Sofia tossed bills to the performers. Later, as she climbed into bed, Cam realized Avery hadn't quite said no.

On quiet nights, Sofia shared her impressive back catalog of dance movie sequels. Cam was floored when, during *Boogie Breakup 3*, Sofia got up and performed a dance routine perfectly coordinated with the movie. Avery applauded and screamed for an encore.

Occasionally, Cam spent solo time with James down in the garage. The space had been converted to a hardware workshop with a smorgasbord of expensive machinery and a vast array of gleaming tools interspersed with hardwood-topped workbenches. While Cam took advantage of the most beautiful 3D printer she had ever seen (leagues bigger and faster than the one she had used at school) to build Specio prototypes, James used every hour he wasn't at work or being hauled along to Avery's latest scheme to create new personal projects.

"Is it another speaker?" Cam asked one evening, looking over at the table James had claimed as his permanent station. Among the tools and screws neatly laid out, she observed what, upon first glance, looked like a decorative white 3D-printed human skull the size of a cantaloupe, made of all flat geometric surfaces.

"Yes, and I just got the amplifier working. Listen." James adjusted a few more knobs, cleverly hidden in the eye sockets, until loud, guitar-heavy music came pouring out of the skull's mouth.

"What kind of music is this?" Cam asked, astonished by the intensity of it.

"Technical death metal," replied James, nodding his head to the beat. His hands twitched on his thigh in a way that Cam realized belatedly was not erratic at all but was keeping time with the high-speed complexity of the song.

The track ended, and James put his completed speaker up on the shelf above his desk in between a cupcake-shaped and a motorcycle-shaped speaker. Cam didn't know if she agreed with his taste in music, but his craftsmanship was second to none.

Marcus remained the most elusive. Cam's interactions with him were limited to passing each other at dinner or the glimpse of him across campus, walking with Wyatt. He even missed the last Tacky Tourist Time, when Avery took them down south to a local festival in the freebie car and they all shared garlic ice cream.

Seemingly out of nowhere, Jennifer reached out to let the pages know that they were almost at the halfway point of the program, and that BIDC, the Beekor International Developer Conference, Beekor's enormous yearly conference where major new products were announced, was coming up. Cam screamed into the phone with excitement as she told her mom about getting full access to the conference, but she also found herself getting increasingly sad about the fact that the program was almost half done, and that she would have to think about what she would do after leaving the house and the rest of the pages.

—

Friday afternoon at the office, Cam was struggling to get anything done. For all intents and purposes, the Three Ts were already on the weekend, and at this point, even Cam could barely muster the energy to pretend she cared about the status of the task "Clear logo usage in influencer outreach packets with legal team." Mercifully, Cam's new phone took that moment to start buzzing ferociously with a series of texts from Avery to the group chat that included Sofia and James. Better not to look divine providence in the eye, Cam thought, and opened the messages.

> *Avery:* Yo, you have plans?
> *Avery:* Tonight?
> *Avery:* Because I have plans for you
> *Avery:* Everyone
> *Avery:* You're going to love it
> *Avery:* Wear something cute~!
> *Sofia:* I am always cute.
>
>   I'm also always cute : **Cam**
> *Avery:* lol
> *Sofia:* lol
> *James:* lol
> *James:* what time?
>   Why is what I said funny? : **Cam**
> *Avery:* let's leave the house at 8pm
> *Sofia:* ok
> *James:* k
>
>   >:C : **Cam**

Back in the page house, Cam decided to go all out. She laid out her entire wardrobe: her original clothing, the pieces from Georges, and even a few new things she had picked up on a vintage shopping trip on Haight Street with Avery and Sofia. An hour later, after trying on several dozens of different combinations, Cam finally landed on one she thought would meet everyone's exacting standards.

She wore a copper-colored scoop-neck shirt with a pattern of small yellow flowers tucked into a burnt-umber denim miniskirt with silver buttons up the front. Underneath, she wore semi-sheer black tights and black kitten-heel booties. She paired this with a small gold chain necklace, earrings she had bought from a street vendor in Hayes Valley that looked like tiny slices of toast, and a purse that was shaped like a toaster. She topped the look with the lightest touch of makeup. She had been practicing, but she didn't feel up to the level of Avery's flaming decal-like eyeshadow or Sofia's brilliant cat eye.

Lastly, Cam pulled out her oversized green plaid jacket, the same one she had worn on the day she arrived at Beekor. She had felt so inadequate in it compared to the rest of the pages back then. It had hung in the back of her closet, a drab reminder of her shortcomings. But now that same jacket, with the rest of her outfit, looked like a statement piece that had always belonged.

After one final look in the mirror and an apology to the future Cam who would have to tidy her room, she headed downstairs. Bubbling with giddy elation, a sensation she had never felt about her appearance before, Cam practically skipped down the stairs to the living room to meet Avery, Sofia, and James. With a rush of exuberance, she jumped down the last three steps, practically floating with happiness.

"All right, Avery, I'm ready to— Oof!" Cam collided with a large, warm body smelling of amber and cinnamon that almost fell over from her momentum before grabbing her shoulders and setting them both upright.

A rumbling chuckle emitted from the firm chest she found herself pressed against and vibrated through her bones down to her toes. "You all right?"

Cam looked up from the hard biceps she had caught herself on and into the laughing face of Marcus. This close, she could see his long eyelashes, the light stubble on his face, and the exact depth of his dimple.

After more than a month of not seeing him closer than the other end of a mentor's-dinner table, Cam had worked to convince herself that the elusive snob wasn't actually that handsome after all. His nose was a little crooked, and his eyebrows were too thick. But once again, this close to him, leaning into the heat of his hard body and gazing up into his dark, mirth-filled eyes, she realized she had been wrong all that time. He wasn't handsome; he was gorgeous.

Cam suddenly perceived that she had been staring at Marcus for too long. Blushing, she practically leapt back from him and almost fell again, before he caught her forearms and steadied her.

"Whoa, careful," Marcus cautioned.

Cam felt her face heating to an unprecedented degree. "Yes— I— Thank you— I mean sorry—" A tiny sliver of her rational brain begged her to stop talking.

"No worries." Marcus smiled and lightly squeezed her forearms once before releasing her. Her skin tingled where he had touched her.

"You two good?" Avery asked slyly, stalking over from the living room in checkerboard-patterned balloon shorts, highlighter-yellow-tinted aviators perched on their head, a loose white shirt, a long denim jacket with faux-fur trim and covered in dozens of embroidered patches of nonexistent brands, and red high-tops. Sofia followed behind them like a graceful egret in gray slacks and a backless white merino-wool sweater.

"Yes, fine, I'm ready to go now!" Cam said frantically, squirming a little under Avery's all-too-knowing gaze.

"Where are you going?" Marcus asked Avery.

"What, don't you have a corporate party in the Salesforce Tower to go to?" Avery quipped. Cam thought they sounded almost a little jealous.

Marcus waved them off. "I'm a free agent tonight."

"How unusual," they remarked dryly. "Well, come on, there is always room for one more. But you have to change into something less business drone. I can't be seen with you in a suit. You ready, James?" Avery looked up at James, who was just coming down the stairs, dressed in one of his vintage sweaters and large headphones, managing, as always, to look comfortably classic.

James just nodded. Avery, Cam, and Sofia gasped as one. It was the least amount of convincing James had ever required. He smirked faintly.

"You'll actually tell us where we're going this time?" Marcus inquired.

Avery grinned like a shark. "Tonight, we're going to a gallery opening!"

Chapter 20

THE GALLERY WAS NOTHING LIKE what Cam had expected.

The ride over had been quick. They got an enormous Beekar that could fit all the pages, with Cam, Avery, and Sofia in the middle seat and Marcus and James in the back. Marcus had indeed changed out of his typical suit-and-shirt combo, opting for a knit turtleneck sweater and thigh-length camel coat, a hint of lavender socks at his ankles. Avery kept up a patter of loud, boisterous conversation, with Marcus chuckling at Avery's antics, Sofia occasionally providing a quip that further encouraged Avery, and James asking puzzled questions with an excessive literalness, which forced Avery into ever more grandiose prevarications. They arrived just as Avery ended their story with "And then I said, I can't take over your praying mantis farm, I'm allergic!" All five laughed and approached a warehouse with a narrow door, a tightly barred metal gate in front of it. They pressed an intercom button and were admitted straightaway. They walked down a claustrophobic hallway before ascending a cramped flight of stairs.

The second floor was a fairy forest. At least that's what Cam thought at first, blinking at the dappled light that filtered through foliage. Taking a second look, she realized the structural pillars of the two-story room had been covered in faux bark. Branches full of artificial leaves hung suspended from the ceiling. The light came from hundreds of tiny strings of LEDs and dark metal lanterns in the shapes of stars. Between the "trees" were little huts, each appearing to be made out of whatever had been at hand—sheets of wood, scraps of corrugated metal, pots filled with actual plants, and even a bike or two—and then painted over in clashing colors of pomegranate, ocher, sea foam, and all hues in between. Some of the huts were on stilts and resembled tree houses, some were shaped like boats complete with portholes, while still others resembled tiny castles. As Cam watched, people flitted in and out of each of the huts, laughing, chatting, and greeting each other.

"Avery! You're here!" A tiny woman with bright blue hair, in black leather pants and a halter top, launched herself at Avery, who caught her up and used the momentum to spin them around in a full circle.

"Of course." Avery set her down. "I just had to show off your work to my friends. Everyone, this is Chi. Chi, this is everyone." Avery gestured back and forth expansively. "Chi is a member of the art-slash-hacker collective that owns this space, DAOTown."

"Marcus, Sofia, James, and Cam," Chi said, pointing at each of them in turn. "The Beekor pages. I've heard of you all, of course. The pics for the article don't do any of you justice." Chi batted her eyelashes at all of them.

Marcus and Sofia seemed unaffected by the recognition, but Cam was still a bit uncomfortable with the publicity. She felt herself trying to hide behind the two taller pages. James was oblivious, distracted by all the creations around them. His toe tapped a drumbeat on the cement floor.

"Flirt later, Chi. Show me your space now!" Avery said pushily as they playfully nudged Chi from behind.

"All right, all right, we'll put a pin in it," Chi pouted, blue hair swishing. "This way—I'm by the windows."

As the group moved through the space, Cam snuck a look into the various huts. Each space contained a small working studio, filled with the tools of each owner's craft, tidied up to make room for them to display whatever current objets d'art they happened to be engaged in creating. Some of the tiny rooms held jars of pigment and showcased paintings. Some showed TV screens playing short movies. James and Cam oohed and aahed together at some of the wildly incomprehensible conglomerations of sculpture, servo motors, and sensors. A lot of the work looked as if it had been hastily brought to a state of completeness for the night's event. James pointed out several loose wires and freshly 3D-printed parts on full display. Chi's collective all built things purely for the art and novelty of it. Cam found herself loving every second of it. James looked like a kid who had just been let loose in a candy shop. He stuck close by Cam, and the two of them fell behind as they excitedly took turns guessing at the function, construction, and unique failure states of all of the bizarre DAOTown artifacts.

Cam was just squealing over a one-foot-tall scale-model animatronic horse-drawn carriage being pulled by an animatronic man in fetish gear, his little legs mechanically pumping, when a familiar figure caught her eye. Lounging by one hut, Daphne from IT cut an even more intense profile than she had at work. She had turned up the dial from casual metal to formal goth. Her black eyeliner was ramped up to eleven, spilling across her eyes in a dark band, and the spiked collar was as spiky as ever. However, she had lost the band T-shirt and replaced it with a fitted black blazer, partially open at the front, to reveal a sliver of bare torso. She had an intense-looking sternum tattoo. Cam was reminded of Avery's talk about how your appearance could be your armor, and she thought Daphne looked ready to battle heaven itself. Daphne caught Cam staring, snickered, and sauntered over.

"Hey, newborn," Daphne greeted her. She did a little spin in place. "You like?"

"You look awesome!"

"Heaven in Flames," a voice interjected.

Daphne's eyes went wide. Cam turned to see James behind her, fiddling with the dials on his headphones. "The portrait of Wyrmwood the Fallen, off Heaven in Flames's first album."

Daphne laughed aloud. "Off the *original self-release print* of their first album!" she exclaimed. "There are only five hundred of those in the world! Once they got a label and a more professional album release, the cover art completely changed."

Cam looked confused.

"He's talking about my tattoo," Daphne explained. She parted her blazer a bit to reveal more of the design. It looked like some sort of wicked, heavily armored demon with spreading wings and a corrupted halo. "Who is this man with impeccable taste?"

"Oh, sorry, I'm being rude. Daphne, meet James!" Cam said. "Daphne works at Beekor too, in IT. She can get you anything. James is one of the pages! That means he's my roommate, and *I* get to steal his insane hardware knowledge whenever I want." Cam smiled with satisfaction. "Apparently, he's skilled with metal of *all* types!"

Daphne laughed, and James gave a small smile of pleasure and a bit of chagrin under their scrutiny. "Um, do you want to get a drink and look at the art?" he asked and almost looked surprised at his own daring.

"Yes to the art. But I'm straight edge, so soda water for me only," Daphne said.

"That's what I prefer too," James admitted, sounding a little more at ease, and stepping out from behind Cam.

Daphne grinned and presented an elbow to him. James looked at it for a beat, uncertain of how to proceed, before eventually sliding his arm through hers to get escorted away. "Later, nerd. Don't wait up for us," Daphne called out. She waved over her shoulder with her free hand at Cam.

Cam stood blinking, then spun to catch up with the rest of the pages and Chi. Sofia looked around her questioningly, clearly looking for James. Cam just shrugged and waggled her eyebrows, to which Sofia gave a small, knowing smile.

Eventually, they stopped near a hut that vaguely resembled a mausoleum. Inside, the space looked no larger than maybe ten feet square. It didn't look like there was anything in there beside a raised platform that occupied the majority of the floor space. Chi reached under a small desk in the corner and pulled out a cold beer for each of them. Then the space went completely dark, and Chi disappeared.

Suddenly, a small light appeared, highlighting a face in the dark. It was Chi. The rest of Chi's body became visible as she crept cautiously through the dark. Her clothes had changed to an explorer's drab olive outfit. Cam thought something about the outfit shimmered for a moment, but she dismissed it.

Chi crept around the darkened stage until a pillar suddenly appeared in front of her. She examined its arcane symbols. Two red embers in the dark became visible off and behind Chi, and a deathly moan played. Chi froze with overstated drama, then spun. The two embers resolved to a gruesomely decayed zombie, who menacingly tottered Chi's way.

Chi screamed and took a terrified step back, only to have another zombie suddenly appear and swipe at her with gnarled claws. Her outfit tore open in the back, olive tatters hanging, and Chi stumbled forward. Then she made a look of resolve, righted herself, and took on a martial-arts stance.

What followed was two minutes of fight choreography involving Chi punching, spin-kicking, and sometimes backflipping her way through a horde of zombies, who all succumbed to her might. Zombie bones snapped, skulls gave way with sickening crunches, and gore sprayed Chi's face as she systematically destroyed the horde. The fury of the battle seemed to crescendo, until Chi and all the remaining horde stood still and a chorus chant kicked in. Then Chi reached down to her waist, activated a bright green laser sword, and commenced slicing the remaining zombies, whose decayed body parts spun through the air before disappearing into the dark at the stage perimeter.

The fight was over. Chi stood center stage, breathing heavily as she looked straight out at her audience. Her laser sword retracted with an otherworldly hiss, and the lights came on simultaneously. Chi stood there, still attempting to regain her breath, but her clothes were completely normal again. The only thing that remained from the show was the red paint splashed on her face.

Nobody spoke for a solid ten seconds after the show finished. Then they broke out in wild applause. Chi smirked.

"How the absolute hell did you do that?!" Cam cried. Her eyes shone with admiration for Chi's combination of technical mastery and performance art.

Chi came down from the stage. "It's all holographic projection and body tracking! I'm working on a zombie game, and I realized I could take the assets and AI and play a choreographed sequence of the game in an enclosed space using my body as input!"

Cam's jaw dropped. She began doing rapid calculations to figure out what it would take to track a body that precisely while combining it with a piece of performance art.

"The blood, though?" Sofia inquired. She pointed at the zombie gore on Chi's face.

Chi winked. "Let's just say not all the zombies were projections."

Sofia arched an eyebrow.

Chi looked as if she were trying to hold it in, but she lost all restraint and burst rapidly into a more detailed explanation of how she had also incorporated drones that were tracked into the same game space and driven by the AI in order to create physical interactions like blood spraying. She and Sofia were instantly neck-deep in technical jargon, in their own private world.

As they chatted, Cam experienced déjà vu. The way Chi incorporated hardware and software creatively, integrating elements across so many different disciplines, she was almost like a mirror version of Cam, albeit one with more money and less of a personal mission. With the support to flourish and do what she wanted, Cam thought, briefly bitter. Cam looked around the space that DAOTown owned. No, Chi wasn't just a mirror version of Cam; she was a version who had appeared to have found a home and a people. And Cam suddenly realized that she had found her people as well. The weird old wizards on the hardware engineering team that she could vibe with about the nerdiest conceivable things, the brilliant pages, even the new people Cam had just met, like Chi and her DAO, creative makers with which Cam found herself rubbing shoulders—they were Cam's people. She breathed deep and took a long look around her, jealousy giving way to deep gratitude. In a way, the realization that Cam had found a home and people was more magical than her surroundings.

Avery looked over to Cam and Marcus. "How about you two check out the rest of the gallery? The warehouse is communal, but each studio space is managed by a different artist. You should see what's here. I'll stay with Sofia; looks like we'll be here a while."

Cam glanced up at Marcus, who smiled and gestured with a nod for her to join him. She suddenly realized that they would be alone for the first time since the photo booth at the pier. A little breathless and thrumming with anticipation, she reached out and wrapped an arm around his. As Marcus spun them, Cam looked back and saw Avery wink at her. She thought she might've even seen Sofia wink too.

Chapter 21

LINKED AMICABLY TOGETHER, CAM AND Marcus wandered without any particular goal. They let themselves be drawn to whatever caught their attention. The different huts around the enormous space all seemed to reflect a completely different mastery of some wizardry, technical or otherwise. The artists and makers that comprised DAOTown had a very broad set of skills, and Cam thrilled with excitement as she got to dig into all the weird, clever, hacky solutions they had come up with in the process of making their respective art. Marcus looked on in amused fascination as she gleefully pumped people for information on how they had built things, and everyone seemed only too pleased to answer all her questions.

One hut featured a vast stone idol, moodily lit, that boomed ominous pronouncements at people before firing off streamers and squirting a tiki drink from his mouth. Another contained a robot cobbled together from random bits of discarded electronics. Cam and Marcus helped it learn to count to ten. Yet another hut had pieces of framed art on the wall that, when touched, would display different wave patterns and produce different sounds. Cam, Marcus, and several random attendees used the picture frames to make a song together.

They walked into a pink mushroom filled with plastic neon kaiju that had tiny screens for bellies. Each kaiju belly featured a different video game. There wasn't anyone attending the space, but there was a giant sign that read "Play Me."

Marcus's eyes sparkled. "Want a rematch?" he asked, gesturing to a pair of glittery purple game controllers.

"Don't cry when I beat you!" Cam agreed, grabbing the one closest to her.

They first played the game on the lime-green kaiju, which turned out to be a side-scrolling fighting game. It wasn't long before Marcus's vast superiority for the game became apparent.

"You've played this before," Cam accused. Her character, which looked like a robot clown operated by a cat, went through a particularly convoluted death animation at the hands of Marcus's character, an Egyptian vampire with spurs.

"I have two younger siblings. This used to be the only thing we'd play all summer when we were growing up," Marcus admitted, and then paused. "Can I tell you a secret?" he asked, looking like a little kid who had snuck a pet into school.

Cam was wholly invested. She absolutely wanted to know a Marcus secret. "What is it?"

"Well,"—he hesitated—"it's a little silly. But as a kid, I used to draw new characters for the game." He looked sheepish.

"Really?" Cam was intrigued. "Like what?"

Marcus let out a cough of a laugh. "Oh man, a bunch? I would also draw them for my siblings and my friends. My favorite was a lion in jeans with a fire mane and a scythe I called King Volcano." He looked like he regretted bringing up this topic.

"Marcus." Cam reached out and touched his forearm solemnly. "Your secret is safe with me." She let a beat pass, then smiled impishly. "As long as you show me those drawings!"

Marcus laughed for real, his dimple ghosting briefly across his cheek. "You pick the next game."

Cam selected a goldenrod kaiju with a cartoony racing game.

"So," Cam began as they scrolled through the driver selection menu, "haven't seen you around much."

Marcus grimaced. "I've been busy." The digital race began.

"Too busy to hang out with us rabble?" Cam punctuated her question by tossing a crate of bananas onto Marcus's character, causing it to momentarily spin uncontrollably.

Marcus cursed. "No, I'm actually trying to get out of a few things." Cam tossed a bottle of glue back at Marcus, resulting in his character being stuck in place for a few precious moments. "Honestly, I'm supposed to be at a party with some overseas investors, but I read up on them and their policies seem . . . unethical. So I ditched."

Cam delivered the coup de grâce when she lapped Marcus to win the race.

"I played with cousins," she said by way of explanation, with smug satisfaction at her restored honor. "Well, I hope you play hooky more often. I like beating you."

"I'm going to make you eat your words," Marcus swore.

They moved across the rainbow of kaiju, playing each game and growing increasingly competitive. They began shouting bad advice, playfully blocking each other's views of the screen, and reaching over to press the wrong buttons on each other's controllers. It culminated in Marcus tickling Cam's side, causing her to screech and drop the pixelated hamburger she was trying to make, giving Marcus the edge he needed to win.

"I am the Emperor of the Chefs," Marcus crowed, arms raised in victory.

"You cheated!" Cam dove into Marcus to tickle him back.

"Hey, we're closing up for the night." Chi poked her head into the mushroom just as a laughing Marcus lifted a squealing Cam up over his shoulder to keep her away from his ticklish spots.

Cam, gasping for air after laughing so hard, looked upside down at Chi. "We have to find Sofia and Avery. Also, we've got to make sure Daphne hasn't sacrificed James on an altar."

"They all left ages ago. And James looked like he still had all his blood," Chi assured them. "You two have a good night, though!" She leered at them, then waved as she headed off to close up her mausoleum.

Marcus effortlessly lowered Cam gently to the ground. She marveled at how easily he could carry her. Together, they walked out of the tiny studio and into the main area. They realized they were some of the last stragglers still there. Someone had already turned off most of the twinkling branch lights.

Suddenly, Cam was overcome with nerves. She had felt so at home among the makers at DAOTown, surrounded by art and creative energies, people pursuing their dreams. Exploring it with Marcus had been electrifying. But when they walked away, the easy camaraderie of the mushroom had become stiff and awkward, a swirling energy with no clear place to go.

"Hey." Marcus looked down at Cam. "You want to see a killer view?"

"Is it trampoline-worthy?" Cam joked.

Marcus smiled back with his whole dimple. "Let's go see."

Chapter 22

"**SAN FRANCISCO HILLS DO NOT** mess around." Cam panted up the steps cut into the slope. Marcus had brought them to a place he called Twin Peaks, but he had had the autonomous car drop them off on the back side of the hill instead of on top to avoid detection. It was after hours and the park was closed, after all.

Marcus, who had practically jogged up the steps, said, "You get used to it," then offered his hand to Cam. She took it gratefully, and he helped pull her up the final steps. He didn't let go when they reached the top, but kept holding her hand casually in his. His warm fingers nonchalantly enclosed hers in a way that made her heart skip.

"Whoa," Cam gasped, finally seeing the view. From here, she could see all of nighttime San Francisco spread below her like a glittering carpet. The crisp night air provided a crystal clear view of the high skyscrapers of the Financial District, the rainbows of the Castro, the bright signs of the Mission District, the blinking lights of vehicles dancing through, the stars in the sky that glittered back down, and, above it all, the moon.

They stood that way awhile, hand in hand, content to just take in the view.

Cam had been out with boys in places they weren't supposed to be before. She couldn't help but think about her last boyfriend, Nick, and how they would sneak into the abandoned bowling alley. But those times had always been quick, fleeting, and more about bragging rights. Here, with Marcus, under a blanket of night, it felt romantic, like it could build toward something more if she wanted it to.

"So," Cam began, talking softly into the quiet space between them, "where'd you get your socks?"

"You like them?" Marcus asked with a childlike enthusiasm she had never heard from him before. He lifted up his foot and pulled up the hem of his dark pants to reveal a pair of socks styled to look like a periwinkle alligator was eating his leg. "I have another pair that looks like otters giving each other high fives."

Cam laughed. "I do like them, actually. I'm just surprised." Marcus looked at her questioningly. "Well . . ." Cam hedged. "You don't exactly wear a lot of . . . loud clothing. You're more of a muted color palette."

"You don't like my clothes?" he asked flatly.

"No! Yes! I mean, I like your clothes. I think you look really good in them; they really show off your best assets." Please, Cam's brain pleaded with her mouth, stop talking.

Marcus laughed. "Don't worry, Diaz, I was just giving you a hard time. I know what you mean." His smile faded, and he looked out pensively over the city.

Finally, he took a deep breath and, eyes on the twinkling buildings below, explained, "My parents are two really driven people. They have their reasons, but suffice it to say they both accomplished incredible things really young. And there's a lot of pressure on me to live up to that."

"But you made it into the Beekor program—aren't they proud of you?" Cam questioned, watching his face.

Marcus hesitated before replying, "It's what they wanted."

"But what does all this have to do with socks?" Cam circled back in confusion.

"There are certain expectations of me. And one of them is a particular air of executive-level professionalism. So while I may like 'loud' clothing, it's not something I can indulge in."

"Hence the socks."

"Hence the socks." Marcus nodded and looked at her with a light smile absolutely devoid of his dimple. "They're a safe spot for self-expression."

"Well, I think that's pretty cute." Cam grinned up at him.

Marcus stared down at her intently. Cam began to worry she had messed up, embarrassed him in some way. But instead of pulling away, Marcus slowly lifted his hand and brushed back Cam's hair and tucked it behind her ear. She felt her pulse quicken, a rattling thrum against her chest. The spot where he had barely grazed her ear burned. She felt light, like she might drift off the hilltop. She was almost scared of floating away entirely as he leaned down, their noses barely brushing. His breath tickled her lips. Heart hammering, she closed her eyes and lifted up on her tiptoes.

"Hey, you! You can't be here!" Cam and Marcus leapt apart. Down the hill in front of them, two figures in brown scythed flashlight beams through the night sky, blinding them.

"Run!" Marcus yelped with a laugh and pulled Cam back down the steps.

"Stop!" one of the park rangers shouted, but it sounded half-hearted at best. It was plain neither of them had any intention of racing up a hill to chase after people who were obviously leaving quickly.

Laughing and panting, Cam and Marcus tripped down the hill and back into the residential area. In the darkness, they crouched half-hidden between cars and tried laughingly to shush each other as they called a rideshare.

"The last time I ran from park rangers, there were fireworks involved. And a lot of goat milk."

"Oh, you have to expand on that," Marcus demanded through a choked laugh.

"No way, that is a third-date story. Minimum," Cam stated, refusing to give in.

"So I only need one more?"

"What?" Cam shouted before Marcus laughingly shushed her. "Where are you getting two dates from?"

"The pier and here," Marcus reasoned.

"The pier absolutely does not count; that was a group. Neither does this," Cam insisted.

Marcus reached up and brushed hair behind Cam's ear. "We're alone now."

Cam's brain short-circuited, which was when the rideshare car pulled up.

The ride home felt endless, but it wasn't really. The whole time, Cam and Marcus sat in the back seat, coming up with excuses to reach across the small space and touch each other. Brush arms, graze knees, and whisper fingertips past each other.

When they finally got back home, they quietly unlocked the front door and tiptoed up the stairs. Marcus walked Cam to her attic room but stopped a step down from the landing.

"Thanks so much for tonight. I had a lot of fun," Cam said, reaching to straighten the lapel of his coat.

"Me too. It's been a while since I've just relaxed with someone." They looked at each other for a moment.

"Can I kiss you?" Marcus whispered in his low voice, looking up at Cam through his long lashes.

"Yes."

This time, she closed her eyes and leaned down and he was the one who closed his eyes and tipped up.

His lips pressed softly, then more firmly against hers, and she could smell amber and cinnamon. His warm mouth sent a tingling zing through her body. She reached out with her other hand to grab both of his lapels and pull him forward more fully into her, deepening the kiss.

Cam had been kissed before and done a fair amount of her own kissing in return. She knew how she liked her bottom lip nibbled; she knew how much tongue she liked. Even so, she had never known a kiss like this. With permission given, Marcus consumed her mouth. Cam lost herself in the sensations as he explored her, and she recklessly explored him in return. His long-fingered hands roved over her shoulders, her waist, her hips. She grabbed the back of his head demandingly as he ran his tongue along the inside edge of her lips. He moaned when she teasingly nipped at his.

He pushed her against the wall and kissed the sensitive spot on her throat just beneath her ear. She gasped loudly.

It was that sound, echoing in the narrow space, that brought Cam to her senses. Gently, she pushed Marcus away.

She liked Marcus. If she was being honest with herself, she liked him a lot. But hooking up with a person that lived in the same house as her while they were both competing for the same prize probably wasn't the best idea. And Marcus was not one-night-fling, consequences-be-damned material.

Marcus looked at her questioningly. Seeing his eyes dilated with desire for her and lips swollen from her kisses almost made her pull him back to her and all the way into her bedroom.

Instead, she just grinned at him. "I think you owe me a coffee date."

Marcus blinked a few times, clearly trying to clear the carnal fog from his brain, before slowly smiling back at her. "I do, don't I?"

Cam put on a mock prim voice. "Yes, you said you would take me to find the most trampoline-worthy coffee in the city." She lowered her voice. "Get me that coffee, and maybe . . . we'll pick up on this again."

Marcus chuckled softly. "Sounds like a plan." He kissed her once softly on her forehead.

"Good night, Cam," he said, walking backward down the steps for a few feet before turning to go to his own room.

"Good night, Marcus," she whispered back.

She retreated to her room and tucked herself in, but sleep was a long time coming.

Chapter 23

CAM WAVED AT THE DIGITAL whiteboard and laughed maniacally. The Three Ts, gathered in the conference room with Cam, clapped. Cam had brought up their project management dashboard and pointed dramatically at the latest bar to have turned green: "Incoming Orders." The Karrygold stream had been incredibly successful, with tons of other VTuber streamers and fans hitting the website to order Karrygold custom phones.

"Is that the last one?" Theresa asked. Rather than replying, Cam just smiled and silently zoomed out the view to include all their goals for the quarter. With that last metric hit, the influencer customization program had gone from deep in the hole to completely on track to hit every one of their targets.

"Bonus time, let's go!" Travis yelled. Terry slapped him five.

"Wait, you guys get bonuses for this?" Cam began, then froze, eyes on the door. The Three Ts spun to see what she was looking at. Wyatt had poked his head into the conference room. He smiled winningly, calculatedly mussed lion's mane looking as magazine-cover-worthy as ever.

"Great work, everybody! Camila! Let's walk." Due to being enclosed in a conference room, their early warning system—the wave of terrified employees that usually preceded Wyatt's presence in a building—had failed them. Cam quickly tried to smooth her hair and tidy her clothes before following Wyatt out. On the way past, Travis met Cam's eyes and nodded once, supportively.

"You're doing phenomenal work with the influencer customization project. Absolutely masterful." Wyatt delivered effusive praise, gesturing with his hands, as they walked through the open-floor-plan office area. Cam looked over to Wyatt's assistant, who made brief eye contact, rolled his eyes, then took an even briefer note.

Cam took Wyatt's praise and used it to bolster herself for what she was planning to do. Outwardly, she focused on projecting cheerful confidence. "Thanks, Wyatt! I have to admit, you were completely right. I had so much to learn."

Wyatt nodded sagely. "David and Kevin have been raving about you. They love working with you." Cam experienced a surge of pride at hearing that. Wyatt led Cam to the coffee shop in her building, a strong candidate for the best one on campus. The café occupied a nook off the side of the building that was open, airy, with massive panes of glass comprising all three walls. White counters and tabletops contributed to the feeling of spaciousness. Wyatt stepped into the line. Every single person ahead of him in line instantly left.

"It's because you're aware of your limitations," Wyatt continued with the charming air of a patronizing parent.

Cam felt the familiar bubble of rage rising in her belly, but she took a tight hold of herself and schooled any signs of it from her face. She reminded herself that while she had not appreciated Wyatt's feedback the last time they had spoken, he had ultimately been right. If these past few months had taught her anything, it was that she needed to actually listen to what people were saying.

"Their output has been nothing short of phenomenal. You've really gotten the entire team humming." Wyatt ordered coffees for the two of them and handed one to her. She took a tentative sip of her drink and was unnerved to realize it was a sweetened pistachio latte with almond milk, her favorite order. Cam attempted to stifle her shock and decided it was best for her mental health to assume this was some sort of coincidence rather than becoming a Wyatt conspiracy theorist.

Wyatt led them to a table in front of a window overlooking the bay. His assistant pulled up a chair to sit behind Wyatt in an unobtrusive manner and continued quietly tapping away at his tablet. From their position, Cam was able to watch the distant waves crashing violently against the rocks beneath the Golden Gate Bridge. She sipped her delicious latte and steeled herself. It was time to make her move, she thought.

Wyatt seemed to sense Cam's intentions. "Is there something you'd like to ask me, Camila?"

This was her moment. Cam took a breath and launched into her pitch. "As you can see, the influencer customization program is back on track." Wyatt nodded. "I'm sure you've kept track of the team's progress, but when I joined, the influencer customization program was failing to meet expectations in literally every metric." Cam continued with hot pride. "As of today, we are *exceeding* expectations in every single category." Wyatt beamed proudly at her and nodded.

"It's true; I did have a lot to learn. And if you'll look at the influencer customization program, I have simultaneously filled the gaps in my knowledge and set up a failing program for continued success." She smacked her fist in her palm excitedly, echoing Wyatt's body language from a prior meeting. "The time is perfect for Beekor to allocate some serious resources to me to run the Specio project!"

Wyatt sat silently, making prolonged eye contact with Cam. He steepled his fingers. He sighed elaborately. "Camila, you trust my instincts, don't you?"

Cam nodded profusely. "A-absolutely," she stammered to get out. She realized it was time to take a different tack. Wyatt opened his mouth to say something, but Cam stayed on the attack. "In fact, I've come to realize just how much of an asset your instincts would be to my project!" Wyatt's mouth snapped closed, and he looked at her skeptically. Cam ignored it and kept going. "Your continued dedication to championing excellent user experience is actually the *exact* thing my project needs." Cam felt herself gaining momentum. "It would help address the largest gap in my experience. What I'm building is incredibly needful for an enormous number of people. And I've already got a captive audience of users ready to go. I can be up and running tests with them to gain valuable insights as soon as I can deploy another round of hardware." A fire lit in her eyes. "My project is perfectly poised to fly! Imagine how far it could go with Beekor resources behind it!"

Wyatt's exasperated sigh instantly deflated her. Cam felt her heart sink. "So, you've still been pursuing this on the side?" he asked.

She nodded with sullen defiance.

Wyatt took on a concerned tone. "Cam, we have to marshal our resources and apply our efforts where they can yield the most benefit. Distractions kill products; that's something you'll learn in the start-up world." Quietly, he added, "And I've also heard you're still spending time with Lee Baker.... The same lesson applies. Managing our time effectively, avoiding distractions, is one of the most essential skills a tech leader can cultivate."

Wyatt continued more loudly. "If you trust my instincts, then you should respect my judgment that there is still quite a bit further for you to go before you can overcome some of the weaknesses I see in you. You've only been on this a couple of months." Cam felt as if she were sinking into a pit. "Do you really think, right as the influencer customization project is starting to turn around, that it's the right time to change leadership?"

She shook her head sadly, recognizing a closed subject when she heard it. Then she broke eye contact and looked at the lid of her latte as she took another sip.

Wyatt placed his hand on the table in front of her so it was in her field of view, as if he were extending a lifeline. He put on a compassionate air. "The team couldn't spare you at this point. You've proven that you can make art when given good clay. But there's still so much road ahead. Operating a team and growing it—now that's a challenge that I want to see you solve." He took on a matter-of-fact tone. "I would want to know that you're truly ready to operate at scale before I put resources behind you on your . . . adapter project." He said the last words in a dispassionate voice.

Maybe she just needed to get over herself, Cam thought. She tried to reassure herself that Wyatt knew what he was talking about. He couldn't have gotten this far and succeeded to this degree otherwise. She forced herself to nod her head yes.

Wyatt's face brightened, and he smoothly transitioned to cheerful and congratulatory. "And when I say I want to see you operate at scale, I mean I want to see what you've got as a leader. I'm placing you in formal leadership of the team, and I'm ramping up the resources we're allocating to the influencer customization project! Let's see what you can do with more people, more money, and even more leads!"

Cam felt absolutely pummeled by the shift from triumph to disappointment and back.

"We're going to massively juice the whole program. Now's your time to truly shine, Camila!"

Cam attempted to put on an excited face.

Wyatt suddenly became very earnest. He looked Cam in the eye soberly. "Camila, it is my solemn promise that we will build you into a talent the likes of which this industry has rarely seen. I elected to extend the opportunity for you to join the Beekor Accelerator Program because I knew we could help you grow and realize your untapped potential." He continued plaintively. "So please, trust that I am using my experience to guide you forward in the best way possible."

When Wyatt's hand slid back to his side of the table, he left behind a set of keys. "Here's a little token of personal appreciation. You can use it whenever, just check the shared calendar. But there aren't many others who have access. Beekor rewards our high performers."

Cam held up the keys, yet again off-balance. "Thank you," she began.

Wyatt shook his head solemnly. "No, thank you. I knew we were right to bet on you."

She took a breath and tried to process everything. Okay, she thought. Wyatt had been right in the past; she had seen that herself. He was probably right about her needing more leadership experience too. She worked to psych herself up. *I can prove that I can do this; then I'll be even better positioned to build and run the Specio project.*

She looked Wyatt in the eye. "All right, Wyatt. I see what you're saying." More excitedly she continued, "Thanks for the opportunity to formally lead a team!"

Wyatt smiled ruefully. "I think we can all use some honest feedback from time to time. Lord knows I could benefit." He laughed warmly and stood up. "Thanks for yet another chance to peek into that brilliant mind of yours!" He walked off, assistant in tow. Cam examined the keys in her hand and realized they were *car* keys.

Consolation prizes they may be, but if Cam were being honest, use of a company test car and leadership of a team were still pretty damn cool consolation prizes.

Chapter 24

BIDC, THE BEEKOR INTERNATIONAL DEVELOPER Conference, was held on the Beekor campus in an enormous dome that Beekor had built specifically for the occasion. With the sound of the enthusiastic crowd bouncing off the dome overhead, the inside of the vast space positively reverberated with an excited roar. Inside the dome, there was a stage with a massive screen behind it. Seating was arrayed around the stage in concentric half rings. Along the peripheries, innumerable holographic fields displayed Beekor devices, historic moments from Beekor history, or directions to the restrooms. Tables with the latest hardware were distributed about.

No active presentations currently occurring meant that the space was a free-for-all of people milling about. The sort of people that had verified check marks on social networks posed in colorful outfits with plastic wineglasses next to the latest-generation Beekor devices. International business leaders in dark suits laughed and jockeyed for position among one another between bright displays that rattled off hardware stats. Tech gurus in deceptively casual, neutral-colored clothing were hounded by journalists for their opinions on the newest software hitting the market. Cam stood transfixed at the edge of it all. Her eyes tracked from the giant video-feed projections in the air that showed testimonials from influencers, tech gurus, and business leaders down to the actual influencers, tech gurus, and business leaders walking the floor. It was BIDC, where the latest and greatest that Beekor had to offer was revealed to the world each year.

Her chest filled with the giddy excitement of being here, actually *here*, and not just watching the recaps on MiTube. The feeling of being on this side of the camera for once, of being right next to the people whose work she had been following for years. Of breathing the same air as some of the greatest minds on the planet. She found herself clenching her hands around the strap of her popcorn-box-shaped purse and forced them to relax. She deserved to be here, she repeated to herself.

Someone tapped her shoulder, and she snapped her mouth closed with a yelp and spun. Sofia stared down at her. She was sporting her usual slicked-back high ponytail and Beekor glasses but had swapped her designer slacks for an umber body-con dress with open back and thin heels. As usual, her look was meticulously curated and executed.

"Okay?" asked Sofia.

"Well, I just—" Cam started. "Everything here is amazing! The displays are amazing! The hardware is amazing!" Her eyes unfocused as her surroundings seized her attention again. "The people . . ."

"Are amazing?" Sofia finished for her, deadpan.

Cam laughed. "Exactly! There is just so much to see I don't—"

"Psst." A whisper from behind her cut her off mid-sentence. Cam turned to look but saw nothing. "Down here." Cam looked down at a very short woman. She appeared to be in her early twenties, and she wore comical, extra-large sunglasses and a bright yellow, loose-fitting onesie. "Fancy meeting *you* here, Cam." She spoke with an arch, exaggerated tone and waggled her eyebrows. It was almost theatrical.

"Uh."

"You don't recognize me?" She dramatically pouted and crumpled. "This is unbearable!" There was something familiar about her voice, or her way of speaking, but Cam couldn't quite place it.

Cam attempted to play it off. "Uh, yeah. Of course I remember you. Good to see you . . . again?"

The short woman wagged a finger, but then the houselights began to fade. "The show is starting," she said in a hushed voice. "Let's put a pause on this until later."

Cam stood there and blinked for a moment as the woman walked off. She gave Sofia a questioning look. Sofia just shrugged. Soon after, the two of them were swept along by the sudden sea of people filing into the adjacent auditorium. Inside, they found James already seated in a lightly cushioned foldout chair at the end of a row, looking like he had been there for a while. He was decked out in a stylish variant of the engineer uniform—a comfortable but well-maintained hoodie, Japanese denim jeans, immaculate-condition developer-conference T-shirt from nearly a decade prior, and a pair of more unobtrusive earbuds. He sat there silently drumming his fingers on his thigh in a convoluted pattern that Cam now knew definitively was the inhuman rhythm of whatever song he was listening to. Sofia and Cam greeted him and sat down next to him as he nodded his head in acknowledgment but otherwise kept quiet. A short distance farther down the row, Cam spotted Avery adjusting the back of their long, striking pin-striped suit as they settled into their seat. Hand to what could only be described as a cravat, Avery shared a quip with their neighbor, none other than the same random person who had intruded on Cam and Sofia earlier. Cam still had no clue who she was.

"You think Avery knows her?" Cam whisper-hissed to Sofia, eyes glued to the two of them as the woman with Avery began laughing.

Sofia just looked at Cam flatly.

Ahead of them in the audience, Cam's eyes caught magnetically on a dark figure with a familiar set of broad shoulders and perfect posture. Marcus stood with his signature tall, easy grace in a sleek navy-blue suit and gray turtleneck sweater among a group of similarly dressed business-development folks. He appeared perfectly at home shaking hands and talking easily with an older man who practically exuded the kind of power that brokered deals and maybe engineered coups in South American countries to keep cobalt prices low.

She hadn't seen him since the kiss they shared the week before. In preparation for the conference, Marcus seemed to be busier than ever. In fact, the entirety of Beekor had felt like a beehive that had been kicked. People all over the campus had been running to and fro to last-minute meetings, running speeches past PR, and pushing out final software updates. Even Cam's team had been busy with a small booth they set up in the conference hall showcasing some of their influencer customizations. Cam had gotten home late each night and fallen asleep exhausted, too tired to think about Marcus. At least, that's what she told herself.

As if sensing her gaze on him, Marcus turned and made eye contact with Cam. His eyes instantly lit up, and he smiled at her. She felt her chest start to flutter and her lips tingle with remembered kisses. He looked away as a man with an orange pocket square engaged him in conversation. He quickly looked back to Cam and signaled he wanted to see her after. She nodded quickly and then internally cursed herself for looking desperate instead of cool and sophisticated. Marcus just smiled again and turned his face back to his group.

Onstage, the presentations kicked off in earnest. Beekor product managers, VPs, and engineers rolled out all variety of hardware and software, one after another. A drone that could navigate the city and deliver pizza. "So now we can move even less?" Sofia quipped. A smart fridge that automatically ordered groceries based on what foods it was missing. "Too bad it doesn't cook as well!" An update to allow the Beekor watch to recharge purely from human sweat. Sofia snickered. "But when will we sweat if the drone has already picked up the pizza?"

All the shiny new tech started to blur together until Cam's hands hurt from clapping. Then the presentations ground to a sudden halt. The applause and excitement reached a crescendo and slowly faded. In the overly long pause after the last presentation, the enormous space gave way to an expectant hush.

Right as the tension became thick enough to cut with a knife, Wyatt came striding out, and the audience erupted. His lion's mane of swept-back graying hair looked especially regal today. His smile and energy dazzled in the lights as the applause poured in. He took his place at center stage and bowed a few times in a gesture of modesty, waiting until the applause died completely down and the entire auditorium grew utterly silent. Into the total quiet, Wyatt finally spoke.

"Good afternoon, everybody," he began. "Sorry if I'm a little late. The team and I were up until three a.m. preparing what I've got for you today. My designers and engineers are so incredibly inspired and excited to share this with you." Wyatt brandished the latest Beekor phone. Lights came up behind him to unveil plain white tables where other variants of the new phone sat, and a camera feed looking down on them was projected on the enormous screen behind him.

"Let me guess," Sofia whispered. "It's faster than the last one?"

Cam giggled.

The new phone looked incredibly sleek and beautiful. Wyatt dove into the features, rattling off tech specs and discussing the implications of Beekor's latest hardware design decisions.

"Surely the camera isn't better as well?" Sofia asked, a microsecond before Wyatt reported from the stage that, yes, the camera and holoprojector were indeed superior to last year's model. Cam clapped and resisted laughing aloud.

After the fifteenth round of applause, Wyatt's eyebrows waggled as he said, "And one more thing."

Sofia and Cam watched as Jennifer, their daily coordinator, walked out onstage carrying a small box. She delivered it to Wyatt, who opened it and took out a pair of Beekor smart glasses. He nodded affably at Jennifer. "Thank you." Then he put them on.

"Here at Beekor, I consider our most important goal to be facilitating human connection. And, even more, to do so seamlessly, unobtrusively, and with minimal fuss." As he spoke, the camera feed coming from his glasses was projected on the vast screen above him. They were seeing through his eyes. "The devices we own shouldn't be the focus of our attention. They should function as an augmentation layer that enables and improves those human connections."

Wyatt turned to face Jennifer onstage. On the screen above him, the feed from his glasses showed Jennifer, followed by a brief, familiar-looking loading indicator. Loading resolved quickly, and then, beneath Jennifer, a sequence of lines of text appeared:

- *Jennifer Sommers*
  - *Human Services—Daily Coordinator*
  - *Last met at meeting titled Keynote Speech Preplanning*
  - *Recently got a new puppy*

Above the text, Jennifer waved. The crowd erupted into applause. "Imagine it," Wyatt uttered, shouting to be heard above the crowd. "A piece of technology that can allow you to effortlessly keep track of everybody you've ever met, supply the context of where you last met them, and prepare you with relevant facts about their lives?" He went on with a note of awe, "Awkward small talk, misremembered names, and social uncertainty could become a thing of the past." He turned to face the crowd, who saw themselves projected on the screen behind Wyatt. "All to get back that"—the names and social data of everybody in the crowd simultaneously resolved, giving a short blurb of context for each and every face in the front row he looked at—"genuine human connection." The crowd went wild. Cam cheered harder than anybody, so proud that

Sofia's project had gone live onstage. Only, when she looked over, Sofia wasn't cheering.

"Sofia! I didn't know your project had already been integrated and was launching today!"

"Me neither," Sofia said, all color leaching from her face.

Chapter 25

SOFIA REMAINED EXTRA QUIET, EVEN for her, throughout the rest of the conference. Cam felt her growing more rigid beside her, as her breathing became disturbingly measured, with exactly ten seconds between each loud exhalation. When the final speaker wound down their presentation and walked off to the requisite applause, Sofia leapt up and nearly ran out of the conference hall. James looked after her with a concerned look on his face but nodded understanding when Cam waved to him that she would handle it. She didn't think Sofia wanted a crowd right now.

Cam chased after but struggled to keep up with Sofia's much longer legs and knifelike precision in weaving through the crowd. Cam was forced to apologize to numerous magnates, bloggers, and first-time conference-goers gaping at all the spectacle while occupying key walkways. Cam spun past a giant phone with legs and arms, accepting the flyer that the man in the mascot suit handed her and emerging from a wall of people just in time to catch a glimpse of Sofia darting into a private lactation room down a quiet hall past the bathrooms. Cam, breathing heavy from exertion, knocked on the door.

"Sofia?" Silence on the other side. "It's Cam. Can I come in?" There was a loud click as the door unlocked.

As Cam entered and locked the door behind her, Sofia sat down on the edge of the lone armchair, which was covered in frilly pillows with duckies embroidered on them. She rested her hands primly on her knees, glasses in one hand, closed her eyes, and began to breathe in through her nose and out through her mouth in unsteady waves.

"Hey, are you all right?" Cam asked tentatively as she stood by the door, trying to gauge how upset Sofia was.

"Yes," Sofia responded during one of her exhales. "I am simply recalibrating." She seemed really upset.

"You . . . you didn't know about the Beekor facial-recognition software," Cam said. It was a statement, not a question.

"That is"—inhale—"correct." Sofia began holding her breath.

"Beekor stole your project." Another statement. Her voice began to grow outraged as reality set in.

"Not necessarily." Sofia let out the breath she was holding in a rush. "This could simply be coincidental. A case of convergent evolution. A need both parties identified and filled. Simultaneous discovery, like Newton and Leibniz both inventing calculus at the same time," Sofia said in a rush, nearly tripping over her own platitudes to assure herself. "This is not uncommon."

Cam reeled a little under the weight of what was practically a deluge of words from Sofia before focusing. "So you were reassigned to work on a different project while Beekor worked on your original project with an entirely different team, to which you were not invited?!" Cam asked.

"It appears so, but it could be a simple mistake—crossed wires or a failure to communicate." Sofia began to take careful, measured breaths once more.

Cam was skeptical. "Didn't you pitch this project to Beekor as part of your application to the Accelerator Program? And here you've been working on tools for the glasses with a remote team and nobody thought to say anything to you?!"

Sofia faltered a little. "No."

"They stole this from you!" Cam was heated. "Beekor has a ton of engineers that could pull this together quickly. I just think this is really suspicious to have happen now, after you've already pitched to them and joined the Accelerator. Why have they kept you in a box this whole time?" Cam was livid.

"Stop," snapped Sofia. "We do not know that. And even if we did, it changes nothing. It's out; everything I built was on their proprietary software and hardware." Cam stepped back as Sofia looked away. With a much quieter inhale, she softly said, "I do not know where that leaves me."

Cam watched Sofia for a moment, then opened her arms. "Hug?"

Sofia let out a puff of a laugh and looked up at Cam. Her eyes were overly bright and looked a little wet. She nodded.

Cam squeezed herself onto the seat that was really only meant for one and wrapped her arms around Sofia. After a moment, Sofia haltingly spoke.

"My brother has always needed a machine to talk. I taught myself programming on his speech device, helping him set up conversation trees. Sometimes rude ones." She gave a watery chuckle. "Using tech to help—I want to keep doing that. It's why I made my facial-recognition assistance software. To help myself and others like me." She dropped her head onto Cam's shoulder. "I suppose Beekor will keep doing that. I just thought it would be me leading it."

"Well," Cam started when it was clear Sofia wasn't going to say any more, "it's a really cool idea, and useful too. Everyone is going to love it. I can see why Beekor is implementing it." She felt Sofia's whole body rise on a shuddering sigh. Cam was still frustrated on Sofia's behalf. But she could tell that Sofia wasn't interested in dwelling on the experience and stewing in anger. Bitterness had never been Sofia's style. So instead, Cam pivoted to one of Sofia's favorite things, compliments. "I mean, honestly, that's amazing that you built that whole feature by yourself! I bet it took them a whole fleet of engineers to get that working."

Sofia had a grim little half smile. "It is cross-device and backward-compatible too."

"Incredible!" Cam boggled. "You must be a one-engineer army."

"True," said Sofia with more of a smile. Then she deflated again. "Maybe I should go home to Hong Kong. Nothing to work on here."

"No, you can't go." Cam was emphatic. "Who will show me all the *Dance* movies?"

Sofia gave a tiny laugh, less wet-sounding than her last.

Cam started thinking quickly. She really didn't want Sofia to leave; she had come to enjoy the young woman's dry sense of humor and wit. But more than that, Cam loved Sofia's honesty and caring nature. She wasn't afraid to tell Cam when she was screwing up, and she was patient enough to assist her in correcting her mistakes. She genuinely wanted to help people. Sofia was too good a person for Cam to let her go home with her tail between her legs.

"What if you join my project?" Cam asked. Pridefully, she added, "I run it now; I can hire whoever I want!"

"Customized hardware that's even more exclusive and expensive than Beekor already makes." Sofia hummed dubiously, spinning her glasses in her hand. "Not interested in influencers."

Sofia's description was pretty accurate, Cam thought. It was the same problem she herself had with the team. She really liked the Three Ts, and the features they were working on were cool and innovative. Someday they would probably trickle down to the regular populace. But none of that work did anything for people like Cam and her mother right now. "Well," Cam proposed tentatively, "how about Specio? My *future* project."

Sofia tilted her head and looked up at Cam quizzically.

Cam felt a rush of energy at the prospect of talking about her project again. Sofia had only briefly seen Cam's original project in the airport, and the two hadn't discussed it much since then. Cam had been too ashamed at

Wyatt's dismissal to talk about it with anyone other than her mother and her friends who already knew about it. But as she continued to work on the adapter at home, with each successful revision to her prototype, Cam had felt her confidence restoring.

She steeled herself. No, she wasn't talking about her project; she was *pitching* it. She was pitching to get Sofia to join her. Cam leapt up off the single couch cushion and began pacing the small room. Unsure how to begin, she chose her words in a rush.

"My family doesn't have a lot of money. For people like us, some of the really cool features of Beekor's newest phones are completely inaccessible due to cost. And that actually ends up costing people like us even more, because we don't get the ability to use a lot of the tools that the more privileged can afford." Cam spoke with increasing enthusiasm, and she began gesticulating passionately, unaware that she had begun to mirror Wyatt's speech-giving movements.

"Tools like holographic teleconferencing are becoming a requirement for collaboration! Not just between businesses, but for an increasing number of jobs and schools. There are tons of kids right here in this country that can't afford the technology that is needed to complete their schooling. And that doesn't even take into account communities in poorer countries. It's incumbent on us to ensure that as many people as possible have access to the opportunity that this technology provides! Opportunities for learning and growth and work should not be limited to only those that can afford them!" Cam realized she was getting louder and talking too fast, but she was too passionate about the subject to restrain herself. "My whole life, I've been figuring out how to upgrade old stuff when we couldn't buy the latest tech; that was what motivated me to make Specio. Making these opportunities available to everybody while also breaking out of the wasteful cycle of new hardware replacements each year ... In a lot of ways, it's the polar opposite of the influencer customization program." Cam unzipped her popcorn-bag-shaped purse and pushed past her new Beekor phone to pull out the latest version of her prototype.

"Check this out. I've made a *lot* of improvements since you last saw it." Cam sounded cocky.

Cam was proud of the strides forward she had made in her spare time, but as Sofia looked at the mishmash of 3D-printed parts, loose wires and an old, off-brand phone, Cam became painfully self-conscious. In Sofia's slim manicured hands, it looked quite rough and messy compared to the flawless finish of a Beekor device. Cam had no need to worry, though. Sofia tilted it this way and that to take Specio in from all angles. To Cam's intense gratification, Sofia nodded appreciatively when she saw the improved clasping mechanism and the streamlined cable management.

Sofia handed the device back and Cam powered up her ancient phone. The two bent over it, and then Sofia smiled with pride for Cam as the ancient hardware booted up, projecting a three-dimensional animated icon, just like the latest brands of Beekor phones.

Cam's eyebrows waggled as she said, "Now watch this!" She pressed an icon, and Sofia's phone chimed. Sofia answered it, and they entered a holochat session together. Cam waved her hand over her prototype hardware, and the small figure of Cam waved at Sofia from her cutting-edge Beekor device. "I got interoperability to allow holochat with Beekor phones working! I want it to let even the oldest, most inexpensive devices work with the same tools that the newest Beekor devices have, leveling the playing field and letting anybody collaborate!"

"I didn't know you had gotten so far!" Holo-Sofia parroted her words through the phone and looked impressed. "Why 'future project' though? This looks like a now project."

"I was pretty inexperienced when I arrived," Cam explained breezily, closing down the call. She was eager to gloss over how wildly understated this was. "So Wyatt put me on the influencer project to learn how to operate a project." She gestured at her prototype. "He said he'll give me the resources once I prove I'm capable of handling them. So in the meantime, I'm working on the hardware and software and gathering data by testing it on a few users. I'm hoping to hit the ground running once I'm given the resources and team to back me."

Sofia took the prototype from Cam and examined it thoughtfully.

Cam felt a sudden sense of internal resistance. Sofia needed something to work on, and Cam had something that needed working on. Between her day job at Beekor and the burden of trying to convert Specio, which was still a relatively rough prototype, into something that regular people could use, she realized a lot of new feature work was lagging behind. She hadn't improved the hardware or added support for new devices or holographic data formats in quite a while. If she honestly looked at things, she needed help. And Sofia was probably the most fortuitous help Cam could have stumbled on. And she had the belated realization that she could also really use someone to talk to and bounce ideas off of. Her mother was encouraging, but she didn't know anything about computer software. Sofia would be perfect.

On the other hand, Specio was her baby. She had ushered it into existence from nothing, and the thought of sharing it was scary, even with some-body she completely trusted, like Sofia. These ideas warred in Cam's mind. Eventually, she said, "I have been struggling a bit with more comprehensive backward compatibility."

Sofia was quiet for a long, contemplative moment. Then she nodded and handed the prototype back to Cam. "I have tackled that problem recently and may have some insights to offer."

Cam's eyes lit up. The idea of Sofia *wanting* to join had her bouncing on her toes in excitement. Cam worked to restrain that impulse, however. She decided to walk things back a bit. "Obviously, I could use the help, and you would be the perfect person to join me, but we should probably both take some time to think about it, and figure out where we each stand when we're not in the middle of tearstained lactation room on the show floor of one of the world's biggest tech conferences."

Sofia laughed, stood, and crossed the room to Cam. She placed her hands on top of Cam's around the prototype. "You are passionate. That is rare. You are passionate about helping others. I respect that." Sofia stared into Cam's eyes. "You will do great things, and I want to be there."

Cam felt her breath catch and her heart swell. "I've never worked with someone before," she said shyly.

"Collaborating is learning to ask for help when you need it," said Sofia. "Or give it." She reached down and pulled Cam into a tight hug. Her voice still trembled a little bit around the edges. "In that regard, you have already been an excellent collaborator. Thank you, Cam."

Cam squeezed her back.

They stood like that for a minute before Sofia let out one last, shuddering breath and straightened herself up.

"We can't stay here all night. We're supposed to be at a party," Sofia said, discreetly wiping at her eyes. "Tomorrow?"

Cam nodded her head in agreement and put her prototype back into her bag. "Tomorrow. But are you sure you want to go to the after-party? We can just go home if you want to. I'll go with you. We can watch *Fevered Nights: 4Life*." Cam did want to go to the party—Jennifer had implied there were going to be acrobats—but Sofia's well-being was more important than that. Plus, Sofia had been there for Cam when she had been miserable.

"No. We must drink." Sofia appeared to shake herself a little, like a bird trying to resettle ruffled feathers. "I will mourn my project." She grimaced and smoothed down her skirt. "And you must celebrate me maybe, possibly, considering joining yours." She patted her hair, checking that it was still in its customary sleek ponytail.

"Hey, shouldn't you be the one celebrating me maybe, possibly, considering asking you to join?" Cam asked with an affected challenge.

"I will drink twice," said Sofia solemnly, and they both headed out to find the party.

Chapter 26

AFTER THREE MONTHS AT BEEKOR, Cam had already seen things she would never have previously believed. She'd met a kid who invented a chores-backed cryptocurrency called MommyCoin to earn anime-watching time in exchange for doing dishes, only to suddenly find that his dumb token had hit a $200 million market cap. She'd experienced a day where the sky was just orange, the entire time. She'd been in the office when a bunch of personal trainers showed up for the Friday happy hour and gave the engineers molly, causing HR to quarantine one whole section of the building to prevent further spread of the twerking outbreak. But all those experiences were completely blown out of the water by the things Cam encountered at the conference after-party.

Once they had their passes scanned at the door, Cam and Sofia entered a giant warehouse with a live band playing onstage in the center. Performers spun on silks and giant rings far above the growing crowd. Ice sculptures in the forms of characters from games on the Beekor App Store served as ice luges for the bartenders to pour drinks through at the open bar. Neon-lit platform paths hung suspended from the ceiling and led to rooms with retro pinball machines, cutting-edge hologames, and couches where people could see and be seen. Models of every gender handed out goodie bags full of high-tech swag ranging from T-shirts to phone accessories to actual phones. Catering staff flowed around and between them all, circling with tiny, delicious appetizers. And all this was only in the first room.

"There you are!" Avery appeared between them like a bolt of lightning, all frightening energy and pizzazz. "The party has missed your charms and your delights, and you have missed the first wave of party bags! But never fear my dears—I snagged one for each of you." Avery tossed a bag at each of them and started shouting, "Shots! Shots! Shots!" Without missing a beat, Sofia joined in, and Cam was swept along, dragged away from where she had been actively goggling at a plinth with a machine on it that would scan visitors in order to generate a gold-printed 3D model of themselves. Cam followed as the two raced to the open bar. The bartender stood behind a gigantic slab of strange marble that glowed from within with an eerie light that transitioned color from white to purple as they approached.

"What's your poison?" Avery asked Sofia.

"Usually? Santa Teresa. Here? Whiskey," Sofia responded.

Avery grinned. "I know a place with a good rum selection. I'll take you there sometime. But for now—four shots of whiskey!" They shouted at the bartender and crammed a generous tip in the tip jar.

"Four shots . . . ?" Cam asked hesitantly, opening up the gift bag.

"One for each of you, and two for me," said Avery, observing as the bartender set up the glasses in a row.

"I am drinking twice," Sofia said, looking at Avery.

Avery looked Sofia in the eye and asked, in an uncharacteristically solemn voice, "Bad as all that, my dear?" By this point, Sofia had regained her customary goddess-like perfection, but she was still pale and a bit brittle-looking around the edges.

"One bad, one good," Sofia replied, meeting Avery's eyes, hands resting determinedly on the bar like she was standing her ground.

Avery watched Sofia for a moment longer before slowly reaching over and grabbing one of her hands in theirs. They squeezed, and Sofia squeezed right back. Avery slowly smiled. "Make that seven shots, if you would be so kind!" they said to the bartender, who nodded and went for more glasses.

Cam gasped and froze.

"What?" Avery asked as both they and Sofia looked over at a startled Cam. "Do you not like whiskey?"

"Did you see this?" Cam opened her gift bag and pulled out a cylinder of metal that gleamed with the greenish-rainbow sheen of an insect in the bar's teal light. "This is an EverWarm temperature-controlled travel mug. Daria Violence signature edition!"

She brandished the mug. "Hello," it said in a breathy robot voice.

"Do you know how much this costs? I've never even seen this color before!" A cool $250.

"Probably exclusive to this event," said Avery, uninterested. They rubbed a thumb over Sofia's hand, still clasped in theirs.

"A Beekor watch too! Are you serious?" Cam squeaked, continuing to go through the bag. Starting price $375.

"Slim-line model. Less features. More fashionable," Sofia said, glancing into her bag.

"This is all free? Are you serious? This is all really expensive stuff," Cam said, looking out over the crowds and trying to calculate how many people and how many gifts. Her brain fried at the thought of all this tech that she could never have afforded just being handed out for free like it was candy on Halloween. And these people didn't even want it. She already saw some people forgetting their bags in favor of taking selfies with the white-chocolate fountain in the shape of Wyatt Ecker's face. Cam felt her stomach tighten.

"Tax write-off," Avery said, clearly more invested in the bar than the state of Beekor's financial records. "Gentlefolk, pick up your shots!" they yelled, downing a shot and holding up another. "One bad!"

Cam stuffed her goodie bag in her purse and snatched up her allotted shots. Sofia lifted hers as well. "One bad," agreed Sofia

"One bad," chimed a dazed Cam. And the three clinked and drank.

Cam coughed as the whiskey burned its way down her throat. Honestly, she was more of a tequila-margarita type, and this stuff kicked.

Avery grinned at the completely unfazed Sofia and raised their remaining shot. "One good!"

Sofia gave a faint smile. "One good!"

Cam, still reeling from the first shot, wheezed, "One good," and again the three clinked glasses. Sofia and Avery threw theirs back with no problem while Cam gingerly sipped a small amount before sneakily placing the rest back on the bar.

"So what do you want next?" Avery asked, eyes on Sofia. "More of the bad or more of the good?"

"Both," said Sofia, never looking away as she continued to hold Avery's hand.

Out of the corner of her eye, Cam saw a flash of gray and quickly declared she was grabbing something to eat before backing away. She needn't have bothered with excuses. The two were already deeply engrossed in ordering their next round of drinks. It looked like Sofia was going to be well taken care of.

Cam skirted a small platform on which a robotic arm was building a miniature castle out of frosting-coated cookies shaped like Popsicle sticks, and darted around a group of people in provocative clothing, corsets, gas masks, and bunny ears to lightly grab Marcus's elbow. He spun in his gray suit and looked down at Cam before smiling warmly at her. His lips, which Cam now knew were incredibly plush, were parted just the slightest bit.

"Hey," he said quietly, his deep voice rumbling through her. "Found you."

Cam felt her face warm under his full focus. "I think I'm the one that found you." She tucked her hair behind her ear and smiled up at him, strangely feeling shy talking to him for the first time since the stairwell kisses.

"I'm surprised to see you alone," Marcus said, looking around them. "Where's Sofia?"

"I left her with Avery at the bar." Cam looked through the crowd and was just able to make out the flash of Avery's red hair.

"Smart of you to retreat. I've seen Avery drink people twice their size under the table. Trust me, you do *not* want to try and keep up." As he said that, they heard a cheer erupt from the bar.

"Yeah, I've made that mistake before." Cam grimaced, thinking back to her first night out with them. "But Sofia seems to be able to handle it just fine."

"How is she doing?" Marcus, who was tall enough to see over the milling people, looked at Sofia with concern.

"She's . . . doing all right. It's kind of hard to tell. I think she needs distraction right now, and Avery is good at that." Cam listened to the chants of a drinking game starting by the bar. "Sofia told you about her project, then?"

Marcus hesitated. "She didn't."

Cam frowned. "Then how did you know she was upset?"

Marcus didn't look at Cam. "She didn't look happy at the conference. I asked Jennifer about it. She told me.

"Hey," he said, abruptly changing the subject. "You want to get something to eat? They've got food trucks out back." Marcus offered her his arm.

"All right," she said, letting him shift the mood. "But only if you show me your socks."

Marcus laughed and obligingly lifted up the hem of his pants.

"Is that the Power Rangers?" Cam questioned, looking at the colorful helmets decorating his socks.

"Did you mean 'Is that from the iconic show *Power Rangers,* which has captured the hearts and souls of children for generations?' Yes. Yes, it is." Marcus lowered his cuff with a flourish.

Cam laughed. "I was more of a PBS kid myself." She looped her arm through his.

Marcus guided them to a pair of large, open garage doors, easily slicing through the crowd with his height and assurance. He led them unerringly past a photo booth where partygoers were throwing water balloons, diving through confetti, or jumping and landing in heroic poses while a high-speed camera captured super slo-mo footage of them, roaring and screaming through clouds of particles like they were in the climax of a superhero movie. Several people waved at Marcus as he passed by. He nodded but didn't stop. Cam tried her best to not look like an awkward accessory. Outside was a large concrete patio space partially covered by a broad, permanent awning made of solar panels. Lined up in neat rows were a dozen or so food trucks. Although "food trucks" only fit by the loosest possible definition. One was a retrofitted double-decker bus that served chicken and waffles on the ground floor and allowed patrons to sit on the second. Another was a truck with a wall made of glass that allowed passersby to see inside to the giant brick oven imported from New York and the delicious pizzas coming out of it. Still another looked like a classic San Francisco trolley from which people served gelato and mochi.

"What would you like?" Marcus asked Cam as they took in the scene.

"I kind of want everything?" Cam confessed. It all looked delicious.

"All right, then I think it's best if we divide and conquer." Marcus put a thumb to his chin and nodded. "You take that half." He gestured to the right. "And I'll take this half." He gestured to the left. "Get at least three things, and we'll meet back at that table." He pointed to a vacant, low wood-slatted table surrounded by several plush outdoor lawn chairs. "Whoever brings back the most trampoline-worthy meal gets a prize."

"What's the prize?" Cam asked dubiously.

"Well, it won't matter because I'm going to win." Marcus laughed and dashed off to the left. Cam cursed and ran off to the right.

Twenty minutes later, the two combatants arrived at the table with their offerings. Each one returned with far more than the originally stipulated three items each.

"I'll admit, this is a strong contender," Marcus said, eating the fries with pork sisig and an egg on top that Cam had brought.

"This, though!" Cam gestured emphatically at the pork-belly bao with pickled daikon and an indescribable sauce that she had just taken a bite of.

Seamlessly, they swapped food and tried what the other had eaten.

"Incredible," Cam effused.

"Oh man," Marcus said simply.

In this manner of camaraderie, good cheer, and mutual appreciation, they ate through their assembled feast. The final winner, it was decided, was a juicy country sausage burger with kimchi that Cam had returned with.

"I am the champion," Cam sang as she wiped her hands clean with a compostable sanitizing hand wipe. "What's my prize?"

"Okay, okay." Marcus laughed as he tossed his own cleansing wipe. He reached into the inner pocket in his blazer and pulled out a surprisingly large and thick envelope. He handed it to her in an uncharacteristically nervous manner. Curious, Cam gently took it and opened up the unsealed flap.

The card inside was of a thick stock, clearly an expensive piece of paper. The outer edges of the card had an ornate frame hand-inked all around, floral and leaf patterns, in an art deco styling. The body of the card, in exquisite calligraphy, read:

This coupon entitles the bearer to
ONE COFFEE DATE

Beneath was a QR code, neatly concealed in the embellishments. Cam pulled out her phone and scanned the card, which took her to a website. The homepage was a drawing of a trampoline; clicking it scrolled the page down over a drawing of Jell-O and to a drawing of a train. The windows of the train slid down to reveal half a dozen photos of coffee, each linking to a different famous or trendy coffee shop around the city.

Cam looked down at what she was holding, stunned. It was a masterful piece of artwork, the card and the website. "Did you make all this?" she asked, looking up at Marcus, who had begun fidgeting anxiously as she had examined his work.

"Yeah, I did. I make this kind of stuff in my free time." He rubbed the back of his neck and looked away.

"It's beautiful. You're a really good artist." And it was. And he was. Cam absolutely loved it.

"It's nothing, really. And anyway . . ." He looked over at Cam and gently placed his hand on her knee under the table. Suddenly, her knee was on fire, sending tingling waves to the rest of her body. She remembered when his hands had touched more of her, sensations she had spent a week thinking about. ". . . I hope you'll redeem it soon."

Cam's breath hitched as she looked into Marcus's eyes. She felt herself leaning toward him.

"Marcus!" someone shouted from across the patio.

Marcus leapt apart from Cam with a start and stood up.

Suddenly, a ball of people pressed in on Cam as she stood, and she was engulfed in the cloud of entourage wannabes that orbited Wyatt Ecker like planets around a star. He was talking, and they were listening.

"Ah, here are some of our bright, young overachievers from the Accelerator Program. Camila, Marcus—having fun?"

Marcus turned. His winning, camera-ready smile was on full display, but the dimple was nowhere in sight.

"Oh, absolutely—" Cam started to answer, but Wyatt had already moved past her and had put his hand on Marcus's shoulder.

"Great things, we're expecting from this one," Wyatt said warmly, and beamed a smile back at his people.

"Thanks, Wyatt," Marcus responded gracefully.

"Come with me," Wyatt continued. "There are some people I want you to meet." And just like that, the Wyatt star moved on, capturing Marcus in its orbit. Marcus looked contritely over his shoulder and gave Cam a "you know how it goes" shrug before following. Then Cam was alone.

She sighed and looked down at her beautiful ticket before carefully tucking it in her now-bulging purse.

Cam still didn't quite understand the way Marcus's relationship with Wyatt worked.

Heading in, Cam stumbled on a segment of the party space that had turned into a full-on club. Tiles on the floor lit up to the beats from a suspiciously familiar-looking European DJ. Of course, Avery and Sofia were right in the middle of it, dancing their hearts out. The short woman from before, during the conference keynote, was with them. James was nowhere to be seen. Cam hadn't seen him since far earlier in the evening, but as the music got louder and the crowd crushed in more, she realized this sensory overload of a party was probably the last thing he would want to be at. He was most likely back at the page house contentedly working on a new speaker in the garage. With a smile at that happy thought, and a reminder to herself to make sure she brought him home a swag bag of his own, Cam set to squeezing her way through the dense crowd of dancers.

"Excuse me," she said for the three-hundredth time as she finally reached the center. Cam stopped in front of Avery and Sofia, and before she could say anything, Cam felt something in her hand and looked down. Somehow, without making eye contact even once, with the supernatural instincts of some sort of party god, Avery had already pressed a brand-new drink into Cam's hands.

"You're right on time, honey," Avery said. "Now drink up." Cam followed orders.

The short woman sidled up to Cam as she tried to finish enough of her drink to make dancing without spilling a possibility. "Psst," she began, spinning around to execute a skillful booty shake. "Do you know who I am yet?" she asked over her shoulder. "It would be em-bear-assing if you couldn't figure it out."

Cam slapped her palm to her forehead. The hyper-dramatic way of speaking, the incredibly strained bear puns. "Karrygold? Is that you?"

Karrygold laughed. "Bingo!" she shouted. Then, quieter, "But keep it down! I'm incognito." She winked and put a finger to her lips. "It would be unbearable if people knew my true form."

"Thank you for trusting me to . . . bear this responsibility," Cam tried back.

Karrygold screamed with laughter and encouraged Cam to do yet another shot with her. At the merest mention of shots, Avery gravitated toward the pair as if summoned. As they took in Karrygold and Cam, Avery's eyes lit up. "How rude of me! Cam, allow me to introduce you to—"

"Karrygold, yes, we've met," Cam interjected.

"Cam is my Beekor bestie!"

Avery looked momentarily surprised and a bit deflated, but they rallied quickly. "Well then, let's get this party continued!"

Chapter 27

CAM FELT LIKE A CORPSE.

The morning sun streamed in through her enormous bay window. Cam cracked one bleary, bloodshot eye and immediately regretted it. She reached for her phone.

She could not find her phone.

Cam lifted her head and began to run a tally. She was not sure how or when she got home last night—this morning? But she was here in her bed with her pajamas on and a big glass of water by her bed. She groaned gratefully, thanking past Cam for her consideration, and began to drink the water before abruptly spitting it out when she realized it was tequila. She lay back down, took a couple deep breaths, then hauled herself up with a defeated hiss to draw the blackout curtains around the bay window closed again and totter to the bathroom to drink a few handfuls of water from the sink. As she brushed her teeth, she considered that, maybe if everything was going to be free, she would have to learn to say no a bit better to infinite drinks. She spat toothpaste and massaged her throbbing temples.

For all that Lee Baker's old Victorian was well maintained, it was still an older house and the floorboards creaked. Which meant Avery and Sofia were aware of Cam's approach down the steps to the open-floor-plan kitchen–living room on the first floor.

"She lives!" said Avery, offensively chipper. They sat seated on a barstool next to the kitchen island drinking a tiny espresso, looking like they had come back from a brisk morning run. Afternoon run? Cam had no idea what time it was.

"Have you seen my phone?" Cam drooped, feeling her energy being leached out even being in the same room as the positively spunky Avery.

"There," Sofia said, pointing with a spatula to a phone resting on the kitchen counter and plugged into the wall. She also looked disgustingly normal with not a hair out of place from her customary slicked-back high ponytail.

"Oh, thank God." Cam stumbled forward to pick up her phone. She opened it to find it in the middle of a cat video. It was 1:00 p.m. She then became aware that Sofia was cooking on the stove. She had a flat griddle going with small, thick yellow pancake-looking things cooking in the middle. As Cam watched, Sofia sprinkled cheese over each pancake thing and folded it in half.

"Darling, last night you were so drunk, Sofia and I decided to take you back to get another Cali-style burrito to sober you up," Avery began as they sipped their tiny espresso. "You ate half the burrito, then cried big, ugly anime-girl tears and said the second half was too delicious to eat. But I distracted you with the story of the last time I was in Venezuela, which, by the way, inspired us to look up how to make these cachapas that Sofia is currently cooking, and you laughed so hard they kicked us out. You ate the rest of your burrito outside; then you immediately cried again when you could not find your burrito and insisted rather vehemently that we rescue it from the raccoon king. It took some convincing, but we brought you home, where you plugged your phone in here and tried to show us videos of cats, but you were laughing too hard for us to see. You then poured yourself a glass of pure tequila and went to your room. Sofia checked in on you there five minutes later and found you passed out in your bed. Ah, lovely, they're done!"

Sofia handed Cam one of her freshly plated pancake things. Cam hastily bit down, mostly to avoid thinking about how embarrassing she had been last night, and immediately burned her tongue.

"Careful, or you will burn your tongue," warned Sofia dryly. Avery just cackled.

Cam tried once again and tentatively took a small, exploratory bite. It was delicious! The cachapa was made of sweet corn and flour with salty cheese in the center. Cam wolfed it down, nearly burning her tongue again.

"Have a few more." Sofia piled a couple more on Cam's plate. "Sober up and then show me your prototype."

Oh yeah, that, Cam thought. Cam remembered that Sofia had agreed to team up. She experienced a complex flurry of feelings around the idea that she wasn't quite sure she was ready to parse yet.

A full meal and several aspirin later, Avery kissed Sofia on the forehead and slipped off to who knew where. Cam, in a state of borderline delirium, watched Avery go, then stared hard at Sofia. "So . . . ?"

Sofia did not acknowledge Cam in any way, clearly having no intention of discussing . . . whatever was going on between her and Avery. She simply headed out to the back patio of the house and proceeded to pull two deck chairs together. Cam, getting the hint, went to fetch her laptop and eventually came outside and flopped into one of the seats. She made a look of distress as the sun beat down on her, so Sofia dragged over an umbrella to provide some cover. Cam pulled up her laptop, and the two settled in to discuss collaboration on Cam's project.

"All right, so let me just get this little chart I made open, and I can show you the main components of what I've built so far," Cam said. A slide deck came up. The first slide had a series of diamond shapes and square shapes with text in them. Some variety of graph. "Ah, ignore this first one; this is a work in progress." Cam clicked through to the next slide. It consisted of several images showing how the holographic tech worked. "As you can see here, the main realization I had was that I could re-create the actual holographic projector myself using this light pipe design and an inexpensive plastic lens I was able to find online from a maker in Germany. It doesn't have the high quality of the precision Beekor glass, so it warps the image. We can still get a decent holograph out of it, though, by calibrating on the software side of things to make sure the images we push to it are distorted in the exact opposite way that the lens will warp them, resulting in a clear final image."

Sofia nodded.

Cam continued. "So if you knew your plastic lens would always pinch an image in the middle, you could just make your software project images that are purposefully warped outward in the middle so the end result would look normal after the image was pinched again as it was projected from the lens."

Sofia dismissed Cam's elaboration with a wave. "I understand. May I see the code for the image distortion?"

Cam was taken aback for a moment. "Sure," she said slowly. It almost felt too soon to let Sofia into her code. As if it were a private space. She opened up a text editor and navigated to the code.

Sofia started to reach over to scroll the file and then just opted to snatch the laptop out of Cam's hands and place it in her own lap. She rapidly scrolled through the file, making occasional thinking noises that Cam had trouble interpreting. Cam experienced an unaccountable degree of nervousness having Sofia inspecting her code base. It was a little bit like letting Sofia read her diary or look into her closet in her recently "tidied" room.

"Here we are," Sofia said as she pointed at a matrix that Cam had experienced particular difficulty with. "This is why what you showed me last night displayed that warping at the edges." Sofia smiled confidently.

Cam was quiet for a beat. "You spotted that in the middle of a dark party?"

"What's that? Why, yes, you are very lucky to have me, and you are extremely welcome." Sofia preened.

Cam sighed and took the laptop back from Sofia. "About that," Cam began.

"Yes?" Sofia folded her hands to give Cam her full attention.

Cam took a moment to collect her thoughts. She worked together with a team at Beekor right now, but this felt different. This was *her* thing. "So, for one, I would never hold you to a commitment made under duress. After the conference, you were obviously at a low point—" Cam began.

Sofia cut her off. "That's not what this is about."

Cam took another breath before beginning, "You're right. Obviously, in every way, you're everything this project needs. But I'm so used to owning this. The idea is mine, the work is all mine, the problems are all mine. It's . . ."

Sofia gave a single nod and looked Cam in the eye. "I understand."

"You do?" Cam wasn't sure she even understood her own feelings.

"Of course." Sofia sounded matter-of-fact. "You have had this perfect vision in your mind all this time, and now you are faced with the prospect of somebody else sharing in the glory of it, or, even worse, changing the vision. Possibly in ways you don't like."

"Yeah!" Cam was relieved. Sofia did understand.

Sofia put on an empathetic look. "Your mental model is completely wrong."

"Huh?" Cam was taken aback.

"You aren't losing a share of the glory when you bring in a partner; you're giving your creation a chance to be so much bigger." Sofia's voice took on heat as she continued. "You aren't going to lose something essential by relinquishing some control of your vision either; you are going to gain the experience and perspective of another person. One that can help temper and shape your vision to address some of the gaps in your own ideas." Sofia flicked an invisible speck of dirt off her shoulder. "And, in my case, that experience and perspective is *very* valuable."

Cam looked off into the distance. "This is about the perspective matrix again?"

Sofia fluttered her eyelashes primly.

"But I *like* struggling with the stuff I'm not good at . . ." Cam began.

"That's your prerogative, if you want to keep Specio as a permanent side project rather than actually getting anywhere with it. Build an actual product, or keep tinkering?"

"You sound like you've done this before," Cam said ruefully. She gave Sofia a slight smile.

Sofia nodded. "Yes." Under her breath, she said, "Those music videos featuring inexplicably frequent occurrences of mannequins didn't film *themselves.*" More loudly she went on, "However, that also gives me the experience to know *I* have a requirement if we are to work together," Sofia said.

That blindsided Cam. "What's that?" she asked.

"Equality."

Cam deployed her favorite stalling tactic. "Uh."

Sofia faced Cam straight on and made continuous eye contact as she listed her demands. "We must be equals. I will own it as much as you." After a pause, she added, quietly, brow furrowed, "Because I *did* just lose a project I had been dreaming and working on for so long."

Cam's chest constricted at the pain wrought on Sofia's normally stoic brow. She reached across and squeezed her friend's hand. Sofia tightly squeezed Cam's hand back and looked at her intently, her heart bared. "I do not want to be in a position where I can have my work snatched away again. I need you to respect my thoughts on this project as much as your own. We won't always agree, but you must agree to listen. It is a requirement if I am to be as invested in our success as you are." Sofia's eyes bore into her with an almost physical pressure. Finally, Sofia eased the tension a fraction with a tiny smile. "As Michiko said in *Karate Tango 3,* 'We will dance together, or we will die together.'"

"You really see this dream as something big enough and interesting enough to invest yourself in it as much as I am. . . ." Cam paused for a moment, took a breath, and started over. "The project would be very lucky to have you, and I would be extremely thankful. Terms accepted." Saying the words aloud, she got that light feeling in her gut again, like a promising future was unveiling itself.

Sofia looked smug. "You see? We could've skipped all that and just gotten straight to thanking me." Then she thrust her hand forward.

Cam shook Sofia's hand to seal the deal and laughed. "I'm glad your unassailable confidence is back. Those cheap lenses are so inconsistent; they will absolutely beat you to shit getting things to look good." Cam suddenly realized she had a lot of work to do to make collaboration with Sofia go smoothly. "So . . . I guess we need to figure out a space to work in now, huh?"

Chapter 28

"RUNNING LATE; BE THERE SOON. Hope you've got a normal-sized head."
Lee Baker's holographic face cackled at a bewildered Cam before
abruptly hanging up. Cam didn't really have a great gauge on the relative
normalcy of the size of her head.

The day was, by most accounts, absurdly beautiful. It was a little bit cool,
but that suited Cam in her layers, and the sun shone bright from a clear sky
on the exhaustively landscaped Beekor campus greenery. There was nothing
to mar the flawless day except for the dim roar of a distant motorcycle. Cam
checked the time.

Cam had struggled to focus the entire day at work. Her attention had
continually ping-ponged between Sofia and Marcus. Her thoughts were a
confused jumble. She was still struggling to process the idea of Sofia as an
equal owner of Specio. The prospect of working with her on her dream was
both exciting and terrifying. And Marcus . . . The roar of the motorcycle
engine grew louder. Cam settled back on her heels.

The situation with Marcus was similarly confusing. When they were together, it felt wonderful and fun and relaxing. She felt like she could do anything with him, hang out and play video games on the couch, go sky-diving in Australia or backpacking through the Amazon. No matter what they did, she knew they would enjoy it with each other. The problem was, it was near impossible to get ahold of him. Even now, after he gave her that beautiful card, she hadn't seen him in the days since the conference. He was constantly being pulled away in other directions, and Cam didn't know where that left her.

The roar of the motorcycle suddenly became intensely loud, cutting through every thought in Cam's head.

Lee Baker screeched to a stop in front of Cam. Her black-and-red sport bike looked like a bird of prey, poised to devour. She leaned back in her riding leathers, placed one booted heel on the pavement, flipped up her helmet visor with a gloved hand, and grinned wickedly Cam's way. "Let's go. We're gonna see the bison." Cam barely caught the helmet she tossed.

It turned out Cam's head was normal sized. Or at least, within the standard range for a motorcycle helmet. It looked like it was going to be another day of sightseeing. Cam didn't know if she was really in the mood. Still, she obligingly made a death grip around the older woman's waist as Lee Baker blazed across city streets, slaloming down one-ways and lane-splitting between cars. Cam was just starting to overcome the existential terror and enjoy the feeling of the ride when they reached Golden Gate Park. Lee took it slower within the park boundaries. Cam relaxed her body as vast tracts of greenery streamed past. Lee slowed and pulled over on the side of a road by a large fenced-off area of rolling green hills.

Cam slid off the bike and pulled off her helmet. Lee stepped up beside her. Lee had not been hyperbolizing. There was an actual herd of live bison, though they looked more like a half dozen brown lumps off in the distance. Cam supposed there was a majesty to them. "So," Cam began. Lee looked at the bison with her and smiled.

"Look at these lazy fuckers." She leaned on the fence and jerked her chin casually at Cam. "So, what's Wyatt having you do these days?"

"Still on the influencer customization program. The perks . . ." Cam trailed off.

"The perks are insane, huh? But don't let them distract you from what you actually want." Lee took out her vape pen and puffed in a cavalier manner over the fence. "What do you actually want?"

Cam thought deeply, and suddenly realized she didn't quite know. What had once seemed a clear road at the beginning of the page program had taken unexpected deviations. What she had once thought was a straight road was starting to mimic a corn maze. She tried to be present and look at the bison, but the weight of her thoughts and everything with Sofia intruded. Her attention skittered, and she crossed her arms and tapped her foot restlessly.

"What's going on?" Lee asked, picking up on Cam's mood.

Cam took a breath. She was too preoccupied to try her usual attempts to flatter or impress Lee Baker. She let it out. "Can I get your advice?"

Lee turned to face Cam fully, attention laser-focused on her young protégé. "Of course. What's the problem?"

Cam started hesitantly, "So one of the other pages . . . Sofia? She had this whole project that she was working on to help her with facial recognition." Gaining confidence, Cam continued. "It basically recognizes the person you're looking at, gives some data about when you last saw them, stuff like that."

Lee nodded.

"Well, the exact same invention showed up at the Beekor conference. Wyatt announced it onstage and everything. But Sofia says she wasn't involved at all." Cam stared at Lee, gauging her reaction.

Lee winced. She looked pensive, then turned and waved for Cam to follow. Together, they crossed the street and entered a thicket. Lee talked as she walked. "The company will take everything from you if it can. *Any* company will. You can give forever, and the company will still want more."

More quietly, "I should know." As they walked, she peered through the foliage, looking for something.

She went on. "It's up to you to protect yourself."

"You think they stole Sofia's project?" Cam asked plaintively.

"Would Wyatt play dirty? Of course."

Cam stopped. "I . . . I don't want to believe that." And she didn't. She didn't want to think the company she was working at, one that had given her access to so much, and one at which she hoped to create amazing things in the future could be . . . bad. Lee continued searching for a moment before she realized Cam had stopped. She turned back to face Cam in the woods. "Maybe it's . . . What did Sofia say? Convergent evolution?" In the light of day, Cam thought the words sounded flimsy.

"*Could* be," Lee said. "Beekor has a lot of fingers in a lot of pies. All those resources go to an absolute fuckton of projects at the same time." Lee resumed checking trees. "Or somebody in legal nabbed it. It's in their job description to seek maximum advantage for the company." The thought put Cam on edge. She had no clue how to deal with her benefactor and likely future employer also possibly being malicious.

At the same time, Cam knew there was some kind of very personal tension brewing between Wyatt and Lee. She still had no idea what it was, but suffice it to say, Lee's clear dislike could be affecting her judgment about the supposedly malevolent practices of Beekor. Cam needed to ask someone more neutral.

"Yes!" Lee exclaimed. She was touching a tree with a rough X scratched on it. She paced a few steps in a different direction, looked around a bit, then looked satisfied as she came across another tree with an X slashed into it. Looking appraisingly back at the first tree, she stepped to the halfway point between them, then walked forward several paces. "Fuck," she shouted frustratedly. She turned and strolled purposefully out of the thicket.

She got back on the bike. "C'mon."

Lee took Cam down several roads within the park and pulled up near a traditional-looking Japanese gate with tiered eaves. The gate was closed. Several tourists out in front strained to reach above the hedges to take pictures of the space beyond. Lee parked the bike. "So what is your friend doing now? The one who got her shit jacked."

"Sofia," Cam supplied. "So," she began, tentatively, "I may have recruited her to work on Specio with me." She said it slowly, as if testing out the words for the first time to see how they felt.

Lee brightened. "A cofounder! That's great news!" she exclaimed excitedly, hands on Cam's shoulders.

Yeah, Cam realized, belatedly, it really *was* great news. Sofia was so awesome, she could probably work on anything, with anyone that she wanted, and she had chosen to work with *Cam*!

"Well, we only just decided it," Cam began a little bashfully. Lee turned and waved for Cam to follow, leading them past the tourists and up to the gate. Cam continued. "I've been struggling with sharing my personal project with someone else, you know? I'm used to being in control."

Lee nodded ruefully. "Oldest story in Silicon Valley. The relationship between founders, your trust for each other, is probably the single most important resource you've got. You need to protect and manage that.

"Building a start-up . . . realizing your vision, employing others, adding something to the world. It feels incredible." Her look grew distant. "But it comes at a cost. The terrible anxiety, stress, and the feeling of being utterly alone. That's where the team comes in.

"You're only as strong as your team. Alone, you can be as impressive as you want." Lee leaned against the gate wall, pointed at her eyes, and then pointed at Cam's. Cam took the hint and furtively scouted the area for any sort of authority figures. The coast was clear. Cam nodded at Lee. Lee slid a thin strip of metal between the doors of the closed gate and fiddled with it until something clicked. "But together, you can be so much more." Lee slid one of the doors open wide. She grinned at Cam and beckoned her hurriedly in.

Inside, the Japanese Tea Garden was a series of pagodas painted a bright, brilliant red, thrusting up to the sky from behind a profusion of immaculately pruned little spherical bushes and trees. There was a picturesque pond with fallen leaves collected at the surface. Low wooden posts sketched the outline of a peaceful, meandering path around and over the pond, toward the pagodas. The two of them walked the path in silence for a moment. Cam felt a peace settle around her heart.

"Not fucking bad, eh?" Lee began to inspect specific posts along the walkway.

Cam sighed. Several feet ahead, she spotted a post with a small arrow scratched into the top of the wood. "Here," she said, and pointed.

Lee smiled amiably. "How very 'disruptive' of you." She wandered off the path into another thicket. Cam kept watch for authorities. She heard branches snagging, leaves rustling, twigs snapping, and then a single, exclaimed "Yes!" Some more snaps and rustling. Then Lee came rushing back out of the thicket. She was clutching an enormous marijuana plant.

"What the actual fuck?!" Cam cried. "We passed three dispensaries on the way here."

Lee laughed. "Where's the fun in that, Cam? A leopard can't change her spots!" She hurriedly made her way back down the path to the entry to the Japanese Tea Garden, and Cam crouch-jogged after her. At the gate, Lee poked her head out the door, then snapped it back in quickly and gestured for Cam to wait with a raised hand.

Lee addressed Cam in a sober tone. "Beekor wasn't just Wyatt and me, you know. There were more of us. Bet your ass we wouldn't have gotten as far without them." Lee tapped Cam's helmet to signal her to put it back on, then pulled on her own, visor still up. She continued. "A great team with a bad idea is better than a great idea with a bad team. A great team can course correct and overcome anything."

Lee signaled that the coast was clear and pushed the door open and strode out of the courtyard at a brisk pace.

"Hey!" a large man in a brown Recreation and Parks uniform shouted at them from down the walk. He began yelling into a walkie-talkie and huffing after them. Cam and Lee sprinted, laughing, to Lee's bike and leapt onto it. Lee started it, revved the engine loud. Cam tapped her shoulder to signal she was in place, and Lee gunned it out of there.

Chapter 29

SUNDAY MORNING, CAM WAS QUITE nervous about seeing Sofia. Despite having lived in the same house for months, been on innumerable of Avery's adventures together, and supported each other through heartbreak and triumph, Cam still worried about something going wrong on their first real day working together. At any rate, Cam had already done all the prep work, and it was time to bite the bullet. She took a breath, then knocked on Sofia's door.

Sofia opened the door looking flawless, as usual.

"Morning." Cam attempted to project chipper normalcy.

"Morning," Sofia confirmed.

Cam gave up. She couldn't just dismiss her trepidation that easily. She wanted Sofia to love the space she had set up and for everything to go smoothly and for this weird, formal shift in their relationship to be effortless and easy, but it was all stacked up in her head and she decided to just vent it instead.

"All right, I've gotta say, I'm a little nervous right now." Cam realized she was sort of yelling. "Let's just see how this goes."

Sofia smiled slightly. "Remember Domina Patronella."

Cam thought for a moment. "From *Dancepocalypse: Nights*? When she dances her first duet with Georgette and, over the course of the song, goes from stumbling over trying to lead to learning to relinquish control and dance in perfect harmony?"

Sofia nodded.

Dance Nights truly did have a lesson to impart for every occasion. Cam smiled ruefully. "You're right. You're so right." She perked up. "Anyway, to my room! Grab your computer."

As they climbed to the attic, Cam made small talk. "What are you doing at Beekor now?"

"The same busywork. I requested a meeting with Wyatt."

That stopped Cam short. "Wow, what did he say?"

Sofia gave an acid look. "'This was all a big misunderstanding.'" She said in a scarily good impression of Wyatt's jovial manner. "I am not so easily fooled." Sofia visibly shook off the anger. "But one good turn deserves another, so let's get building!" She gestured Cam forward to the office reveal.

Cam had been, demonstrably, very busy. Cam had asked Jennifer for what office supplies she could have, and Jennifer had cheerfully replied that Cam only needed to file a ticket with IT, and it would automatically be charged to the Accelerator Program account. Jennifer implied that the account didn't really have a limit, as long as she wasn't buying a spaceship. But even that was negotiable. So Cam filed a ticket with IT to secure a whiteboard, two desks, extra-large screens for each desk, attached via boom arm and fully connected to power supplies, as well as the fully loaded version of the office chairs that Beekor used, with lumbar and neck support adjustment knobs.

Daphne from IT had arrived in a truck with all the items. "I just wanted to see where you all live. This shit is nice. Yeah, no, I'm not helping you bring it upstairs." Daphne had simply reclined across three barstools in the kitchen and swiped through her phone as Cam slowly hauled everything she had asked for to the attic. Partway through this seemingly Sisyphean task, James emerged from the garage workshop with a large pair of rainbow-sheened metallic headphones over his ears.

"James," Cam panted. "Could I ask you to help me?" She was in the process of pushing one of the armchairs across the living room to the stairs.

James looked at the chair, looked at the direction Cam was headed, and said, "You can ask. But I will say no."

Daphne broke out laughing. James froze and looked over at the reclining young woman. Daphne lowered her feet off one of the barstools. "James, NecroTopolis has just dropped their latest album, come over here and listen with me." James obliged, sat on the edge of the proffered chair, and took his headphones off.

"So, how's your computer doing? Any new glitches? You seem to get a lot of them," Daphne inquired with a smirk.

James made a noncommittal noise before suggesting, "You want to listen to it on one of the speakers I made? They're down in the garage."

"Hells yes," Daphne enthused, jumping up from her stool. "Lead the way."

Cam, meanwhile, had continued to make round trips until everything was upstairs, and Daphne had returned to campus. Although Cam noticed that Daphne had left with a speaker that looked like a skull cradled reverently in her arms. In her room, Cam had pushed aside the vanity to make space for the two desks, installed the power strips, set up the whiteboard, attached the monitors, placed the chairs, and even put down a vase with a couple flowers from the garden.

After all that work, Cam held her breath when Sofia entered the space for the first time, watching for Sofia's reaction. Sofia stopped as if stunned. After a beat, she walked up to one of the two desks and slid the chair aside. On the desk, Cam had already placed a fresh Danish and a cup of coffee. Cam had done an early morning café run to ensure everything was perfect for their first day. Sofia held up the Danish. "Incredible," she whispered, her back to Cam.

Cam laughed in relief and rubbed her eyes. As she took in Sofia, holding a Danish, standing in their office, she felt a dam break. Cam's first office of her own! She shook it off, then placed her computer on the desk beside Sofia. "Let's make sure everything works! Plug in."

While Sofia was booting up, Cam turned on the whiteboard and opened it to the project management dashboard she had set up just for them. After a moment, Sofia noticed, and she grinned while shaking her head. "You didn't."

Cam laughed like a madman. She had customized the project dashboard with a *Dance Nights* theme. Don Julio; his mother, Georgette; and Snake Malone were dispersed all across the top of the board in the banner area and the margins, each one in respective states of dance ecstasy. An animated image of Don Julio was doing spins on the top of the user-count bar graph.

Cam rubbed her hands together with wicked glee. "I'm just getting started, cofounder!" As soon as she said it, she felt her heart flutter and her breathing hitch a bit. It felt really good to say. She had a cofounder! She wanted to yell it out loud, but she decided she had already done enough embarrassing things today already. She let the feeling warm her for a moment before getting down to business.

"All right, let's get you invited to the project so you can see all my files!"

Cam got all the files and project management tools shared with Sofia, then began actually walking Sofia through the way installation of Specio worked. Sofia took copious notes and asked many questions, some of which hit Cam in a weird way. All of a sudden, the embarrassment and nervousness she had briefly experienced when Sofia had looked at her matrix errors the other day returned with a vengeance. Cam wasn't ready to feel so exposed like that.

"Look, there are reasons why I ended up doing it this way," Cam suddenly found herself protesting.

Sofia put a hand up to stop her. "No judgment." She paused for a moment and looked thoughtful. "Even I, a genius, have committed code atrocities."

Hearing it called "code atrocities" made Cam feel, if possible, even worse. They continued with the installation process, and Cam worked hard to keep her cool, but she struggled with the building sense that what she had made was full of too many weird hacks, flaws, and shortcuts. It felt like she was displaying all her dirty laundry to Sofia, and she kept finding herself feeling defensive about every weird installation step that Sofia tsked at or took notes about.

Eventually, she succumbed. "Yeah," Cam found herself saying as they reached yet another embarrassing step in the installation. "I wrote almost all my code for splitting the holographic data up to send different streams to the light pipes using an old library that ended up adding all these weird extra installation requirements for the user, but I was too far along at that point to rewrite everything—"

"The best code is no code," Sofia said cryptically.

"Huh?"

"The best code is no code. Everything we write is a mess, or, if it's beautiful, it becomes subject to entropy. Or it ends up being written for one reason, only for us to realize we actually need something different later on." Sofia nodded, seemingly to herself. "But since we must write code in order to achieve our goals, we must accept that we will make a mess."

Cam tried to take it to heart. "Right . . ."

"And don't get me wrong, this is a *real* mess." Sofia laughed. The tension broke, and Cam laughed as well. "But that's why you have me." Sofia paused for a moment as if considering something. "Your cofounder." She said it like she was trying out the word too, getting a sense for how it fit, the same way that Cam had. Sophia gave Cam a sweet smile.

Chapter 30

OVER THE NEXT TWO WEEKS of nights and weekends, the value of a fresh set of eyes on the code for Specio became abundantly clear. Under Sofia's ownership, things that Cam had been too deep in the code to notice, or things that Cam just hadn't had time to do, started coming together one by one. Installation got easier. Performance improved. Sofia even set up automation tools that made it so every time she made a change, it would update a connected device immediately without needing to manually click, drag, or otherwise move things around to test the new code on the device. As a result, iteration time dropped and it became far easier to change things and see how they worked, vastly increasing the pace of the project. Tickets on their *Dance Nights*–themed project management task board moved into the done column faster and faster.

And just like that, Cam and Sofia were ready to release their first new build to their users. That is, to Cam's mom. And maybe her study group, but Cam wasn't holding her breath. Now that Rosa could actually, finally, receive holochat calls, Cam arranged to do one with her mom to talk about the new changes. Cam put an event on her and Sofia's calendar. "User Feedback Interview." That Cam would get the opportunity to introduce her shiny new cofounder and best friend to her mom as well was just a pleasant side effect. As Cam and Sofia readied themselves for the call, Cam thought she caught a moment where Sofia actually looked nervous, although her signature impassive expression quickly reasserted itself.

Cam initiated the call. Rosa answered after two rings, and then her face was projected in the air in front of Cam and Sofia. She appeared to be reclining in their living room. Her hair was a bit mussed and hastily tied back. Cam realized that, holding this call at night after work and classes, her mom had probably already washed her face and moisturized for the evening. Rosa looked a bit tired but cheerful as ever.

"Cammy, ¡mi amor!" she enthused. "I'm so excited to do our first holochat!" She squinted close to the view feed, and her face came close to Cam and Sofia. "What have you done to your hair?"

Cam smiled wide and turned side to side, framing her new hair for her mom to see. "You like? Avery helped!"

"It's wonderful!" Rosa crowed, then fanned her face. "Oh, my beautiful baby." With a visible effort, she composed herself again. "And is this supermodel friend of yours Avery?"

Cam beamed pridefully and put her hands on Sofia's shoulders. "No, Mom, this is Sofia. My *cofounder!*"

Rosa erupted into laughter and sounds of happiness, clearly proud of her daughter. The resemblance was unmistakable, as Cam bounced up and down in time with her mom, jostling Sofia all over. Sofia gave a tiny wave while the overwhelming waves of happiness from mother and daughter washed over her.

"Good to meet you, Ms. Diaz," Sofia finally managed to get a word in after the cheering petered out.

Rosa dismissed Sofia's formality with a hand wave. "None of that Ms. Diaz, please. Call me Rosa!" She made a thoughtful face. "Thank you for being such a good friend to my daughter; she's told me all about you."

"Oh?" Sofia looked at Cam.

Cam laughed. "Only good things, I promise!"

Rosa nodded vigorously. "Mm-hmm. I'm so proud of my Cammy, making such great, supportive friends." The image shook suddenly, and the microphone picked up fumbling hand noises all over Rosa's phone. "How—how do I take a screenshot with this?"

"It's the two buttons on the side, Mom. Press them together."

They heard the camera shutter noise of a screenshot. "All right, moment captured." Rosa reappeared in the holographic video projection. "So, Sofia, are you making sure to protect Cam? She can expect too much from herself, too fast, and she gets disappointed when it doesn't happen."

"I've observed." Sofia sounded wry.

"I'm right here, Mom," Cam said, exasperated.

Rosa continued as if she hadn't heard Cam. "She has always been a bit more optimistic than is reasonable about what she could achieve, and in how long."

"Motivation," Sofia said.

"What's that?" Rosa inquired.

"Motivation," she repeated. "I think that optimism and self-belief is what keeps her so motivated and gives her the temerity to try ambitious things."

Rosa was quiet for a moment. Then, "Cam, your cofounder is very wise!" She spoke cannily. "But she also didn't answer my question."

"I promise to protect Cam from getting too far ahead of herself and becoming disappointed when reality doesn't quite live up to her optimistic vision." Cam looked nonplussed.

Rosa nodded, satisfied. "Good, good. Now, Cam, you were saying you have a new version of your software for me to install?"

Cam excitedly peered into the holographic field projecting her mother in front of her. "I sent you the new installation steps! You'll notice there are only twenty-seven steps now." She laughed haughtily. "All thanks to the improvements made by my new cofounder."

Sofia pantomimed taking a bow.

"You only need to do the second part of the installation since you already have the hardware, and you just need to update. Oh, and can you share these with the study group? I'm hoping maybe it will be easy enough for them to try too."

Cam and Sofia gave a quick explanation of the new steps, and Rosa left the call to try them out. It only took thirty minutes and a few panicked texts for help before she had gotten things working again. To Cam, it felt like a major sign of progress.

Chapter 31

"HOW IS THE NEW PROTOCOL work going?" Sofia asked from the doorway.

"Uh," Cam replied distractedly. She was deep in thought at her laptop and didn't bother to turn around.

"I hope you're at a stopping point," Sofia continued, and then paused.

"Hmm." Cam thought she had an idea where her code was flawed. She swapped over to a different file and found the issue.

"Because you need to stop now." Sofia said it with finality.

"Huh?" Cam turned in her chair. Sofia was dressed as an extremely tall, extremely glamorous bee.

Cam was as eloquent as ever. "Wha?!"

Avery poked their head into the doorway behind Sofia. They were at the center of a voluminous ring of bright pink petals. They put one leaf-shrouded hand on Sofia's shoulder. "By the way, it's Tacky Tourist Time. Let's *go!*"

Cam exhaled long through her nose and highlighted the stuff she needed to change in her code. Maybe she would get to it later in the day. She looked over to see Avery hefting a bottle labeled "Pollen" to take a swig of something that smelled poisonous even from here. Avery laughed. Maybe she would get to the fixes tomorrow, Cam thought resignedly.

The pages assembled downstairs for Sofia to give them all the rundown. James was seated at the kitchen island, examining a Japanese robot toy that could transform. Cam flopped on the couch. Sofia and Avery stood in the open area between kitchen and living room.

"As you know, I am an avid runner," Sofia explained.

James made brief, pained eye contact with Cam. Cam took his cue and asked, "So we're doing a . . . marathon for Tacky Tourist Time today?"

"Technically a 12K," Sofia replied.

Avery laughed. Marcus took that moment to come in through the front door, looking determined, as if he were in the midst of an arduous task.

"Thank you for coming, Marcus. I will require you to change into something more appropriate in short order," Sofia said with precision.

"Uh, appropriate for what?" Marcus asked, clearly shaking his thoughts free from whatever was plaguing him.

Avery cackled. "Bay to Breakers, baby!"

Marcus looked as if he were about to say something, then just nodded.

Cam felt the familiar fluttering in her chest from seeing Marcus again, looking as though he had stepped from a magazine. But this time, it was, strangely, accompanied by a vague feeling of annoyance. Surprised at her own reaction, Cam tried to cover it up by dubiously looking at Sofia's and Avery's outfits. "Don't we need, like, athletic gear?"

Marcus went over to her on the couch and put one big, warm hand on her shoulder. Hands she had become familiar with in her dreams. Cam felt a zing go down to her core at that touch. She looked up at the mischievous glint in his eye and, inexplicably, felt her face want to crumple into a scowl before she willed it to neutrality.

"Don't worry about that," Marcus advised. "Just prep some of your margaritas to go."

They arrived at the Embarcadero via separate Beekars a short while later. The financial epicenter of the city and one of its most easterly districts with a view across the water to San Francisco's sister city, Oakland, it was clearly the "Bay" part. Cam didn't know where the "Breakers" were. Given only thirty minutes, the vague directive to "put on a costume, and it better be good" from Avery, and whatever they could find in the house, James, Marcus, and Cam were dressed to various degrees of success. Cam, used to wearing clothing a decade out of date, rummaged through her old wardrobe and managed a convincing re-creation of a pop star who had been all the rage when she was a child, complete with ponytail and wispy bangs. James had cobbled together a hoodie-casual re-creation of a classic video game character who dressed in green, though his crowning achievement was the sword he made from a cardboard box and aluminum foil. But by far the winner was Marcus, who had found purple balloons from somewhere and attached them to a tank top so he looked like a bunch of grapes. An incredibly sculpted and delicious-looking bunch of grapes with arms cut from rock. Really, thought Cam, grapes had no right to be sexy. Or at least, ones made out of quick craft supplies shouldn't be. And yet, there Marcus was, a sexy bunch of grapes sliding out of his Beekar to stand next to Cam. She again felt that flickering burn of resentment toward him.

"Everybody ready for the race?" Avery asked through a shit-eating grin. At least a dozen random passersby responded with whooping cheers. Embarcadero itself was bedlam. They were in front of a vast skyscraper right up against the ocean waters in the bay, and they were surrounded by a great throng of people who appeared to have failed at the race before even having started. People dressed as dinosaurs, ghosts, monkeys, and more mundane casual clothes milled about, drinking, yelling, and emitting vast clouds of weed smoke.

"Okay, ready, set, go!" Avery shouted, waving a beckoning leaf forward. Cam couldn't tell if Avery's face was red from makeup or if they were already half-drunk.

"What, we just go? We don't need to register or something?" Cam queried. Although it didn't look like most of the throng who were starting to stream down the street had numbers on their . . . costumes. James, for his part, was doing his best to keep a six-foot distance from the rest of the jostling crowd.

"C'mon," Sofia called back to them. She was already well ahead, moving at a comfortable jog.

The pages struggled to follow her even at her most relaxed pace. All around them, people dressed as hot dogs, video game plumbers, and many, many completely naked people raced past, laughing or screaming. Avery was probably one of the *least* drunk people in the crowd, Cam observed. The race started off downtown among tall buildings in the Financial District. Even this early, all around them, runners were giving up and either stopping to drink and hang out right where they were, or just walking.

Cam struggled to speed up to reach Sofia. "How . . . *long* is this?" Cam managed to gasp.

"Around seven miles," Sofia said easily, not even winded.

Avery interjected, flower petals hitting Cam in the face. "Don't worry about that. Nobody actually finishes the race."

The pages didn't run for very long. Sofia could've gone forever, it appeared, but James, in particular, was huffing and struggling in short order. His efforts ended in an unexpected climax. A helpful man dressed as the pope at the side of the road was offering drinks from a pitcher. Grateful for some water, James went up to the man and requested a cup. After reciting the required three Hail Marys, James received his cup and returned to the waiting pages. He took a sip and immediately spat it back out. "Vodka," he said with a blank look. Cam took the cup from him, unwilling to waste free vodka. From that point on, they all walked.

As the pages walked from the downtown area to increasingly residential areas, the giant, roving party devolved. The actual serious runners still streaked through but everybody else was walking, and house parties on all sides spilled out onto the sidewalks and into the vaguely mobile throng.

People dressed as eggplants and jelly doughnuts aggressively freaked to loud music blaring from windows and roof patios. Cam saw an alien kissing a corncob on the front steps of one house, and a pink gorilla kissing a human banana on the ground by a bus stop. And always, naked runners wove in and among them all.

Avery made the rest of the pages wait as they ducked into a random house party. They emerged a short time later with a refilled bottle of "pollen," everybody in the party cheering for them. On reuniting with the rest of the pages, Avery made a sloppy, uncoordinated bow, flourishing leaves and petals to offer the bottle up to Sofia, who took it and chugged massively. Marcus laughed and put an arm casually around Cam. Cam, delightfully buzzed from the vodka and her margarita, squeezed several of the balloons aside and leaned into him, relaxing easily into his warmth. Any ill feelings she had toward him earlier in the day were washed away by jovial camaraderie.

The pages, flanked by their cacophonous procession, eventually arrived at the panhandle of Golden Gate Park. James, whose enthusiasm had rapidly depleted during the course of the walk, became very alert all of a sudden. Finally, he spotted his target and made a beeline for a young woman in black who was reclining under a tree on a blanket with some friends gathered around a familiar-looking skull speaker. As she turned to look at James with a smirk, Cam recognized her as Daphne from IT. Cam looked sharply between James and Daphne as he flopped onto her blanket, accepting a bottle of actual water from Daphne, and did not bother looking back. Maybe it was no longer "Daphne from IT" and more like "James's Daphne." "Bye," Cam yelled at James's back. Daphne waved once at them.

Inside the park, there were stages set up along the trail with live music playing. The pages wove in and among them, briefly erupting into dance during particularly good songs. Cam lost her empty margarita jug some-where along the way, and while she was attempting to get her eyes to focus, Marcus put his hands on her hips. She grinned and popped several of his balloons so she could dance close against him, going low along with the extremely raunchy song that was playing. They both paused to watch as a swarm of human butterflies swept past Avery, each one flapping wings in Avery's face. "Nature truly is beautiful," Marcus opined.

Sofia danced up to Avery, wings and stinger athrust. "I require more pollen."

Avery hefted the bottle, but it was, once again, empty. "My reserves are out," they said sadly.

"Perhaps I could get some direct from the source." Sofia looked devilishly into Avery's eyes, then bent down to take Avery's face in hands and kiss them among the petals. It went on for a while.

"You know, if this were accurate, you would be rubbing your ass on my face," Avery said after they broke.

As the two of them walked off, Cam heard Sofia reply, "That can be arranged."

Electronic dance music built to an epic crescendo as Cam and Marcus faced each other. With no thought at all, simply that she knew she wanted it, Cam put a hand to his face, and they crashed together. Tongues sought each other and lips pulled, a tiny island of two from within the inebriated crowd.

He felt so good; why weren't they kissing like this all the time? Cam thought as she sucked at his plump lips. Oh yeah, it was because she hadn't seen him since the conference after-party. One of Marcus's hands crushed her to him, and the other pulled up her thigh to wrap around his waist. The party where Sofia had been so upset.

Cam separated them, panting, with one hand on Marcus's broad chest.

"You know, I've been thinking about something," she began, the ground swaying even though both her feet were planted firmly.

Marcus smiled in anticipation. "What's that?" His hands rested on her waist and gently squeezed, his thumbs rubbing in small, delicious circles.

As if unable to control what she was saying, she continued on. "I've been thinking that you knew what was going to happen to Sofia." Abruptly, Marcus stepped back, dropping his hands. He looked pained. Part of her was screaming for ruining whatever was happening between her and Marcus. But another part, freed by the power of alcohol, was giving vent to feelings she hadn't even known she felt. And had felt for a while. Feelings that had been leaking out all day. It was like her mouth was attached to an entirely different part of her brain. "You seemed to know her project was going to get stolen. But you didn't warn her."

Marcus furrowed his brow. "What good would it have done?"

"So you *did* know." Suddenly, that hidden anger welled to the surface in a dark ooze. "It would have possibly helped prepare your *friend* for some awful news," she spat. "So your *friend* wouldn't have to deal with it on the show floor during a conference." She realized she wasn't just angry, she was livid.

"That's not my job," Marcus shot back.

Cam sneered. "And only your job matters, right?" Stop, please, the more rational part of Cam thought. But it was like a chain-link fence trying to hold back a tidal wave. "That's why you choose Beekor over your friends!" She built to an angry yell. "That's why you're never around!" She almost said "Not even for *us*," but finally managed to bite her tongue.

Marcus flinched as if struck; then his face became passive. A cold wall dropped down between them, and he took a step back. "Some of us have a future to think about." The lack of emotion in his voice hurt Cam more than his anger. "I suggest you call a car to get home." He spun and stalked off.

Cam trembled with rage and spent adrenaline as she watched his form disappear among the crowd.

Chapter 32

CAM'S USUAL PUNISHMENT FOR PEOPLE when they angered her was to ignore them. It was typically pretty effective. Rosa would wait for Cam to cool off, and Cam would wait for Rosa to understand how she had upset her daughter. Then Rosa would make something delicious as an apology, and Cam would eat all of it to show she accepted the apology. Only this time, Cam's ignoring tactic was useless in the face of Marcus's complete absence. If this hadn't been his exact same behavior as before, Cam would think Marcus was the one ignoring her.

Sofia, wandering casually out of Avery's room the next day, seemed to sense that something had happened between Cam and Marcus. But intuitive as she was, she also sensed that Cam didn't want to talk about it. Instead, Sofia helped Cam funnel her excess energy into Specio.

Which is how late the next Saturday afternoon found Cam and Sofia up in their attic office. It had gotten a bit hot, so Cam had opened the sliding door of her deck a crack. With the open window on the other side of the room, the cross-breeze shifted some papers on Cam's desk. Cam was explaining how some of the hardware worked. She had a 3D model up on her computer for Sofia to look at.

"If you look at this part of the chassis, it holds the lens assembly in place, with a series of light pipes underneath it, as well as the interface that plugs into the phone." She pointed to the blocky, homemade-looking shape that held the lens in place pictured on the slide. "You can see that it basically snaps down over here. . . ." She traced a specific hinge on the image of colorful plastic and made a snapping motion with her hands.

Sofia cocked her head. "Can you show me that on the prototype?"

"Sure, just a second." Cam fished in her bag for the prototype, and when she pulled it out, a piece immediately fell off. "Shit!"

"Can you fix it?" Sofia asked a little dubiously.

"Yeah," Cam began. Then she suddenly felt overwhelmed as she recalled all the work she had to do to help out Rosa's study group. One of them, Rudy, had actually managed to install his own Specio, which meant they were at a whopping two whole users! But a couple others had gotten stuck, and Rosa had set them up for a call with Cam to walk through everything. Cam took on a harried look as she contemplated taking the time out to set up a new 3D print job and watch over it.

Sofia, by now accustomed to Cam's distraught look of being pulled in multiple directions, said, "I warned you about this."

"Warned me about what?!" Cam felt almost like she was being scolded.

"We are a team now. And teams do not let individuals struggle alone. Individual suffering collapses the entire team. But individuals are also responsible for asking for help. You must ask the people around you and your friends. They would enjoy assisting you."

Cam got it. "We should ask James."

Sofia smiled slightly. "We should ask James."

They found James downstairs in the basement garage, in his customary spot. Even after having used it for weeks, Cam still had to make a conscious effort not to ogle the 3D printer humming away in the corner. James was bent forward, hands drumming a beat under the table as he scrutinized some complex mechanism exploded out across several parts on the bench. He acknowledged them with a wave as they approached, but didn't look up, minutely adjusting the positions of the various objects on his workspace. The object looked a bit like a robot, but also a bit like a truck.

"Hey, James," Cam began. "We missed you last night after the mentor dinner." He had disappeared before Avery dragged Cam and Sofia to a live theater re-creation of an '80s action movie. Sofia had gotten selected to play the main character, a taciturn placeholder prop around whom the play revolved around requiring minimal involvement. Sofia had absolutely killed it for her two lines, "Whoa" and "Whoooa."

"Sorry about that, I was a bit too tired to take on crowds and lots of noise. . . ." James adjusted some bits in front of him, but he seemed at ease. "I decided to head home to try to deal with some computer issues. . . ."

"Computer issues, or computer people?" Sofia asked wryly.

Cam snickered, and James made a small, private smile. Cam realized just how much more open and comfortable James had become around her. It was like a wall had come down.

"What are you working on?" Cam asked.

James lit up. "It's a speaker shaped like a truck but . . ." He took off his headphones and began to shift some pieces around. "It transforms into a robot!"

Sofia blinked. Cam clapped with delight.

"How's your Beekor work going?" Cam asked.

James looked vaguely annoyed. "Finished my project. Last week, actually, and I haven't had an assignment since then. My adviser keeps rescheduling our meetings."

Cam shook her head, still unsure how to take the inconsistency in tasking between herself, James, and Sofia. "What do you think of it all so far?"

"This is great," he said gesturing to the hardware. "And being surrounded by so many people that just want to build, like me . . . I like that part."

Cam nodded energetically. "I know *exactly* what you mean." She'd had the same feeling upon meeting other engineers and makers just like herself since coming here. Face-to-face, around so many talented people, it was possible to exchange knowledge and learn from each other in ways she had never suspected. She had grown so much more capable as a result.

"But what they have me doing has been menial. When they have me doing anything, that is." He sounded frustrated.

"Well," she started, "if you're sort of in a holding pattern, maybe you have the time to look over my project?" She started backpedaling immediately. "If not, that's totally cool. I don't want to take up your precious time—"

Sofia cut Cam off with a hard look.

Cam took out the busted prototype, and James went utterly still, with his eyes trained on the pile of tech. "I think I already showed you this mechanism I made to snap a projector and lens assembly onto a wide range of variously shaped phones. Obviously, it's really bulky and inelegant. Not to mention, uh, broken." Cam handed James the prototype, several pieces now hanging off.

James took the prototype delicately and held it close to this face. He made a thoughtful "hmm" noise as he touched one of the dangling plastic pieces. Then he angled the piece back into position exactly where it should have been. "Hmm."

He rotated the device around. He looked down the barrel of the lens assembly and shifted it a bit. "Hmm." Then he actuated the snapping mechanism where the holder was attached to the phone. He made another noise, this one somehow more contemplative and intrigued-sounding. "Hmm."

As James began to take on the problem and run with it, Cam knew exactly what to say. "Do you think you could see a way to improve on the design here? Or maybe come up with something even better?" James's eyes gleamed. Critical hit.

"I'll take a look," James said quietly.

Sofia clapped. "Excellent. Welcome to the team."

"I'm still waiting on feedback from my adviser. I'm sure there will be more for me to do to prepare for commencement," James said as he put down the prototype and began to tap his heel again. "Whatever my adviser assigns is priority zero," he said resolutely. "But," he acquiesced in a softer tone, "absent that, I'll make this priority one."

"Of course." Sofia smiled. "Once you get feedback from your adviser."

James looked up. "I came to work for Beekor. I don't want to jeopardize that."

Cam decided to try a different tack. "I get you completely. We don't want you to risk your work at Beekor. However"—she stretched the syllables out, singing the word—"I recall that you wanted to work on making hardware more accessible to more people, something that they're not really letting you do." She paced a bit around the garage. "Specio is the same for me. But where you're aiming for physical accessibility, I'm aiming for cost accessibility, making holographic tech available to people that can't afford Beekor phones. Which begs the question . . ."

Cam stopped and spun, facing Sofia and James. "¿Por qué no los dos?"

James was quiet for a beat.

Cam began, "That means why not both–"

"I figured that," James cut her off. Eventually, he replied, "I'll need access to your files." He slid the speaker he was working on aside for the moment. "And we should probably discuss constraints a bit. I'll want to know how your projection system functions, as well as what device sizes need supporting."

Chapter 33

IT WAS SATURDAY MORNING, AND the pages were up early. The view from the deck was a complete, unobstructed view across the bay. A few fluffy, photogenic clouds scudded past, and sailboats dotted the water. The day was, inexplicably, even more perfect than usual. Cam was ready to seize it. She headed to the garage to find James.

Just a few days prior, after the twentieth time taking the stairs down three floors to the garage to chat with James and then back up in a single afternoon, Sofia's patience had finally run out. Cam and Sofia had vacated Cam's room and moved their Specio desks and screens down to the basement. James had been compelled to help carry furniture this time. Cam had taken a look around the newly emptied corner of her room, her first office, and felt an instant wave of nostalgia. Somehow, the thing they had created there had left some kind of mark on the space.

Which was why she now found James at his workspace in the garage cozily tucked between her own and Sofia's stations.

Cam gasped, "James, you're a magician!"

James looked up, and in his hands was a prototype that shaved a full inch off the obtrusive size of the adapter. She ran over for a closer look.

He gave a subtle smirk. "I realized we could achieve the same goal with the light pipes if I routed them around this side of the phone." He gestured with his hands. "Wrapping them flush with the edge allowed me to achieve a fifty-five percent reduction in overall device depth. It's still by no means pocket-ready, but I have some more radical concepts in mind, including grips or variants to accommodate users with disabilities."

Cam couldn't help but thank Lee Baker. She had been absolutely right. James and Sofia joining the team had already enabled her to achieve so much more. Their ability to deep dive on things she hadn't had the time for was paying massive dividends.

James attached the adapter to a test phone mounted and waiting on a custom jig. The test graphic appeared in short order.

"Holy . . ." Cam leaned in to inspect it, then gasped. "The image is sharper! This is incredible!"

James adjusted his headphones and looked down. He gave a rare, full-on smile. It was a great look for him. But Cam was getting distracted. Time to get focused on the task at hand, she thought.

"I need you to stop working right away, though."

James looked dismayed.

"No, no, you're doing great. *We're* doing great, but it's Saturday and I wanted us all to do something fun!" She decided to channel Lee Baker again. "Let's make sure to enjoy the city while we're here! It's not just work!"

James gave a long suffering sigh and began to pack away his tools. Cam thought about how James was always dragged with the rest of them and decided to approach the day's outing from a new angle.

"This time around, let's do what you want. What sort of activity would *you* enjoy?"

James stopped tidying up and pulled his headphones off. After a moment of thought, he replied, "I would like to go to a park."

Cam smiled brightly. "Done! I'll make a picnic for us. Sound good?"

James nodded.

"All right, I'll get ready. Leave in an hour?"

James nodded again with a small smile of his own.

On the way back from the garage, Cam swung past Avery, who lounged on the couch, decked out in neon-green leopard-print shorts and a long-sleeved button-down. They wore what appeared to be a bush hat, also neon green. "Hey, Avery. Do you know a good—" Cam began.

"Dolores Park," Avery replied instantly, without looking up from their phone.

Cam's mouth snapped shut. She stared at Avery.

"What? I have good hearing! You might be leading this trip, but I'm still the one who knows all the good places!" Cam continued to stare. Avery twisted to make eye contact. "And *I'm* the one with a car, thanks to all my powerful and mysterious connections." Avery put down their phone and grinned devilishly at Cam.

Cam smirked. "The one we took to Fisherman's Wharf?" she asked, solicitously.

Avery waved their hand vaguely. "The very same."

"I think I can get us something more suitable," Cam said cryptically.

"Huh?" Avery looked momentarily off-balance, but Cam swept out of the room before they had a chance to request clarity.

"We're leaving in an hour. I'm gonna talk to Sofia and make some food!" Cam declared loudly throughout the house.

Despite herself, Cam's thoughts strayed, once again, to Marcus. He was as absent as ever as yet again all the pages—sans Marcus—had plans to hang out. Cam wondered if his lifestyle ever left him feeling lonely. She shook her head to clear her mind. He was an adult; if he wanted to be different, he could do something about it. Besides, she was still furious with him. She had been right before to swear off boys; they were only a distraction and had no place in her life currently. Right now, it was about her having a good time with her friends. She kicked all thoughts of Marcus to the edge of her brain, where she hoped they would stay for at least a little while.

A short time later, the four pages stood outside of Avery's cinder block of a car, toward which they had not grown fonder for the time apart. Sofia and James looked dubiously at it.

"Nice car, Avery. But maybe we can take mine this time?" Cam grinned, dropping her cooler full of food and tossing a set of keys casually in her hand.

Avery looked at Cam quizzically. "You have access to a car?"

"Of course." Cam spun and gestured at a vehicle parked across the street.

Yesterday, Cam had finally decided to book time to borrow the car Wyatt had given her access to. And her reaction last night when she went to pick it up from the campus's concealed underground parking lot was similar to Sofia's and James's now—awe at the sleek, futuristic, and insanely expensive-looking car. Although maybe it was more accurate to call it some sort of land rocket. Avery looked distinctly surprised, and a little bit miffed.

"I got connections, baby!" Cam yelled, deliciously pleased to have an excuse to both show off and treat her friends. "It's the latest Beekar prototype. It's supposed to go into production sometime next year."

James, in a black T-shirt of the softest cotton and a pair of fitted shorts that came to just above the knee, opened a door with reverence and claimed one of the back seats. He began applying sunscreen. Avery stood, conflicted for a moment, before giving in and climbing into Cam's car beside James. Sofia, with an air of a visiting royal dignitary, took shotgun.

Cam beheld her shiny, awesome vehicle from the driver seat. The inside of the car was even more posh and elegant. The interiors were soft, warm leather, and there was an enormous tablet screen mounted on the dash.

She pressed a button, and the top slid smoothly down, folding in on itself like an insect's wings. Avery looked around and nodded their head, impressed. They looked at Cam for a moment, squinting, as if seeing something they hadn't quite expected for a moment.

The ride over was gorgeous. Cam had opted for a simple outfit of sandals, high-waisted black jeans and belt, and baggy striped shirt with collar. For this particular outing, though, she elected to elevate the look with a bag that was shaped like an orange. It had a green leaf. James at first tried repeatedly to return his blond hair to its orderly perfection but eventually abandoned the effort. Sofia, on the other hand, let her black hair fly free in the wind as she quietly enjoyed the view of the passing city, making waves through the air with her hand as they crossed the metropolis. Even Avery, normally effusive, was content to pass the time in companionable silence.

Dolores Park was a city block of bright green grass bordered on one side by a rail line for local transit. The entire park was set into the hill, with the descent from the utmost corner being relatively steep, until the grade evened out farther down. At the base of the hill, there were several tennis courts. Across the street lay Mission High School—a block-wide white-and-gold building with a tall tower that looked like it should have a bell. The park had a playground on one end, low buildings with, presumably, restrooms, on either side, and was split by a tree-lined foot path. There was also a vast, bizarre building with a shiny dome across the street that looked like a secret society should be operating out of it. Several of the cars parked nearby appeared freshly broken into.

The park was busy. There were people reclining on blankets all over the grass. Somebody was attempting to maintain balance as they walked across a slack line strung between two trees. A person in a boxy metal robot suit with speakers in its torso was dancing and getting its ass spanked by an incredibly drunk-looking batch of twentysomethings. Kids slid down an enormous slide in what easily qualified as the most bougie playground Cam had ever seen. Drunken Santas were arriving and departing in droves.

"Wow. This is free?" Cam asked, bewildered. She was used to parks, especially grassy ones maintained by sprinklers, that required an entrance fee.

Sofia and Avery gave her weird looks.

Avery pointed out an ideal spot toward the center of the park, partially shaded by a tree, and currently unoccupied. As they descended down the steepest part of the grass, blankets and cooler in hand, Avery played the tour guide. "This area is gay beach," they explained. The hill was studded in studs. Clusters of perfectly groomed, Speedo'ed, and muscular men lounged around the area.

"That's where the drugs are." Avery pointed to some tables at the mid-point of the park with voluminous clouds emerging from them. "Also there. And there. There too, I think."

"Joints! Weed!" An entrepreneurial fellow with a cart made the rounds, hawking his wares. "Hey, Avery!" he shouted. Avery waved and continued their tour.

The pages found a spot and laid out blankets. Cam had discovered a closet back at the house with two picnic blankets and a synthetic bearskin with a waterproof lining. James took extra care to align them all. Nearby, a man in a homemade karate gi practiced his katas for what Cam could only assume was the most thoroughly ineffective, bargain-bin martial art that had ever been invented.

Cam cracked open the cooler and distributed Italian sodas. They tasted incredibly refreshing in the hot sun. James reclined on the bearskin and watched the clouds go past. Dogs streaked around them, fetching balls or making friends with one another. He sighed once, peacefully.

The erstwhile karate man did a sequence of kicks interspersed with rolls across the grass. He then, bizarrely, pantomimed a motion of chopping an invisible foe with invisible twin sabers.

The pages joked as they sipped their sodas, then chatted idly about Beekor, the Bay Area, and life in general. Finally, when the time seemed right, Cam sat up straight and cleared her throat. The other pages listened attentively.

"I bet you're wondering why I've gathered you all here today," Cam began.

"Weather!" Avery shouted.

"Friendship!" Sofia shouted.

"Food!" James shouted, eyeing the cooler.

"Yes. But quiet!" Cam popped open the cooler. "This is a *celebration!*" Cam took out four individually packaged containers of what looked like a fruit salad, along with some spoons. "We hit our first user target for the newly kit-ified, easy-to-install version of Specio!" Sofia and James clapped. "We got my mom and her entire study group to install it and use it! That's seven users.

"It wouldn't be possible without Sofia taking on a lot of the software work and taking care of so many things that I didn't have time for."

"You're welcome," Sofia said loftily.

"Or without James taking my messy files and setting up a 3D-printing pipeline that is actually sane and reusable."

James smiled a small smile.

"I prepared something for everybody." Cam began to distribute the fruit cups. "This is gazpacho moreliano! It's a kind of fruit salad I made." James looked slightly nonplussed as he examined the combination of different elements. "Just try it out," Cam urged.

James took a bite, and his eyes went wide. Avery chewed and looked at the fruit salad in Cam's hand with an incredulous face, as if they had been betrayed.

Sofia smiled lightly, as if reality had matched her expectations. "Onion."

Cam laughed maniacally. "And *hot sauce*," she said with glee.

"Holy *hell* it's good!" Avery exclaimed.

James nodded and kept eating.

The park ninja began to make loud mouth noises as he executed a devastating flurry of air punches.

As they all ate, Avery stood. "I also have an announcement to make," they said. Everyone waited expectantly, and Sofia and Avery made brief eye contact.

"Welcome to the team, me," Avery said, and clapped.

"Uh, welcome?" Cam asked, taken aback.

"Now that you've"—Avery tapped Cam's nose—"hit your limits on user acquisition, it's time for me to lend my expertise."

Cam blinked and looked surprised. "Avery, how did you know—" She looked over at Sofia, who shrugged in a "they asked, I told" kind of way. Cam turned back to Avery. "Well, you don't have to help just—" Avery silenced Cam with a flourishing gesture in the air like a conductor signaling their orchestra to come to silence.

"You're the one that's actually chasing your passion," Avery explained. "Nothing more Valley than that. That's the sort of energy that can make a real difference." They smirked. "With some elite-level help, that is."

"I . . ." Cam was at a loss for what to say, blindsided by Avery's candor and zeal for the Specio project, and a tiny bit irritated at the way Avery was yet again presenting their assistance as a gift which Cam had no choice but to accept.

"Sofia told me about what you all have been working on. And I think it's amazing." Avery looked at Cam, dropping all their usual grandiose bravado and speaking sincerely. "You've identified a need, and you've got a solution that has the potential to help hundreds of thousands of people, maybe even hundreds of millions." Cam felt her breath catch; she had never thought of Specio in terms of huge numbers like that. The scale felt wild for something she had started building in her cramped little bedroom.

"I don't understand hardware or software," Avery continued, "but I do understand people, and I want to give you the connections you need." Then they grinned, their cocky showmanship back on display. "I haven't even shown you my best trick yet," they began. They whipped out a phone from behind their back. It was a non-Beekor phone, with one of Cam's holographic adapters already installed on it. "Behold! I have gone through the installation steps myself and thus increased your user base by over ten percent *already*." It was true; at just seven current users, Avery's new install increased the total installed base by around fourteen percent.

Cam tamped down some of her irritation at being treated as if she needed help, again. It *would* be great to have somebody managing new user acquisition, and it was obviously one of Avery's greatest strengths. What was she even thinking? She had another person who *wanted* to be on the team. This was a moment for excitement! "Great to have you on the team, O Most Excellent One!" She lifted her fruit salad in a cheer. "To Avery!" Everybody else raised their fruit salads, and Avery posed with fists on hips, basking in it. "Thanks for increasing our team size by thirty-three percent!"

"Which means it's also time for a team name. What have you got, my little lambs?" Avery peered around expectantly.

Sofia and Cam looked at each other, stumped. It was James who piped up. "Ofanim."

"What's that?" Cam asked.

"It's the name of an angel in the Bible that is a wheel consisting of eyes. It makes sense because our first product is Specio."

Cam got it. "Oh! Because they're both about seeing!"

"Unique. Related. Memorable. I like it," Sofia concluded with a nod.

Avery cackled, "It's perfect! An uncanny angel with too many eyes will definitely look great on hats."

Cam swelled with love. Love for the project, and love for the friends who were helping her. "Ofanim it is!"

As they finished their homemade fruit cups and discussed plans, the martial artist finally went too far. Avery was explaining some of the people they were already in contact with who might be interested in helping Cam test, but they cut off as the man, with a look of complete concentration on his face, stumblingly punched and jump-kicked his way toward them in slow motion. Avery leapt up and body-checked the man before he bumbled and fell on Sofia.

"Don't you have a sensei to go duel or something?" Avery asked, having fully lost their cool.

The man looked darkly at Avery. "David Bowie called; he wants his everything back!"

Avery barked a laugh. "Great! Why don't you run off and tell him how good your Cob McGraw training is going?" The man turned and stalked off.

James's eyes shone with admiration, until Avery took notice. "What?" they asked.

"Teach me your ways," James said.

Sofia laughed. Avery asked, "You want me to explain how to eject unwanted attention from your life?"

James nodded profusely.

Avery laughed. "Step one: Discern their greatest insecurity. Step two: Ruthlessly exploit it . . ." they began.

It eventually got dark, and unexpectedly cold. The pages packed up everything, disposed of all their garbage in the proper receptacles, and headed to the car. It looked to Cam like her team, Ofanim, had grown.

Chapter 34

WITH AVERY ON BOARD, THE Ofanim team charged ahead. And stumbled to get their footing. The team started off by sitting down to decide on a feature road map as well as their new KPI goals. Cam suggested fifty users. Avery laughed full in her face.

Cam flinched. "You want more than fifty? We just reached eight; let's be realistic," Cam reasoned.

"Realistic? Let's start off conservative, then. A thousand users," Avery said with a straight face.

Cam visibly balked.

"Trust," Sofia said. Avery looked deadly serious.

Cam took a long breath and reminded herself about how good she was supposed to be about trusting and relying on her team now. She nodded, finally, and they were off to the races. Under Avery's efforts, users came flooding in. In just two days, Cam found herself spending every waking hour not in the Beekor office (and increasing waking hours *in* the Beekor office) 3D printing and shipping new hardware, disseminating instructions to new users, or helping them troubleshoot problems. It was lucky that James and Sofia had entered the drift because Cam no longer had even a second to spare to do any engineering work anymore. Desperately, she tried to unbury herself.

First, she put up a basic website with installation instructions and an FAQ for common problems. Sofia looked at the site and winced slightly.

"What?" Cam asked.

Avery bounced a ball off the garage wall for the six hundredth time that day. Cam gritted her teeth.

"It's a good start," Sofia said eventually.

Then Cam set up a deal with a 3D hardware print-on-demand service that Chi and DAOTown knew. They would print and ship Specio for new users practically at cost, including several of James's different variants and grips for those that preferred or needed different hardware shapes. Cam made a MiTube video to explain how to order and get the hardware. She even tried out adding her own title cards, transitions, and video effects.

"Huh," James said over her shoulder.

"What?!" Cam snarled.

James jumped. "Thank you for doing that," he said into his shoes as he retreated back to his workbench.

Next, Cam set up a chat server for her users, started running weekly town halls, and appointed some of the more knowledgeable users as community managers who could help point newbies to all the necessary resources, as well as offer some basic troubleshooting advice. She made the header art and all the little announcement graphics herself. Her mom was the first one in.

> **rosalita:** *wow, you did this all yourself!*
>
> *yeah. why?* **:cam [mod]**
>
> **rosalita:** *it's wonderful* ♡

None of Cam's efforts to reduce her workload dealing with new users worked. Or least, never enough. Every new improvement she instituted was met with yet more new users to fill the gap and consume her free time. She left her work at Beekor on complete autopilot. Her mom complained that she spoke to Sofia on the phone more than her. As more users joined up, the entire community came together around the project in amazing ways that Cam hadn't expected. They shared their stories about how Specio had changed their lives with one another. They cheered Cam and one another on, and they celebrated each new milestone (a hundred users, two hundred, three hundred) with Cam and the team.

To commemorate the upcoming milestone of five hundred users, Cam took a moment to set up a tool for the office whiteboard that displayed a social feed on it. As users joined the Ofanim chat server, pinged the dev team, or made posts on social media, they would all appear, streaming past, on the whiteboard. Watching the ongoing feedback of her users provided an intense feeling of gratification, a boost to morale and motivation for the team. For Cam, they were a respite from the harrowing workload. Finally, one Friday evening, as the onboarding of the five hundredth user became imminent, Cam kicked off a holographic live stream.

"How many people are watching?" Avery asked.

"Thirty-seven," James said.

> ***karrygold:*** *hey hunnies! we got a party going on here?*
> *ill bring some friends.*

"Two hundred and eighty now." James's eyes popped.

Avery sprang into action. "Welcome, everybody. I will be your elegant, effervescent, and exceptionally eloquent concierge to this singular experience." Avery smirked and posed. The users went wild for Avery's outfit (a beautiful suit with a full-bleed floral print in pinks and yellows). Avery led the stream on a tour of their work space. Sofia appeared statuesque, a bit mysterious, and dignified, like a cold mountain wind. James practically fled.

Mentally, Cam reviewed her task list and felt a bit mournful that she couldn't knock anything else off it while the stream was live. She thought wistfully about the day she could work on Specio full-time and no longer have to try (and fail) to balance it alongside her day job with the Three Ts. Cam's eyes unfocused, and she drifted.

"Not a woman of many words, are you?" Avery was saying, projecting at full TV-presenter volume.

Cam came to from her exhausted stupor. "Huh?" Congratulatory messages from the chat were coming in a torrent on the whiteboard. Sofia was even clapping.

"How does it feel to have reached five hundred users—fifty percent of our current user goal, in just three weeks?!" Avery prompted.

"We did it?!" Cam asked. She leapt up. "Yesss! Thank you, everybody!" She hugged Avery, then Sofia, and even James, who only put up a mild struggle.

After a bit more revelry, the party eventually wound down and Cam finally ended the stream. The space immediately grew quiet, and each one of the pages sagged in place, as if they were marionettes whose strings had been cut.

Something Cam had been neglecting suddenly occurred to her. "Just a moment!" The pages gathered around as she logged in to the FTP server and directly updated the html for the Specio website. Then she brought the site up on her screen and hit reload. "500 Users!" it said in enormous font, right at the top of the homepage.

James attempted to smile.

Avery sucked their teeth.

Cam snapped. "What?! What is it? What am I doing wrong?!"

Sofia looked downward. James had taken several steps back. Avery, on the other hand, met Cam's angry gaze with an utterly even look. "The site doesn't look very professional . . ." Avery began.

Cam shot up from her seat. "I'm doing my best!" she bellowed. "What the hell else do you want from me?!"

Sofia stepped directly into Cam's personal space and placed a hand firmly on her shoulder. She looked into Cam's eyes and said, "We talked about this."

As Cam met Sofia's gaze, she realized she had screwed up, but she struggled to disarm her own defensiveness. "Talked about what? The fact that I can't design worth shit?"

"We talked about sharing the load."

Sofia's and Avery's disappointed looks and James's visible, intense discomfort defused Cam's anger, and she suddenly felt like a complete asshole. She sank back down into her chair.

She gave an exhausted look around. "I'm drowning in all this, plus Beekor."

With a visible exertion of will, James faced them and spoke up. "That's no excuse to be a jerk."

Cam nodded. "You're right. It's not an excuse."

Sofia typed something on her computer, and Cam got a notification. She looked at her computer screen.

"Ticket 'Recruit Graphic Designer' has been created," it read.

Cam sighed. "All right. I'll get started—"

"No," Sofia said.

"No, you don't want me to actually start?" Cam couldn't keep a note of irritation out of her voice.

"No, I don't want you to continue working yourself to death." Sofia sounded stern and unyielding. "*We* need you to be well rested and functional." She turned to go. "Then *we* can talk about how we're going to address the need for a graphic designer *together*. Good night." She walked out without a look back.

Cam looked around chagrined. "I'm sorry, guys," she said.

Avery shrugged. "Water under the Golden Gate." They left with James.

Cam took one last look at the messages on the whiteboard. "Happy 500!" She followed the other pages out.

Chapter 35

REALIZING HOW HARD THEY HAD been pushing, Cam instituted a recurring group relaxation session each Saturday. Which was how that particular brilliant morning found the crew getting ready to spend the warm hours picnicking in the Botanical Garden in Golden Gate Park. Cam had just finished packing a batch of empanadas she had prepared for the outing when she looked up and happened to catch an elusive sight through the kitchen window: Marcus reading a book in the back garden.

Cam made a lightning-fast decision. She grabbed the bag of snacks and threw it at Avery, who had just come down the stairs to the main floor. "Sorry, something came up. Have fun without me."

"I— What?" Avery fumbled with the bag before catching it. "You're not going to work are you?" they shouted up the stairs at Cam's retreating back.

"No," Cam hollered over her shoulder before pounding up the last steps to her room. There, she delicately picked up the coffee ticket she had received from Marcus weeks ago from where it resided on her bedside table and sprinted back downstairs.

"Have a good time!" she shouted at Sofia and Avery as she careened past them. The two other pages exchanged a look between themselves and didn't say anything as Cam flung open the door to the outside patio. James simply blinked in confusion in her wake.

Outside, Marcus looked up in surprise at Cam's approach and blinked as she thrust her coffee ticket under his nose.

"I would like"—pant—"to redeem this"—wheeze—"please," Cam managed to gasp at him.

Marcus blinked a couple more times before regaining his composure. He gave Cam an even look. "I thought you were mad at me."

Cam sat on her heels and held up one finger as she regained her breath and tried to quickly formulate her thoughts. Finally, only a little huffy, she said, "I am still a little mad at you. You're not the one who hurt Sofia, and I do think you should have said something before. But"—she gulped several more breaths—"you're not the one truly to blame."

Marcus looked pained for a second. "You weren't . . . entirely in the wrong." He heaved a sigh. "I'm sorry too. I thought a lot about what you said. I wasn't seeing things from Sofia's point of view. And"—he hesitated and scanned the garden in a distracted way—"I realized you're right. About friend stuff." He reached up to rub the back of his neck, self-conscious and abashed in a way Cam had never seen from him before.

He sighed and continued. "As I've said, my parents have a lot of expectations of me. They've had those expectations my whole life. And it's resulted in a lot of . . . very specific organization around my friendships."

Cam stared at him. "Your parents choose your friends?"

Marcus grimaced. "Not exactly. But in essence, most of my friendships have a specific script. That is, except for you." He looked up into Cam's eyes with such intense sincerity she felt her chest flutter.

"Cam, I'm sorry I haven't prioritized you. Us." The word "us" hung heavily in the air between them. "I'm new to—to more organic friendships." He fumbled for words. "I want to do better."

Cam looked at the heart Marcus had laid bare and felt her own constrict. She thought about how close she had grown with the other pages, especially Sofia. Who did Marcus have? Being pulled away from the page house all the time had left him isolated. They hadn't even thought to invite him to the park today—they had just stopped expecting him at all. She thought about the events surrounding Sofia from his angle. Sofia was someone he seemed to get along with, but when did he have the time to get to really know her, to tell her what was happening to her project? Not for the first time, Cam contemplated how lonely Marcus might be.

"All right," Cam said, coming to a decision. "I'll forgive you." Before Marcus could fully smile, she cut him off. "But I have a condition. Next time you want to apologize, you come find me. Friends don't wait for friends to apologize first," she spoke in a manner that was both playful and threateningly serious.

"Agreed," Marcus said warmly. "Do friends hug?"

"They do." Cam leaned down to hug him, and he wrapped her in his arms. She luxuriated in his smell for a moment before straightening.

Marcus laughed nervously. "Honestly? I didn't think you were ever going to talk to me again. I was such an ass, leaving you there in the park. I'm really sorry." He looked pained.

"So make it up to me," said Cam as she brandished the card again. "You free right now?"

"As of three seconds ago, no. A cute girl asked me out on a date." Marcus broke into a smile. One with that pace-quickening dimple. He lightly tapped his book on the top of her head before saying, "Let me go put this in my room. Meet you by the front door?"

Ten minutes later, a much more composed Cam met Marcus, now crisp in dark jeans, dark shirt, and long gray coat, on the front steps. Cam had also changed into a shirt commemorating a field trip to an observatory in '73 tucked into dark emerald-green pants with an ocher cardigan over it all. Cam gripped the strap of her purse, which looked like the sun with solar rays. "Anywhere in particular you want to go?" she asked.

Together, they grabbed a Beekar to take them to a trendy café that had been on Marcus's coffee-ticket website. It served hot chocolate with melting clouds of peppermint-flavored marshmallows. Cam turned to Marcus and asked, "So what were you reading out there?"

"Ah." Marcus looked a little embarrassed. "A comic book."

"Really?" Cam asked. "Which one?"

"One Dream." He didn't elaborate.

Cam frowned. "Isn't that the comic about the pirate who sails through dreams in search of his dad? Didn't that come out when we were kids?" She saw his shoulders loosen the tiniest bit.

"It started coming out when we were kids. It's been going this whole time," Marcus relented.

"Wow, you've been reading it for years? You must be an überfan." Cam was impressed.

Marcus laughed a little. "Not the whole time, no. Actually, my parents banned me from reading it. So I'm kind of reading it behind their backs. Don't tell them, okay?" he whispered conspiratorially.

"Banned? I didn't think it was particularly violent." Cam thought back on her own experience reading the issues that had made it to her local library. She had loved the colorful artwork and the adventures of Captain Nuro as he flew through dreams with his first mate, Navi Gator, a talking alligator. She had only stopped reading because the library didn't have anything past the fifth volume.

"No, it's not. *I* was banned because I kept drawing the characters on my homework assignments." Marcus grinned crookedly. "I was not a good student. So my parents forbade me from reading it and got me a tutor. I had forgotten all about it until I read an article saying that the latest volume just came out. Right now, I'm catching up on everything I missed."

Cam was fascinated. "What's happening? I only got up to the part where the dual-wielding swordsman joins the crew. Spoilers are okay."

"Mister Cutting Edge? So much has happened. It turns out he's actually the Sword Princess in disguise. They travel to her kingdom to help her reclaim her throne from Wet Stone." All reservations gone, Marcus opened up animatedly about the trials of Captain Nuro and his ever-changing crew. After so much stress at both of her jobs, existential fears about her place at Beekor and whether Ofanim would ever amount to anything, just spending time with Marcus in the bliss of their newly patched . . . whatever they were to each other and getting swept up in his enthusiastic retelling of a comic book had Cam feeling calm and peaceful for the first time in a long while. She sighed.

"Wait, I didn't lose you, did I?" Marcus sounded legitimately worried.

"No way!" Cam cried. "So what happens to Madame Delicatessen?"

"I don't know. I need the next volume." Marcus admitted.

Cam weighed her options, then asked, "Would it be rude if I said we should table coffee and go get that next volume instead?"

Marcus smiled bright enough to challenge the sun. "It's your date. And I know a place!" He typed a new destination into his phone, and a short while later, they pulled up to a glass-walled storefront. Inside were three floors of comics on bright shelves, lit by skylights from above. Scattered through the space were red couches and beanbag chairs where adults and kids sat reading samples of the merchandise.

They made a beeline for the section with Captain Nuro and found the volume Marcus had gotten up to. He flipped it open, and Cam leaned over his arm to read alongside him.

"I had forgotten how cool the art is," Cam marveled, looking at the bright pages.

"It's more than just the art, though, look at the flow." Marcus started pointing to the pages. "See how this word bubble is placed here? It lines up with Captain Nuro's sword. It means you read the dialogue and naturally your eye follows down along the sword and to the next panel. And here the rope bridge curves to the next panel. Because the flow is so natural, it's really easy to read, meaning even people who have never picked up a comic before will be able to read it. It's some real genius level of skill." He was smiling, full dimple out. Cam wanted to kiss it.

Why not? Cam thought. Without letting herself overthink it, she got up on her tiptoes and kissed his sweet little dimple. Cam rested back on her heels and looked up at him to gauge his reaction.

Marcus looked a little startled, but then he smiled down at her in a softer, more intimate way. Slowly, he lifted up his free hand and gently cupped the back of her head, allowing her to break away if she wanted. She didn't. Achingly slowly, he bent down and kissed her. She closed her eyes and breathed in the sensation. This kiss wasn't like the crashing, combative kiss of the race, nor was it the tentative, exploratory kiss on the stairs. This one was the slow, magnetic movement of people who had already learned each other's lips and knew exactly how to fit them together. Cam felt like a stone with a heavy, undeniable river slowly running over her, gradually wearing her down and changing her shape into something more soft. He parted his lips and gave her the lightest of nips on her bottom lip. Cam gasped.

Marcus pulled away leisurely and gave her a satisfied little smile. Then he dropped his hand to grab hers. Interlacing their fingers, he asked in a neutral, pleasant tone, "Do you want to check out the rest of the store?"

Cam nodded, knees a little unsteady.

They explored the rest of the store, occasionally splitting up to examine separate corners before reuniting to show each other their finds. Marcus found a comic book that broke down the history and structure of comic books. Cam found a comic book about building tiny arcades with microscopic, hobbyist single-board computers. Together they laughed over a collection of newspaper comic strips, and both were equally confused over a superhero comic that purported to be issue 1, but clearly referenced at least fifty years of previous material.

Finally, they went to the cash register with their chosen items. Marcus didn't even ask; he primly grabbed Cam's books and placed them next to his. Cam tried to protest, but he waved her off.

"You sidetracked coffee to come do something I wanted to do. It's the least I can do to repay you," he said, tapping his phone on the register to pay.

Cam didn't think that was what had happened at all, but it was too late. She thanked Marcus profusely as she accepted her bag of comics from the sales clerk.

As they stood outside on the curb, Cam turned to Marcus, who was pleasantly humming as he flipped vaguely through a volume of Captain Nuro. "Hey, Marcus, do you think you could do me a huge favor?" She was a little nervous about asking a newly re-friended Marcus, but the date—and it was definitely a date, not a friend hang—had gone really well.

She had his full attention. "What is it? Need help getting rid of a body?"

Cam huffed a laugh. "Not this time, no." She cleared her throat. "Actually, I kind of need help building a website?"

"Don't you have a grandson or someone that can help you?" he deadpanned.

Cam groaned. "I can build a website just fine. I have! But I don't know how to make it look good."

Marcus raised an eyebrow.

Cam was really starting to regret asking. "Look, I made a website for my passion project, and it looks like a boiled turd. It functions, but it's not functional. You know what I mean? People have a hard time navigating it because it's so messy. I don't know what to do." Cam said all of this in a rush. "But I remembered your coffee-date website. It looks so nice, and it's fun to use, and I was just wondering if you could give me advice? Anything, really." Cam deflated. She thought she had gotten better about asking for help, but apparently that all went out the window when it came to making yourself vulnerable in front of a cute boy whom you really, *really* wanted to kiss again.

"Okay," said Marcus.

"Really?" Cam straightened hopefully.

"Yeah, sure. How bad could it be?" Marcus asked with a smile.

—

"Cam, this is really bad," Marcus said mournfully a little while later.

Once they had arrived home, Cam had brought her laptop up from the garage as she hadn't wanted to subject Marcus to the controlled chaos that was their makeshift office. She had plopped herself down on the couch in the living room and opened up the Specio website. Marcus had sat down next to her and scrolled through it with increasing dismay.

"Cam, what is this, Web 1.0? Are you using Papyrus? This isn't even retro awful; this is just awful." Marcus clicked through a couple of the links. "Why is this doing this? What are these graphics? How do I go back to the homepage?"

"You can hit the back button?" Cam wasn't sure why Marcus was asking such a basic question.

Marcus stared hard at her. "You mean users have to hit the back button a bunch of times? There is no homepage button."

"Uh." When Marcus put it like that, it did seem a little silly. It was a system that worked fine for her, but that didn't mean it was intuitive or easy for most of her users. "Look, I don't want you to think I'm trying to use you." Like some of his "friends" in the past, Cam suspected based on their earlier conversation. "You can totally walk away from this right now, and I wouldn't blame you. But also I really need help. Help, please?" she practically begged.

"Oh, no, you need me." Marcus sighed and looked at his designer watch. "I've got to get going to a thing, and I'm booked tomorrow. But do you want to go over this Monday at lunch? You can walk me through the user flows then."

Cam also sighed and nodded. Marcus leapt over the back of the couch, pausing to lean over and kiss Cam quickly on the lips.

"See you on Monday." He waved, dimpled smile on full display, and skipped up to his room.

Cam waved back in a daze, thinking that maybe now was a good time for a cold shower.

Chapter 36

MONDAY ROLLED AROUND, AND CAM'S productivity was at an all-time low. She found herself continually checking her computer, her phone, and the large display clock made out of a pendulum. She was seeing Marcus in two hours. One hour and fifty-eight minutes. One hour and forty-two minutes. One hour and— Why was time moving so slowly? It was untenable.

While Cam sat fidgeting, the Three Ts were having a discussion among themselves. Finally, the conversation intensified, with Terry looking understanding but firm, Theresa fierce and determined, and Travis fighting a tide he was clearly losing. The end result was Travis approaching Cam tentatively.

"Hey, Cam," Travis started, and then looked over his shoulder to Terry and Theresa, the former giving him a big thumbs-up and the latter only scowling. Travis turned back. "Can we have a quick chat?"

"Sure," said Cam distractedly, looking at the time on her phone. "I've got time."

"Great, great." Travis beckoned, and the two went into a small conference room where one wall was covered in a three-dimensional bubble-wrap pattern with different colored bubbles spelling the word "Beekor." Travis and Cam both settled into ergonomic chairs. Travis clasped his hands and stared at Cam. He appeared to be sweating lightly.

Cam wasn't sure what she should do in this instance, but she was struggling not to check her phone again.

Travis finally broke, throwing up his hands. "This is supposed to be Terrance's job. I can't do this." He sounded beyond exasperated.

"What needs—" Cam started to ask before she was cut off.

"Cam, where are the notes from your meeting with your last influencer, SoSoBaby?" Travis was grabbing the armrests of his seat in a viselike grip, looking ready to puke.

"Oh, uh," Cam started guiltily. She had talked to SoSoBaby last week but hadn't gotten around to transcribing her notes. "I'm basically done. I can give it to you after lunch."

"And have you followed up with the hardware team for the custom bounce light for Savvy_Snavvle?" Travis asked, barely listening to her excuses.

"I—I was. It's on my calendar," Cam hedged. She was a bit behind on that.

"And does software know about the TOS updates needed for the hand-tracking app they are making for TheFlyingFr0g?" Travis was on the edge of his seat now.

"No, they don't." Cam was seriously behind on that one. She felt a hot sun of shame rising in her chest. She hadn't realized quite how thoroughly she had been ignoring her responsibilities.

Travis pulled out his cell phone and unfolded it a few times to make the screen bigger. Then he flipped it around to show her their task board. Almost everything was in the green, with a few yellow priority tickets.

"That was two months ago," Travis intoned with gravity. "This is today." He swiped the board, and suddenly it was all red. "Our off-site to Tahoe has already been canceled. I had to return the skis I bought."

Cam winced. "I'm really sorry, Travis." And she truly was. She had also been eyeing that off-site wistfully and hadn't understood why it had gotten canceled.

Until now.

Travis sighed and rubbed the back of his neck. "Look, I hate having these confrontation talks. We got swamped with so many orders after the conference. We really can't afford to be a person down. Is there something distracting you?"

Cam took that moment to check her phone to see if Marcus had texted, and offered, "How about we do lunch, all four of us, and go over the work we've got so we can—"

Travis was cut off by the alarm chime on Cam's phone. It was time to meet Marcus. "I have to go." She stood up quickly. "I'm so sorry, Travis. I hear what you're saying, and I will do better. See you after lunch." With that final platitude uttered, she dashed off. Travis resembled a plant that had been overwatered—wet and sickly.

As Cam grabbed her laptop and dashed off to meet Marcus, she swore to herself to try harder with the influencer project. Just because she was going to leave the influencer project soon was no reason to leave it in tatters. She also wondered who would replace her after she was gone. Travis was right; they needed someone to hit the ground running. Maybe she could gather all the notes she took when she was first starting and compile them into a guide for new team members.

Outside, Cam grabbed one of the electric scooters that sat in front of all Beekor buildings and used her badge to unlock it and ride to the Omni building across campus. She met Marcus there just as he was walking up.

"Hey," Cam said, and tried to discreetly adjust her muted-color striped pants and dark red sweater into seamless perfection, hiking her bag shaped like a hot-air balloon self-consciously on her shoulder.

"Hey yourself." Marcus smiled back. He looked as good as always in a sea-foam-colored suit with white shirt.

"Sock check," Cam called, and looked down.

Marcus laughed and lifted a hem. His socks looked like a colorful painting of a dozen or so cakes on pedestals.

"Wayne Thiebaud?" Cam was impressed. "Culturally relevant and cute. Nice."

"Thank you." Marcus grinned, obviously pleased Cam recognized the reference.

They both walked into a building that looked like a stack of plates that were in the process of falling apart with glass windows set haphazardly in the cracks. They went through the lobby, past an installation piece that consisted of a pile of tents and trash labeled *House the Unhoused,* and to glass elevators that took them up to a private top floor that Marcus's key card had access to. Marcus led Cam to a wood-paneled hallway that, upon seeing Marcus slide one panel open, she suddenly realized must have been filled with hidden doors. Beyond the panel Marcus opened was a pleasantly appointed room with a wall of two-way windows looking out over the campus and onto the city beyond. It was filled with cushy seats around a dining table for four, as well as two individual reclining sofas, a large-screen TV, an abstract shag rug, and a mini fridge with wine. Cam could tell it was wine because the door was glass. Cam stood stunned by the door while Marcus walked to a tablet on the table. He quickly swiped through it before handing it over to her.

"This good?" he asked. On the tablet, there was a profile for Cam that included the most common meals she ate at each of the dining halls. She touched a drop-down and found a menu that even showed how frequently she used the restroom and her average use time. She was stunned. She clicked out and found entries for others on campus too, including the Three Ts. Their positions were plotted in real time on a map.

"What the fuck is this?" Cam asked, bewildered.

Marcus looked chagrined. "I hadn't even realized not everybody is privy to that."

"You mean this massive violation of privacy?" Cam exclaimed.

Marcus winced. "Yeah, it does look like that. But it's for internal use only, higher-ups exclusive." Cam stared at him. "Look, Beekor makes a device that's in everybody's pocket, and it has always-on location tracking and a full suite of sensors. It looks bad but . . . it's sort of to be expected . . . ?" He trailed off under Cam's icy glare.

Eventually, she gave in and just selected the recommended meal on the tablet. It was, in fact, exactly what she wanted, although she eyed the Wagyu beef and puzzled over the tasting menu on offer. Was this really how Marcus ate regularly?

Marcus proceeded to pull out his laptop and place it on the dining table.

"Do you always eat here?" Cam asked Marcus as she sat down on the corner next to him.

"Sometimes. When I'm meeting with someone internally. But a lot of my afternoons are off campus." Marcus clicked through his laptop before spinning it to show Cam the current version of the Specio website. "Okay, let's start off by having you tell me the basic-use case of the site. Show me a typical user flow."

Cam walked through the website with Marcus and described to him what information needed to be on each page. Marcus labeled sticky notes with page names and laid them out on the table. He took copious notes on each sticky and continually moved them around with new information from Cam.

After a while, the food arrived on a cart. The server, whom Marcus greeted by name, lifted the lids to the serving trays and carefully placed the plates on the table. He seemed used to having to navigate around laptops and strewn notes.

When the server left, Cam picked up her fork and looked over at Marcus, who was beginning to chow down on half a roast duck with sauce. "So exactly what do you do every day?" It was something that had been bothering her since she had found out that Sofia's and James's days were so different from hers, and since it was increasingly obvious that Marcus's days were even more unique.

"Well, I wake up, and I pick out my socks for the day—very important—and then I go to the gym—" Marcus began his recitation before Cam cut him off.

"Very funny. But I'm serious. What do you do all day? I hardly ever see you at the page house, you're constantly with Wyatt, you're always running off to some meeting or other. What, are you training to be Wyatt's bodyguard or something?"

Marcus laughed. "He's got enough of those already. No, I'm kinda like a glorified assistant. I follow Wyatt around wherever he goes." He seemed almost bored with the details. "But he's out of town this week, so I've got the free time to help you out. Speaking of which, what is this site for? You said you're building a holographic phone adapter?"

"Yeah. It basically attaches to older phone models and allows them to use the more modern holographic tech at a way lower price point. I started with making one for my mom, and then her friends, and it kind of grew from there." She shrugged and ate some of her lunch. She felt oddly nervous talking about this with Marcus. He was obviously clever, and she didn't want to seem like an unprofessional fool in front of him. She wanted him to be impressed with her.

"Hmm." Marcus looked at the website. Carefully, without looking at her, he asked, "Is Wyatt aware of what you're doing?"

Cam was confused by his weirdly neutral tone. "Yessssss." She dragged out the word, hoping to get more information out of him. "But he knows I'm leaving my current project soon. We've agreed that I will once I've proven my capabilities."

Marcus's shoulders relaxed just enough that Cam realized they had been tight.

"Well, it's a good project to learn on. You've got hardware, communication issues, software, and customers." He listed points off on his fingers.

He seemed to be contemplating all the factors and possibilities. "It's great practice."

"Wyatt thought so too." Cam grimaced and stuffed her face determinedly with rabbit ragout. She still didn't feel great talking about her inexperience. She was slowly coming to terms with it, and she had had a plethora of smart, talented people placed around her to help her grow. She was no longer the naive newbie she had been when she arrived, but she wanted to appear sophisticated in front of Marcus, who never appeared less than suave and capable. She wanted to be taken seriously and respected by people the way he was.

"Anyway," Cam said, blatantly changing the subject, "can we get back to my website? You know, the one that looks like a turd?" Well, in some ways her svelte image was irredeemably ruined, and she should come to terms with that.

Marcus chuckled. "I think some product photos are in order. They'll help the site look nice and let people know what they're getting. I also think I can whip up a logo."

They spent the rest of the lunch hour talking over the website, user flows, and what a potential logo might look like. She couldn't wait to implement some of his ideas as soon as she got back to the page house. Thinking about home made her realize how many hours she still had left in the day. She thought guiltily back to Travis's talk with her this morning. She really had to put in some work on the influencer project.

Marcus took a picture of his makeshift diagram and grabbed up the sticky notes. "I'll make a mock-up for it. Ask me about it tonight, maybe over dinner?"

Cam agreed in a blasé fashion, secretly thrilling inside at the idea of dinner together with Marcus.

Just the two of them.

Chapter 37

THAT NIGHT, CAM GOT HOME a little later than she wanted. The amount of work that had piled up on the influencer project really was pretty bad, and she ended up spending the entire day trying to address the highest-priority items. Realistically, thought Cam, even if she did stay on the project, they needed at least one more person to help. The team was too small for the volume they were handling. Ideally, Cam wanted another copy of herself, but as she thought it through a bit more, she realized that somebody that just focused on the project management tasks—the dissemination and sharing of information—would free her up to focus exclusively on working with influencers to refine their ideas and needs down into coherent product ideas that the engineers could deliver on.

With this buzzing in the back of her head, she went to her room to get dressed. She opted for a green skirt with belt, a big sweater with her community college logo on it, and a denim jacket. She accessorized with a pair of high-tops and a purse that looked like a hamburger. Just a touch of makeup completed the look. Twisting in the mirror, she thought she looked really cute. Cute enough for a date with Marcus.

She headed downstairs to the kitchen to work at the bar top until Marcus got home. She sent him a quick text before settling in with her laptop. Sitting there swinging her legs, Cam was around when James came in, went down into the basement, then came back upstairs and headed out the front door, muttering something about needing IT to reinstall some equipment along the way. Cam wasn't sure who James thought he was fooling, but it wasn't her. She sent another follow-up text to Marcus, just to let him know where she was. Cam was around when Sofia came down the stairs in a slinky off-white backless sweater dress and nude pumps. Her earrings, which looked like tiny gold daggers, matched her small gold shield clutch. Cam was around when Avery burst in through the front door with a bouquet of blooming flowers in every shade of white. They handed them with a flourish to Sofia and kissed her hand with a bow. Sofia smiled her small smile and put the flowers in a vase in the kitchen. The two of them waved goodbye to Cam, Sofia serenely, and Avery like they were the cat stealing the cream, as they sauntered out the front door. She sent a text to Marcus politely asking if they were still on for tonight. Cam passed another forty-five minutes getting back up-to-date with the Ofanim chat server to see if there were any fires that needed putting out.

Cam checked her phone yet again, completely fed up. Was Marcus blowing her off? Where was he? He hadn't responded to her texts at all. She tapped her foot in indecisive irritation before finally breaking down and deciding to holocall him. If he was going to be so rude, the least he could do was make his lame-ass excuses to her face.

She heard Marcus's ringtone distantly upstairs. Disbelievingly, she got up and ascended the stairs, following the sound until it led her to Marcus's room. She waited a moment listening to the musical trill, then knocked on Marcus's door. She heard a brief rustle of noise; then her holocall was rejected. What the hell?

Cam knocked more forcefully. "Marcus, I know you're in there." Did he think he could just ignore her? Hide up here like a coward? She was beyond pissed. After all that talk of him trying to make an effort to put in the time for them, he flaked at the first chance. About to knock again, she was halted by the abrupt opening of the door.

On the other side was a bleary-eyed Marcus, who stood barefoot in a loud graphic tee for a band Cam had never heard of and patterned pajama pants the colors of a '90s kids show.

"Nice jammies." Cam wasn't sure what to say. He clearly had been dead asleep.

Marcus snatched his bonnet off, radiating embarrassment. He looked at Cam, plainly confused. As she watched, she could see his brain revving up and processing. Finally, he looked appalled. "Shit, what time is it? I'm so sorry, Cam. I meant to take a power nap. My alarm must not have gone off." He looked betrayed at the offending phone still lying on his bed.

"I actually think it did." Cam huffed a laugh. She could feel her anger ebbing away. Marcus was obviously contrite. "You slept right through my texts and call."

Marcus groaned. "I am beyond sorry! Do you still want to go out? I can be ready in five." He looked appreciatively at her outfit. "You look great."

Feeling mollified and, suddenly, magnanimous, Cam waved him off. "Stay in your pj's. I'll see what's in the kitchen that I can make."

"I'll help," Marcus swore.

A few minutes and one pantry expedition later, Cam and Marcus were in the process of making sopa de fideo. While Cam gathered ingredients and opened up cans of fire-roasted tomato, Marcus attentively listened to her instructions and chopped onions and minced garlic.

"So who are the Burning Tigers?" Cam asked.

Marcus looked down at his shirt and laughed. "It was a band my friends and I were in."

Cam was intrigued. "You were in a band?"

"I say 'I was in a band,' but really my high school friends and I just talked about what it would be like to form a band. Who would play what, who would be the front man, you know. We got as far as coming up with a band name, but never had a practice." Marcus grinned as he reminisced.

"Doesn't sound very far at all." Cam smirked.

"No, too disorganized." Marcus laughed ruefully. "Besides, my parents wouldn't have let me form a band. None of our parents would have." Marcus shoveled his chopped bits into the blender with Cam's ingredients.

"Sex, drugs, and rock 'n' roll?" Cam raised an eyebrow.

"Hmm, maybe. But mostly they wanted us to study. We were all competing for valedictorian." Marcus turned on the blender, effectively ending the conversation. Cam took the hint. She had begun to realize his parents, and their expectations for him, were a touchy subject. She thought again of his admission of having "scripted" friendships and wondered if these were the same friends he had been thinking of.

After she finished with the blender, she spooned out some of the mixture into a saucepan with olive oil. "So where did the shirt come from?"

Marcus loosened his stiff posture and grinned at her a little self-consciously. "I made it."

"What?! Really? Let me see," Cam demanded. Marcus turned obligingly toward her. It was an illustration of a three-headed tiger shooting fiery laser beams out of its eyes to burn down a school.

"I gave them to my friends when we graduated," he explained.

Cam roared with laughter. "That's so good! And you're a really skilled artist—I thought this was a legit band." She really meant it too. It looked really professional.

"Thanks," he said, clearly embarrassed. "But how about you? Were you a part of any bands?"

"I wasn't that cool." Cam poured in the fideo pasta. "But my cousin was a bouncer, and sometimes he'd let me sneak in through the emergency exit to watch bands play at his bar."

"Did your mom know?" Marcus helped Cam pour the rest of the soup mixture into a pot. All the ingredients began mixing together. The smell was incredible.

"Of course not! She thought I was doing community service." They laughed together companionably, and Cam even got to see Marcus's elusive dimple.

While they waited for the soup to finish cooking, Marcus got his laptop out on the table to show Cam what he had been working on before he fell asleep. It was a clickable mock-up that mimicked the proposed flow of Cam's website. Cam was stunned at how, even with stock placeholder art, the website looked and felt so much better to navigate. She didn't have the words to describe why it was so much better; it just was.

"How did you do this?" Cam asked, flabbergasted.

"There's a lot of software out there that you can use to make a wireframe pretty easily," Marcus explained, clicking through a few more pages. "Here's where we'll put the photos."

"No, I mean, how do you know all this stuff? How it should look?" The more Cam observed Marcus's handiwork, the more she could tell he actually had quite a lot of experience in design.

"I took some graphic design classes in college. And a couple on website design." He explained, "And here is where you can integrate the most recent messages from your message board."

"Your parents allowed that? They seem . . . pretty strict." Cam knew she was stepping into dangerous territory, but she was genuinely curious.

"I was required to take a certain number of classes outside my major to graduate, so I picked graphic design," Marcus responded stiffly. Cam could see that he was starting to clam up.

"Look, I know you said your parents have high expectations for you, but you seem really good at this stuff. And even more important, you seem to like doing it. I guess I'm just wondering . . . why aren't you pursuing it more . . . full-time?" Cam could tell she was making a huge blunder of this.

"Design is just a hobby," Marcus snapped. "Do you want my help or not?"

"Yes, of course I do—" Cam stumbled over her words just as the alarm on her phone went off. Gratefully, she rushed back to the stove and poured two bowls. She added creme fraiche, avocado, and a few other garnishes to each bowl before coming back to the table.

They ate in a tense silence, the camaraderie from earlier evaporated. But in Cam's experience, good food could wear down even the hardest of hearts. And Rosa's recipes made for very good food.

"Is there enough for seconds?" Marcus asked, a peace offering stretched out ruefully.

"I always make enough for seconds." Cam smiled and took his bowl, her fingers brushing against his.

Just then, a tornado crashed through the front door. Avery came spinning in, holding Sofia in their arms like a bride across a threshold and singing a bawdy pop song at the top of their lungs. They were actually quite good.

"Hello, Cam. Hello, Marcus." Sofia waved serenely from Avery's arms.

Avery whipped around, saw Cam and Marcus, and came charging over. "I hope we're not interrupting anything." Avery waggled their eyebrows in an obscene way and eyed Marcus's pajamas.

"Marcus was just showing me his mock-up for the Specio website," Cam supplied hastily. She gestured at Marcus's still-open laptop.

Sofia tapped Avery's shoulder twice, and they gently tipped Sofia onto her feet. Sofia clicked through the mock-up and began nodding her head.

"Good," she said in her usual loquacious manner.

Avery, who had been looking over her shoulder, chimed in, "I know a guy who can take the pictures. Owes me a favor."

"I like it," James said from Sofia's other side.

"James! How did you get here?" Avery yelled jovially to the quiet page, who had managed to sneak up on all of them.

"The front door was wide open," James replied, deadpan. "Let me see the rest of the site."

Cam smiled enthusiastically as Marcus looked on quietly. She was finally going to have a badass website. Let them try and complain again.

Chapter 38

THE REST OF THE WEEK flew by. By day, Cam struggled to stay afloat with the influencer project. It was becoming increasingly difficult to stay interested in the problems of wealthy individuals when the Ofanim message boards were constantly being flooded with new, excited users sharing stories of how Specio was changing their lives. By night she worked with Avery to find new users, Sofia to provide new software updates, James to improve hardware and accessibility for different users, and Marcus to clarify the visual brand.

Marcus had seamlessly slipped into the team. The first night he came down to the garage workspace with Cam, he had instantly charmed Sofia with a few well-chosen compliments and made James feel at ease by asking about his fidget gadgets. His easy banter with Avery cemented him in the circle. He had even charmed Cam's mother on a user research call that ran far longer than Cam would've expected and, for some reason, required that Cam leave the room so as not to "skew the results." Cam heard Marcus laughing loudly through the door. Afterward, Marcus had exclaimed to Cam, as if it were truly surprising, that "Rosa seemed really supportive of you!" Unsure what to make of the statement, Cam just nodded her head.

Throughout the week, Marcus sat in the middle of the group and intermittently worked on the website while exchanging horrifying childhood stories with Avery.

"And then"—Marcus was almost crying, he was laughing so hard at this point—"Avery came out of the ski lodge in a penguin suit and said, 'I'm running away to the North Pole!'"

"I WAS SEVEN!" Avery hollered back, though they too were laughing. "And anyway, the penguins WOULD have adopted me. Look how cute I was." Avery pulled out their phone and found a picture of themselves, a chubby-cheeked age seven, in a penguin suit. Their face seemed to emerge from the penguin's mouth.

Sofia grabbed the phone and let out a high-pitched squeal, the likes of which Cam had never heard come from her. "I need this photo."

"I was cuter." James held out his phone, which displayed a photo of him as a toddler dressed as a box of popcorn. His giant blue eyes staring out doe-like between large fake kernels.

What followed was a heated discussion of the cuteness factor of each of them as babies, along with a desperate one-upping of who had the worst baby photo of all time. Cam couldn't remember who won or lost, only that her sides were hurting from laughing so much. But best of all was Marcus's hand squeezing hers under the table.

With no clear indication of who started it, Cam and Marcus had begun kissing each other whenever they thought they were alone. Sneaky kisses behind the CNC machine, quick kisses in the hall, playful kisses on each step down the stairs to the kitchen, deeper kisses on the living room couch. Always, they sprung apart when they heard someone approaching, an unspoken desire to keep the extent of their relationship a secret from the rest of the pages. Actually, Cam didn't even know if it was a relationship. She kept meaning to ask, but every time she was with Marcus, all she could think about was his mouth on hers, his hands roaming over her body, and his amber-cinnamon smell filling her lungs.

A few days later, Marcus sat down next to Cam in the garage and showed her a mostly completed website. "It's not perfect," he warned. "There is way more than could be done in a week. But this should help a lot."

"Marcus this is incredible," Cam said, and meant it. There was a visual cohesion throughout the site that made it not only beautiful but also enjoyable to use. Cam found herself exploring the site repeatedly just because the navigation was so seamless and fun. Marcus had even hidden a few little surprise animations for those who knew which photographs of the Specio adapter to click. "I really wish you had the time to check out the UX of the installation and software for Specio too." They had briefly discussed it, but as Wyatt came back in just a few days, they had decided Marcus's time was best prioritized on the website. Marcus shrugged.

"Hey." Changing the subject, Marcus turned his body to Cam and rested his hand on the back of her chair. "I want to apologize about the other day for not taking you out to dinner."

"Oh?" Cam responded coyly, looking around the room to make sure they were alone before turning to rest her knees in between his.

"I want to make it up to you." He lowered his voice and bent over her.

"How are you going to do that?" Cam leaned into him, her lips just a breath away from his.

"Let's go out tomorrow." Marcus reached over and rested his hand on her thigh just above her knee. "I'll pick you up at six?" He squeezed, and Cam heard herself gasp.

"Yes, six. Yes, that sounds great." Cam struggled vainly to speak articulately while Marcus's thumb moved in slow, firm, delicious circles on her inner thigh.

"Perfect." Marcus smiled one of his dazzling smiles with his dimple on full display. Then he took one of his long, slow kisses. His methodical ones, which caused Cam's toes to curl and her insides to melt into a hot pool of desire. Too soon for Cam's liking, he pulled back and gave her a flirty peck on the nose. "I'll see you tomorrow."

He got up with a spring in his step and left Cam to go take yet another cold shower. She seemed to be taking a lot of them these days.

Chapter 39

CAM WAS NERVOUS. HAVING A full day to overthink her upcoming date with Marcus that night had made her anxious with anticipation. Any sort of work she had caught up on with the influencer project this week was completely obliterated, as she kept thinking about her date in the evening. Back in her room that night, Cam was trying on outfit after outfit, dissatisfied with each and becoming more stressed about the time. Time, which had moved so slowly though the day, was now whirling quickly out of control. She was ready to start crying in frustration when Avery knocked and quickly let themself in.

"Darling, I hope that wasn't your plan." Avery looked up and down at Cam, who had two different shoes on in a vain attempt to decide which matched the outfit better.

"Plan for what?" Cam hedged.

"What you're going to wear on your date," Avery said bluntly.

"What date?" Cam attempted evasion, but Avery was having none of it.

With a roll of their eyes, they said, "I'm not an idiot. You and Marcus have been dancing around each other for months now. It's good to finally see it getting somewhere. Although Sofia thought it would happen sooner and James thought it wouldn't happen at all. Which means they lost our bet and they owe me a bottle of seventy-five-year aged whiskey in the brand of my choice."

Before Cam could react to this revelation that not only was her secret relationship not so secret but the other pages had been gambling on it, Avery was picking up and thrusting articles of clothing at her. "This, this, and this. Change." They had absolute authority in their voice.

Cam's back stiffened. "I can pick my own outfit, Avery." The fact that she sounded petulant when she said it irritated her even more. Galvanized into decisiveness by her anger, she selected her pieces one by one, pointedly not selecting any of the options Avery had picked out. Avery backed off and watched. Soon, Cam was dressed in a pleated yellow miniskirt, a dark russet scoop neck, and a white biker jacket. She accessorized with white booties. Avery offered up a pair of tiny pepper stud earrings and a purse that looked like a bottle of hot sauce with enough of a humble air that Cam accepted them as the peace offering they were. "Thank you," she said with less heat. She examined her look in the mirror as Avery watched. Finally, Cam broke down and asked, "Can you help me with my makeup?"

Avery smiled without any smugness, sat Cam down, and got to work. After a beat, they said, "So you and Marcus, huh?" They picked out an eye shadow from a palette they had brought.

Cam sighed, understanding that the price of this timely makeover was gossip for Avery. "Any red flags I should know about?" Cam figured if Avery could ask questions, she could too.

Avery paused, considering the question as well as Cam's face with the eye shadow they had just applied. "He's got a lot of pressure on him from his parents."

"I noticed," Cam said wryly. "Your parents know each other; do yours pressure you too?"

"Mine are different." Avery pulled out a black eyeliner pen. "They want me to succeed, and they'll use their influence and connections to help me in any way they can. I've got nepotism helping me, for sure, but we gave up on trying to understand each other years ago." They examined their handiwork. "If you ask me, Marcus should push back against his own parents more. I think he makes good choices when he decides for himself."

"So you and Sofia . . ." Cam said, deciding to switch the topic.

"She is a gem, is she not?" Avery practically gushed, touching up Cam's face with light concealer, blush, and contouring. "Her perfection is unrivaled, she is a queen and the world is her queendom, she is the apple of my eye."

"So . . . is she your girlfriend?" Cam mumbled between applications of lipstick.

Avery paused and got a soft look in their eyes. "I've traveled a lot—known many people—but I don't stay anywhere for long. . . . I've never had anyone like Sofia." Avery looked suddenly vulnerable in a way Cam had never seen them be before. They went on. "I don't—I mean—we're still figuring it out. Labels aren't either of our thing. But yes, she is important to me."

They shook their head and seemed to inflate themselves back to their usual boisterous overconfidence. "Enough of that, look at yourself." Avery guided Cam to a mirror.

Cam had been worried Avery might apply the same lilac-and-silver floating flame eyeliner to her—a look that was incredible on Avery, yet Cam didn't feel she had enough gravitas to pull off—but she needn't have worried. Avery knew their craft. She was the same Cam as before, only the slightest bit enhanced.

Cam hugged Avery. "Thank you." She hesitated a moment, then added, "I really appreciate you. And I'm happy to hear about you and Sofia." She paused. "But if you hurt her, I'll delete every single contact in your phone."

Avery laughed in appreciation of the threat and hugged her back warmly. "Noted," they said, then stuffed something into her hot-sauce-bottle-shaped purse. "Now go, or you'll be late," they crowed.

As Avery shoved Cam out of her bedroom door and down the stairs, she looked into her purse. It was positively overflowing with condoms.

"Oh my god, Avery, who even needs this many?" Cam screeched, and felt herself blushing. It certainly wasn't the first time that her purse had carried protection, but it was the first time she had had a friend give them to her so cavalierly.

"This many what?" Marcus asked, stepping out of his room, wearing a pair of slim-fit slate-gray wool slacks, matching wool suit jacket, and a casual gray cotton crew-neck shirt underneath. In short, he looked absolutely delicious, and Cam couldn't help but think about all the little foil packets in her possession and their intended purpose.

Cam snapped her bag shut as fast as she could. "Nothing!" Avery only cackled, not helping at all.

"Shall we go?" Cam dashed forward and looped her arm through Marcus's, practically dragging him out of the house before Avery could come up with a new way to embarrass her.

"Bye, kiddos—have a good night!" Avery waved at them from the door. Cam flipped them the bird, and Avery blew kisses back.

Outside, Marcus laughed. "Don't let it bother you. Avery only heckles people they really like." He summoned a Beekar.

"I feel sorry for their enemies," Cam muttered as the car pulled up.

A short while later, they pulled up in front of the California Academy of Sciences. Marcus explained that once a week the natural history museum would close for the day, then reopen its doors for the evening date crowd. Food stalls, pop-up cocktail bars, and a DJ or two were always on hand, though the main attractions were the animal life and specimen collections.

"They have an albino alligator?" Cam leaned over the enclosure with amazement. A white alligator floated lazily, surrounded by several equally lazy turtles.

"Don't accidentally feed him your mai tai," Marcus warned with a laugh.

They wandered through the rainforest biome where Marcus marveled at the insects and Cam kept a healthy distance. They wove through the aquarium and decided which fish best represented their friends (they agreed Avery was a peacock mantis shrimp). They admired the rock collection and laughed at the penguins' antics.

"My mom would love this," Cam said as they stood in a holographic projection of the inside of a blue whale. The projection began with the skeleton, then slowly added the vast nervous system, the pulsing circulatory system, the digestive system, and so on until they were encased inside the vast breathing hologram of a giant sea creature.

"Rosa's studying nursing, right?"

"Yes, she told you about it?" Cam asked as a humongous lung expanded above her.

"She told me about how she uses Specio to look at holograms of human anatomy," Marcus explained. "It's clear she's really proud of you."

"Well, I'm really proud of her." Cam watched as holographic muscles formed around them. "She basically raised me by herself. We don't have a ton, but she's always given me everything she can. Like when she got me my first radio to pull apart. Or when she gave me the bedroom of our apartment in high school so that I could have a private space to study. She's wanted to study to become a nurse for years, but she said she wouldn't until after I graduated college. So, I'm happy to finally be the one supporting her." Cam smiled at Marcus.

Marcus gave her a look of slightly dazed wonder. "The Diaz family is made of some incredible women," he said, tucking her hair behind her ear.

Cam felt her cheeks go pink.

"Come on," said Marcus. "Let's go check out the roof."

They walked up a flight of stairs into the brisk night air. Above them, the dark sky was clear with a twinkling of stars; beside them was an undulating grassy rooftop. Cam blinked.

"Cool, isn't it?" Marcus asked in an eager way, like he completely expected Cam to agree with him.

"Why is the roof shaped like this?" Cam asked.

"It's a living roof! It was designed by the architect Renzo Piano to mimic the hills of San Francisco." Marcus leaned over the railing separating their terrace area from the rest of the roof. He began gesturing energetically to features as he pointed them out. "See the round windows in the hill? Those open to help regulate the temperature in the building below us, but the moist and compacted dirt means the visitor area stays cool and doesn't need air-conditioning." Cam stopped looking at the roof and just watched Marcus. The way his eyes shone, his face animated, his skin practically glowing. "All the plants up here are also native to the area, and more species show up all the time thanks to the birds and insects that visit."

"You really like this stuff. Design, I mean," Cam said. She didn't know if she had ever seen him so full of vigor. So *alive*.

"I just love seeing ways design can do good, you know?" He looked at Cam, dimple on full display. "How art can elevate what's already there and help us appreciate it."

Cam reached up with both hands and pulled his face to hers in a deep kiss.

Marcus was stiff with initial surprise but quickly melted and enthusiastically kissed her back. Cam dragged at him, hungry for the passion he showed when talking about art. Eager to taste the zeal of his heartfelt words on his tongue. Marcus complied, spilling his energy into her in a way Cam had never felt from any of his kisses before. He thrummed with intensity, his kisses going deeper, his arms pressing her fully into his warm and hard body. She gasped as he nipped at her lip, sending a tingling sensation ricocheting down to her toes.

Marcus pulled back from her the barest amount, and Cam looked up at him dazedly.

"Should we . . . go home?" He sounded a little bit ragged, and Cam realized her hands were under his shirt grabbing his waist.

"Yes. Yes, we should." Cam nodded emphatically.

Chapter 40

THE RIDE HOME WAS SHORT but intense. Cam and Marcus couldn't keep their hands off each other, exchanging kisses and touching every piece of exposed skin on each other's bodies. Cam was practically in Marcus's lap by the time the Beekar finally rolled up to the page house. Thank God for driverless vehicles, Cam thought as they tumbled out of the car and up the front steps.

The inside was dark, the rest of the pages having gone to bed. They tripped out of their shoes, attempting to be quiet while continuing to kiss their way across the living room. It was a lost cause, as Cam nibbled Marcus's ear and he groaned low in his throat. She felt a delicious satisfaction at being able to break through his pristine shell and see his eyes shining with raw desire. A desire for her that was intoxicating.

He retaliated by biting her neck in a sharp, sweet love bite, sending a wave of need coursing through her body. She gasped. He chuckled a deep bass rumble against her neck. Their progress up the two flights of stairs to her room was slowed as they pushed each other up against walls to kiss deeper, more forcefully.

Marcus's knee thrust between her legs as she was pinned to the wall almost made her tear his clothes off in the hallway. The way he rocked his thigh into her had her legs trembling with the sweet building sensations, threatening to collapse underneath her. His lips stretched into a grin as he felt her arch against him.

Two could play at that game. Cam shoved him off her and pressed him into the stair railing with her body. She began to confidently rub the hard length of him that had started to strain against his pants. It only became harder under her ministrations and had Marcus panting into her open mouth. She swallowed it all and reveled in her power over him.

With a growl, Marcus picked Cam up and carried her in his arms the last steps to her room. He stopped on the platform by her door and looked down at her questioningly. His eyes were full of lust, but even through the haze, she could see he was willing to put her down, go back to his own room if she sent him away. She didn't even hesitate in opening her door for him.

They tumbled in, Marcus barely managing to kick the door closed before they fell onto the bed in a tangle of limbs. Marcus rolled on top of her and pulled down her low neckline and bra to expose her taut nipples to the cold air.

"I've been wanting to do this for ages," Marcus whispered against her skin before taking a hard bud into his mouth. Cam gasped as he sucked and sent pulsating waves of pleasure to her core. She clung to his shoulders tightly as he moved to her other breast and repeated the process. She felt her hips begin to rock involuntarily against him, eager for even more.

He released her and sat back on his heels to peel off his jacket. Cam rose up with him, tracing her hands up his sides to strip off his shirt, following with kisses over each freshly exposed rib. Her hands felt the muscles of his broad warm back as she rained kisses over his collarbone and neck and he tossed his shirt to who even knew where. As her hand reached down to unbutton his pants, he caught her wrist and brought it to his mouth to kiss. As tingles ran down her arm, a part of her brain registered surprise that that part of her body could be so sensitive.

"Not yet," Marcus rumbled, and grazed his teeth lightly over her delicate skin, causing yet more tingles to ricochet from her arm to her center. He pushed her back onto the bed and leaned over her with one hand by her head as he reached under her skirt with the other. Gently, he stroked across her through the thin fabric separating her from his roving fingers. She gasped and grabbed his shoulders.

Where Marcus had been all passionate haste a moment ago, he abruptly slowed and began carefully and methodically exploring her. He stared down at her intently, watching every expression flit across her face as he caressed her. Under this onslaught, Cam felt herself begin to hum with desire. Just as she was about to kick off the offending fabric, Marcus pushed it aside and began to traverse her folds with the same attentiveness, watching her face for the effects of his efforts. Cam wasn't thinking anymore, only wanting; she felt her nails dig into his shoulders as she began to pant.

Finally, he slid a finger into her. Cam moaned at the welcome sensation. He began to pump slowly, a jolt of bliss with every thrust, and built her up until he was able to slide in a second finger. Cam grabbed Marcus's face and began kissing him fiercely. Probing him with her tongue as he plunged into her with his fingers.

Abruptly, Marcus broke the kiss and moved to lower his head between her legs. He pulled off her underwear and, without any more preamble, touched his tongue to her, lightly at first, then with increasing force, while continuing to thrust with his fingers. He curled them inside her as if beckoning her to him. Cam lost control. Her hips bucked wildly. Marcus responded by pressing her down into the mattress with the palm of his free hand against her pelvis. He transitioned from licking to sucking as Cam moaned her way through an orgasm the likes of which she had never felt before. Her entire body seized and arched, trembling at each peak, her nerves chiming like one vast tuning rod.

After an eternity, Cam lay panting, damp with sweat. Marcus sat back and laughed richly, arm under Cam's leg, holding her thigh against the side of his face.

She had had satisfaction by herself, and with other partners, before. Her last boyfriend, Nick, had gotten the job done. But there was a world of difference between the consummation she felt after a quick session in a pickup truck and the drained, full-body humming sensation she felt after Marcus had touched her. Like the difference between a puddle and a turbulent river. Her hearing in her left ear was momentarily muffled.

Cam smiled happily and lethargically as Marcus got up and slowly and carefully helped her remove the rest of her clothes. She felt boneless and intensely sensitive to all sensations. Sensitive to his hands sliding over her arms, his thumbs brushing over her nipples. To his light caresses down her spine, awakening her anew. Fully naked before him, she leaned in to kiss him deeply. This time when she reached for his pants, he didn't stop her, but groaned as she helped set him free.

"You're a lot," Cam remarked as she ran her fingers over the hard, velvet surface of him.

Marcus chuckled. "Let me get a condom." He looked around for his jacket that he had thrown somewhere.

"I got it." Cam leaned over and retrieved her purse from the floor. The catch was stuck on something. Cam gave it a couple of good yanks, and the purse exploded outward in a shower of condoms.

They both stared at the bed. Marcus broke first, laughing long and hard. Cam laughed with him as she cleared them a condom-free zone in the middle of the mattress. Marcus picked one up and began to ease Cam back onto her back.

"No, like this," Cam insisted, switching places with him and pushing Marcus down. He easily acquiesced.

She knelt above him and took his length in her hand. Feeling the rigid, pulsating heat in her palm, she stroked the whole of him. He groaned, head leaning back. She felt powerful, holding and controlling his reactions. She leaned in to take him into her mouth and suck. He cursed under his breath and moaned as she continued to stroke and suck him.

His thighs suddenly clenched, and he begged her to stop. "Please, for the love of God, stop. Stop. I'm so close. God," he panted beneath her. His hands gripping the headboard like his life depended on it. Cam almost ignored his request, but her core pulsed. She wanted him inside her too.

Almost reluctantly, she let him go and opened the condom, carefully sliding it over the whole of him. Then she straddled him. He grabbed her waist to help ease her down as she guided him into her. She was so well prepared for him, his girth slid into her easily, stretching and expanding her so exquisitely she almost unraveled when she reached the hilt of him. Marcus was no better, eyes squeezed tight with concentration as he held her hips firmly in place. They stayed that way for a few moments, breathing heavily, locked together, reveling in the feeling of being joined so intimately. Then they began to move. Slowly and only a little bit at first, then faster and harder. Marcus's hands pulled her down to help set pace, his thumbs digging into the sensitive nerves in her pelvis and driving her wild.

Without warning, Cam felt her core detonate as she orgasmed for the second time, even harder than the first. She saw stars and fireworks behind her eyes. As the tidal waves of pleasure subsided, she found herself quaking on top of Marcus, him still throbbing deep inside her.

Cam looked at him and found him staring in awe at her. He reached up and brushed her hair back from her face.

"That was the hottest thing I've ever seen," he confessed.

"That felt really good," she confessed back. She was too euphoric to feel embarrassed by her admission or his compliment.

He grinned in an extremely self-satisfied way and helped ease her off him and down next to him. She felt unbelievably heavy and infinitely light at the same time, every part of her body tingling with rapture.

Marcus took himself in his hand, clearly prepared to reach his own climax by himself, before Cam stopped him. "Please, give it to me," she requested, too wrung out to articulate herself any clearer.

Marcus looked at her lethargic body, which practically glowed with satisfaction. "Are you sure?"

"Yes," she heaved. "I need more." And it was true. She felt a hunger inside her, one that told her she wasn't done yet, even though another part of her couldn't believe she still wanted more.

Marcus saw the voracity in her eyes and nodded. Cam lifted one leg invitingly, angling her hips in a way she knew would have him hit all the right spots. He obliged, leaning over her to slide himself in easily. She almost screamed at how good it felt.

With very little buildup, he was ratcheting into her. His thrusts pushed him deeper and deeper into her, pounding her into a level of bliss she hadn't even known was possible. She felt wound too tight, her skin too sensitive, her body too filled with pleasure. Just when she thought she would die from the sensations of it all, she reached her peak and something snapped. For the third time that night, she climaxed harder than she ever had before. If her other partners had produced puddles, she had felt a river, an ocean, and now a tsunami in a single evening. Pleasure crashed in wave after wave of ecstasy, so intense that she only vaguely felt Marcus shudder and join her over the edge. Contented, she sighed and rode the sensations into oblivion.

A short while later, Cam woke to Marcus handing her a glass of water. She took it gratefully as he slipped under the covers with her. They sat propped upright, cuddling, passing the glass back and forth between them.

"So," Marcus said, placing the empty glass on the nightstand. "Your bag. Pretty ambitious," he teased.

Cam groaned in embarrassment and looked at the foil packets strewn about the bed and floor.

"I consider that a challenge." He leaned over and started playfully kissing her neck.

She laughed and turned her head to kiss him back, hands already tracing his sides.

Chapter 41

SUNSHINE BEAMED THROUGH THE HALF-DRAWN curtains of Cam's bay window. She squinted at the sun and burrowed her face back into Marcus's shoulder. Marcus obligingly rolled over and put his back to the window, creating a pocket of shade. She hummed appreciatively as he pulled her closer.

"Morning," he murmured into her hair.

"Morning," she mumbled into his chest. She lay in a state of utter, languid comfort. It was a full-body relaxation she hadn't felt in weeks, not since before the conference. Maybe not even since before Beekor. Actually, maybe not ever. She felt herself drifting back to sleep.

She blinked. It seemed like just a moment, but the angle of the sun implied more time had passed. Marcus rumbled, "What time is it?"

Cam muttered something nonsensical, then squawked a protest as her warm, living pillow turned over to grab his phone. He whispered apologies, and she sighed contentedly as they resettled into their previous positions.

Cam was still half-asleep, but she could feel Marcus's body tensing as he looked at his phone over her shoulder.

He cursed softly. "It's late. I have to get going." He disentangled himself from Cam and rolled out of bed stiffly, all the relaxed grace of just a few moments ago gone. As he searched about the room for his various articles of clothing, she could practically see him returning to the more cool, professional Marcus she was used to seeing. His work face was at odds with the more open and passionate side she had been glimpsing more of in the past week and had spent the entire blissful night with.

"Where are you off to?" Cam asked groggily, wondering what had caused him to change so abruptly.

"My parents want to see me," he said offhandedly. His mind was clearly somewhere else as he stepped into his pants and buttoned them up.

"They're here?" Cam squeaked, sitting upright.

"No, Napa cabin." He looked up from chasing socks and froze. Something happened to Marcus as he looked at Cam sitting on the bed, shirtless, blankets strewn about her, tousled bedhead, with morning light streaming behind her. His face gentled, dropping his detached mask and returning to the compassionate lover of the night before.

"Come with me," he said softly.

"What?" Cam croaked. Her clear reluctance broke the spell, and Marcus shook himself free of his blind admiration.

But even so, it just caused him to repeat, loudly and with more conviction, "Come with me. I want you to come with me." He came over and sat down next to her on the bed.

"I— You mean to see your parents?" From what little Cam had gleaned about Marcus's parents, they sounded strict, and nothing like her own mother. She wasn't sure she was ready to meet them, especially after a night of so little sleep.

"Yes, I want to introduce you to them. They love smart people, so they'll love you." Marcus grabbed Cam's hand and squeezed. "And I . . . I would just really appreciate having you there." He looked at her so earnestly, the fun, creative Marcus shining out through his eyes, that Cam felt her will crumble.

"Fine." She sighed. "I'll go meet your parents."

—

This is not a cabin, Cam thought a couple hours later as she beheld the sprawling, ranch-style home that sat on a hill overlooking rolling fields of photogenic vineyards below.

The first sign that Marcus had been understating the scale of the "cabin" was when a private, two-seater autocar had come to pick them up from the page house. It wasn't a Beekar. It was something else. It radiated disturbing expense.

"Sorry it's a little tight," Marcus apologized ruefully. "I didn't think to ask for one of our larger cars. It's usually just me."

Cam mumbled something about it being fine as she slid rigidly into the leather-lined interior that was, in truth, wonderfully spacious. She had lost some of her nervousness on the hour-long ride over, Marcus holding her hand as they listened to music and talked about bands they liked. Marcus surprised her with some of the more eclectic musicians he was into.

"I can't believe you've seen Trap Spider Monkeys live. I'm so jealous," Marcus practically gushed.

"I told you, my cousin's a bouncer. I'm surprised you've even heard of them—I thought you only listened to classical music." Cam grinned playfully.

"Alas, I *am* a classically trained pianist." Marcus looked dramatically pained, and Cam had to laugh. "But I've always fancied being a bass guitarist. Every band needs one! They are the glue that can make or break a band's whole sound, and they can *destroy* a solo."

"But the lead guitarist gets more fun bits," Cam reasoned.

"Fine, let's start a band. You lead from the front, I'll support from the back, and the whole crew of us will go platinum." Marcus whooped and kissed her.

Cam's good cheer evaporated as they pulled through the gated driveway of the "cabin" and into a freestanding garage that looked like it could have engulfed the entire apartment in which she had grown up three times over and still have room for more. The two-seater slid between an SUV and a luxury stick-shift sports car. Cam didn't get a good look at the other three cars in the garage, but she didn't need to to start calculating astronomical costs in her head.

As Cam got out of the car, she looked over at Marcus stepping out in a pale orange linen suit. In the ride over, he had been casually slumped, limbs spread wherever they fell. Now, he appeared wound stiff and tight, every muscle held in precision. Cam felt her own spine aching in sympathy, or maybe she was just as tense.

Marcus led her out of the garage and up the gravel path, past a gurgling fountain, and to the front door. He hadn't even rung the doorbell before the massive hardwood door was opened by a tiny, middle-aged woman with her brown hair in a bun and wearing a maroon suit. She looked nothing like Marcus.

"Welcome home, Marcus!" the woman beamed up at him and ushered them into a spacious foyer.

Marcus smiled back down, dimple and all. "Thanks, Laura. I didn't know you were going to be here."

"Your mother is planning on staying here until your commencement and is thinking about a few renovations, so she asked me to come along. I heard your car coming up the drive and knew I had to see you before you get swept up by your parents." Laura glanced at Cam and then expectantly up at Marcus.

"Oh, right—sorry!" Marcus startled. Then he looked at Cam and gestured to Laura. "Cam, this is Laura. She's our estate manager, and she's known me since I was little." Marcus reversed. "Laura, this is Cam, ah, a fellow Beekor page." Cam snapped her head over at Marcus's slight stumble. What had he been thinking of saying?

Laura reached out and shook Cam's hand. "It's a pleasure to meet you, Cam. I used to be the Davidsons' housekeeper before they sent me to get my degree, so I am well aware of the troublemaker Marcus was as a boy. I hope he hasn't given you too much grief." Her eyes twinkled, and Cam began to think she had also observed Marcus's verbal trip.

Cam smiled at the petite woman, who reminded her of her own mother and felt at ease enough to tease. "I'd love to hear some of those stories."

Laura's eyes sparkled with mischief. Before Marcus could do more than groan, however, a rich voice called down from the hall, "Is that Marcus I hear?"

In rolled a heatwave. That was the only way to describe the woman who looked like a fine-boned and delicately aged version of Marcus with microbraids swept up into a bun. In gold heels and a white tailored power suit, she exuded the confidence and power of the sun.

"My son!" She strode across the foyer in long powerful strides and squeezed Marcus's arms in an embrace as she kissed him on both cheeks. Finally, she held him at arm's length to look at him, almost eye level with him. "How are you? Your emails are so short, but Wyatt's been keeping us apprised. Your brothers are now thinking of grad school at Yale; I think they just are looking for excuses to not come home. I want to hear more about the Knox merger."

When Marcus's mother took a pause for a breath, Laura jumped into the gap with practiced ease. "Mrs. Davidson, please let me introduce you to Cam, another Beekor page."

The woman looked over at Cam, and Cam almost buckled under the full force of her regard. This morning, Cam's plaid slacks, oversized button-down shirt, cable-knit sweater vest, and purse that looked like a bottle of wine had felt the right amount of sophisticated-casual. Now in a building that was closer to a manor than a cabin, in a room full of people in suits, Cam felt like Marcus's mother was seeing into her very soul, where she was still wearing her hand-me-down T-shirts from the community thrift shop.

After a pause, the woman looked back to Marcus, whom she still held, and said neutrally, "I thought you said you were bringing Avery."

"No, I said I was bringing a friend. You were the one who decided it was Avery." Marcus kept his eyes trained on his mother.

"Ah." Another pause. Then his mother let go of Marcus and turned to extend a hand to Cam, placing the full heat of her attention on the young page. "A pleasure, Cam. I'm Mrs. Davidson, Marcus's mother. We're glad you could join us for lunch. I'm sorry you can't stay for dinner, we already have plans, and I didn't realize Marcus was going to bring a new, ah, friend over."

Cam shook the proffered hand. "That's all right. Thank you for having me." Cam wondered if the stutter over the word "friend" was hereditary.

Mrs. Davidson released her from her gaze, and Cam felt like the room temperature dropped by several degrees. The older woman pivoted to Laura. "Laura, I hate to ask, but could you let Maria know to serve lunch in the formal dining room?"

Laura didn't blink before saying, "Of course." But Cam could tell by the way Marcus clenched his fists before forcibly relaxing them that something about the request was unusual.

"I'll see you at noon, honey. We must show your friend proper hospitality," Mrs. Davidson said over her shoulder as she swept out of the room. Laura followed close behind.

Cam waited until she could no longer hear the women's footsteps before reaching out to touch Marcus's hand with hers. He jumped, clearly startled, before laughing at himself and rubbing the back of his neck.

"Is something wrong?" Cam asked.

"No. It's just that usually we dine outside here if the weather is good. The dining room is reserved for more formal occasions or . . . It's nothing. Don't worry about it." Abruptly, he turned to her with animation. "Let me show you the view."

Marcus led her through the house into a vast, open living room with numerous couches that transitioned seamlessly into a mosaic-tiled patio and large pool. They walked past a stone gazebo with curtains tied back to reveal a dining table laid for four and onto a grassy lawn that overlooked miles and miles of vineyards only lightly broken up by buildings and roads. Under a clear blue sky, it was breathtaking.

"Your mom doesn't seem to like me," Cam began.

Marcus's face shuttered, leaving nothing but blank neutrality. "She doesn't know you, and you don't know her."

Cam decided it was best to drop it, at least while they were here. "So, are your parents wine-rs? Or whatever? Do you make wine?"

Marcus relaxed a fraction and gave her a tiny half smile. No dimple. "Vintners, and no, they're lawyers. The vines are leased out; they only wanted the view." For the next hour, Marcus showed Cam around the property and they stayed on neutral topics like the production of wine. For all that Marcus said his family wasn't vintners, he seemed to know a lot about the business of it. But mostly, Cam got the impression he didn't want to be confined indoors any longer than he had to.

Finally, it was time for lunch. Marcus led her back inside the cool house, past marble statues and an enormous display of fresh flowers, and into a large dining room with a long table that appeared to be a single slice of a massive tree. Already seated at the head of the table was a stout older man with closely cropped hair and beard who had Marcus's eyebrows. Mrs. Davidson sat to his left. They both stood as Marcus and Cam approached.

"Father, I'd like you to meet Cam, another Beekor page." Cam noticed that he had dropped the word "friend" altogether. She shook Mr. Davidson's hand.

"Pleasure," he said, and looked calculatingly at her. His stare wasn't fire the way his wife's was, but an arctic cold that had Cam's insides shivering. Cam had only been in this couple's presence for a few minutes and she was a wreck of nerves. She couldn't imagine having grown up with them as her parents.

They seated themselves, Marcus at his father's right, across from his mother. Cam was on Marcus's right and across from no one, giving her a clear line of sight to the gold statue of a wolf biting into the neck of a deer.

The meal started about as well as Cam expected. She tried to stay polite and hedge where she could, but they were lawyers and she felt herself being interrogated on her own personal witness stand. Very quickly, they found out the facts of her entire life's story, wheedling out tiny details she had never discussed before, like her cousin's parole violation and her grandpa's death due to lung cancer. But the thing that annoyed her the most was the way Marcus sat through it all and didn't say anything at all to stop it.

Desperate to avoid further examination, Cam pulled up the main thing she had been thinking about for months.

"Did Marcus tell you about Specio?" That got Marcus's attention. He put down his fork and stared at her. Mrs. Davidson looked to Marcus and then back at her.

"No, he didn't."

"Specio is the project I've been working on since before I got to Beekor." Cam reached into her purse and pulled out her old, non-Beekor phone. It was clad in the latest prototype adapter hardware from James, which was still bulky but was leagues more streamlined and sturdier than the one she had first presented. "Holographic technology is incredibly powerful and useful, but right now it's prohibitively expensive in the latest Beekor devices. So I'm developing a way to turn older phones from as many as five or more generations ago into holophones." Cam typed on her phone, and a moment later, a holographic display of the central nervous system of a cat came up. "The hand-gesture shortcuts aren't properly integrated yet, but Sofia thinks she'll have a solution soon."

"Sofia Ly from the Beekor Accelerator Program?" Mr. Davidson questioned.

"Yes, she's my cofounder," replied Cam. "And James is the one who made this version of the prototype."

"James Foster, also from the program," Mrs. Davidson stated.

"Yes." Cam really didn't like the way Marcus's parents were staring at her. She decided not to mention Marcus's or Avery's contributions given she knew they disapproved of his design interest and they personally knew Avery.

"Does Wyatt know about this?" Mrs. Davidson asked, her voice flatly professional.

"Yes." Cam was irritated that she kept getting asked this. "He gave me his go-ahead."

"What did he say exactly?" Mrs. Davidson insisted.

Cam furrowed her brow. "He said once I learned what I needed to on the influencer project, he would give me the team to work on Specio. Although," Cam admitted, "he wanted to name it something else."

"You cannot be this naive," Mr. Davidson said dryly.

Cam saw Mrs. Davidson looking grim, and Marcus looking aghast at her.

Mrs. Davidson saw the look of confusion on Cam's face and took it into her hands to break it down. She held up one finger. "Firstly, Wyatt isn't going to fund competition against Beekor."

She raised another finger. "Secondly, he isn't going to support something like that, which is a clear deviation from the Beekor brand of luxury and sophistication. That"—she gestured to Specio—"looks like the site of a car wreck."

"Thirdly"—she raised a third finger—"the team Wyatt is dangling in front of you was already promised to Marcus before the program started."

Cam looked to Marcus for an explanation. He couldn't meet her eyes.

For the first time, Cam saw a genuine look on Mrs. Davidson's face, one of startled bafflement. "Don't tell me you didn't know Marcus is meant to win this so-called competition. Isn't that why you're cozying up to him? So he'll get you a good job at Beekor? Or are you aiming to stick around until he becomes CEO of Beekor? You won't last that long."

Cam's head spun, and she felt dizzy. "What?" she asked weakly.

Mrs. Davidson's brows furrowed in confusion over Cam's obvious lack of knowledge. "The page program is a PR opportunity for Beekor. They choose promising candidates who they know the press will like and set them up in the company. And it's a good way to promote select people, like Marcus, quickly. So that he'll be in a position to take over as CEO later." She stated bluntly, "Wyatt selected Marcus over a year ago. He's training Marcus to be his replacement. Everyone knows this."

Cam felt herself undergoing a full-body panic. She felt trapped and claustrophobic and far too short of breath.

"I, uh, think I need some air. Excuse me." She pushed back from her barely touched lunch and dashed through the house and out the back door before finally collapsing beneath a gnarled tree. She put her head between her knees and took several deep breaths. She heard the sounds of feet approaching and looked up to find Marcus.

"Did you even submit a project to Beekor?" Cam asked.

Marcus paused, then seemed to come to a decision. "No," he said.

Seeing how upset she was, he began speaking quickly, almost rambling. "You've seen my parents. They're super-type-A personalities. They planned this all out with Wyatt years ago, for me to go to the right schools, graduate with the right grades, come here, win the program, and be promoted in. The trajectory is for me to be trained to take over as CEO in a decade or so...." He ran out of words and finished limply with "Cam . . . I . . . I really thought you knew this. You hang out with Avery all the time."

"What does Avery have to do with this?" Cam demanded.

"Avery's parents got them in too. We came here together. I thought you knew," he repeated more quietly.

Cam hadn't known. She had suspected something was amiss about the Accelerator Program. There were hints that something was off, such as the way all the pages seemed to have wildly different workloads and schedules, the snarky comments from the previous graduates, and the way Sofia and James had had their projects treated with zero care, either being outright stolen or ignored, respectively. But even with her suspicions, Cam never would have guessed anything of this scale. That, she realized bitterly, was because she was naive and hopeful. Her stupid optimism wouldn't have allowed her to see this possibility because she wanted to believe that if you worked hard enough, you could make it. You could rise to the top. She didn't want to believe it was all back doors and handshake deals.

"I thought you said you were training on the holographic phone adapter. I thought you said your Beekor project is the influencer customization team," Marcus accused, cracking the knuckles of his fingers in a nervous habit Cam had never seen before.

Cam looked at Marcus dumbfounded. "No, the influencer team was for training. My end goal has always been to work exclusively on Specio."

They stared at each other across the gulf of their misunderstandings and misconceptions.

"What, did you think Specio was some kind of phase?" Marcus looked away, and Cam felt her blood begin to boil. "Did you think I was losing sleep and stressing over something I planned to forget in a week?"

Marcus muttered something unintelligible.

"What?" Cam demanded.

"I said I thought you were going to join my team. After the program. I was going to ask you to join my new project."

"Do you know what you're going to do with this team of yours? Or is that something Wyatt is going to pick for you?" Cam asked acidly.

Marcus remained silent. Answer enough.

The hot rage coursing through her veins gave Cam the strength to stand up and face Marcus.

"Am *I* just a phase to you?" Cam nearly spat in his face.

Alarmed, Marcus turned to look at Cam with bright earnest eyes. "No, Cam, of course not." He went to tuck her hair behind her ear, but she pulled back before he could touch her.

"Is that why I'm just your *friend*?" she demanded. "Are you ashamed of me? Heir apparent to the mega corporation can't be seen with the

PR-opportunity poor girl?" Cam felt molten tears burning the back of her eyes, but she refused to shed them.

"No! Cam, believe me, I'm not ashamed of you. You're smart and talented and beautiful and funny. It's just that . . ." He trailed off, unable to complete his sentence.

Cam nodded. "That's what I thought." She turned away from him. "I'm taking the car back by myself. Give your parents my thanks for that enlightening conversation. Have fun at dinner."

She walked away, feeling the door on her and Marcus slamming shut behind her.

Chapter 42

ALL DAY SUNDAY, CAM'S MIND ping-ponged through every emotion—despair, disillusionment, betrayal—before finally deciding to settle firmly on rage. Rage meant she didn't have to work through her feelings about Marcus. Rage meant she didn't have to think about what this meant for her future. Rage meant she could go to work boiling with anger and send an email to Wyatt demanding a meeting without thinking about the consequences.

At her desk the next day, as she mechanically did user research and moved tickets around, all she could think about was what a sham it all was. Her project, *her promise*, none of that had ever mattered to Wyatt or Beekor. She was just a destitute girl Wyatt could use to launder his image. She was ashamed of herself for trusting Marcus, Wyatt, and even Avery. The Three Ts seemed to sense her mood and gave her a wide berth.

Then Wyatt showed up. He said something to her, but she had gone distant in her numbing fury and missed all of it. All she noticed was the look of fear on Terry's face as they looked at Cam to see what the matter was. Cam turned to Wyatt and made eye contact and just nodded. He smiled his fake, perfect smile and did his dynamic visionary act, gesturing grandly as he spun around and strode off, expecting to be followed. Cam trailed behind woodenly.

She walked with Wyatt as he did his whole thing. It really was like a personal TED Talk every time. Cam wasn't surprised to find that he could just keep going with nary a reply on her end. Finally, he gestured to his assistant and led Cam to one of the small, private meeting rooms. This one just had two easy chairs in it, awkwardly positioned facing each other. He sat in one, and Cam obliged him by sitting in the other. With the door closed, the space was dim and stuffy.

"Camila, is something wrong? In your email you seemed upset." Wyatt was projecting empathy, warmth. Cam took a moment internally to applaud whoever had programmed him. He seemed almost human. Very lifelike.

"Yes, something is wrong," Cam finally replied.

Wyatt leaned forward and turned the dial on "soul-searching gaze" up to 10. "What's wrong?"

Cam shook her head, as if to herself. She was done with the bullshit; she decided to be straightforward. Cam trained her face into a semblance of her normal, composed, perky self. "Wyatt, I want to work on my holographic adapter project again."

Wyatt's empathetic act turned off instantly, and he leaned back.

"Is Lee doing this to spite me?"

"What? No. Lee has nothing to do with this." Momentarily derailed by Wyatt's non sequitur, Cam focused on what she wanted to say. "*I* have been refining and improving Specio, turning it into a user-friendly upgrade kit on the side, and I've built a team. The pages and some others outside of Beekor. We've been releasing once a week and have just exceeded a community of a thousand incredibly engaged users." Despite her anger, her passion for what she was doing began to reassert itself. She leaned forward and spoke with increasing enthusiasm. "For many of those users, we have made a *real* difference in their lives. Content creators, people connecting with loved ones, and *students*! So many students—"

"Let me cut you off right there, Camila." Wyatt's eyes blazed with anger, but he kept his voice tightly schooled. "So you've been spending your time and energy, using equipment that Beekor owns, to just . . . do whatever you please?" He looked theatrically outraged. "*This* is why the influencer customization team's numbers have been dropping?"

Cam felt herself losing her cool. "My *numbers*? The project only got back on track thanks to me! Because you said I had '*gaps in my experience,*'" she spat.

Something must have clicked for Wyatt because he stopped and took a different tack. He steepled his fingers and spoke more quietly and evenly. "Camila, the reason why I rejected your project is because it runs counter to one of Beekor's primary principles. Every product we make needs to look, feel, and function beautifully." Cam's gut dropped as she realized Mrs. Davidson had said the exact same thing. If she had been right about that, it only made sense that she would be right about everything else.

Livid at all this implied, Cam thrust a finger at him. "You just want your walled garden full of rich assholes," she accused.

"Because I can control everything that happens in a walled garden!" Wyatt bellowed. For the first time, Cam got the sense that he was finally expressing an authentic emotion.

Cam laughed cynically. "What about the people left outside of it, though? I'm building Specio for all of *those* people."

Wyatt stood up. "I don't have to explain myself to somebody to whom I've given every opportunity."

"Sure," Cam sneered. "Throw me being a *charity case* in my face."

Wyatt sighed. "Far from it. You have done great work with the influencer customization team. Forget about your holographic adapter project altogether and come to Beekor full-time to run that team," he said flatly, as if he were ironing all emotion out of his voice. "You'll get a job offer at the conclusion of the program. I can't remember what Product Manager Level One salary is—one fifty? Three hundred? Whatever. You'll get it. And we can restart this entire relationship on a different footing."

"What about Sofia?" Cam practically leapt out of her chair. "You stole her project from her. You're a thief!"

It was then Wyatt appeared to crack. Every last ounce of humanity seemed stripped from him, and he looked down at Cam with an icy stare devoid of all feeling. He spoke softly, almost monotonously.

"Sofia Ly is a brilliant engineer, but Beekor was already working on facial recognition software before her project came to our attention. Even if Beekor were to have released a product with some features that bore resemblance to hers, there is no court of law that will take her side." Wyatt paused and smiled cruelly. "Speaking of legal standing, are you familiar with California intellectual property law?"

Cam looked confused.

"Camila, let me be clear." He gently laid a hand down on the table. "I own everything. This room, this building, this campus, the house you are sleeping in, the laptop you are using, the machines you print with, the very food you eat. I. Own. Everything." He emphasized the last words with light taps of his finger. "And most of all, I own everything you have created the entire time you have been here."

Cam felt her stomach drop.

Wyatt leaned in and stared at Cam with cold, dead eyes. "Any intellectual property developed using hardware that Beekor assigned to you is the property of Beekor. If you had familiarized yourself with California's laws, you would have already known this."

Cam's face went pale.

Wyatt nodded. "Yes, that means everything you did for your little adapter is now Beekor property. And I say it's time to stop working on it." He said the last part gently, almost like a father telling his child it was time to put down the toys and go to bed.

He straightened. "Now then, Camila, be a dear and fix your influencer numbers, all right? You've been falling behind." He started to walk away before stopping beside her. "Oh, and one last thing. If I hear that you or the other pages are still working on the adapter project, I'll fire and blackball all of you. None of you will ever work in the tech industry again." Cam felt as if she had been slapped.

Wyatt walked out. The door fell closed again behind him. Cam sat in the dim, stuffy room and began to tremble in fear and rage. The voice in her head was wailing. She couldn't bear to be sent back home. She couldn't bear to lose Specio. She had made a life and found her people, and it was all about to be snatched away.

Chapter 43

CAM FELT BOXED IN, TRAPPED. Some of that insecurity she felt from her early days at Beekor returned, along with that yawning gulf of terror at the thought of being sent back. Why had she directly challenged Wyatt? She sat at her desk hyperventilating, panic rolling through her in waves. She thought she had become more worldly, but she realized with complete shame that she was still the same naively idealistic child she had been when she first arrived. She felt sick.

By the time Cam finally looked up, the rest of the day had passed. She stood and wandered mutely through the empty office space. In a haze, she collected her things from her desk and considered the unoccupied space where she and the Three Ts sat. This wasn't what she wanted, but it wasn't such a bad corner of the world. Beekor was still a pretty great consolation prize, she told herself. Travis, Theresa, and Terry were all decent people. She did like seeing them every day. And while the influencer project wasn't exactly changing lives, it did make people happier.

She felt numb.

Cam got home late. As she entered through the front door, she took a look around the house—the spacious, well-appointed place that she had come to call home, along with the rest of the pages. She stopped off in the kitchen and grabbed one of the canned Italian sodas. She drank it in the dark but didn't taste it. From somewhere in the house, she heard muffled sounds of people talking.

Cam tossed the empty can in the recycling and walked through the hall and down the stairs to the basement garage. She pushed the door open to a scene that had become commonplace. User chatter streamed past on the whiteboard. Sofia was leaning on a bench, looking at something on James's computer, while the two discussed some implementation detail or other. They both stopped and looked up at her as she came in.

"What's wrong?" Sofia asked immediately.

Cam wiped her face and realized she had been crying, most likely for a while. She strode over to her desk and slammed her laptop shut, then disconnected it. Sofia touched Cam's shoulder.

Cam turned to her, face streaming with tears. "It's over. I'm shutting Specio down."

"What—" Sofia was taken aback. James looked at Cam in silence, headphones down around his neck.

"We're done," Cam repeated.

Sofia spread her hands, pleading. "Why are you—"

Cam yelled at her, "I said *we're done.*"

Sofia darkened. She straightened and said evenly, "We agreed to equal ownership. We agreed that we're doing this together." All of a sudden, she was seething. "You still think this is your little toy project that you can pick up and put down again whenever you want? You're not the only one carrying this!" she ended in a shout.

Cam felt herself explode. All her bottled-up feelings suddenly came uncorked and poured out in a slurry of vitriol and self-loathing. "A toy project? A toy? This is my life. And I have been burning the candle at both ends to keep everything afloat for months. I've been building the influencer project and scraping Specio together from nothing. The road only gets harder from here, and I'm *so* fucking tired." A distant part of her brain tried to stop her, but she shoved that voice aside, reveling in the pain she was inflicting. "Honestly, I never should have thought we were suitable to be partners. The stakes for me are *actually real*," she almost screamed.

"What are you talking about?" Sofia demanded.

Cam sneered and spat out, "Unlike you, I can't just leave here and return to my family's multimillion-dollar apartment in the Mid-Levels in Hong Kong, or whatever you called it. If something goes south for me here, that's it. I'm fucking done; I don't have a cushy palace to go back to." She instantly regretted saying it, but the jealousy and rage had erupted out of her, impossible to control.

Sofia looked terribly hurt. She took a step back, and her lip quivered once. "Don't hold my background against me. That's unfair."

"Why can't we keep going?" James demanded, punctuating Cam and Sofia's angry exchange. Cam turned to see James looking bewildered and pale. He was utterly still. "I thought you actually cared about making something accessible to everyone." His voice rose to an acid intensity; a bellow as far as James went. Cam suddenly realized that, for James, to trust and become close with them had been *his* risk, and she was betraying him.

"We fit together," he continued, more plaintively.

A wave of shame and self-pity threatened to wash Cam away. She struggled to steel herself. "I learned the truth. And Wyatt wants this *done*." She swept her hand to indicate the whole room and said, in a spiteful singsong, "He told me in no uncertain terms to shut this whole project down. Or else."

At that moment, Avery came into the room in their usual grandiloquent manner. "Hey, what's—" They took in the entire scene in bewilderment. As soon as they saw Sofia, tightly clutching her own elbows, they rushed to her side. They wrapped their arms around her, attempting to support her and block her from Cam at the same time.

Cam's rage flared up uncontrollably, seeing Avery. "I am shutting Specio down. But you knew that," she spat. "You knew what was up all along, didn't you? You knew this Accelerator was all a sham. You knew what we were being funneled into from the start. You knew this wouldn't be allowed."

Avery turned to face Cam, all pretense of bombast and playful arrogance discarded. "Yes. I understood the game we were playing." Avery crossed their arms, whether as a defensive measure or as a form of self-soothing was unclear. They muttered, "Or at least, I knew what was planned for Marcus."

Cam hissed. "No need to tell me that, though?"

Avery laughed angrily. "Oh, come on. How did you not know? Was it like Marcus being the favorite was a secret?" Avery looked around the room. "A part of you chose to not look too closely. Taken in by all the money and the great dinners and free phones. You didn't ask what price you had to pay for all those perks because you didn't want to know."

Cam shook her head. It felt like everything was spinning around her. Avery was right that she had known something was off but had repeatedly avoided asking too many questions.

Avery continued. "Anyway, if you just want to detonate everything here, that's fine. Your loss." They sounded sad but cold. "I wasn't planning to stay at Beekor either way. Unlike you, I entered the Accelerator with my eyes open and my goals clear." They slapped the back of one hand in the palm of the other to punctuate each point. "Enter the program. Make the necessary connections. Add the achievement to the list. Exit." Avery laughed sadly. "It was your fault that I lost sight of that. Caught up in your dream of doing something bigger. Helping people."

"Oh, I'm sorry for not being sufficiently grateful that you've deigned to help me after your parent's *connections* got you into this program. I'm not your charity case, Avery!" Cam bellowed.

Avery flinched and was quiet. They held Sofia, who trembled slightly.

James looked cold and distant, his wall up once more.

The feelings of shame, rage, jealousy, and self-pity reached a crescendo, and Cam began shaking uncontrollably. She hated everything she had done and said but had no way to take them back. *I* am the victim here, she thought. *I* was the one that was betrayed, she reasserted to herself. *I'm* the one that has to go back to the tiny room, the coupon clipping, and no opportunities, if this doesn't work out.

But she *had* known something was wrong, a tiny voice in her head said. *She* chose to ignore it so she could get the perks, get the man. So she could do what she wanted. Cam looked around the room at the office space that they had made together, their beautiful work all over the benches and on screens. She looked at the friendships that she had just shattered, the three people she had betrayed utterly. She sobbed and ran out of the garage.

Chapter 44

ASHAMED, AFRAID, AND DISGUSTED WITH herself, Cam went straight to her room and fell miserably asleep. The next day, she hurried to work early. James was in the kitchen, but she hustled past, avoiding eye contact. On the way across campus, her phone pinged with notifications as messages from the Ofanim chat server came in. Cam angrily dismissed the first few, before finally uninstalling the program from her phone altogether.

As the day wore on, Cam threw herself fully into her tasks, and she found a sort of peace in it. The distraction of complete focus was a respite from the painful memories of the things she'd said and done to her friends. And respite from the project on which she had worked so hard, only to be forced to walk away from it. Cam stayed late that day, ostensibly to wrap up all the loose ends that had accumulated during her long period of negligence but more to avoid the situation at home. When she did finally leave, Cam grabbed some food from one of the dining halls on campus to eat alone in her room.

Arriving through the front door, Cam was in the process of taking off her shoes when she looked up to see Sofia and Avery in the living room. They stood still and watched her, silently, Sofia with a look of mingled sadness and anger, and Avery with a furrowed brow, as if they were experiencing a feeling to which they were not accustomed. Cam dashed up the stairs, past the ghosts of kisses with Marcus, to her attic space. Alone in the room, she relaxed back into a blob of sadness and ate her cold meal sadly, occasionally sobbing.

The next week proceeded much the same. Cam brought everything about the influencer customization project that had frayed back into order. David and Kevin were unblocked. Influencer feedback was collated and turned into fresh new design ideas. The Three Ts seemed thankful, but Cam could see, in the corner of her eyes, the ways that they exchanged worried glances when they didn't think she noticed. She knew she wasn't projecting her usual chipper positivity, but there was nothing for it. She just wasn't feeling very chipper or positive at the moment.

She tried to fake that. There were always team events happening on the campus—kegs and wine available for some team or other that had achieved a new milestone or just come out the other side of a harrowing deadline. From among all the teams she worked with, it was easy to find one that was throwing an event. So Cam threw herself into drinking and hanging out with similar abandon. She attempted to take solace with all her people that she had finally discovered in the hardware and software engineers at Beekor. All those people she had bonded with and seen herself represented in, people who had come to this place because they loved the same things as her, the ability to create things and see their ideas and effort made manifest, were a fun diversion, but didn't address the deep wound she felt like she was walking around with. She missed Tacky Tourist Time. She missed her friends.

Marcus repeatedly texted her, but her feelings were in such a jumble. She had no regrets about their night together, but she couldn't see a future for them. She hated what he represented: continued nepotism. Hated what he had hidden from her, unwittingly or not. In some ways, being together with him felt like giving up every aspect of herself to the corporation that was Beekor. And she didn't think she could do or say that. So she didn't even bother to open his messages.

Cam looked herself over in the mirror before heading out to the group dinner that Friday. She was almost ready to go, wearing an expensive emerald turtleneck dress and black heeled boots, gold hoop earrings, and subtle lip shade. There, she thought, as she picked up the costly little black clutch that would complete the look. It was too small to hold anything but her Beekor phone.

Cam arrived alone at the beautiful restaurant. She was, as always, ushered past the main dining room, this time to a long steel table that was directly in the kitchen. Food was prepared all around them, but the process was oddly quiet. The space to which Cam was ushered was surrounded on all sides by vast windows so passersby could see them.

As Cam entered the kitchen dining area, she saw that everyone was already seated, Wyatt at the head, Marcus at his side, and holding court for several executives and powerful types that had already arrived. He got up when Cam arrived and gestured to the open space on his other side, opposite Marcus. "Please, Cam, join us up here." He smiled graciously.

My reward for being brought to heel, Cam thought. She felt her wall of iron composure crack just a bit, the rage behind it all threatening to escape. Outwardly, she smiled broadly and walked past the other pages at the foot of the table up to the top. She accepted the seat and then laughed in delight as an initial appetizer, a single spoonful of bird's nest soup, delivered in an actual bird's nest, lacquered on the inside for watertightness, was promptly placed in front of her. Down the table, Avery laughed loudly and with abandon, as they exchanged barbs with yet more former-pages-turned-Beekor-employees, to all appearances oblivious to Cam's arrival. James sat with his face down, tapping out one of the most complicated rhythms she had ever heard. Sofia, on the other hand, looked directly at Cam with quiet intensity. Cam felt her charming new smile begin to slip, so she turned abruptly away. She refused to look at Marcus at all.

Course after course arrived, and they were, without fail, incredible. Cam exchanged all her weird jokes, newly acquired *Dance Nights* factoids, and excited engineering stories for bland anecdotes and feigned laughter at the cynical witticisms of the powerful people around her. She pretended engagement with the investor's long, rambling explanation for why his sailing team wouldn't be able to compete in the America's Cup for another year. She acted duly awed by Wyatt's sporadic visionary utterances. She even made empathetic noises as the CEO next to her lamented about how the school of clowns he had invited to take over the company building for the week had, rather than achieving the desired morale boost, actually caused *more* employees to stay home, many of which cited a fear of clowns as the reason to HR.

Against her will, Cam's eyes wandered across the table and briefly connected with Marcus's. Cam felt her heart being crushed. For just a moment, his eyes reflected a deep, desperate sadness, before he could put the wall back up. Cam tried on her cool smile one more time but couldn't quite make it stay. Down the table, Sofia and Avery talked animatedly, until James said something that elicited Sofia's high musical laughter. Cam suddenly felt utterly awash in misery all over again. She excused herself and made her way to the restroom.

Even the restroom was beautiful. An artful wabi-sabi arrangement of three small branches from trees native to the head chef's home, a single candle, and a scattering of duck's feathers on a granite sink all contributed to the most artistic setting in which Cam had ever cried. "I can do this. I can do this. I can do this," she repeated to herself. Cam made a valiant attempt to salvage her makeup in the borderline-useless lighting, then steeled herself to stagger her way back to the table.

As she returned to the table, a man in an immaculate suit was in the process of telling some other inane story that slid right off her in her thoroughly dissociated state. Marcus cut a tiny, concerned glance her way as she sat down; then he returned to acting rapt about the subtly self-aggrandizing narrative as it ramped to a crescendo. And suddenly, Cam was hearing what the man was actually saying: "Anyway, we don't need *another* exec with weird hair color and too many opinions, now do we?"

Wyatt chuckled amicably but responded professionally, "Now, now, big personality aside, Lee's work was an important part of Beekor's history. We both agreed that was where her contribution would remain." Wyatt speared a beautifully seared and dressed prawn with his fork. "For a massive entity like Beekor, it is paramount that there be no confusion about who provides direction. The kingdom thrives when everybody knows where they fit."

Cam bristled. The way he accepted the insult against his cofounder with good cheer, then filed her away in a box labeled "Beekor History," like it was all dusted and done with? At the same time, the mention of Lee's compliance with Wyatt's manipulations struck a chord. Cam suddenly felt the scales fall away from her eyes. The occasional pauses and diversions in their conversations, the way Lee would always hint that Wyatt was capable of bad things, but shy away from a direct assertion—*Lee knew where she fit.* And Lee knew where Cam fit in Wyatt's kingdom too, she thought. Lee knew that Specio didn't have a chance all along. And the dam fully broke, rage and sadness roaring back out. Cam felt herself struggling to breathe.

Cam gasped out an excuse. "I'm sorry, I'm really not feeling well." She abruptly stood, causing all heads to turn. Avery gave her a concerned look. Cam made a brisk exit and ran around the corner and down a block to ensure nobody would attempt to check up on her. Then she called a car to pick her up. As she waited out on the street corner on a cool downtown San Francisco night, the sidewalk sparkling with some kind of ingrained glitter, a stew of feelings threatened to drown her. She took deep breaths and felt some of the anger fade, only to be replaced with hurt. She took out her phone and sent a text.

Chapter 45

Can we talk? *:Cam*

LeeB: something on your mind?

You could say that . . . :Cam

LeeB: wtf . . . right now?

This is serious :Cam

LeeB: say no more. come here

LeeB: [user shared location]

Be there in fifteen :Cam

CAM GOT A BEEKOR AUTONOMOUS car to Lee Baker's location. It was fully dark as she pulled up to the bar in the Mission. The place was called the Tex, and there were a lot of women inside that looked like Lee. The bar was divey in a comfortable way. Chandeliers on chains gave an impression of a sort of faded opulence. Stage lights on the ceiling, aimed at the bar and at large poles around the space, hinted that rowdier stuff sometimes went on.

As Cam entered in her emerald dress, all eyes turned toward her. She ignored the attention as she strode directly up to Lee Baker's side at the bar. For Lee's part, she appeared contrite and only briefly eyed Cam's look. It appeared that she had an inkling of what was bothering Cam.

"You had to know, right?" Cam began resignedly.

Lee took a moment answering. Just then, the bartender, a woman with short hair, aggressive tattoos, and powerful arms, slid a second whiskey their way. Cam took it and sipped it without breaking eye contact with Lee.

"I said it before. Wyatt can make you money, but that asshole will always protect himself and his bottom line."

"Explain." Cam stared. It was a little closer to a rude demand than a request, but Lee let it slide in the face of Cam's obvious distress.

"Look, I didn't want to break it to you and screw up a good thing—"

"I don't need to be protected. Please, explain," Cam bit out.

Lee looked down into her drink while she spoke. "As soon as you said Wyatt was tasking you directly, I got an idea of what he might be doing."

"That's not normal."

Lee shook her head and took a sip of whiskey. "It's not. I think the bottom line he was protecting is obvious."

"What do you mean?" Cam asked, although she was afraid she knew the answer.

"Your project, Specio? It's a direct challenge to Beekor's business model. Wyatt doesn't give the littlest shit about making the holographic revolution accessible to more people. He cares about exclusivity. That's what makes him money." Cam realized Mrs. Davidson had been right again.

"Which is why he was never going to let me move forward with Specio. So he brings me into the Beekor Accelerator and then pressures me to sideline the project. . . ." Cam's eyes went distant.

Lee nodded ruefully. "He gets the project killed and avoids the terrible PR that would come with attacking a young woman of color in court to kill her homemade project." Lee laughed angrily as she realized another wrinkle in Wyatt's plan. "And that's not to mention the fact that he also gets a talented leader for a pet project of his at the company. Two birds"—Lee took a sip—"one fucking stone." She looked at the bartender and raised her empty glass to request another.

Cam felt hurt and disgusted all over again. Hurt that so many people she had worked with and trusted might have known what was going on, Lee especially, but had thought it better not to tell her out of some sort of perverse desire to protect her. The idea that people thought of Cam as some sort of innocent child, to be sheltered from the truth, burned in her throat. Disgusted at the way Wyatt had completely manipulated her, made her question herself. She took her drink over to a couch against the wall and sat down.

Lee got her next drink and joined Cam on the couch. "I didn't want to break it to you so harshly because you really do have a good thing here, if you want it," Lee said imploringly. "I know what it's like to need the money." She hesitated.

Cam took a sip of her whiskey, savoring the burn for a moment. "Oh?"

"Wyatt and I, we started out small and scrappy. But as Beekor got bigger and bigger, something changed in Wyatt. Or maybe it was always there and I had just been blind to it. . . ." Lee swirled her drink. "At any rate, Wyatt still saw as sharp and as far as ever, except that the goals he aimed for changed." She tilted her glass back to her lips. "It wasn't about building the new, exciting thing anymore. Technical innovation was never as important to him as it was to me, which is fine, but it wasn't about changing the world for the better anymore either. It became all about providing the ideal accessories to an elite lifestyle. Shaping the trappings of eliteness and serving it."

To Cam, Lee's face looked lined.

"We began to clash constantly. In private and sometimes in public. In meetings. With the board of directors. I wanted us to keep pushing the technical envelope, and most important, I wanted us to open up more of our tech and more of our platform to allow more people to take part. To relinquish some of our ownership in exchange for far greater reach." Lee looked at Cam. "That was the beginning of the end. Maybe it was the money;

maybe he just got more serious about what Beekor represented and became paranoid about losing control of it. . . .

"In the middle of the power struggle, my dad got sick. It was bad. Beekor, the success we had . . . it made it possible to get him the best care in the world." Lee's voice came out throaty and choked. "And when that didn't work, it made it possible for me to spend his last few months with him, doing everything he wanted, in as much comfort as could be afforded."

Cam nodded sadly.

"When I came back, Wyatt had me sidelined. That snake-fuck shifted almost all my responsibilities off to others. And I—" She looked away, ashamed. "I finally just accepted it. I had made my money, made my mark. Maybe it was all right to let go for a bit, I kept thinking."

A lot of Lee's behavior made more sense to Cam now. Lee was at the start of a whole different chapter of her life, a post-Beekor chapter, despite still being very much attached to it. The days spent completely slacking off fell into place.

"But this isn't about me." Lee shifted direction firmly. "You've gotten an incredible entry into a whole new world. If you just stay on task and follow Wyatt's plan for you, you'll have the money and freedom to pursue whatever you want in no time." In a hushed tone, she said, "If you could endure working with that prick for a little bit." After another pause she proceeded, "Buying your mom a new house? Sending your cousins to college? Taking family vacations to other countries? That would be no problem." Abruptly, Lee stopped. Then she looked Cam full in the face.

"I apologize for treating you like you weren't ready to deal with the full knowledge of what was going on. That was shitty of me."

Cam scrubbed her face with her hands. "I—I'm glad you're being real with me now at least." She looked Lee in the eye. "Don't lie to me ever again," she said seriously.

"I promise," Lee said hurriedly, crossing her heart. Then, "Hey, you've been through some shit. I'm sorry for my part in it. Come here." Lee spread her arms, and Cam accepted her embrace. Lee hugged her tight, and Cam felt some of the feelings of hurt, mistrust, and anger swirling inside of her sort of squish out. She felt supported by the older woman. Cam hugged her back, hard. When they parted, Cam wiped a few tears from her eyes.

Lee Baker suddenly got a cocky smile. "In the interest of our newfound candidness, I would like to reiterate one point."

Cam crossed her arms, cocked an eyebrow, and looked at Lee expectantly.

Lee took on a conspiratorial tone. "There's a reason why Wyatt wanted to stop you. It's because you're an actual threat. You're formidable; that's obvious. There is a world where you carve your own path." Lee spoke slyly and looked up, as if she were peering at the outlines of a possible future.

"It's not easy, but if Silicon Valley is about anything, it's about blazing your own path, Cam." Lee stopped and looked back at Cam. "Call it hubris or stupid-ass confidence, whatever, but for better or worse, there's no problem a founder from out here didn't look at and say, 'I bet I can fix this.' The essence of Silicon Valley is ignoring what we all think of as 'reality' in order to change the status quo.

"And there is no status that is more fucking quo than Beekor." Lee smiled winningly. Then she let the smile slowly fade as she came back down to earth.

"There's no shame in taking the great job, though. The assured paycheck. You'll be a wealthy highflier, just like any of the other former pages at the group dinners." Lee took a sip from her glass and leaned back, looking outward rather than directly at Cam. "There's a real price to taking your own path." She sounded thoughtful. "Usually, you fail. You end up ruined financially. Even if you don't fail, there's still the mornings waking up with your stomach twisted up from the stress. Depression. Burnout." She hesitated a moment. "Betrayal."

Then her expression brightened. "But when you succeed, holy shit! You can change the whole world!"

Cam rested her head against the wall and gazed at the ceiling as she thought things through. "I get it. It's sort of passion versus security."

Lee smiled and nodded at her.

Cam shook her head. "But it's not even possible. Wyatt said—"

"Forget what Wyatt said for a minute," Lee interrupted. "I want to know what *you* think."

Cam tried to keep the quaver out of her voice. "Well, Specio isn't a product I want to sell for profit. That would defeat the purpose. And if I don't make anything—" She began, then redirected. "The stakes are really high for me. If I have to go back—"

"There are options," Lee cut her off. She leaned in. "There's fundraising. You could still take a comfortable salary, even as head of an open-source organization, with all your hardware plans and software fully shared, freely— the way you currently operate." Lee held out a hand before Cam. "You don't need to sell anything to your users. You can operate as a nonprofit if you'd like, although it may be very hard. Or you can run a for-profit open-source company, where you make money off partnerships with large corporations, setting up their hardware and consulting for them as they roll your work out to their organizations." Lee cocked her head to the side. "And that's just off the top of my head." She looked at Cam again. "The point is, there are ways forward if you want to go your own path. Ways that don't involve you going hungry."

Lee made an empathetic face. "It's up to you to make the choice. Passion versus security. Whichever you choose, I'll be here."

Chapter 46

CAM GOT HOME LATE. SHOE evidence by the front door implied the rest of the pages had already gotten home from the mentor dinner. Conversation with Lee still buzzing in her head, Cam could see that she at least had some options, but she was still completely torn about which way to go.

The idea of continuing to work for Wyatt made her skin crawl. She was still shocked after the realization of all the ways he had lied, manipulated, and gaslit her. If she could separate herself from that, however, and simply soldier on, there was a vast pot of gold at the other end of it.

Specio on the other hand was her heart. She had been working on it since before she had joined Beekor, and she had come so far with it, but, if she pursued it, she would have to deal with the very real prospect of enduring an incredibly difficult slog. These months had already been a grueling effort that showed no sign of letting up soon. And all of it could still potentially lead to complete failure. Lee had assured her that a failed company didn't actually mean much in Silicon Valley—it was always possible to take another swing, and it wouldn't ruin your reputation if you gave it an earnest try—but she had stated in no uncertain times how harrowing the grind was trying to operate your own start-up, especially if it started to tank. Actually keeping Ofanim running and growing would not be an easy task.

And then there was the way she had completely dynamited her relationships with the rest of the pages. . . . Better not to think of that. It still hurt far too much.

On a whim, she headed down to the garage. Cam looked around at the chaotic space where all their hopes had been piled up for so many weeks. It sat empty now. That felt wrong after the life they had breathed into the project together there. Various versions of the adapter, organized by James in order of increasing newness, sophistication, and tininess, were lined up on a rail beneath the whiteboard. Cam saw that the digital whiteboard was still on. The social feed widget she had installed in the run-up to the five-hundred-user party was still active.

> *GlowKeeper: hey, any word on where cam was this afternoon? i was really looking forward to the town hall*

Cam felt a pang of guilt. The question had received a flurry of reactions and was followed by many other users with similar questions.

> *Zev [mod]: i'm sure she's all right! don't worry, we'll figure out some news and share as soon as we know more*
> *aiur2x [mod]: she's already shared the updated roadmap. we should be able to answer most questions!*

> ***lakewood:*** *I made a video showing how I've been using my Specio for the Community Spotlight. Where do I send it to make it into the upcoming video?*

Cam sat down and scrolled the feed up. After she had missed the weekly meeting, the chat server had gone into a state of mild panic. Her mods had spent the day working desperately to calm everybody and reassure them that things were okay. She felt a numb dread. She had let all these people down.

"Hey, can I come in?" said a voice from the door.

Cam turned and saw Marcus standing tentatively in the doorframe, clearly unsure of his welcome. Cam was also unsure of his welcome. But after ignoring him for the better part of a week, she figured she could let him say his peace.

He came in and sat next to her, placing a laptop she just now realized he was carrying onto the table. They sat in silence side by side. Finally, Marcus breathed out and stepped into the breach.

"Wyatt told me you two talked," Marcus stated neutrally.

"I suppose you could call it that." Cam grimaced sourly, wondering where he was going with this.

"Cam." Marcus paused to gather his thoughts. "Do you resent me?"

Cam swiveled to look at him. "No!" she cried plaintively, then quickly reconsidered. "Well, maybe. A little." She shook her head. "I don't know; it's complicated." She gesticulated in frustration. "I don't resent that you have had more opportunities than me. I don't even resent that you got your whole life of successes laid out for you like some perfect life roadmap. I know you had to give up a lot too. But I do resent that you expected me to just give up my dreams and follow you into the sunset."

They sat there, thinking. Wordlessly, Marcus opened up his laptop and slid it over to Cam. On the screen was a logo. Marcus had created a simplified, stylish version of the Ofanim angel, a wheel of eyes. He had made it look sleek and cool.

"Did . . . did you make this?"

"The other day, you asked why I don't pursue design professionally and I got defensive. I'm so used to my parents' criticisms, I lashed out at you as a reflex. But that anger shouldn't be directed at you, and I'm sorry." He began cracking his knuckles nervously. "I've been thinking about what you said, and I've been thinking about how much I loved working with everyone on Specio, as part of the Ofanim team, how much I enjoyed the work itself. I've been thinking about my whole life at Beekor, constantly putting off what I like doing in pursuit of what others tell me I should want." He took a deep breath, appeared to center himself, and looked Cam full in the face with his usual reassured confidence. No, thought Cam, he suddenly was even more steady. He looked more solid than he ever had before. Like before he had only been a hollow vessel and was now filled to the brim with an undefinable energy.

"After you left that day . . . I had a couple days alone with my parents to think. I realized how miserable it's been, having nothing for me." He flexed his hands. "Becoming the CEO is their dream, not mine. I don't really have a plan." He huffed a laugh in a sort of bleak way. "Hell, they'll probably disown me." He straightened. "But I know now that what *I* want is to pursue design and work with you guys on Specio. More than anything. And I have you to thank for helping me realize that.

"So as a sign of my commitment," he continued a little sheepishly, "I made a logo for the company." He motioned to the laptop screen.

Cam was stunned. She couldn't believe that Marcus, of all people, was willing to give his parents the middle finger.

"I— Marcus, are you sure about this?" She didn't know what else to say.

"I've never been more sure of anything in my whole life." He grinned, his dimple deep enough to swallow all of Cam's own doubts.

She felt herself choked up with emotion, touched by his gesture. "Thank you, I . . . This means a lot to me." She let out a watery laugh. "Although there's not much of a company left."

"Really? It looks like it's going well to me." Marcus pointed at the board behind Cam.

While she had been talking to Marcus, she had had her back to the board. She turned back around and looked. On social media, submissions for the Community Spotlight were still pouring in. Users were sharing the way Cam's invention had touched their lives, improved them. Some of them were simple things. Some users just talked about being able to watch holographic cartoons or read 3D comics. Many others were people just like the members of the study group Cam's mother was in, though. One user posted about how Specio had made it possible for him to take a class remotely and make up a missing credit in order to graduate on time. Another person talked about how much it meant for her to be able to be close with her girlfriend while she was studying abroad. Cam saw that one had gotten a lot of likes, and it turned out Karrygold had reshared it.

Messages from the Ofanim chat server kept coming.

> *DoubleOhSixtyNine: hey all! new here! have been using specio for a while now and*
> *DoubleOhSixtyNine: wanted to try messing with the codebase. anyway, i built this selfie filter thing for it*

DoubleOhSixtyNine posted a pic. In it, she appeared to be a college-age woman who was posing in a very messy room. She had applied a filter that added little flapping angel wings off the sides of her head and gave her enormous, soulfully glistening anime eyes. Her picture garnered an instant flurry of heart reactions from other users that were currently online.

> *Zev [mod]: woah that's awesome! welcome to the server!*
> *Zev [mod]: the team reviews new features made by the community for inclusion into the main codebase during their weekly town*

> *halls. there should be one coming up next*
> *week!*
>
> **DoubleOhSixtyNine:** *yesss okay! i would be*
> *really proud to make my first contribution*
> *to an open source project!*

Cam watched the messages streaming past, a glowing sense of pride and happiness warming her center. She had helped make this. She and the team had brought people together, and the community they'd all built was flourishing. She couldn't possibly leave all those people behind, she realized.

Cam felt a great weight lifted off her shoulders. She knew. She knew she had to keep going, to keep making, to keep creating, to keep helping. She heaved a sigh as she began mentally preparing herself for the road ahead. She knew there would be an inevitable confrontation with Wyatt, then her ejection from Beekor. Most stressful of all, she contemplated the apologies she was going to have to make to her friends in order to make up for the trust she had betrayed.

Cam stood, elated. Then sat back down in crumpled defeat.

"No." Dejectedly, she continued. "It still won't work. Wyatt said Beekor owns Specio and all related intellectual property. Even if I wanted to, I couldn't. Not without somehow getting him to relinquish it." Regardless of her resolve to pick the project back up, that roadblock looked insurmountable. She felt herself sinking back into a pit of despair.

"About that," Marcus started. "I think I might have a solution."

Cam looked at him, the flutterings of hope lapping at the edges of her heart.

"And I'd like to officially join the Ofanim team. If you'll have me." He held out his hand to shake, appearing a little anxious. "Pending everybody else's approval, of course. . . ."

Cam felt herself break into her first genuine smile in a long time.

Chapter 47

THE NEXT DAY, CAM GOT up early. She darted around town running errands in the predawn light. For several sleepy store clerks, she was the first customer to arrive.

When she finally got home, just as the sun was rising, she immediately got to work in the kitchen. Chopping, cracking, brewing, boiling, mixing, and general cooking commenced in a flurry of activity.

Soon the sounds and, more important, the delicious smells lured the rest of the pages downstairs and into the kitchen, where Cam was in the process of laying out a feast: a pot of coffee, a pitcher of horchata, refried beans, rice, tamales, quesadillas fritas topped with crema and sauce, chilaquiles, scrambled eggs with onion and chili pepper, and two dozen mochi doughnuts that spelled out "SORRY."

Sofia looked over this assembly, sat down wordlessly, and poured herself a cup of coffee. James soon joined and explored the food options. Avery came down as Sofia was serving herself a tamale and immediately ate all the doughnuts forming the first "R." Marcus arrived last. He walked over just as Cam set the last plate on the table and squeezed her shoulder reassuringly before sitting down to serve himself. They weren't on the same physically intimate terms they had been before, but they were finally professional equals meeting each other on level ground. They had stayed up late talking, actually opening up to each other about their hopes and dreams. The damage and mistrust was not fully repaired, but Cam could see a future where they were stronger for it. She hoped the same could be true for the rest of the pages.

Cam stood before everyone at the table and took a deep, steadying breath. The assembled pages put down forks, spoons, and, in Avery's case, a gravy boat full of sauce from which they had been taking surreptitious sips, and turned to her expectantly.

"I'm sorry." Cam figured that was as good a place to start as any. "I was backed into a corner and scared. You're my friends, and I should have come to you for help instead of hurting you. At least," Cam said wryly, "I hope you're still my friends."

James and Avery both looked to Sofia, who simply looked at Cam as if to say, "Go on."

Cam geared herself up to explain. "When I realized Wyatt wasn't being honest with me, I confronted him. He told me I had to abandon Specio and become a team lead on the influencer project. That I'd—we'd all—be kicked off campus and blackballed." James made an O with his mouth. "I've been imagining for months this dream where I could pursue my ideal project with my best friends, fully supported by Beekor, and all of a sudden I was told it was all a lie. I kind of lost it." Cam took another soothing breath. "But I've been doing some soul-searching, and I've realized that I don't need the money, or the stability." She paused, then continued quietly. "The money and stability would definitely be nice, but it's not enough for me.

"I came here with a dream to make a difference for people like my mom. To make the world more accessible—to connect people that don't have the means to do so. And if that can only happen outside of Beekor"—her voice took on a steel note—"then I'm leaving Beekor." She paused and looked around. "I want to take our work and forge a new path, to formally incorporate Ofanim and bring over our customers." More quietly she said, "To continue to work on our dream to make the world better for everyone."

Cam tried to keep the quaver out of her voice. "I'd understand if none of you are ready to fully commit to that path. I'm ready to do it on my own if I have to." She looked into each of their eyes before stopping on Sofia. "But I'd really like to have my cofounder there too."

Emotions warred on Sofia's face, as if she were wavering but working to remain resolute. Cam held up a hand to forestall anybody interjecting.

Cam turned to James first. "James, I apologize for betraying your trust in me, and in us, as a team. I had no right to disrespect your commitment and contribution like that." She took a breath. "I know that building something accessible to everyone is just as important to you as it is to me." James looked up to meet Cam's eye and nodded once.

"Avery." Cam looked at them. "I'm sorry for being a jerk to you and implying you were intentionally lying to me. You're right that, to some degree, remaining ignorant suited me. I've also resented that you treat me like your personal pet project, but I should have said that to you openly instead of letting it fester. I won't let it happen again." Cam spoke with resolve.

"I'm sorry too, Cam. You're right: I didn't treat you with the respect you deserve," they said solemnly. "I-I'm more used to having connections than friends." Avery gave a tiny smile that managed to convey both contrition and wickedness in equal measure. "I promise in the future to bring you in on my subterfuge."

Cam returned the smile briefly before turning to Sofia and looking her in the eye. She inhaled one long breath and went on. "Sofia, I'm sorry to you most of all. What I did was incredibly unfair, throwing your affluence in your face." Cam's vision became blurry with unshed tears, and her voice shook. "I may sometimes struggle with the gap between opportunities we had growing up, but I never, never believed that it in any way diminishes your commitment to our dream, or your support for me as a friend." Sofia quietly nodded, shaking free a tear to streak down her face as well. Cam began to openly wail. "So please can we go back to being friends and making this amazing thing together?!"

Sofia stood up, fully crying, and crushed Cam against her. The two hugged for a long time, shaking, until Avery also joined in, then Marcus, and, after an even longer period, almost tentatively, James. They stood like that for a while, Cam basking in the warmth and smell of her close friends, until nobody else shook with tears and a feeling of deep catharsis settled, like a city street after having been scoured by a torrential rain. They all stood back, red-faced.

Cam took another deep breath. "Even with the chance of getting black-balled, you're still in?"

"What is my privilege to escape back to Mid-Levels for if not to use it to throw my weight around?" Sofia mocked, and sniffled. Cam winced to have some of her words thrown back at her, even lightly. "I am your cofounder; I am with you."

Avery leapt in immediately after. "And I'll get you so many outside investors, you won't *need* to worry about Wyatt." They flourished their fork like a wand. "Good luck blackballing *us* after we've gotten enough powerful people in our corner to make our own damn Beekor!" They smirked.

Cam looked at James. His hands beat a rhythm under the table. He made eye contact and, after a struggle, Cam saw his wall slowly come down once more. He nodded once, emphatically. "I want to work together again." He smiled a little bit. "But this time I want a contract. You'll be stuck with us!" He placed one closed fist on the table. "No escaping when you feel bad."

Cam grinned. "That seems like a good deal to me."

Finally, she looked to Marcus. He just smiled up at her. Dimple showing.

Chapter 48

"HEY, HONEY!" KARRYGOLD'S GOLDEN BEAR avatar appeared in the holographic field, accessorized with a monocle and top hat this time around, with hundred-dollar bills raining slowly down in the background.

Cam couldn't help but laugh. "Hey! Long time no see. How are you?"

The bear made an overly dramatic thinking pose, then said, "I'm good. I'm feeling *generous*."

Cam held up her hands. "Wait! Let me actually do my pitch!" Karrygold shook her head no forcefully. "Since when did you start investing?"

Karrygold shrugged exaggeratedly. "Other streamers are doing it, and I thought it would be cool to try it out! Besides, you're, like, incredible! Your community engagement is through the roof!" Karrygold spoke as if utterly awestruck. Her eyes actually turned into spinning stars for a moment.

Cam reddened. She spoke into her shirt, "I just made what I needed and didn't have, and I realized I could supply it to others too." It made sense that Karrygold would look at Cam's work through the lens of community management, because it was exactly what she did day-to-day.

Karrygold shook her head profusely, speed lines appearing. "Sweet, so you'll let me help!"

In the end, Karrygold gave the verbal handshake that she would be committing a check to the cause with minimal fuss. One down, a lot more to go.

At the first of their investor debriefs, Avery congratulated Cam on her first check. Cam cheered along with Avery but worked to temper her excitement. "Karrygold is investing in me, which is great, but I'm worried that I haven't necessarily learned much since I wasn't challenged."

Avery nodded thoughtfully. "That's fine. Part of the goal of starting off with friendlies is to help you get comfortable in there with investors. Were there any parts of the pitch that you would like to refine a bit?"

Avery had been as good as their word and immediately filled up Cam's meeting queue with a ton of investors. As they hashed out strategy together, Cam grew increasingly aware of just how astute Avery's insights into people were.

"Making and maintaining connections with people, it's not just idle socialization for you. It's an active process," Cam said.

"Obviously!" Avery sounded almost caught off guard. "Wait, have you just been freestyling all this time?" They looked appalled.

"Well . . ."

"Of course it's an active process! It's also showing others respect to explicitly plan time to keep up with them, to seek to understand them and their ambitions." Avery looked at Cam with slight admonishment. "And to ask them directly for ways that they can support you, which is what we're working on with you right now with these investors."

Chastised, Cam mused about the way the nature of their relationship had changed. Avery was still confident, sarcastic, and decisive, but now Avery expected more of Cam. They were also solicitous of Cam's thoughts and opinions in a way that they hadn't been previously. It was taking time for Cam to adjust to it all.

"Parties are work for you too, aren't they?"

Avery nodded once, sharply.

"I've seen the way you play the host at all times, bringing people together and engaging people in the group that are being left out, making yourself vulnerable in order to put others at ease."

At that, Avery looked distinctly pleased. "Ah, so you've noticed my vital work!" They waggled their eyebrows. "So many awkward nerds out here, somebody needs to play the nerd whisperer to keep things flowing!"

Together, they ran through the deck again, making improvements as they went, until Cam was satisfied. In the end, Cam and Sofia had come to the conclusion that they would make Ofanim into an open-source foundation. Everything would remain fully free for individual users like Cam's mom or her study group, but as Lee had described, they would eventually make money by consulting for large corporations that wanted special features or assistance deploying Cam's hardware to their workforce.

Cam's next meeting was with Avery's friend Chi and her art collective DAOTown. As a bunch of makers, Cam knew that her work, and the open-source nature of the project, along with the way Cam had slowly begun to recruit more builders from within their community, would most likely resonate with Chi. Cam prepared her pitch to stress that particular aspect of the project.

Chi and Cam met back at Chi's makerspace in the Mission. The large warehouse space appeared totally different during the day, when it wasn't set up in party mode. Everything looked unfinished. The entire space was rough plywood and exposed electronics. As Chi led Cam back upstairs and to her personal space, Cam noticed some pretty advanced fabrication tools, though. The kind of stuff that could give even the page garage a run for its money.

Chi sat Cam down at a table shaped like a big mushroom and brought her an herbal tea, then Cam got started. For this meeting, Cam found herself actually going through her slide deck. The talented team of Beekor pages was an obvious bright spot, one of which was Chi's friend Avery. But Chi actually made her dig in quite a bit on her expansion plans and the economics around making a single hardware unit and shipping it. Cam found herself lacking some of the information Chi would want, but she felt that she had hit pay dirt when she started talking about the traction she was getting with her growing community and the way it was doubling as outreach for more makers to contribute to the foundation. Especially with makers in the accessibility space like James. "It's a snowball rolling down a ski hill!" Chi exclaimed. As soon as she started suggesting more ways Cam could creatively grow the foundation, she knew Chi was won over. She left with another handshake and promise of a check from DAOTown's community treasury.

Two handshakes in (Avery had prepared Cam by telling her that, when it came to pitching in the valley, a handshake is a legitimate commitment, and people that go back on that risk their reputation), and Cam was feeling incredibly good about fundraising. After the meeting with Chi, Avery and Cam went over their growth cases and economic models a bit more thoroughly in order to ensure Cam had her talking points down. They also noted that Chi was pretty much a perfect investor fit for Ofanim. That is, Chi was both aligned with Ofanim's mission and a great strategic connection for gaining access to maker spaces, tools, and other hackers.

Cam's next meeting was also in person, with a somewhat more difficult potential investor—Avery's friend Oleg. The two of them met during the day in a coffee shop. She had debated setting the meeting in the same bar they'd met all those months ago, but she eventually concluded that it might be unprofessional to kick off a formal relationship with an investor in a place with a significant amount of porn on the walls (although the sloth was probably okay).

The coffee shop was a beautiful, massive, airy space with multiple floors and a ton of the floor space devoted to sacks of beans and equipment for roasting or grinding. It was ironic that she was there, asking for money, when people that were either fiending for a fix or actively starving were also beg-ging for smaller change right out front, but she wasn't sure what she could do about that. She wondered if perhaps the issue could be improved if local government were to prioritize buying or building social housing and more shelters, regardless of local homeowner protestations, and expedite the path into shelters each night rather than requiring months-long wait lists to get in, but it seemed out of Cam's remit for the moment.

Oleg showed up on time. The blond man looked as dashing as ever. He came up the stairs and shook hands with Cam graciously. Pleasantries out of the way, Cam launched into Ofanim's slide deck with Oleg. As they sipped coffee, she projected the slides above their table with her phone using the latest model of the Specio adapter that James had assembled. It was sleek, elegant, and beautiful. Oleg took a moment to appreciate the quality of work. As Cam went through the slides, however, Oleg interrupted repeatedly to get more information about each point. As the Ofanim pitch became increasingly bogged down in Oleg's questions about minutiae, or challenges for every one of Cam's assertions, Cam was stuck with the grim feeling of watching her entire pitch go down in flames.

In the end, as expected, Oleg elected not to write Cam a check. "Yeah, I'm sorry. I love what you're doing and I think the mission is great, but I just don't see the right DNA in your team to scale."

Cam shook his hand woodenly, thanked Oleg, and left.

Back out on the street, Cam felt demoralized after her first no. Avery met her out front and Cam gestured to Avery to walk with her while they debriefed. After a pensive moment, Avery said, "Believe the no, but not the why," cryptically.

Cam tried to puzzle that one out for a beat. "What?"

Avery continued. "This is something I've worked to internalize over the years. When somebody rejects you, you can believe the fact that they said no, but you shouldn't necessarily give much credence to their explanation of why they did it." Avery's eyes grew distant as they explained. "Half the time, they think they are trying to protect you from hearing something difficult, or maybe the reason is actually personal, or maybe it's just plain stupid, like bad vibes or something. Regardless, don't take anybody's stated reason too much to heart, unless you're running into the same sort of trouble repeatedly," they finished.

Cam nodded. "Right, that's probably decent advice for dating too," Cam began. After a beat, she said. "I appreciate your advice, Avery."

Avery preened but in a vaguely abashed way. "We all have our skill sets," they eventually said, with warmth.

"And as a show of my gratitude, I booked us a session here!" Cam spun and pointed at the cat café she had stopped them in front of. In the window, a diverse range of cats lounged, played on various cat furniture, or eyed them to ascertain whether or not they might be the next pair of treat dispensers. Avery yelped with delight as Cam said, "Even though this last one didn't work out, I still wanted to say thank you." Avery looked genuinely touched.

Soon the two of them were seated in the middle of a room full of friendly felines and were reviewing the pitch itself and reassessing if there was something that could be simplified, some factoids that Cam was missing, or anything else that could be sharpened or refined. Of course, cats swarmed Avery and made themselves at home. During a brief moment between pitch refinement and fulfilling cat demands, Avery stared at their tiny espresso. "You know, I appreciate what you've done for me too."

"Hmm?" Cam asked. She idly waved a string on a stick around for a mackerel tabby to lazily bat at from a reclining position on the floor. His collar said that he was named after what Cam was pretty sure was a Japanese horror movie.

Avery's voice was momentarily free of bombast. "I'm great at making connections, and don't get me wrong, it's not like everything is transactional with the people I try to bring into my orbit, but there's often a . . . a pretext, you know?" They sipped their tea in calm silence.

A second mackerel tabby joined the first, jumping over him to block his access to Cam's string. Her collar seemed to say she was named after a Japanese citrus fruit. She began leaping about after the string with gusto.

Avery continued. "Tacky Tourist Time was a good excuse to get to know each other at first, but then I really started to enjoy it. It felt freeing to just do something fun with no other motives or goals." Avery eyed Cam's cats. "To just go places with people because it's enjoyable to be around them."

"That's what we call friends, Avery," Cam said.

Avery laughed. A third mackerel tabby, with white paws and a pink nose, yowled at them. When Avery gestured to their lap, the cat's tail went straight up, and he settled in, purring loudly. He seemed to be named after . . . some kind of cheese?

"Well, friends aren't something I've always had. Or family. Even when we settled somewhere, it seemed like my parents were in a real rush to get rid of me; send me to some rich people summer camp or private school. So thanks for being a friend, Cam." Avery dutifully administered the requested pets. "I'd like to keep doing Tacky Tourist Time whatever happens with the company."

"Deal!" Cam replied with gusto.

—

Georges came next. Acting off her knowledge of Georges, what he stood for and cared about, Cam went in with a plan to play up the aspect of Ofanim's efforts around repurposing existing hardware, rather than locking users into a treadmill of constant, expensive, new phone purchases with obsolescence built in. She absolutely nailed it. Georges was in.

"I also have something for you," Georges said, and he pulled out her ratty old backpack he had taken from her months ago. Except it was no longer ratty; it was pristine and bespoke. It had artistic patches and embroidery of fruits and vegetables. Cam took it with reverence.

"Georges, it's beautiful." And it was.

"Use this as a reminder that the old can be good; it just needs a little help sometimes."

Cam threw herself at Georges and enveloped him in a giant hug.

As the week progressed, she met with a blur of investors from all walks of life. Some were angel investors like Georges; others were institutional investors, with large pools of wealth to allocate. The meetings were up and down. Bigger investors balked at open source, somewhat, but Cam would point out some recent open-source projects that turned into enormous successes. Small investors that had the privilege of owning the best equipment at all times would question the need for Ofanim's work in a world with Beekor phones, but Cam would point out the massive percentage of the world that could only afford non-Beekor phones, which amounted to a gargantuan addressable market. As the investors started to become further from their value pool, they became increasingly less friendly, and a lot more rejections rolled in, but Cam continued to find success from time to time. The debrief sessions with Avery began to feel more and more like therapy as Cam ran the gauntlet 24/7.

At the end of two weeks of nonstop, frenzied pitching, complete shirking of daily work at Beekor, and the Ofanim team being forced to fend for themselves, the situation was grim. Cam had found some success, locking in quite a few small checks, but as she sat down to do the math to calculate their burn rate—the monthly cost to pay her team, pay rent on a space, and afford all other operational costs such as equipment, utilities, marketing, etc.—she would barely have enough to run for three months, and that was even assuming she paid the entire team the same low (relative to cost of living) salary that she was planning to pay herself. The goal was to get eighteen months of runway.

Late at night, Cam was sitting at her desk, head in her hands. Cam was tormented by the feeling that she was being pushed inexorably toward a cliff, as the Beekor Accelerator Program ran to its completion and Cam still hadn't secured enough money to operate for any meaningful period of time. She and the rest of the team would all be sent packing, having burned their bridges with Beekor and thrown away the opportunity from the Accelerator Program. Sofia, who had just arrived home from dinner with Avery and was stopping by the office to grab something, came upon Cam in this state, struggling with personal failure. She approached Cam slowly and put a hand on her back.

Cam looked up from her desk with a face of utter defeat.

"Investor trouble?" Sofia whispered.

Cam just nodded woodenly.

"How bad?"

Ruefully, Cam replied, "Well, if I can just spend two weeks raising money every three months, we'll be okay . . ."

"What if I didn't take a salary?" Sofia began.

Cam shut it down instantly. "No. That is not a fair sacrifice to ask of you." Her voice took on force. "You've all already given enough by turning down the lucrative Beekor job and potentially making Wyatt an enemy."

Sofia was quiet a moment. "Well, think about it."

"Thought about it. The answer is no." Cam's voice brooked no further argument.

Sofia sighed. "Well, I guess . . . we just try to raise money every three months?"

Cam despaired as she felt their dream slipping through her fingers.

At the corner of her desk, her phone buzzed.

Chapter 49

THE DAY WAS BRIGHT AND beautiful on Beekor campus. The grounds were as vibrant and perfectly trimmed as ever. In the same open area on the campus that had been tented for the conference, another small stage had been set up with concentric rows of seats around it for guests. Commencement was a smaller affair than the conference by far, but actual seats were limited, with extreme exclusivity—only direct invitees of Beekor, staff linked to the Accelerator, or the two guests allotted for each page. Outside of the main area for commencement, there was a small crowd of Beekor employees at the periphery, but otherwise, Beekor work life proceeded apace all around them.

The event was fully live streamed—something that Beekor had begun doing in recent years. Cam had reviewed a couple of the prior events just to get a sense of how things would play out. She found her stomach fluttering over and over as the event actually began in earnest. Jennifer was onstage at the podium, a structure of chrome pipes with a transparent platform at the top and a microphone, giving some comments about this year's batch, but Cam couldn't focus on what she was saying. She and the other pages were seated at the front near the stage.

Cam looked down the row at everybody. James tapped his feet rhythmically and gave a small smile, projecting support. Avery vamped in absolutely gigantic sunglasses, a rich floral-print coat in blacks, reds, greens, and pinks, with enormous black lapels, on which they had two roaring lion heads embroidered. They also wore a thick collar with lion heads on it. From the mouth of each lion depended chunky, bejeweled crosses. Marcus looked his usual self, in a perfectly tailored suit. Without looking at Cam, he silently lifted one pant leg to reveal a sock featuring Captain Nuro, flanked on all sides by the rest of the cast of One Dream. Cam smiled to herself. As Jennifer wrapped up her introductions and called Wyatt onstage, Sofia met Cam's eyes and projected a silent, calm confidence that immediately buoyed Cam.

Wyatt strode onstage with his usual polished, vibrant energy. The man looked much the same as usual, completely composed, salt-and-pepper hair calculatedly tousled and swept back, outfit both casual and exuding an air of cost and care. Cam tried to calm her nerves as Wyatt began his address.

"Let's have a round of applause for this year's batch of graduating pages!" he began. The attendees surrounding Cam applauded warmly. Cam looked around a bit, and everybody smiled her way, except for Amari and Keloa, who stared through her as if she weren't there. Fake-ass vampires, Cam thought. After the applause ran down, Wyatt continued. "And what an incredible batch you all have been! In many ways, this has been our most successful cohort in the Beekor Accelerator Program to date." Applause. A screen slid down behind Wyatt.

"This year, our pages generated"—he triggered a slide full of bullet pointed text to appear on the screen behind him—"four new patents. Two thriving business units. Fourteen new partnerships with external parties." He gesticulated with one hand to emphasize each of his points, then triggered the slide to disappear. "But most important, we've helped to realize the stupendous potential of five future leaders." Wyatt met Cam's gaze, and his eyes glinted.

"Each and every one of the pages this year will be offered the opportunity to continue on with the teams in which they've been embedded here at Beekor as full-time employees." Applause. "And they'll be among excellent company with some of our graduating pages from prior years." Amari and Keloa waved from their seats. "Together, we'll work to further hone their talents."

"But let's cut to the chase here. As you all know, the stakes this year are higher than ever. Our star page for the batch will be awarded a three-million-dollar starting budget and the pick of the litter of available company resources in order to build a team to work on a project of their own choosing." More applause. Cam's stomach fluttered again in anticipation.

"So, without further ado, I'd like to announce our star page for this batch of the Beekor Accelerator Program. Congratulations, Marcus Davidson!" Applause broke out in earnest. Marcus looked around, smiled his professional-grade smile, and waved. Cam met his eyes for just a moment. He winked at her.

Wyatt gestured toward the stage. "Marcus, why don't you come up and say a few words?"

Cam couldn't understand how he did it. Her hands were shaking just watching as Marcus strode up on stage with the same sort of gracious energy that Wyatt consistently projected. He shook hands with Wyatt warmly, and the two appeared to quietly exchange pleasantries, or thanks, then Marcus took his position at the podium.

"Thanks, Wyatt," Marcus began. A beat for applause. "It's been an incredible honor to get the opportunity to work with Wyatt, as well as all of the Beekor staff during these last six months." Marcus looked at each of the pages. "I believe I can speak for the entirety of this year's cohort when I say that we've had an incredible education, for which we are grateful." Amid everybody's applause, Marcus looked at Cam, and his smile suddenly became genuine, dimple again on full display. Her stomach flipped. Off to the side, Wyatt, who was also clapping, noted the exchange of looks.

"However," Marcus continued, "I'd be remiss if I didn't turn things over to the real star of this batch of pages." Wyatt's smile dropped for a moment before he managed to regain his equilibrium. "Camila Diaz!" He gestured at the podium. "Please, Cam." The audience broke out in applause yet again, somewhat confused but otherwise unaware of the deviation from the script. Wyatt looked a bit strangled as he also clapped for Cam. Sitting in the front row, Jennifer looked around in bewildered terror, the whites of her eyes visible. Cam stilled her shaking fingers, got up, and strode purposefully up to the platform and to the podium. As she passed Wyatt, he somehow managed to smile magnanimously while simultaneously staring daggers at her. Cam gave him a wave, then shook hands with Marcus and took the podium. Marcus moved back and off to the side, flanking Cam's other side, opposite Wyatt.

Cam took a long, slow look out at the crowd. She met eyes with each of the pages, Lee Baker, Chi, Georges, and various Beekor executives, journalists, and people she had come to think of as friends. Cam's voice quavered as she began, "Marcus is certainly right: The last six months have been quite the education." She continued more smoothly. "Six months ago, I was back at home, working in isolation on the barest glimmers of a dream that I had. A dream about making life-changing technology, life-changing *opportunities*, accessible and available to everybody." Suddenly, Cam felt that passion rising in her again. The one that imbued her words with force and made her feel alive, that sense that she was doing what was right in her heart. "I didn't have access to computing resources, money, or expertise to build it, but the dream sustained me."

Cam looked at Wyatt and smiled an earnest, warm smile. "Beekor changed that." The audience clapped. "In the Beekor Accelerator Program, I no longer felt that I had to do it alone. Here, I found my people.

"My fellow builders, hardware and software engineers who were excited to nerd out on the same esoteric CPU thermal density statistics as me." In the audience, David and Kevin whooped. "My fellow pages, who were just as excited to learn about this crazy city where even the wildest dreams can flourish."

"My pleasure!" Avery called out into the gap between words, and Cam laughed along with the rest of the crowd.

"And today, I would like to declare that my dream *has* flourished, become *our* dream," Cam said with relish. "Over the last six months, the rest of the pages and I have assembled to work on that same project on which I had toiled away at home, alone, for so long. The adapter that we've been building, Specio, a tool that can grant access to the holographic revolution to even old and outdated phones, has taken enormous strides." Cam lifted the remote and pressed it with satisfaction. An image appeared on-screen. It was a picture of the device she and the team had built together, attached to a non-Beekor phone, through which a delighted child was interacting with a virtual classroom.

Wyatt's frozen smile looked increasingly brittle. His eyes glinted with rage as he looked up at the decidedly inelegant Specio device projected on-screen in the middle of his Beekor ceremony. Cam could feel his murderous stare on her back. He would probably be tackling her off the stage, right now, if the entire event weren't being live streamed for the world to see.

"As of right now"—Cam checked her own phone—"we've served one thousand three hundred and fifty-six users." Scattered applause. "Many of whom have become active members of our community. They're just the first. Those users are starting a movement with us, contributing to the project, supporting one another, and sharing their stories." Cam paused a moment, then imbued her voice with force. "Beekor unlocked the door," Cam began, then finished, in a shout, "and our users are helping us to throw that door wide open!" The crowd began to clap in earnest. Cam continued straight through. "We're sharing the revolution with everybody.

"My fellow page Sofia Ly, my incredible cofounder, and an unparalleled genius"—Sofia nodded her head once, forcefully—"has both improved the software by leaps and bounds, and also taught me what it means to share a dream with others and accept and embrace support." The crowd began an unending, rolling applause. "James Foster, our hardware expert, joined up and made my flimsy adapter into a sleek, sturdy, and *far smaller* device. He taught me how rare and precious it is to find people that have the same vision as you, but see it from a different angle, and how important it is to protect that." James looked down, but a smile was clearly etched across his face. The crowd cheered. "Avery Giroux, my resident fixer, applied their particular charms to seeking out and finding perfect communities with which to share the early versions of what we've built." Avery stood and bowed gallantly. The crowd roared.

"And Marcus, finally." Cam took a moment and looked at Marcus, who gave her a smile of support. Then she looked at Wyatt, who practically shook with rage. "Marcus took my ugly engineer art and made everything beautiful, cohesive, and *usable*. My God, it was bad before." The crowd laughed. "Marcus taught me about how vital it is to be true to yourself." She paused. "And how much bravery that can take at times.

"All of this adds up to what I believe to be an unprecedented outcome to this year's Beekor Accelerator Program." Cam didn't believe, she knew. She had flipped through all the news articles for the previous batches. "The *entire* batch"—she stressed the word with relish—"of pages has expressed their desire to join together to work full-time on this brand-new venture. Today, our fully incorporated company, Ofanim, is open for business."

The cacophony the crowd let loose at this unexpected event was unparalleled. Wyatt's face fluctuated rapidly between rage, hatred, and artificial good cheer.

Cam's voice took on a note of trepidation. "The road forward for an open-source foundation is a difficult one. Getting investment isn't easy." She took a long breath. "Which is why I'm especially proud to announce that we've already closed our initial funding round, led by Beekor cofounder and my personal mentor, Lee Baker."

The applause continued. In the crowd, Amari and Keloa looked around, stunned.

Lee stood up, bright purple hair, freshly shaved on the sides, on display. In her dark suit, she looked particularly dashing. She waved, smiled, and mouthed "Good fucking job" to Cam.

The applause of the commencement crowd eventually died down. Cam spoke into the calm. "And, again, I cannot thank Beekor enough for making all of this possible!" One last round of applause. "I'd like to hand the stage back to Jennifer to close us out."

Cam stepped back from the podium and took Marcus's side. He smiled at her and squeezed her hand once as Jennifer stood up woodenly from her front-row seat and looked about. She made eye contact with Wyatt, who gestured forcefully with his head. Jennifer jumped as if shocked, then made her way ungracefully to the podium. She seemed to regain her composure as she leaned forward and said, "Our graduating batch of pages!" Through the applause, she spoke in a tight voice. "Let's get everybody up here for photos!"

As the pages started getting up, Wyatt strode to Cam and Marcus.

"You had to do it," he hissed through gritted teeth. "Don't think appearing on a live stream is going to protect you." His face was purple with barely contained rage. "I already told you, I *own* you. Everything you've built is *mine*, made with Beekor hardware."

In openly defying Wyatt, Cam finally felt free. She met his enraged glare with an unconcerned smile. "Nope."

Marcus leaned forward. "You see, Wyatt, the Beekor Accelerator Program isn't actually run directly by Beekor. In fact, none of the hardware or even the page house is owned directly by Beekor either."

Wyatt looked puzzled, then spun angrily to glare down at Jennifer. She looked as if she wanted to self-immolate on the spot as she met his eyes with a look of abject terror and slowly nodded. The pages began arriving onstage.

"The way it works," Marcus continued enigmatically, smiling wide and gesturing with his hands, "is that the Accelerator is operated via a separate

501(c)(3) charitable organization called Grow Unlimited, to which Beekor donates hardware, real estate, and employee resources. All, no doubt, for a tidy tax write-off. But as a result, you never had even the slightest claim to any of our IP." Marcus barked a single laugh, and Wyatt, who had taken on a distant look of smoldering hatred, jumped. Lee Baker arrived just then and, from behind Cam, slid into position to intersect with Wyatt's gaze, smiled, and waved.

Cam picked up where Marcus left off. "We were never even on the clock for Beekor, since we took nothing but a living stipend from the charitable org that actually runs the Accelerator." Cam pointed outward then and continued cheerfully. "Anyway, photo time!" The assembled pages, Jennifer, and Lee Baker all looked out from the stage at the same time. Wyatt slowly turned, looking as if he were actively in the process of clenching every muscle in his body simultaneously. Cam smiled serenely, and Lee Baker looked intensely satisfied as the crowd applauded and journalists and a Beekor photographer captured the moment for posterity.

Epilogue

"HAPPY 5,000!" THE CELEBRATION TEXT appeared in big, virtual balloon letters and went flying up over the heads of everybody on the live stream, accompanied by virtual confetti. In the live stream's chat, congratulatory text and emotes went flying past in an impossible-to-follow flurry. Karrygold, who was in the office in person, running the stream from her phone using the custom VTuber technology Cam had built for her to allow her to do a real-life streaming while using her golden bear avatar, centered Cam, Sofia, James, Avery, and Marcus all around herself as each of them, in party hats, posed together and blew on party-favor noisemakers. After the months it had taken to reach a thousand Specio users, setting the team's next goal at five thousand users seemed incredibly optimistic at the time. But here they were, hitting five thousand just one month later, and accelerating.

"Toast, bitches!" Avery yelled, and cracked open a bottle of champagne to spray over everybody. Cam dove at it with a paper cup to attempt to catch the spillover as it ran out of the bottle. She was still very wary of damaging the new office space.

The Ofanim team's third office was a massive upgrade over the first two. Cam had gotten an excellent deal on some unused warehouse space in SoMa that had previously been home to a small mobile game company.

The space still had the warehouse loading dock, but the rest of it had been converted by the previous tenants to include lots of glass, hardwood floors, and artfully exposed dark steel girders. The walls inside were done up with a faux brick. The foundation had picked up the cheap lease on the space for an entire year, which only became possible because Lee Baker joined the funding round with a large check. After that, it became significantly easier to raise money from institutional investors with deep pockets who clamored to get onto the foundation's cap table with the influential Beekor cofounder. "Pattern matching," Lee Baker had said to Cam, with a sneer. It sounded a lot more like just copying the cool kid to Cam.

The lease secured, Cam and company had gotten tons of supplies like desks, holographic projector screens, and even 3D-printers from other businesses in Lee Baker's network that needed to sell equipment after shutting down, moving location, or upgrading.

It all added up to a beautiful space that Cam and her team had decorated with relish and made all their own. Marcus had added art accents all over the place—large custom signs with the logo he'd designed, bits of pop art, and a big, vintage-looking roadside attraction sign that said "Eat" in light bulbs that he and Cam had stolen from a Beekor dumpster for laughs. Avery and Sofia had set up a welcoming common area with chic furniture and a wine fridge to host guests. James had deployed a range of custom speakers of his own design, from Baphomet surrounded by animatronic children at play to a chrome pyramid streaked in resin blood to an enormous penny, all throughout the space. And they had room to grow! Chi and the rest of her art collective were planning to utilize some of the additional free space to build a holographic performance art installation for the big grand-opening office party Cam was planning to throw for their friends and investors. The foundation didn't have the resources to provide Michelin-star chef meals each day, but Cam had a new restaurant from the neighborhood cater their lunches each Wednesday, and the rest of the week, the team ate lunch in the city wherever they liked.

Paying no heed to Cam's frantic attempts to prevent the champagne from spilling everywhere, and on camera for all to see, Avery touched a single lacquered nail to Sofia's chin and said, "M'lady."

"Gentlethem," Sofia replied, and the two kissed while Cam desperately attempted to wrest the wildly tilting and spilling bottle out of Avery's hand. The live stream chat went absolutely wild for it.

"Cammy baby, I've got this," Rosa called out as she came with towels to wrap around the soaked bottle. Then she hugged Cam tight, swept up in the moment.

When Karrygold brought the stream over to the mysterious goth girl who was fiddling with an oversized flashlight that emitted a dim light that pulsed and changed color to the beat of the music emanating from it, the chat filled up with "?????" and "who is she?" Daphne, in dark eye shadow inset with glitter that dramatically spilled out across her cheekbones, and a spiked collar with a heavy metal pentagram dangling over a band T-shirt, leaned against James's desk and, at Karrygold's prompting to talk to the chat, merely stuck out her tongue and gave them the finger before returning to the speaker. She did make several later appearances, however. She seemed to have a sixth sense for when James was getting overwhelmed and swooped in every time without fail to save him by diverting either the camera's or others' attention away.

As the party devolved into unstructured merriment, everybody got the chance to toast the camera. Chi in a holographic space marine outfit, and even the Five Ts, bolstered by the addition of two new members, Tyler and Tarin, got a drunken moment with the chat.

Midway through, the roar of a motorcycle pulling up signaled Lee Baker's arrival. She came striding up the stairs from the loading dock entry, massive bong in hand, yelling, "Congratulations, motherfuckers!" The party ratcheted up in intensity, and Karrygold was forced to shut down the stream due to risk of TOS violations with the streaming service for display of drug paraphernalia, drunken debauchery, and, probably, excessive fun.

As the night waned, partygoers slowly filtered out. Some went to other bars; others just headed home. By the end of it all, Cam found herself alone in her office, in the dark, unwinding but also trying to commit everything to memory. This was a moment that she would want to be able to replay when looking back on her life. It was a major milestone in this big, ambitious journey that Cam and her friends were undertaking together. They had grown close through hardship and shared ambition. They had become a family.

Marcus quietly entered the office. These days, he was still wearing his customary wild socks, but he had also started wearing colorful shirts. Some he even designed himself. Seeming to sense the moment, he came to Cam's side without speaking and put a hand on her shoulder. Cam leaned her head against his hip and let herself be held for a while. Finally, she pulled him down to her. Marcus kissed her long and deep. He made to rise again, but Cam pulled him down for one more. As he eventually straightened, Cam smiled smugly.

"We did good, boss," he said.

"Oh God," Cam groaned. "Don't call me that after kissing me."

"You're right." Marcus chuckled throatily, dimple shining like a star. "We should disclose this relationship to HR, shouldn't we?"

"I'll review it at our next company all hands," Cam vowed.

"Or I could just put my hands all over you." Marcus swooped in and picked her up, spinning her around and around.

"That's embarrassing." Cam laughed. As she came back to her feet, she looked into Marcus's eyes, thoughtful.

"I'm glad to be along for the ride with you," Marcus said into the silence.

Cam smiled knowingly. "Now the real journey begins."

Acknowledgments

FIRSTLY, WE HAVE TO THANK our agent Thao Le for believing in us and helping us find our perfect duet.

No amount of thanks would be sufficient for our editors, Augusta Harris and Cassidy Leyendecker, for their trust, patience, and positive energy. So much of this book can be attributed to their influence.

We'd also like to thank our friends for knowing when we need a cry and when we need a party, because good friendships have both. Your stories really helped to make our world more rich and fun.

We'd like to thank our families, especially those who didn't get a chance to see this published but were always supportive. Thank you, Grandpa.

Lastly, we're grateful for the San Francisco Bay Area. With all of its charms, problems, ridiculous events, scenery, delicious food, and its willingness to try everything at least once, this could only have happened here. We thank everyone who has made this place what it is and what it will be!